GODFATHER
DEATH
M.D.
I0716170

ALSO BY
JACOB DEVLIN

MIDDLE GRADE

A Thousand Dreadful Curses
Roses in the Dragon's Den
Brambles in the Wishing Well

YOUNG ADULT

The Carver
The Unseen
The Hummingbird

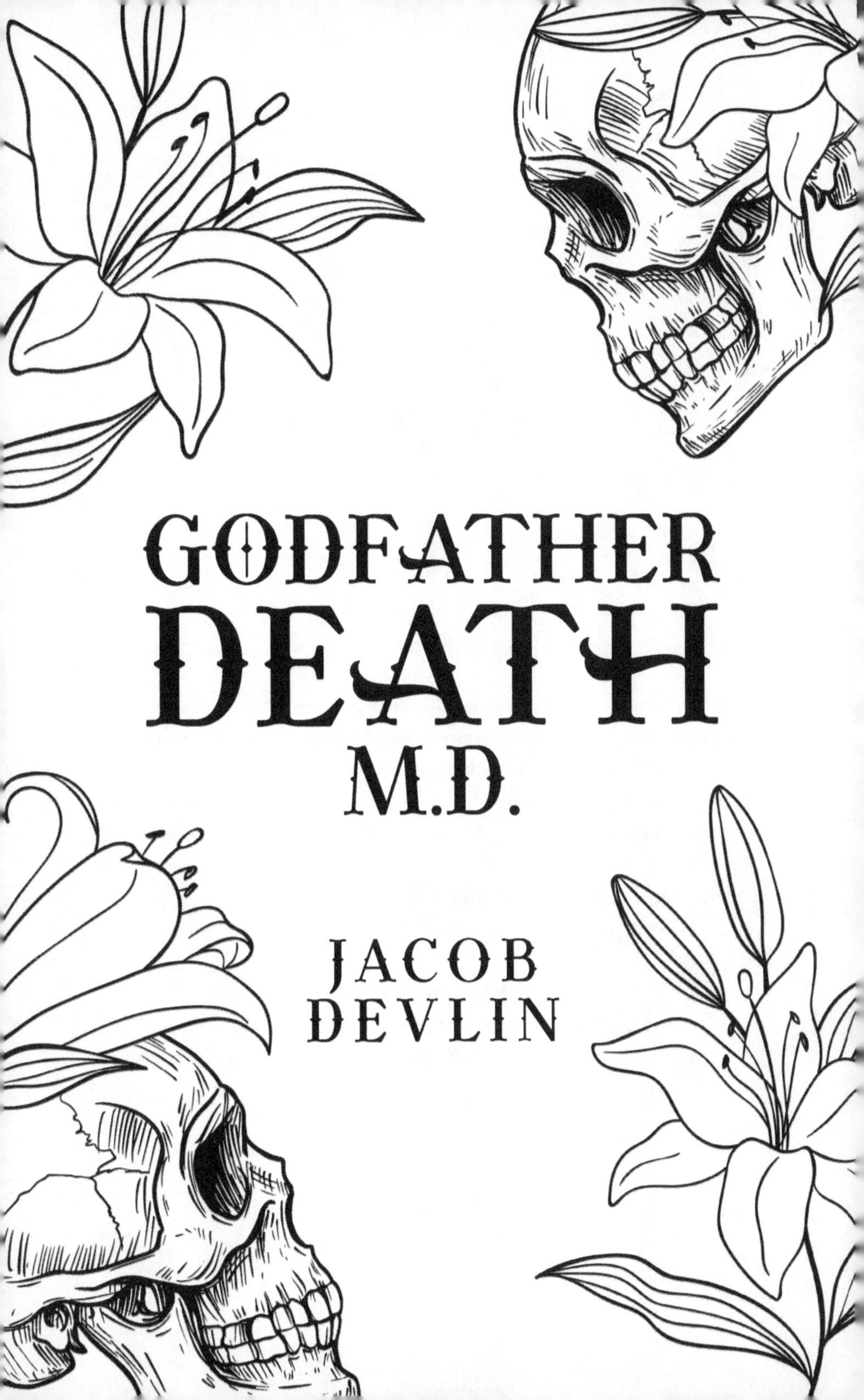

GODFATHER DEATH M.D.

JACOB DEVLIN

GODFATHER DEATH M.D.

Copyright © 2024 Jacob Devlin

AUTHORJAKEDEVLIN.COM

Editing by Silvia Curry

Cover and Interior Design by We Got You Covered Book Design

WWW.WEGOTYOUCOVEREDBOOKDESIGN.COM

TO THOSE REMEMBERED,

THOSE WHO REMEMBER,

AND THOSE WHO BRING US COMFORT.

AUTHOR'S NOTE

An earlier draft of GODFATHER DEATH, M.D. was originally published as a serial on Kindle Vella. While the content follows one narrative arc, each of the three parts represents a "season" and a slight shift. So, you can either think of this as a series omnibus or as a single novel. Both are true!

Because I tend to write lighter stories aimed at younger readers, I want to be transparent about the heavier/more adult nature of this story. Content warnings include death, grief, and strong language. While not intended to be gratuitous, each reader's comfort level is unique and valid. **Please be gentle with yourself as you read**. I might even recommend pouring yourself a soothing beverage like Aunt Cass would make, warming up your favorite comfort food, and taking a deep breath.

We're going to be okay.

With kindness,
JACOB

PART ONE

*"Pale Death beats equally at the poor man's gate
and at the palaces of kings."*

HORACE

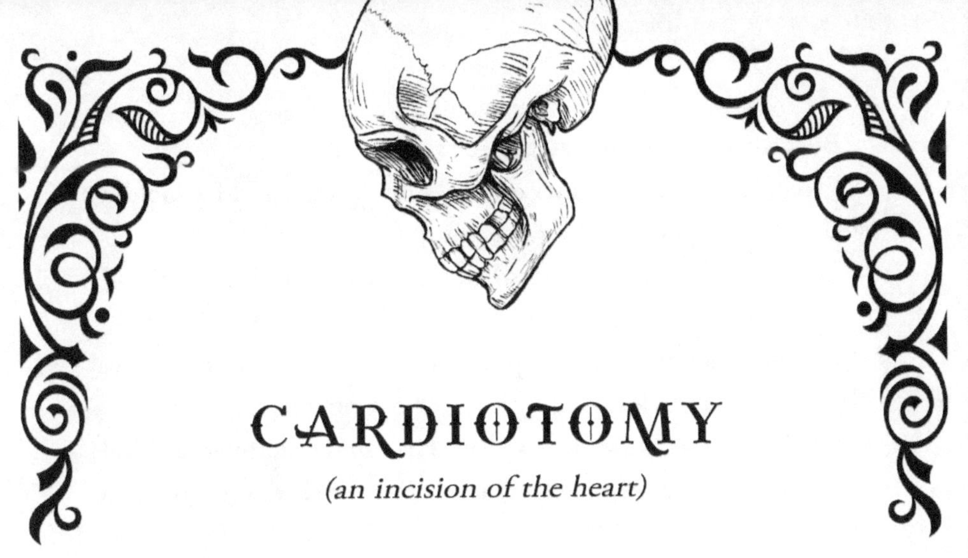

CARDIOTOMY

(an incision of the heart)

Daniel experienced four stages of grief in Mrs. Golden's English class—and they haunted him like ghosts.

Denial: He watched the sluggish hands of the clock wriggle along, and he told himself there couldn't possibly be thirty-five minutes left in the period.

Anger: Mrs. Golden called on Billy Schubert to share his rhetorical argument, her latest torture device disguised as learning. Daniel's temperature climbed as Billy sauntered to the front of the room.

Bargaining: Daniel told the universe he'd give up his phone or his beat-up old car—anything he still had—to escape hell a little early.

Depression: Billy cracked his stupid little know-it-all smirk, and Daniel buried his head in his arms.

Billy cleared his throat with theatrical gusto. "Good morning. I'm Billy Schubert, as you all obviously know—heh—and my report today is about the harrowing incident on the Grimm Memorial Bridge."

Daniel's lungs tightened. He felt the staggering weight of every eye in the room converging on him.

Is Billy serious right now?

"Ooh, how fitting," Mrs. Golden said with a sparkle in her eye. "And timely, too. I just heard on the radio that it's been ten years already. Such a fascinating topic."

Billy cut a side-eye at Daniel. "For sure, Miss."

"Well, I eagerly await your expert take on the matter." Mrs. Golden grabbed her clipboard. "Go right ahead, Billy."

Daniel raised his hand. "Ma'am, honestly, I kinda feel like this is—"

"Please don't interrupt, Daniel," Mrs. Golden scolded. "It's rude. And kindly remove your hat, please. I want everyone to remember the *one diva, one mic* rule. Billy has the floor right now."

Daniel slumped down in his chair. His cap did nothing to shield the intrusive gazes of his classmates. He took all that energy and stared daggers up at Billy.

Billy straightened his crisp stack of papers, snapped them in front of his face, and read.

"Life. Death. The fine line between. Since time immemorial, mankind has been obsessed with this line, especially when it is crossed far too soon. Such was the case when, one fateful day, a massive family decided to travel across what we once knew as the Costa Linda Bridge. Ten members of this family crossed the fine line between life and death, though they did not cross the bridge."

A muffled chorus of *oohs* rippled through the classroom. Half the class looked at Billy, while the other half stared at Daniel.

Daniel gritted his teeth and his knee rattled under his desk. "Ma'am, can I go to the bathroom?"

"You're interrupting again." Mrs. Golden held up a finger. "One more time, and I'll be docking your points for the day. You can hold it for five minutes. Hat, please."

"But—"

"Billy, please continue your beautiful analysis. That was an impressive hook, by the way."

"Thank you." Billy put a hand over his heart. "Oh, man. I lost my place. Where was I?"

"'They did not cross the bridge,'" Mrs. Golden prompted.

This has to be a joke.

Macy Sterling's bangles rattled when she raised her hand. "Can I say something?"

Mrs. Golden sighed and closed her eyes. "What is it, Macy?"

Macy put her fingertips together, her voice calm and her posture straight and tall. "Okay, real talk? This presentation is messed up. It's insensitive to some people in the room. There's a time and a place, Billy, and this ain't it."

Billy clamped his lips together as if he were holding in a snicker.

"Macy," Mrs. Golden said, "I hold the deciding vote on such matters, and Billy is pursuing his fundamental right to an education. The assignment was to craft a rhetorical analysis based on something real, and that is exactly what he's doing. Please show him the same respect that you were given during your presentation."

"Billy was on his phone the whole time," Logan Thane countered. "Just saying."

Mrs. Golden picked up her clipboard and scribbled some notes, her eyebrows high and thin. "The next person who talks out of turn is coming in for lunch detention every day for a week. Do you want to come in and read to me, Logan?"

Silence descended on the classroom. At some point, Billy had taken a seat on Mrs. Golden's desk, his legs swinging and boots scuffing the tiled floor. He thought all of this was a comedy show. Everything was Billy's playground, and Daniel had grown tired of The Billy Show in the fifth grade. That was the year Billy had started calling him the Reaper, and the nickname had spread like fungus.

"Billy, get off my desk, please." Mrs. Golden rubbed her brow. "Continue."

"Thank you. I hadn't even finished my opening paragraph yet. Let's see." Billy scanned his paper. "Oh! Ten of them crossed the line between life and death, though they did not cross the bridge. Like this fine line between life and death, the media is similarly divided about whether this fateful event was accidental. In this essay, I will attempt to argue that it was not."

Daniel sprang from his desk. "Is this a fucking joke?"

"*Daniel Grimm!*" Mrs. Golden eclipsed Billy at the front of the room and slammed her clipboard on her desk.

The class stirred with a mix of excited *oohs* and awkward stares. Heat flushed Daniel's body and his jaw was tight.

"Your anger is disrespectful." Mrs. Golden pointed at the door. "I've had it up to here with your outbursts. You're going to Mr. Jerricks's office right now. I will be advocating for your suspension."

Daniel rolled his eyes and scooped his notebook into his backpack. He didn't bother zipping it up on his way to the door. "Time away from here?" he scoffed. "I don't think I'm that lucky, ma'am."

Daniel marched down the hall, his feet feeling like lead.

He expected to hear the door slam, but instead, a clump of bootheels and a smack of flip-flops quickened behind him.

"Hey, wait up."

Daniel spun on his heel and looked into the faces of Macy and Logan.

"No, you two," he groaned. "What did you do? Go back to class."

"We're coming with you," Macy said matter-of-factly. "That was messed up, and Jerricks needs to know about it. We're gonna back you up."

Daniel hooked his thumbs through the straps in his backpack and looked at each of his friends in turn. He knew Mr. Jerricks wouldn't side with them on this. Mrs. Golden had been at Costa Linda High School for thirty-five years, though Daniel still didn't understand how.

Unlike Logan and Macy, most people only knew how to talk to Daniel in one of four ways.

Pity: *Oh, you poor thing. You must feel like death is following you everywhere.* He'd seen this written on so many faces that he almost started to believe it.

Fear: *This guy's cursed, and I'm in his path.* He knew that Mrs.

Golden had started keeping a rosary in her desk this year, and that it was specifically because of him.

Disaster tourism: *Tell me every detail, especially the gory ones.* That was where people like Billy Schubert dwelled.

Superiority: There was a gym teacher at Costa Linda named Mr. Mikes. Even though Daniel had never interacted with him, Mr. Mikes had clear, vocal opinions about Daniel's life. *Well, imagine being the eleventh child in any family. First of all, that's just plain irresponsible. I don't care what kind of money they come from or who they work for. There oughta be laws against having so many kids. And if you ask me, being number eleven cursed him from the womb.*

Ten years had taught Daniel that countless people considered themselves experts on his story and his pain. The internet housed a messy mosaic of details, both true and false, and all of them readily available at one's fingertips. Even if a thousand news sources worded the events differently or crafted their own details, the takeaway was always the same: Ten years ago, a large family drove three cars onto the Costa Linda Bridge one winter afternoon. A semi-truck swerved into the wrong lane and caused a pile-up that destroyed two of those cars, killing eight of Daniel's siblings and both his parents. The only survivors were Daniel, his two eldest siblings, Aunt Cass, and his godfather, Miguel.

The media endlessly turned the screw about the truck driver. There were prime-time news specials and a few podcasts about him…how he had been perfectly lucid that day. How he'd never touched a drop of alcohol in his life. A conspiracy claimed that the Grimms had leaked heavy government secrets and that the driver was hired to kill them, which was probably Billy's clumsy thesis. It was all an excuse to keep the story alive. The driver had no connection to the Grimms, no motive.

Daniel knew the fascination wasn't with the driver or the collision— road accidents happened every day—or even his parents' mundane engineering work for the government. No, the real obsession was with the size of his family. Had Daniel not been one of eleven kids, the media might've glossed over the accident and he could've faded into obscurity.

Instead, he became The Grimm Reaper.

Billy Schubert and Mrs. Golden were the icy tip of the glacier, and Daniel was exhausted. He knew he should've stayed home today.

"What if they suspend you, too?" Daniel asked Macy and Logan.

Logan shrugged. "Then we get suspended."

"I never thought I would hear you be so casual about that," Daniel said. "What about your college applications and stuff?"

"They'll get it," Macy said. "I know how to kick up some dust."

Daniel could've hugged Macy and Logan. They were the only part of high school he would cherish forever.

They sat together outside Mr. Jerricks's office for a brief eternity. The secretary watched them with a vulpine grin, like they were mice walking into a cat's domain. Through the frosted window, the principal paced back and forth and swung his phone cord, his words unintelligible.

Finally, Mr. Jerricks hung up his phone, dabbed his sweaty forehead with his sleeve, and nodded at the secretary, who smirked. "Mr. Jerricks will see you now."

The principal opened the door, releasing an odor of garlic and stale french fries. The redness in his face nearly matched the shade of his thinning hair and his bushy mustache. Something had already riled him up.

Daniel took the middle chair while Mr. Jerricks reviewed a set of notes on a legal pad. "Daniel," he said by way of greeting, "did you drop an F-bomb in your English class?"

"Sir, Billy was out of line, and—"

Mr. Jerricks swatted at the air. "Ms. Sterling, I asked Daniel."

"I did," Daniel droned. He already knew how this was going to end. "But yeah, Billy was out of line, and so was Mrs. Golden."

"That doesn't make it okay." Mr. Jerricks sucked in his teeth. "Glinda has been teaching at Costa Linda for thirty-five years, and she deserves every ounce of your respect. Frankly, even if she'd only been here for a day, that wouldn't give you the right to snap at her."

"You weren't in the room," Logan countered. "Billy's report about the bridge was insensitive to Daniel, and Mrs. Golden knew that. I mean, on the anniversary of the day he lost his family…? That's the most messed up thing I've ever heard."

Mr. Jerricks frowned and looked at his desk. "I see."

Daniel's breath hitched. "You agree?"

"Now hold on," Mr. Jerricks said. "I didn't say I agree. I trust that Glinda had a good reason for allowing Billy to continue his report, regardless of whether you agreed with her. With that said, I do understand that you're delicate about this subject."

Macy folded her arms. "Is he delicate, or was the subject wrong?"

"Is this how you were talking to your teacher? Because I'm not feeling respected right now." Mr. Jerricks swiveled a bony finger between Macy and Logan. "And frankly, I expected better from you two. All you've accomplished—all that brilliant potential—and now you're mouthing off and rebelling during your last year of high school? Come on. I can see Mr. Grimm's anger is rubbing off on you."

"What does that mean?" Daniel asked.

"Now don't misunderstand, Daniel. You're a victim of terrible circumstances, and anyone in your shoes would be a troubled young man." Mr. Jerricks glanced back at his notes. "Now, it's my understanding that you've already been through extensive counseling. I recommend you continue. Seeking mental help is a brave thing."

Daniel rolled the tension from his shoulders. No amount of prompted journaling or venting in a healing circle would save him from the Billys and Mrs. Goldens of the world, no matter how therapeutic it was.

"Wow—" Logan began as Macy took a deep breath.

"Guys." Daniel held up a hand, silencing his friends. "Sir, that's not the point. Yes, counseling is wonderful, but that's not what I need right now. What I need is for you to transfer me out of Mrs. Golden's class. Regardless of my mental state, which is crystal-clear right now, I'm not comfortable in that room. I'll take the standard English."

"I don't think that's the best solution at this time," Mr. Jerricks said, and Daniel scowled. "Don't give me that look. Our job at Costa Linda is to prepare you for real life. In real life, you will not always see eye to eye with the people you work with, and you will not always like them, but you will have to learn to work with them anyway."

Daniel tilted his head back and closed his eyes.

"Real life, huh?" Logan said. "As if everything Daniel's been through has been some sort of practice run? He's probably lost more than you and me and Mace put together. He's the last person any of us have a right to lecture about *real life*."

"Logan," Mr. Jerricks said. "I want you back in class. You, too, Macy. I never want to see either of you in my office again unless it's to practice graduation speeches. As for you, Daniel, Glinda has advocated for your suspension, though I'm inclined to give you another chance. However, your anger has no place in my school, so knock it off. I seriously doubt this is the vision your parents had for you."

Daniel stood, his jaw sore from clenching. Mr. Jerricks's Adam's apple shifted with a silent gulp.

"You know nothing about what my parents wanted," Daniel muttered.

"Enlighten me. I'm certain it wasn't swearing at your teachers," Mr. Jerricks hissed. "You're under the care of your godfather, no? I will be calling him immediately to discuss your behavior."

"That's some kind of choice," Daniel said. "Tell him I said hello and ask him how his last ten years have been."

Mr. Jerricks's mustache twitched, his face reddening behind it.

"My mistake. Your *aunt*."

"Oh my." Macy crossed her legs, a smug grin spreading across her face. "I can't wait until she hears about all this."

"The queen herself," Logan added.

"Go back to class, I said!" Mr. Jerricks used his legal pad to shoo Daniel and his friends toward the door. "And be kind to your English teacher. I don't care if Death himself is teaching you rhetoric; I'd still expect you to give him the highest respect."

Daniel scoffed. "Honestly, if Death himself walked among us, I'd give him the same thing I'm about to give to you."

Mr. Jerricks rested his fist against his temple. "And what, pray tell, would that be?"

Then Daniel paraded both his middle fingers in front of him and marched out of Costa Linda High School without another word.

At long last, he thought. *Acceptance.*

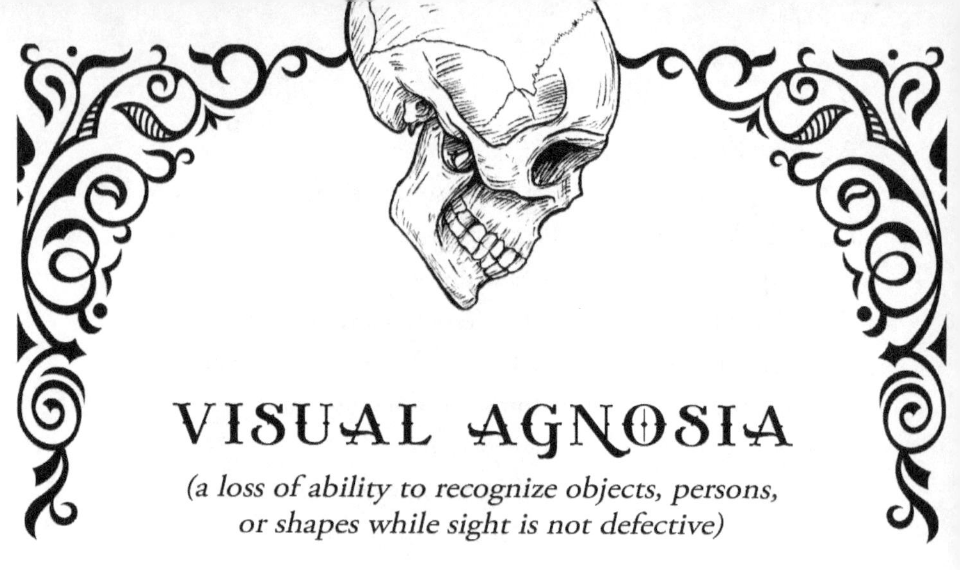

VISUAL AGNOSIA

*(a loss of ability to recognize objects, persons,
or shapes while sight is not defective)*

The crisp breath of autumn whispered through the Crescent Gate Cemetery, blowing dried leaves and flower petals at Daniel's feet. He walked among the storied headstones with his hands in his pockets, the grass soft under his boots. The dull ache of coming here never seemed to wane. Aunt Cass always promised him he'd learn to carry it, so he started bringing a backpack.

Near the bottom of a flowered hill, the ornate family monument stood in smooth black granite. GRIMM adorned the top in regal white letters, followed by a column of names. Daniel unzipped his backpack, fished out a checkered blanket, and spread it out in front of the grave. Then he sat cross-legged on top and breathed in the scents of soil, roses, and bread. A sugared loaf of *pan de muerto* sat in front of the grave, letting him know someone else had been here earlier. Whoever it was, they had also left ten white roses in the vase. Daniel and Aunt Cass had never celebrated Dia de los Muertos, but he knew about the tradition. An offering such as the *pan de muerto* was said to invite the spirits back to the land of the living for a short time.

"If you talk to them and then you listen quietly," Aunt Cass once said, "you'll hear them answer you in the wind."

"Hey, fam." Daniel brushed a finger over the cool granite. "It's been a little while, and I'm sorry I haven't been visiting more often. That's on me."

He studied each name in turn. Hope and Jonathan, his parents. Nancy. Alexander. Victor. Samuel. Monica. Ruthie. Bobby. Elena. Eight siblings, from oldest to youngest. He wondered if Katie and Zeke—the two eldest—remembered today was the tenth anniversary.

"I see someone's been by to visit you all," Daniel said. "I'm glad. It's an important day. Unfortunately, it hasn't been a great one."

He sighed. The conversation with Mr. Jerricks grated like bamboo under his fingernails. Would his parents be disappointed in him? Daniel wasn't sure. Education was a priority for them, but so was pride and standing up for one's beliefs. They would've hated Mrs. Golden, but they probably wouldn't have loved Daniel's attitude toward her, either.

Shortly after he stormed off, he'd received the email that he'd been suspended for three days. Then he treated himself to a milkshake to celebrate.

"We should probably talk about it," he continued. "Technically, it's only a few days. I don't know if I can ever go back, though… or at least, not to that high school. It all sucks, guys. It sucks that you're just a research paper for some people. It sucks that the system favors authority, especially when they abuse their power. It sucks that I don't know how you would feel about any of this, because I can't ask you. I know one thing, though; I wish you could've met Macy and Logan. I'm not sure how I'd survive high school without them."

The two of them had offered to come with Daniel to the cemetery after the fiasco with Mr. Jerricks. They knew today's anniversary was a big deal, but they also knew this conversation was his alone.

As Daniel talked about his friendships and memories, he played with the old lighter in his pocket. It used to be his dad's. Daniel was always mesmerized by the little phoenix engraving, which appeared to breathe fire when Dad lit it up for birthday cakes and the occasional cigar.

Daniel rarely needed a flame, but he always carried the lighter. The grooves of the spark wheel soothed his fingers and his nerves on hard days, and he liked to believe it fired up a little luck, too.

"I didn't come here to talk about myself, though," Daniel said. "I wish there was some way you could tell me about *you*. You know, the multiverse is becoming a topical thing lately. Logan tried to explain it to me with quantum physics one day, but I prefer the fun stuff, like comic books and whatnot. I like this idea that there are infinite worlds out there. It just sucks that I'm stuck in one where I lost you, but it helps me to think that maybe you found the Perfect Universe. I've spent a lot of time dreaming this up. You made it across the bridge, and you're happy. I imagine Bowser joined you when he died."

Daniel wished Aunt Cass would get a dog. She'd confessed sometime after Bowser died that she was reluctant to take him in after the family tragedy, but he nestled his way into her heart because of how fiercely he protected Daniel. Bowser was a tiny little guy, but he thought he was the king of the neighborhood.

He kept playing with the spark wheel while he described the Perfect Universe. Wherever the Grimms were now, they were living a sitcom life. They joked, and they had casual misadventures that could all be resolved in thirty minutes or less. The shadow of death was explicitly forbidden from darkening their bubble.

Wherever they were, the twins were scheming goofballs. Victor was a slick-haired, leather-jacket-toting rockstar, and Ruthie's arts and crafts weren't just a hobby, they were a production. The world would finally hear Nancy's music and read Sam's writing, and every sibling had found their niche. Disorderly chaos was normalized, but always comedic…lidless kitchen blender fiascos and summer barbecues where everyone ended up tangled in the pool with their clothes on.

Daniel would forever search for this universe in stories and songs and dreams.

He talked until a gust of wind ruffled the blanket and sent ripples through the grass. Up on the nearby hill, a sycamore tree stood bathed in golden, autumn-touched leaves, and the breeze rattled them.

A man leaned against that sycamore.

The man wore a black felt coat, a baseball cap, and a surgical-grade face mask. He held a to-go coffee cup and kept the other hand tucked into his pocket. Even though he wore dark shades, Daniel could feel his gaze, pointed and direct. And when they made eye contact, the man did not look away.

The sycamore tree was a lush, peaceful spot to enjoy a coffee, but out of all the places to rest one's attention, did he have to stare right at Daniel?

Daniel looked away and tried to put the man out of his mind.

"Where was I? Nancy, I think about how I'm almost as old *now* as you were when the collision happened. But I get into these spirals where I'm like, in the Perfect Universe, are you the same age you were when you left? Because that would make me older than *all* of you now, and you all used to call me the baby. So, that kinda hurts my brain. I always thought you all seemed so grown up. And now that I'm seventeen, it's weird…Am *I* supposed to feel grown up right now? This is the kind of thing I wish you could teach me. Aunt Cass is my favorite person alive, but I miss having siblings—even the ones who hog the TV and the hot water. It's stupid how sometimes I used to want more attention, and now here I am, just one guy sitting here rambling and," a knot lodged itself in Daniel's throat, "and screaming into the wind."

None of them would ever hear this. There was no Perfect Universe where the Grimms survived. And in this one, death was a sharp and hideous cut to black. There were no post-credit scenes and no encores; there were only ashes under mounds of dirt and cold family headstones strangled by weeds. Who among the Grimms would ever smell the roses in the vase? Who would savor the *pan de muerto* or follow a trail of marigolds?

These rituals were for the comfort of the survivors. They did nothing for the dead.

Through hot tears, Daniel glanced back at the sycamore.

And the man stared back, his coattail fluttering in the breeze.

A chill prickled Daniel's arms. Aunt Cass had been wrong. The dead didn't answer him in the wind, but the living would never stop thriving on his pain. *This is disrespectful.*

"Excuse me," Daniel called. "Can I help you over there?"

The man didn't budge. He might as well have been a statue.

Daniel waved an arm. Maybe the stranger was wearing a pair of earbuds he couldn't see. "Sir? Hello?"

The man lowered his mask to take a sip of his coffee, revealing a thin dark beard. He smacked his lips, replaced his face cover, and continued staring.

Daniel clenched his fists. "You know, I'm used to all the disaster tourism, but some people come here to mourn the dead. Do you mind?"

He considered the idea that maybe the man intended to spook someone in the graveyard. Some people never grew out of the urge to be assholes for no reason, like Billy Schubert. And the thought boiled Daniel's blood.

He stood and marched up the hill without a real plan for what would happen next. "Hey, you want to show some respect? I don't know who you are or what your deal is, but you must be a real piece of work to spend your time this way. Do you have nothing better to do?"

Without a word, the man turned his back on Daniel and started to walk away.

"Hey." Daniel picked up speed. "I was talking to you."

"Apologies," the man muttered, his voice barely above a whisper.

Daniel planted his feet by the sycamore. The man strode away and cleaved a path through the graves until he reached the parking lot. There, and without looking back, he tossed his coffee cup into the trash and then jumped into a midnight blue sedan.

"Good riddance!" Daniel called.

At least it wasn't a reporter. A few of those tended to show up every anniversary, like moths to a flame.

When Daniel caught his breath, he detected the lingering traces of the man's scent. Something about the combination of rain, spices, and cedarwood had a faint aura of familiarity.

He looked back toward the family's grave, his stomach lurching. Was the stranger there to mourn the Grimms from afar?

"Did one of you know him?" he whispered.

His parents did have their share of secrets, and keeping them was part of their life's work.

A cool gust of wind caressed Daniel's cheek.

"If that's a sign," Daniel said to the monument, "I don't know what to make of it. But I won't keep you. I promise I won't make you wait too long before the next visit, and I love you all forever."

He shook the dry grass off his blanket and packed it up. The earthy scent clung to the fabric, but it paled in comparison to the stranger's smell lingering in Daniel's nostrils. Long after he got in his car and turned the heater on, the smell gnawed at the back of his mind. It would haunt him until he figured out where he knew it, like a name on the tip of his tongue.

He drove toward home, cycling through radio stations to ease his mind. At the end of a tangle of commercials and news reports—one of which featured the anniversary of the Grimms' deaths—Daniel settled on an old rock ballad that tapped on the corners of his memory:

"I have stood here waiting for you and now I'm holding strings, picking up the pieces of our hearts and broken things…"

He didn't know the words or who sang it, but the melody had been collecting dust inside his mind. He once knew someone who was obsessed with the tune. Daniel could hear someone humming it—no, playing it on the harmonica. They smelled like rain, spices, and cedarwood.

"You live with your godfather now, no?"

"Tell him I said hello, and that I hope he's enjoyed the last ten years."

Daniel veered into the nearest gas station and shut off the car, his heart rioting.

Between the mask, shades, hat, and the years that had blurred together, Daniel hadn't recognized the stranger on the hill. But sometimes names, scents, and melodies dislodged memories Daniel didn't even know he'd shoved into the cracks.

He looked in the rearview mirror, wondering where that blue sedan was now.

That couldn't have been…

"Miguel?"

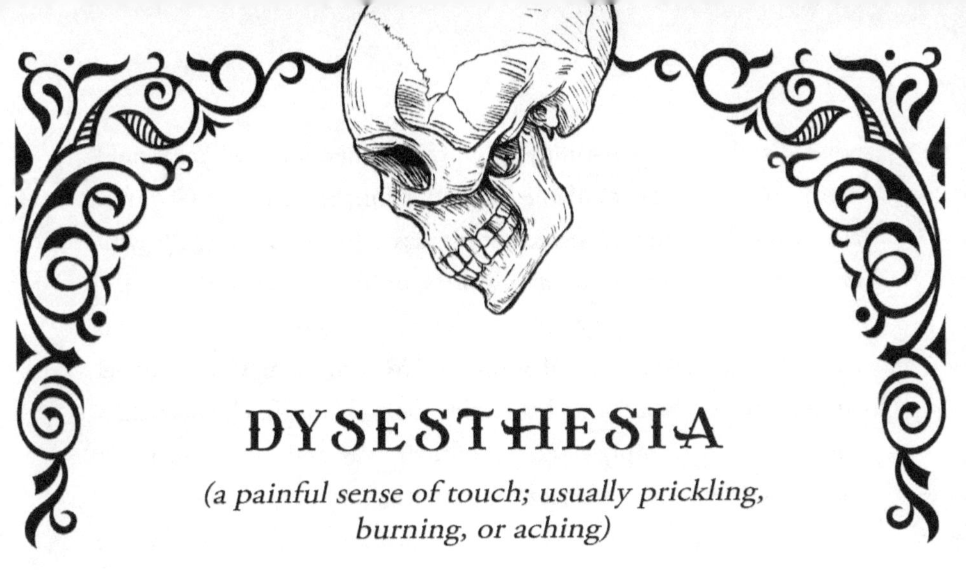

DYSESTHESIA

*(a painful sense of touch; usually prickling,
burning, or aching)*

A night of amateur internet sleuthing revealed that Dr. Miguel H. Mortiz, M.D., was an emergency physician at Hope Haven Medical Center, which was only fifteen minutes from home. The website displayed a picture of a dark-haired man wearing a crisp white coat, a link between the youthful, bright-eyed groomsman in the Grimm wedding photos and the masked, bearded stranger from the cemetery.

Like clouds of cream in a dark cup of coffee, memories of Miguel bloomed in Daniel's mind.

Daniel liked what he remembered about his godfather, even when the memories were only fragments, scents, or general feelings of warmth. Some people left footprints that way. Dad smelled like coffee and had a presence like a crackling fireplace. Mom was all bright laughter and fresh laundry. Victor—one of the oldest brothers—was hair gel and free-spirited charm, while Ruthie was cinnamon and fruit and endless optimism. The twins were grass, and Sam was a beat-up, well-worn hoodie.

There was a time when Miguel felt like a part of the family. He brought gifts for Christmas and birthdays, which seemed to happen every other day in the Grimm house. When the oldest siblings were booked with dates, part-time jobs, or school functions, Miguel would sweep in as the next available babysitter for the youngest Grimms. He'd wrangle them with ease, casting masterful attention spells with intricate pillow forts, immersive stories, or his old harmonica.

After the tragedy, the once-crowded Grimm house was sold, and Zeke, Katie, and Daniel all went to live with Aunt Cass. Miguel visited once or twice, but his demeanor was a little cloudier than before. Then, he simply faded out of their lives, and Aunt Cass never mentioned him again. Sensing the subject was taboo, Daniel never asked about him and, like the songs at the bottom of his playlists, he forgot Miguel existed.

Until the cemetery.

As far as Daniel could tell, Hope Haven's website was his godfather's only digital footprint. There were no social media profiles, no phone numbers, no hits on the search engines.

Why had Miguel disappeared?

Katie and Zeke each left Costa Linda to start something new—to get away from the pervasive memories haunting them everywhere they went. Sometimes Aunt Cass teased the idea of doing the same. It was nearly impossible to go anywhere without noticing the hollow spaces where his family should've been.

But Miguel hadn't left the city. He'd been practicing emergency medicine only minutes away the whole time.

There were some wounds medicines couldn't treat—only time could repair those. Who would know better than a doctor?

Daniel drifted to sleep pondering all these questions and more.

The next morning, he awoke to a light knock on his bedroom door. He stumbled out of bed and threw on yesterday's shirt. When he opened the door, Aunt Cass looked up at him in her baker's uniform—a light shirt and dark pants, with a creamy white apron folded in her arms. Her eyes were round, and her lips curled into a thin pout, a puppy-like expression of guilt.

"Hey, you," she said. "I'm sorry to wake you. Would you hate coming in to help me at the café for a few hours? Everyone's calling in sick, and I could really use the back-up. You know how weekends get."

Daniel pressed the heels of his hands over heavy eyelids, his mind still booting up to compute Aunt Cass's request.

"I'm sorry." Aunt Cass winced. "You don't have plans today, do you?" She steepled her hands in front of her. "I only need a couple of hours."

Daniel stifled a yawn. In another universe, he would've thought this was punishment for his suspension. Breaking the news to her had been a little awkward. She'd been almost stoic about it, hiding her thoughts behind a tight-lipped expression. A few minutes later, she had Mrs. Golden on the phone.

"Yes, *Glinda*, I understand that you feel this is an appropriate scenario to explore research and make effective rhetorical arguments, but as Daniel's aunt—and as someone who personally experienced the traumatic events in question—I am effectively arguing that it is not appropriate to force him to sit through a whole paper about it! Cite me!…Sure…No…Absolutely not…Okay, then I think I'll *research* going to channel nine and *explore* having them run a story about this whole thing. Goodbye."

Then she hung up, massaged her brows, and told Daniel, "I thought Glinda was supposed to be the good witch."

When he told Macy and Logan about that, the group chat combusted.

Aunt Cass asked Daniel what he wanted to do about school. He was inches away from the finish line, and he had his friends. But she also worried that Mrs. Golden and Billy were blights on his mental health, and she asked him to consider finishing his senior year online. He decided to think it over. He planned on taking a gap year before college anyway, which Aunt Cass fully supported. Somehow, he'd won the aunt lottery. The least he could do was spend a few hours helping her at the café whenever she asked.

"Yeah," Daniel finally croaked, his voice rough with sleep. Sunlight hadn't even pierced the blinds yet, but someone had to fire up the ovens before sunrise. "Yeah, I got you, Aunt Cass. Let me shower up real quick."

"My hero." Aunt Cass bowed her head. "Thank you, thank you, thank you. I was gonna drive us over there, but I don't want to keep you all day, unless you wanted to take the bus home. You wash up and come on by when you're ready. I'll get some coffee ready for you, sleepyhead."

Daniel threw his aunt a thumbs-up.

Daniel set off after a quick shower. At this hour, traffic was comfortable and easy, and there was something magical about watching the rest of Costa Linda wake up. That godawful bridge was a blemish on his vision, but it was fun to watch the lights checker the skyscraper windows on the other side of the river.

A helicopter descended on Hope Haven Medical Center, and Daniel thought about how to bring up his godfather to Aunt Cass. There had to be a reason she never mentioned him. Upon reflection, Daniel realized that Aunt Cass always avoided Hope Haven the same way he avoided the bridge. She had sliced her thumb with a santoku blade one evening, and Daniel insisted on driving her to the hospital. Aunt Cass evaded the idea for over half an hour, after which her finger still pulsed blood around her nail.

"You really need stitches," Daniel had said. "I'm driving you."

"Fine." She wrapped a hand towel tight around her thumb. "But don't take me to Hell Haven. That is the ninth circle. Take me to Costa Linda General instead."

"Aunt Cass, that's another twenty minutes out!" And moreover, it was across the bridge. "Your thumb has a drumbeat."

"Costa General, or we deal with it here at home."

She wasn't usually one to invoke the iron tone with Daniel, but when she felt the need to use it, there was no sense in arguing. Daniel had half a mind to drive toward Hope Haven anyway. She wasn't the type to cause a scene in public, so what was the worst Aunt Cass could do? Get on a bus and refuse to go inside? But in the end, Daniel respected her wishes and took her to Costa Linda General. They cleaned her up, glued her wound shut, and sent them on their way.

Now, Daniel wondered if Aunt Cass's aversion to *Hell Haven* had to do with one Miguel H. Mortiz, M.D.

He parked at the café and tapped on the window. His aunt peeked over the counter. She bustled to open the door, wiping one floured hand on her apron and carrying a paper coffee cup in the other. The bell chimed, and then the rich aroma of coffee beans and cream hugged Daniel's soul.

"Here." Aunt Cass handed him the cup. "Your fave."

Daniel took a sip. A stir of chocolate. A splash of vanilla. A pinch of warm spices, all wrapped in a dark, silky brew of coffee. "*Mmm, magic wake-up juice.*"

It was this level of service that made Queen of Cups an award-winning gathering spot in Costa Linda. Aunt Cass not only knew her nephew, but she knew her regulars as well—she memorized their favorite beverages and pastries, their families, their stories.

She pointed to a cardboard box on the corner stage, where the café was known to host everything from acoustic guitarists to poetry readings and stand-up comedy. Daniel would never forget the night Aunt Cass made him, Macy, and Logan join her for a round of theater improv. "Would you mind helping me with the holiday decorations? I'm giving you full artistic liberty."

Daniel sifted through the garland and picked up a can of fake snow spray. "Now, Aunt Cass? It's November second."

"Exactly!" Aunt Cass's eyes brightened. "It's time to promote peppermint drinks, and I have an author coming this afternoon to sign copies of her Christmas romance novel. Would you humor me? Plus, I can't reach the tops of the windows without standing on the chairs." She put on a forced pout. "Go wild. Put your *magic wake-up juice* to work."

Daniel savored another sip, then unpacked the box.

"So, I was thinking." Aunt Cass worked her kitchen like a sorceress, conjuring her brews and firing the ovens. "Now that you'll have all this extra time at home for a while, we should spruce up the house. I want to paint the living room. We need fresh color…something more alive. Would you help me out next weekend? I'm thinking Friday night?"

Daniel gathered a spool of red garland in his hands. "Yeah, sure thing. Whatever you need, Aunt Cass."

"It's about time we get rid of the gray, huh?" Aunt Cass said. "Great. I'll order in some Chinese or something, and we'll make it an event. It'll probably take up most of the weekend, but there's no rush."

Daniel smiled. It lifted his heart to see Aunt Cass excited about decorations, paint, and new projects. She even put on some pop music while she iced her pastries, and Daniel lolled around the café looking for creative ways to arrange the lights, ornaments, and menorahs.

At the bottom of the box, Daniel found some Christmas stockings with the employees' names written in glitter. One of them shared a name with one of his sisters, Monica. With only a glance, he could smell the Christmas seasons from his childhood—peanut butter cookies, watercolor paints, and a crackling fireplace.

He wished he could remember where his parents found space to hang so many stockings. Every year, another detail faded from his memories, like Miguel had. What else had he forgotten? What would he forget next?

Daniel sat on the stage and ran the furry stocking through his fingertips.

"Hey, Aunt Cass?" he said. "Can I ask you something?"

Aunt Cass looked up from her mixing. Her hands moved mechanically and independently from her gaze. It was almost like she had a radar. She could crack an egg, separate it, and whisk in the sugar and milk, all without looking down. "What's up?"

Daniel rubbed the back of his neck. "You know how I told you I stopped by the cemetery on the way home yesterday?" he asked as Aunt Cass reached for an egg. "Well, I forgot to tell you there was a man there. He was kinda watching me from a distance. I wasn't positive because he was all covered up, but I think it was Miguel. My godfather."

Silence.

The room thickened as if Daniel had uttered a curse. For the first time, Aunt Cass faltered. She dropped the egg, the shell imploding and oozing its goopy mess onto the floor. She grasped the counter with both hands.

Daniel swallowed, his mouth suddenly dry.

"I was wondering if you could tell me why he doesn't come around anymore," he added softly.

Aunt Cass's long lashes fluttered as she blinked a few times, like she was coming out of a trance. She pursed her lips. "Daniel, you know you can talk to me about anything, right? Sex, drugs, politics…I welcome it all. But the name you just invoked?" She waved her hands around the café as if conjuring a ward. She peeled off her plastic gloves, then tossed them aside. "That is off limits in this space, in our home, and everywhere."

"I'm only curious what happened—"

"Off limits, I said." There was a warning in her voice.

"Why is it so taboo?"

"Daniel, I am begging you—"

"I'm only trying to understand—"

"Because you're *my* boy!" Aunt Cass slammed a palm on the counter, rattling a pile of silverware and kitchen utensils, and Daniel jumped. When he looked up at Aunt Cass, her eyes glistened with tears.

Daniel ran his hands through his hair. Aunt Cass had never raised her voice at him—not like this.

"You're *my* boy," Aunt Cass repeated, this time barely above a whisper. "Isn't that enough? Haven't I done a good job raising you? I always thought it was the one thing I got right…" Her lip quivered.

Daniel rushed up from the stage, smearing the broken egg with his heel before he caught Aunt Cass in a hug. "I'm sorry. That's not what I meant. You're perfect. You've done everything right."

Aunt Cass scrubbed a wayward tear from her cheek and looked away. "Gosh," she said. "Look at me. Snapping at you in my sanctuary. I'm a disaster."

"You are not a disaster," Daniel said. "I honestly don't know how you do everything. You hold everything together. You raised *me* pretty much single-handedly for ten years, and you still make a badass Aztec mocha."

"It didn't keep Katie and Zeke here," she said. "I haven't heard from them in years. Did they hate their lives here that much? And now you're wondering why you ended up with me."

"Zeke and Katie are complicated," Daniel said. "I never thought about how much it probably hurt *you* when they left. But I don't think it had anything to do with the life you provided for us. I think they were just trying to go their own way and get away from all the bad memories." He gathered some paper towels to clean up the egg. "And I didn't mean to suggest that I'm unhappy here, either. I couldn't have asked for anything better. I only had a memory of Mig—my godfather—and I was curious about what happened to him. That's all."

Aunt Cass dabbed her face with a napkin. "We could still leave, you know."

Daniel scrubbed the broken egg yolk from the sole of his shoe, then tossed the napkins.

Every time she talked about leaving Costa Linda, Daniel wrestled his thoughts. A fresh start meant no Billys, no bridge, no more death chasing him. But it also meant no Macy and Logan. No Queen of

Cups. No reminders of the *good* memories he still had.

Aunt Cass sighed. "I didn't mean to yell at you. For that, I apologize." She leaned back against the counter and looked at the ceiling. "The man you know as your godfather is complicated. I'm sure you remember the good things—gifts and music and ice cream—but don't paint him with a holy brush, Daniel. You didn't know the whole man. And you don't want to. You can take my word for it."

The coffee sloshed around in Daniel's belly. Suddenly he felt queasy.

"If you see him again," Aunt Cass continued, "walk the other way. Remember how I always told you not to play with a Ouija board?"

Daniel nodded. Ouija was one of the only things Aunt Cass had ever been strict about. He'd been curious before, and desperate for a sign that his family was happy. Logan had insisted that 'you can't text the dead,' and deep down, Daniel was squeamish about the idea. He never tried it.

"Well, this is the same thing." Aunt Cass pursed her lips and pulled on a clean set of gloves. "You should never get tangled with things you don't understand, and that includes your godfather. *Especially* your godfather. I'm sorry that doesn't answer your question, but that's all you need to know."

But why? Daniel's mind screamed.

Miguel Mortiz was one of the last living people connected to the Grimms. Daniel craved a fresh perspective on his family. He wanted to sample the memories he never got to make. In a world where the news outlets, podcasts, and the know-it-all teachers wouldn't shut up about the Grimms' deaths, Daniel had found another person who knew about their lives.

For the first time, Daniel believed Aunt Cass was wrong.

He had to go to Hope Haven Medical Center and talk to Miguel, if only for an hour or two.

Why meddle with a Ouija board when he had a living godfather in town?

A doctor…someone who could heal wounds?

Aunt Cass cleared her throat, straightened her posture, and glanced at the garland-strewn café. "The decorations look great. Would you help me ice the scones, please?"

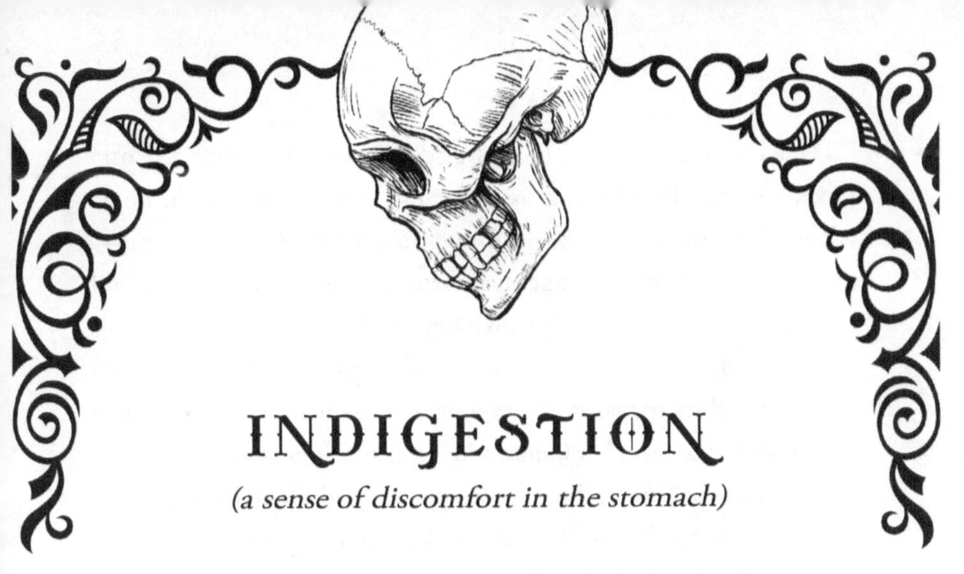

INDIGESTION

(a sense of discomfort in the stomach)

**At Hope Haven Medical Center,
you can count on us...for life.**

Daniel stared at the billboard, and the billboard glared back. He felt like its trio of grinning doctors were shaming him. Parking here had been a direct violation of Aunt Cass's trust. He lingered for a minute with his head against the steering wheel.

Why am I here?

What if Miguel didn't even want to be found? Or what if Daniel found Miguel and learned something he didn't like? Both options were possible.

But it was also possible that today could be wonderful. This risk could be the start of something great—an opportunity to peel back new layers of memories about his family.

In the end, Daniel left it all to fate. If he went inside the hospital and found his godfather, then it was meant to be. If Miguel wasn't there, then the universe didn't want Daniel to keep digging. He promised himself he would walk away and forget the whole thing. Such gambles were risky, and Daniel didn't usually believe in them. Sometimes, the universe just sucked. And if there was a cosmic significance to everything, then fuck the universe for the incident on the bridge.

Daniel went inside, and he was glad Miguel didn't work at Costa Linda General. That hospital assaulted the senses as soon as the doors opened. He remembered wading through a gauntlet of clashing odors—the stink of asparagus and dubious cafeteria meatloaf, the earthy blend of gift shop flowers, and the dizzying punch of cleaning chemicals that prickled the eyes. Plus, all the unsettling paintings in Costa Linda General's lobbies triggered his trypophobia. By the time he had taken Aunt Cass home from her knife accident, Daniel's stomach felt like the bizarre, holey paintings. The hospital probably admitted more patients because of the smells and the artwork than anything else.

Hope Haven emitted a different feeling. The pleasant scent of lemon soap lightly misted the air, and the paintings soothed him with their pastel tones and creamy textures. A rock water fountain trickled by the door, muffling sniffles and drowning out any anxious silence.

Daniel studied the hospital directory.

FIRST FLOOR
> **Admission**
> **Clinical Laboratory**
> **Emergency Services**
> **Sleep Medicine**
> **Cafeteria**
> **Restrooms**
> **Chapel**
< **Oncology**
< **ICU**
< **Surgery Waiting**

Where would someone find Miguel? The web mentioned he was an emergency doctor, but Daniel didn't think he'd be welcomed if he barged into Emergency Services.

Daniel must've stared at the map for a while, because the woman at the check-in desk cleared her throat with increasing violence until he acknowledged her. She peered at him over thick-framed glasses, gum smacking and eyes powdered with all the hues of a peacock. "Can I help you?"

This was the point of no return. Daniel approached the desk. "Yeah, I'm looking for Dr. Miguel Mortiz? Do you know if he's around today?"

The receptionist narrowed her eyes. "Do you have an appointment?"

"It's, uh, not really a medical thing." When the receptionist kept staring, Daniel added, "So, no, I don't have an appointment."

The receptionist's gum crackled like firecrackers in her mouth. "You do realize this is a hospital."

"Oh, wow. I didn't notice the sign outside." Daniel rolled his eyes. "Look, uh, Jan. No, I don't have an appointment. I'm here for a personal thing."

"There are sick people waiting to be treated, and you want to cut in front of them for a *personal thing*," Jan said. "Great. Let me go find the doctor."

"Wait, really?"

The receptionist blew a behemoth of a bubble, then shook her head.

"Fine," Daniel scoffed, "I get your point. Can I at least leave him a message or something?"

Without a word, Jan procured a pad of sticky notes with a Hope Haven watermark, then slid it across the counter with a blue pen.

"Thanks." Daniel picked up the pen and clicked the top a few times. What in the world could he express with a single sticky note?

Hi. It's your long-lost godson.

Long time no see.

Btw, why does my aunt hate you?

Let's have coffee.

Daniel scrawled a few words:

This was stupid. Did he want his phone number and personal life in the hands of this mean lady at the hospital desk? Daniel yanked the sticky note off the pad, crushed it into a miniscule wad, and flicked it into the trash. It landed in a wet paper cup, then bloomed into a soggy blob. He pushed the materials back to Jan.

"Never mind," he muttered. "Thanks, anyway."

Jan swept the pad and the pen out of sight. She looked at him like he'd wasted five years of her life, and he felt like he'd wasted a day of his own.

Daniel left Jan alone. The universe had spoken through a desk lady who probably hated her job. Jan was Daniel's only direct line to Miguel, and she denied him like a bridge troll. Fate had echoed Aunt Cass.

Stop looking.

In need of a pick-me-up, Daniel stopped at the vending machines on the way out. The first machine spat out a chilled can of iced tea. The second machine nudged a bag of chips within about an inch of freedom, then let them dangle. Some vending machines worked more like claw machines—sick games of risk designed to crush the soul.

"Come on," Daniel muttered.

Defying the warning labels, he latched onto the machine and attempted to rattle his chips free. He knew Jan would see him and have some words soon. But so help him, he would get the snack he paid for.

The universe owed him that much.

"You're never gonna believe this," a voice said behind him. "But if you unplug the machine and plug it back in, that usually finishes the job."

Daniel stopped shaking the machine, turned around, and did a double take.

Dr. Miguel Mortiz stepped around Daniel, took a knee, and jimmied the plug free from the wall. He wore a long white coat over a light blue button-down and navy slacks, as well as a dark face mask. When he plugged the cord back in, Daniel's chips and several other snacks plummeted from their spots.

"Dr. Mortiz," Daniel said. He wasn't sure if he could use his godfather's first name here.

The doctor put his hands in his pockets. "That's me. I understand you're looking for me?"

Daniel's tongue dried up. He hadn't planned out his words or even expected to find Miguel today. He cracked open his tea and took a sip to wet his throat. "Look," he said. "My name is Daniel Grimm, and…you probably don't recognize me other than…yesterday, when you were at the cemetery, and I kind of snapped at you, and that was messed up. I wanted to come and apologize, and I also remembered sometime after that moment that—"

"Danny," Miguel whispered.

A swell of warmth bloomed in Daniel's chest. A nickname implied a sense of family or closeness. His godfather had used this name before.

Daniel nodded. "Yeah. You're my godfather."

Miguel opened his arms and waved a hand in for a hug.

Daniel was never an enthusiastic hugger, so he was surprised at how natural it felt to meet Miguel halfway. He almost spilled some of his tea on the back of Miguel's coat.

"Gosh." Miguel gave Daniel a big squeeze. "It's good to see you. Do you think you can manage to call me Miguel instead of Dr. Mortiz?"

"Yeah." Daniel chuckled. "I think I can manage that, Miguel." He collected the snacks from the vending machine—his chips, a few packs of cookies, a pouch of trail mix, and some gum. He kept the chips and held everything else out to Miguel.

Miguel considered the variety of snacks. "That…is a nutritional nightmare." He took half of the cookies and the trail mix, then motioned for Daniel to follow him through the lobby. "But we should enjoy a little treat, shouldn't we? Shall we walk? Come sit with me for a minute."

Daniel followed Miguel into the cafeteria, a waystation of bleary-eyed patients, stone-faced doctors, and hopeful nurses. They stood in lines with colorful salads, umami burgers, and hearty pastas. Miguel scooted into a booth and motioned for Daniel to sit across from him.

"Miguel," Daniel said, "about yesterday—"

Miguel waved a hand and opened his trail mix. "Say no more. I didn't mean to intrude on your space yesterday. I was certain you wouldn't remember me if I approached. It must be startling to see some mysterious figure from your distant past watching from afar. I apologize."

"Me, too." Daniel's chin dipped down. "How have, uh…how have you been, I guess?"

"Ups and downs." Miguel moved his finger in a wave, lowered his mask, then popped a peanut into his mouth. "The past few years hit hard, as you can imagine. But we fight on. And you? You're happy and healthy?"

"I'm hanging in there," Daniel said simply.

"That's great," Miguel said. "I have to say, I feel like I'm looking at your father right now. Watch, turn your head this way…Yep, that's his jawline. But then here…" Miguel waved a palm in front of his face. "That's your mom's smile. Every inch of it. It's bewildering. You look great, Danny."

Daniel looked down. People knew the senior Grimms' faces from the news, but few had truly known his parents. Consequently, nobody had told him anything meaningful about his resemblance to them. Aunt Cass probably thought about it often, especially with the way she looked at him as he got older. But their conversations didn't tend to run sentimental or nostalgic. She cared for him like he was her son, but they often bantered more like brother and sister.

"Thank you. That means a lot," Daniel said. "And you know, you look almost exactly the way I remember you. I think the hat and the sunglasses threw me off yesterday. Maybe the beard. But you've barely aged a day. What's your secret?"

Without missing a beat, Miguel deadpanned, "A couple packs a day, and a steady diet of bourbon and junk food."

Daniel popped a handful of chips into his mouth. "I thought so. So that thing about an apple a day…it's all a web of lies."

Miguel doubled over in a fit of rich, joyful laughter. "There it is. I was waiting to see if you had your father's mouth. Man, we used to joke like this all the time. No matter how sarcastic I was, he would always fire it right back with a straight face. Your mother eventually started doing the same thing. Gosh, they were fun. They could be snarky, or they could be earnest. They wore all kinds of masks when they needed them. But above all, they were sweet."

"That's how I remember them, too," Daniel said. "They must've needed some thick armor to deal with eleven of us every day. Kindergarteners, pre-teens, and high school juniors all at one dinner table. Total chaos."

Miguel played with the ring on his finger, a smooth wooden band with a thread of silver in the middle. "That may be true, but they never thought of you all as a handful. They only had love for their kids, and you all treated each other very much the same way. Any family should be so lucky to have the bonds you all had. *Have.*" He nodded. "I was lucky to be a part of that. Those were some of the best days of my life. I think about them every day."

A trio of beeps chimed, and Miguel reached for his pager. His brows drew together, and he then slid the rest of his trail mix over to Daniel. "Gosh. I know we just sat down, but I have to take this. I'm so glad you stopped by. This was a beautiful surprise. Thank you."

"Likewise." A heavy feeling descended on Daniel's shoulders. They had just started talking about the family. For a minute, he'd forgotten that this was Miguel's place of work. Daniel wanted more time. "Can we catch up some more soon?"

Miguel stood, shoved his hands into his pockets, and bounced on the balls of his feet. "I would love nothing more. But in all truthfulness, we probably shouldn't be speaking." He worked his jaws. "I've been under explicit orders to never contact you."

Daniel scraped a hand over his face. "Aunt Cass?"

In retrospect, Daniel noticed Miguel hadn't asked about her.

Miguel pursed his lips, his head bobbing lightly. "It's rather complicated."

"Please." Daniel leaned on the table. "Talking to you right now was…it was like having my whole family here with me again. I want to know everything you can tell me about them. Besides, you didn't contact me; I contacted you."

Miguel shook his head. "Danny, no matter how technical we get about it, I have to honor the intent—"

"One cup of coffee." Daniel held up a finger. "Just one coffee when you're free. I'll even pay. I'm old enough to decide for myself who I want to talk to. Aunt Cass doesn't have to know."

Daniel could see the gears grinding together behind his godfather's eyes, his gaze suddenly evasive.

Miguel sucked in his teeth and blew out a deep breath. "Here. I'll do you one better. Let me treat you to a meal after school next Friday. But I have two conditions: Number one is that it's on me, of course. And secondly, you can't tell your aunt. She'll eat me alive, and I respect her too much to put her in distress."

Daniel raised his right hand. He didn't have the heart to mention that he wasn't in school anymore. "Scout's honor," he said. "Of course. Deal. That sounds great."

Miguel pointed toward the hospital entrance. "You know the little memorial park across the street? After school, meet me there by the angel statue, and we'll go from there. Does that time and place work for you?"

"Friday's good for me," Daniel said. "At the memorial park after school."

Miguel's pager beeped again. "Then duty calls, my friend." He swatted Daniel on the shoulder, and the clean scent of hospital soap drifted from his palms. "I'll see you Friday. And make sure you come hungry."

Miguel hurried away, and Daniel leaned back in the booth.

The universe was *singing* to him now. This meeting couldn't have gone better. Miguel was awesome.

Daniel already couldn't wait for Friday.

But wait.

Friday. Daniel had already agreed to help Aunt Cass paint the living room on Friday. A pang of guilt stabbed him in the gut.

He'd figure something out.

But how? How could someone as warm as Aunt Cass have such a bone-deep falling out with someone like Miguel?

Daniel tore open a new bag of chips. Maybe a little salt and grease would quell the rioting in his stomach.

DELIRIUM

(a sense of sudden confusion)

And there you have it. After several years, the disappearance of the DiLegno family remains wildly under-reported, and above all, unsolved. What happened to them, and what did their strange next-door neighbor have to do with their disappearance? Join the conversation on WowFeed and let's unpack some theories. We'll be back next week with a brand-new mystery on Strange Universe. *Stay curious, my friends.*

Logan stopped the recording on his laptop, whirled around in his chair, and faced Daniel and Macy. His feet were curled underneath him, and his hair was a little wild today—all spiky and windswept. "So," he said. "Feedback on the first episode, please."

Logan had been talking about starting a podcast since forever. His joy had been endearing.

"Dude," Daniel said. "How come I didn't realize your radio voice would be so soothing? Can you read me to sleep tonight?"

"Yes!" Macy gave him snaps, her bangles rattling. "Lowkey, I could listen to you narrate for hours."

Logan blushed and spun in his chair. "Shucks. The story didn't put you to sleep, though, did it?"

"No," Macy and Daniel said quickly.

Logan stopped his chair and raised a brow. "But?"

Macy threw up her hands. "But I need answers, Logan Thane! You can't just set up a mystery and then cut to black! Do you know what that does to me on a spiritual level? I'm gonna lose sleep over it!"

"I have to echo Mace," Daniel said. "I feel incomplete."

"That's kind of what I'm going for," Logan said. "The whole point is that they never end up figuring these things out, and then it sparks action. People need to be talking about the DiLegnos. For that to happen, people need to hear their story in a compelling way that also infuriates them a little bit."

"Some people like pain, I guess," Daniel said.

"And those people are wrong," Macy said. "You need an investigator to join you. Danny and I will go get the answers. You just keep narrating with that lush, beautiful baritone of yours."

"Well, I have ten cases for the first season," Logan said. "There are some wild stories people need to know, and it's the kind of stuff people wouldn't believe. It's kinda like your multiverse, Danny. Do you guys know about the so-called Pumpkin Prince of Belhaven? Or about the train that disappeared in Europe? Mysterious blackouts in New York? Because if you have any way to get answers about those things, then let's hear it, my friend."

Macy grabbed her purse and pulled out a small rectangular box. "Oh, I'll get you some answers. It's time for a practice sesh."

"I love ya, Mace, but your tarot cards will not solve *any* of my podcast mysteries. These may be weird cases, but there are logical explanations for all of them."

Macy opened the box and shook a thick deck of cards into her hand. "But wouldn't it be fun? We can do like a *Cards with Macy* segment."

"I wish that was more alliterative," Daniel said. "Can it be *Magic with Macy* instead?"

"It's not magic." Macy shuffled her cards. "It's science."

Logan made an X with his arms. "No cards on my show."

"Fine, then. Okay, Daniel, let's go. We'll answer *your* mysteries today since Logan's wearing his cranky pants."

"Logan's wearing his cranky pants," Logan parroted in a shrill voice.

Daniel shook with silent laughter. When Macy narrowed her eyes at him, he stopped, rolled his shoulders, and squared his body against hers. He never really believed in tarot, but it was becoming one of Macy's beloved hobbies.

Macy cleared her throat and tucked a lock of hair behind her ear. "First, my dear, my standard disclaimer: These cards are tools. This is a weather report. Whatever I'm about to tell you, remember that *you* ultimately have the power. The cards do not. Let's begin."

She asked Daniel to tap on the rose on the back of the deck. Then Macy picked up her cards, cut the deck in half, and shuffled. The matte rose artwork danced through her fingers.

A card jumped out and landed face down.

"Oops." Macy put the card aside. "The cards are talkative today."

"Or maybe you're just clumsy," Logan said.

"Nope." Macy fanned the cards out in front of her. "Draw three, boo."

Daniel wiggled his finger around, then chose his cards.

Macy tapped each card one at a time, then flipped them. "What is known…the ten of swords. What is unknown…The Devil. How to proceed…The Tower."

Then she flipped the card that jumped out while she was shuffling. "Death."

With a weary look in her eyes, Macy picked up her water bottle and drained it. Daniel found it unsettling how a single reading could cut Macy's energy in half, like sprinting a marathon or pulling an all-nighter. Daniel didn't like that.

Macy set down her water bottle and leaned in. "Well, this doesn't necessarily surprise me. The ten of swords in this position tells me that you've seen tremendous loss in your past. I know without the cards that you're a sweetheart. The warmth literally *radiates* from your eyes. It's all over your face. The people who recognize this aren't sure if it's because of your past or in spite of it, but the fact of the matter is that life has done you wrong." She tapped the first card for emphasis. "You don't like it when others define you by this incident, but for better or worse, it was the start of your hero journey. Tragedy has shaped the man you have become."

Daniel looked at his lap. "Mace, are you really getting this from the cards?"

"They look at you like you're bad luck," Macy continued, "but they're wrong. It takes maturity to become the man that you are, despite your difficulties. Nothing will ever justify what happened to you and your family. Fortune can be cruel and vindictive, but you are not. Remember this because I want to talk to you about The Devil."

Daniel studied the second card: a red, horned man holding a black rose.

"I feel like there's someone new in the picture," Macy said. "A stranger. And there's a mystery there. You find it hard to concentrate on what you knew before. You don't know all this person brings or what their true intentions are, and that's causing some inner turmoil. Daniel, is this true?"

Daniel thought about Aunt Cass's reaction to him asking about Miguel. *The name you just invoked…that's off limits.*

"Yeah." Daniel bounced his knee on the bed. "That's scarily accurate, actually."

"And who is this person?"

"It's…my godfather."

"What?!" Logan snapped out of the cocoon-like position on his chair. "You've never mentioned a godfather in your life."

"It's breaking news," Daniel said. "And I need you two to swear you'll never mention it in front of Aunt Cass."

Macy nodded her understanding. "Okay, I'm going to finish this reading, and then we're going to unpack what you just said." She tapped on The Devil card with a long fingernail. "I don't know anything about your godfather, but speaking purely from the cards, I do advise caution. If you're going to continue pursuing that relationship, you need to know yourself. If you're not careful, he may lead you into something toxic, and you may not be able to come back from it. If something feels off, raise your hand. Ring the bell. Set your boundaries. And if your godfather doesn't respect all this, then it may be a sign that it's time to turn around and walk. Sometimes it's better to keep some doors closed, no matter how much we want to know what's behind them."

Daniel couldn't help but notice the opposite was happening. Aunt Cass was the one putting up the boundaries, shutting down the questions when Daniel pried. But Macy still made a lot of sense. And he imagined these readings never got one hundred percent of the details right. He knew how his life fit into the cards, but anybody could fit their life into a tarot reading.

Macy moved on to the third and fourth cards: The Tower, and Death. The Tower reminded Daniel a little of Hope Haven. "Now these two concern me the most," Macy said. "If these ones didn't show up, I might not have been quite as worried about your godfather. But when Death jumps out in this position, it isn't usually a good thing, and it heightens my awareness of everything else we just talked about. The Tower indicates some sort of call to action or adventure. So, if your godfather invites you on a trip, or asks you to do something major, recognize your boundaries because of *this guy*.

"Now the common misconception is that when you see Death, it means somebody you know is about to die, and I want to shut that down right away. The thing with this card is that it means something is about to come to an end. End of cycle. New beginnings. Change. It could be a relationship running its course, or it could be as simple as losing your phone on the bus. But it could also mean you might lose a grasp on your current worldview and the way you understand things. Any one of these events could be a metaphorical 'death.'"

"Could it *actually* mean death though?" Daniel asked.

"It could," Macy admitted with a nod. "But I don't want that to scare you. The good thing is that now you have this weather report." She waved her hand over the cards. "You know the clues, you know yourself, and if anything about this feels foreboding or scary to you, remember that *you* have the power to shape where it's going. It doesn't mean you can change what's coming, but when you know there's rain on the way, then you can prepare. If you can't stay home or detour around it, then at least you can pull out your umbrella."

Logan clapped his hands slowly. "Good performance, Mace. You really know how to sell the baloney."

"It is *not* baloney, thank you very much," Macy huffed. "My mom has been doing this for years, and she's never been wrong."

"That's because you can literally make anything fit into your interpretations of these things," Logan said. "But hey, you do you."

"Stop killing my joy!" Macy hurled a pillow at Logan's chest, which he caught and hugged. "Now, spill the tea, friendo. Tell us more about your mystery godfather."

And with that, Daniel told his friends about Miguel. How he was Daniel's godfather, and how he used to be a part of the Grimm family. How he disappeared after the bridge incident. How Aunt Cass wanted nothing to do with him and completely shut down when Daniel started asking questions.

How they had plans to share a meal on Friday.

"And the thing is," Daniel said, "I don't know why, but I need this. I don't have a whole lot of family left, and Miguel knew them all. He might even be able to tell me things about myself that I don't know...or at the very least, about my parents."

When Daniel finished talking, Macy and Logan were silent for a minute.

"Dang," Logan murmured.

"Oh, Daniel," Macy said, "it sounds like there's some big drama there. Aunt Cass is probably one of my favorite humans on the planet. If someone managed to make her mad—"

"Then they probably had it coming," Logan said. "Like Mrs. Golden."

"That was kind of spicy." Macy gave some snaps again. "Cass for president. But what are you gonna do?"

Daniel shrugged. "I'm gonna hang out with him on Friday and see how this all develops. And somehow, I have to keep it from Aunt Cass."

"Ugh." Macy shook her head. "I can't stand an unsolved mystery."

"Right? The more my aunt insisted that I shouldn't contact Miguel, the more I wanted to know why," Daniel said.

"You know, when you put it that way, it's almost like your aunt was actually begging you to look into this." Macy beat her fist into her palm. "It's reverse psychology. You want to push the big red button."

Logan held up a palm. "Uh, Mace, hi. Remember your Tower? I don't think we should encourage our boy to go against Aunt Cass. *I* wouldn't even go against Aunt Cass. This doesn't feel right."

"Oh, now you like the baloney?" Macy rolled her eyes. "Forget the Tower. Just to play devil's advocate—heh—how bad can this be? Honestly, literally every family in the world has drama. Sometimes it's straight-up trash TV. Take it from the Sterling sisters."

"And the Thanes," Logan said. "Look at my mom and Grandpa Weston. They weren't even on speaking terms when he died."

Daniel frowned. "I didn't know that."

"It was stupid," Logan said. "But it's not like my mom loved him any less. Family's just a mess sometimes. Trash TV, like Mace said."

Daniel had fond memories of Logan's grandparents. Afterschool sandwiches loaded with potato chip crumbs. Swimming pool summers. The game room where the sun didn't shine, where he and Logan played video games into the bright hours of the morning, eyeballs fried and thumbs achy…The Thanes had been like Daniel's second family.

"What do you think Aunt Cass wants to protect you from, Daniel?" Macy asked. "Didn't you say he's a doctor?"

"But just because someone's a doctor doesn't mean they're a good human." Logan put his hands up in the air. "That's one of my upcoming podcast stories. I'm just saying."

"Well, we stand by you," Macy said. "Remember my weather report. I think you should enjoy this wonderful new relationship with your godfather. Just, you know, maybe take an umbrella with you."

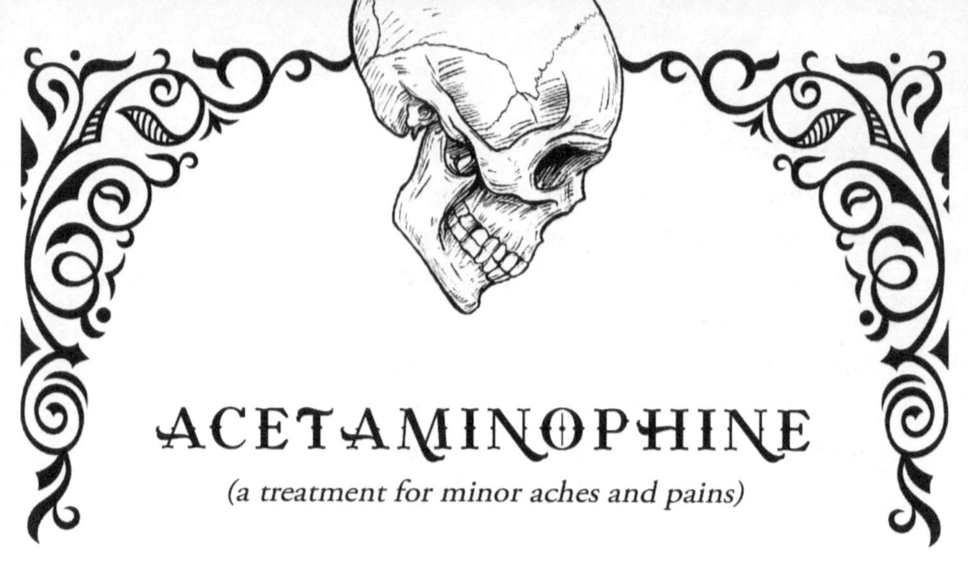

ACETAMINOPHINE

(a treatment for minor aches and pains)

On Friday afternoon, Aunt Cass's living room sprouted a playground of tarp, blue tape, and paint rollers. She had a whole production planned, including an upcoming trip to the furniture store. It was time for a new era. She worked the baseboards and traced Daniel's steps while he used his height to drench the corners of the walls in fresh paint. Aunt Cass had opted for a creamy beige, almost like her cappuccinos. They finished one wall together and jammed to an eclectic playlist before Aunt Cass suggested a break.

"Hey, you," Aunt Cass said. "I don't know about you, but I could eat a planet right about now. Do you want to go pick up some Red Lantern, or maybe some pizza? What do you feel like?"

"Actually…" Daniel said, "I'm sorry to leave you in the middle of this, but I need to shower up and pop over to Logan's for a few hours. Is that okay?"

"Oh?" Aunt Cass wiped her hands on her apron and reached for a rag. "He doesn't want to come over here? He can paint, or not paint. He can just eat all the yums with us. He's more than welcome."

Daniel fidgeted with a dry roller brush. "It's probably better if I see him in private. He's dealing with something kind of personal."

"Aww, poor thing." Aunt Cass scrubbed a sleeve over her forehead, leaving a thin beige crescent above her brows. "Well, no worries. I guess I'll just warm up some leftovers, then. We can keep working tomorrow and do pizza or something. Give Logan all my love."

"I will, Aunt Cass." The lie curdled Daniel's stomach like old milk. Not only did he hate lying to her, but now he'd yoked in a friend, and Logan hadn't been enthusiastic about the Miguel news to begin with. Daniel dropped Logan a quick text and included Macy.

Don't come around today. Aunt Cass thinks I'm at Logan's.

"Love you," he said. "I won't be out too long."

"Love ya too, Danny Boy." Aunt Cass tilted her head and leaned in. "Hey. You okay, by the way? Ever since the whole Billy thing, my *auntuition's* been going wild."

Oh, Aunt Cass. So heroic, she had her own version of Spider-Sense. Daniel winked. "Don't worry about me. Everything's great."

"Okay," Aunt Cass said. "But I've got my eyes on you."

Macy 'hearted' the text a few minutes later, then responded, **Omg! Have so much fun today!**

Logan didn't answer.

Daniel arrived at the memorial park early, which was little more than a patch of grass, an angel sculpture, and a few benches. He'd brought a few prints of old family photos. He'd meant to frame them, but in the end, he resorted to a sandwich bag. Still, hopefully Miguel would like them, and hopefully, he was still coming today. Sometime after their first meeting, Daniel realized they had never exchanged phone numbers.

Meanwhile, there was someone else Daniel had meant to reach out to. Cass's emotional confession at the café had been weighing on him—not only her thoughts about Miguel, but about his brother and sister, Zeke and Katie.

Daniel stretched his legs out on one of the benches and opened a new text for Zeke.

Hey Z, long time no talk. How have you been? I know this is

out of nowhere, but I'm about to have lunch with Miguel. Do you remember him?

His brows rose when the phone rang only a few seconds later. Phone calls usually made him scowl, but it warmed him to see Zeke respond so quickly.

Daniel answered the call. "Hello?"

"Hey, little bro, how you doin'?" Zeke was the kind of guy who never needed a microphone. "Saw your text and thought it might be good to hear your voice for once. Everything goin' well?"

"Sure," Daniel said. "It's nice to hear from you. Everything good for you, too?"

There was a brief pause on the other end before Zeke responded, "Eh, same ol', same ol'. You know how we do. We're survivors. Am I right?"

"Surviving, not thriving?" Daniel asked.

"Always surviving," Zeke confirmed. "But hey, I see you're going to lunch with Miguel?"

Daniel walked a circle around the angel to pump some warmth into his legs. "Yeah! It's all kind of weird how that fell into place. A bit of a long story, and I'm not sure how much time I have because he's on his way. Do you remember him?"

"Sure," Zeke said. "From what I remember, he was a cool guy. Really sweet and friendly. I feel like he might've been the one who brought me that signed baseball from the Mavericks at one point. And he always had the new Pokémon cards, too. Man, I should've kept all those—*and* the baseball. All that stuff is probably worth a fortune today."

Daniel felt a release of tension in his shoulders. He didn't know what he'd been expecting Zeke to say about Miguel, but it was nice to hear that his brother had positive memories—so different from the darkness Aunt Cass seemed to be strangling. He smiled. "You got rid of all your Pokémon cards when you could've given them to me? C'mon, man."

"I know, I know," Zeke said. "But hey, listen. I'm guessing you haven't talked to our sister yet?"

Daniel wrinkled his brows. "Is Katie okay?"

"As far as I know," Zeke said. "But since you're asking about Miguel, I suggest you connect with her. She has a theory about the guy, and we had a conversation about it sometime ago. I don't know how much weight it holds. Some weird alignments, for sure, but I don't know."

A gust of wind blew through the park, and the hair stood up on Daniel's arms. "Is it a bad thing?"

Zeke paused. "I don't think we can assign some huge cosmic value to what all comes down to a coincidence. It's kind of like rolling a Yahtzee, right? It's rare, but you're not supposed to change your whole religion when it happens. Better that you hear Katie's side of things, though. I don't want to take away her thunder or put words in her mouth. I'm sure she'd love to hear your voice, though."

Daniel bowed his head. "Yeah," Daniel said. "And on that same note, you should probably call Aunt Cass sometime. She's been missing you."

"Oh, Aunt Cass…She's a saint. I wish she knew how perfect she was, and I hope you're taking good care of her." Zeke cleared his throat, then sniffled. "It's just hard, you know? Carrying the history we live with. I spent two or three years meandering around Costa Linda like a zombie. Everywhere you go, you keep trying to redefine yourself over and over again, and the people won't let you. You're the cursed guy. I can never go back to Costa Linda, Danny. I see Ma and Dad and the kids everywhere. To this day, I *hate* myself for driving the car that survived."

"Zeke, I—"

"You know my leaving had nothing to do with you and Aunt Cass, right?" Zeke asked, his tone serious. "Because that's all I need to know."

"I get it," Daniel said. "All of it. But number one, I don't like that you're blaming yourself, because as far as I'm concerned, you saved our lives. I'm still here because you were driving that car. And number two, everything you just told me, you should probably tell Aunt Cass."

There was another pause on the other end, and then Zeke let out a sigh as powerful as his voice. "You're right. You're absolutely right. I'll reach out to her soon. Thank you for listening. I didn't mean to get all dark on you."

"It's fine," Daniel said. "I know you just said you can never come back to Costa Linda, but if you don't have Christmas plans, I'm sure Aunt Cass wouldn't mind hosting you here for the holidays. Just saying, there's an open invitation."

"That's a nice thought," Zeke said. "Hey, I'm gonna let you go. But it's good to hear from you, Danny. I don't know where time goes, but man, you've grown up. It's wild."

"Shucks," Daniel quipped. "Thanks for calling, Z. Don't be a stranger."

"Take care."

The call ended, and Daniel rubbed his forehead.

He considered the stone angel. She had some cracks in her arms, and weeds bound her feet to the ground. Somebody had carved their initials into the back of one of her wings. She'd been through her share of storms, but somehow, she was perfect.

"Excuse me, sir."

Daniel jumped, then turned to see Miguel standing behind him. In lieu of his white coat, Miguel wore jeans, a flannel, and a jacket made of rough brown suede. He wore the same shades he'd worn at the cemetery, yet Daniel still sensed the gleam in his eye.

"Hey!" Daniel said. "I didn't even hear you coming."

Miguel went straight for the hug, blanketing Daniel in that scent he remembered from years before. "Good to see you. You hungry?"

"I'm starving, actually." Daniel's stomach bucked.

Miguel chuckled and cocked his head to the side. "Then let's roll." He fished a set of keys from his jacket pocket and clicked a button. The lights on a dark blue sedan flashed. "I have a reservation at one of my favorite places to grab a bite. I guarantee you've never been there. Pardon the mess in my car, by the way."

Daniel opened the passenger door, revealing the cleanest, sleekest interior he'd ever seen. The leather still smelled new, and the floors appeared freshly vacuumed, with soft lines pressed into the floor mats. A single coffee cup lay on the floor, and Daniel raised a brow. "You call this a mess?" He could see himself in the windows, and not a single fingerprint marred his reflection. "I'm a little afraid to sit down in this thing."

Miguel waved it off. "You're fine. I never have passengers, so I thought I'd clean up a little bit. I'm aiming for a five-star review at the end of the ride."

Daniel stepped inside and buckled his seatbelt. The seat supported him like a marshmallow, and he melted right into it.

"Feel free to play with the heater and the radio. Make yourself comfortable." He did a shoulder-check, put the car into reverse, and drove away from the memorial park. "How was school, by the way? Are you at Costa Linda High?"

"I am," Daniel said. Technically, he *was* still enrolled. "But you know how the senioritis gets around this time. I'm ready to be done." He hoped Miguel didn't have any more questions about school. He didn't want Miguel to look down on him already.

"Sure, sure," Miguel said. "That's fair. A little unsolicited wisdom, though. Time goes fast. Try to enjoy what you have left if you can. I know everyone hates this question, but what's next? College? Work? Tell me everything."

Miguel was right; the question usually gave Daniel cold fingers. "I don't know yet."

"And that's perfectly fine. There's more to life than getting a credential, and you don't have to plan out your whole future this year." Miguel tapped the sunroof of the car as they pulled up to a red light. "But I think sometimes our inner ten-year-old is the best guide to what's in our hearts. You know what I remember about you as a boy, Danny?"

"Am I about to be embarrassed?"

Miguel shook his head. "You wanted to be a doctor."

Daniel's brows drew together. "I had a doctor phase?"

"You sure did. You had this little plastic stethoscope, and you'd walk around trying to listen to our heartbeats. I gave you a real one and you just about burst. And then your mother put together this box of cartoon bandages, and you walked around bandaging *everything*. Sam accidentally unplugged the TV one day, and you said it was broken, so you bandaged it." He chuckled. "You put so many of those things on one of Elena's dolls, she looked like a mummy. You told everyone she was sick. That's how I remember you."

Daniel thought for a minute. He remembered owning a stethoscope as a kid, and the mummified Barbie seemed familiar. These were faraway glimpses from another life. Maybe he still wanted all that in the multiverse—the *Perfect Universe* he'd dreamed up, where everyone was still alive and happy. "I forgot all about that."

"And there was another phase where you wanted to be a detective. You had a magnifying glass, and everything was a clue." Miguel scratched his chin. "Now that I think about it, it's no surprise that you tracked me down."

That was mostly the magic of the internet, but Daniel sat tall and grinned. "I'm glad I did."

The rest of the drive passed comfortably enough that Daniel and Miguel never even turned up the radio. Daniel wondered what he would've heard if he did. Was Miguel a country music kind of guy? Hip-hop and R&B? Smooth jazz and talk radio? If Daniel had to guess, he'd say folk and 80s hair metal, but he couldn't articulate why. He couldn't wait to discover clues about his godfather's life, and along the way, his own.

Daniel realized Miguel never told him where they were going for food—not until Miguel had turned on a quiet side road in the hills.

Miguel pulled over and pointed at the house at the end of the road. Daniel thought of a cozy Italian villa, complete with Roman archways, immaculate hedges, and a spacious balcony on the second story. "So that right there is my home," Miguel said. "And the way I see it, we have two options. I can cancel our 'reservation,' and we can turn around and go anywhere you'd like. Or we can go inside, look at some old photos of your parents, and share the bounty of mac and cheese in the crock-pot."

Daniel's mouth watered. He could feel stars popping out of his eyes like the emoji. He'd reached out thinking they'd enjoy a quick coffee and some small talk, but a home-cooked meal in a beautiful house? "I *love* macaroni and cheese."

Mac and cheese was his favorite—his comfort food.

And the promise of photos? Snapshots of the Perfect Universe? Daniel could've hugged the man.

"Some things never change." With a soft smile and a nod, Miguel pulled the car up to his driveway.

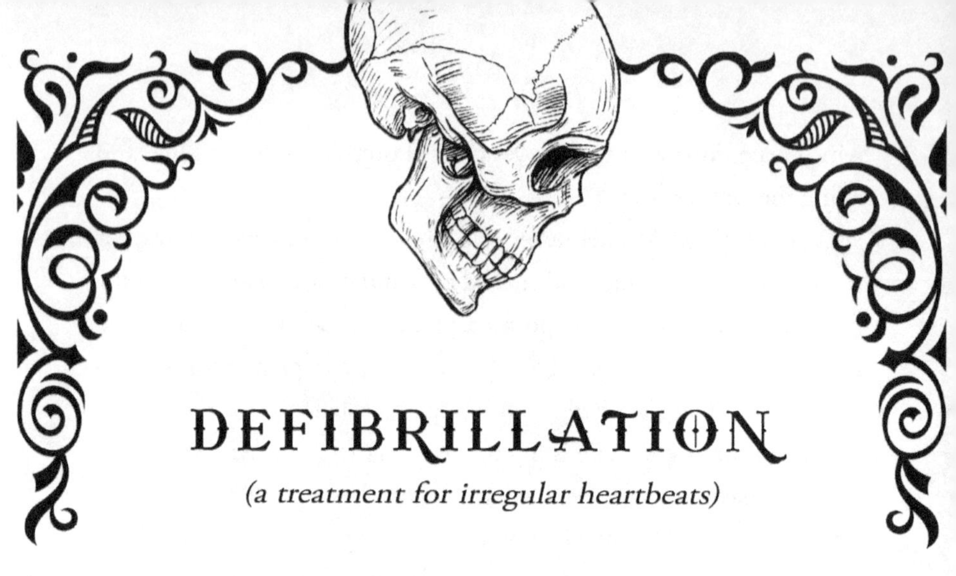

DEFIBRILLATION

(a treatment for irregular heartbeats)

The inside of Miguel's house looked nothing like the outside, but it reminded Daniel of a hobbit's home—cozy, warm, and inviting. Wood lined the walls and created a cabin-like ambience, while columns of stone contained the fireplace. The faint smell of leather hung in the living room.

Miguel hung up his jacket and pointed out some key amenities for Daniel. "Coat rack. Bathroom. Fridge. Shoes on or off, whatever makes you comfortable."

When Miguel slipped his shoes off, Daniel followed suit. A cat with fur the color of gunmetal appeared, seemingly melting out of the shadows, and it greeted Daniel with an inquisitive meow.

Miguel crouched and stroked the cat behind the ears. "Hello, my friend. Would you like to say hi to my godson?" He picked up the cat, and it nuzzled into Miguel's neck. "Gosh, forgive me, Danny. I completely forgot to ask if you're allergic. I can send Dorian to my bedroom if we need to. And of course, I have some medicine ready to go."

"Nope, I'm good." When Daniel stroked the cat, it purred happily, arching its spine into his fingers. "He's a cute little guy. His name's Dorian?"

With a proud nod, Miguel released the cat from his arms and

watched him bound around the living room. "I rescued him out of a dumpster behind the hospital about six years ago, and I named him Gray—I wasn't feeling overly creative that day. But the little guy hasn't aged a day since then. He can also be quite dramatic when he wants something. So, I call him Dorian now."

"As in Dorian Gray?" Daniel asked. "That's fitting. Do you have a painting of him somewhere?"

"I'm impressed!" Miguel's eyes gleamed. "You know your literature."

Daniel didn't enjoy anything he was forced to read in school, but he did enjoy the tale of the vain young man who sold his soul for eternal youth. Of course, that was all *before* Mrs. Golden.

"Speaking of which," Miguel said. "How 'bout I give you a tour of the bottom floor, and then we'll go eat upstairs in the library?"

"You have a library? That I can eat food in?"

"You'll see."

Daniel followed Miguel through his cozy home. With every room, the blurry picture of his godfather grew sharper and clearer, and a bittersweet mosaic emerged.

Miguel collected an assortment of trinkets—wooden figurines, old coins, keys, and candles. He displayed them with care in shadow boxes and on shelves. Every surface was free of dust and polished to a high shine. When Daniel asked him where he'd collected so many keys, Miguel joked, "Past lives," and left it there.

He had ample space, including an expansive backyard with a firepit, a rocking chair, and a swimming pool.

Miguel took pride in his kitchen and stocked it with every kind of spice, gadget, and oil. Here, Daniel smelled the buttery, nostalgic aroma of steaming pasta in Miguel's crock-pot. Miguel took it out to add cheese and threw it in a broiler for a few minutes. When Daniel saw the spinach and artichokes mixed in, a lump lodged itself in his throat. Normally, he didn't care for either of the greens, but Mom always used to mix both into her mac and cheese. The result was always a tangy, mouthwatering dream.

Miguel's library was a *different* kind of dream.

The first thing Daniel noticed was that the spacious inside seemed to defy the outside—like it shouldn't have been able to fit in Miguel's house. Wooden shelves lined the walls from floor to ceiling, and Miguel had filled them with books: Autobiographies. Mysteries. Adventure. Classics. Westerns. He collected everything, and he seemed to *read* everything, too. Every spine was cracked and well-loved, every page turned.

Miguel tidied up a stack of books and medical journals on a coffee table, then took a seat on an L-shaped couch. When Daniel joined him, Dorian curled up in the corner, eyeing the bowls of pasta.

Miguel cracked open his iced tea and held up the can. "Hey, cheers," he said. "To reconnecting, and to your family."

"*Our* family." Daniel clicked his can against Miguel's. "Cheers."

His godfather took a deep swig of his iced tea, then pointed at Daniel's pasta. "I don't think you've touched that yet. I'm waiting with bated breath to hear your thoughts."

"Well, if it tastes even half as good as it smells…" Daniel picked up his fork, and the cheese stretched like a rubber band.

The first bite was an explosion of earthy and tender artichoke, salted penne, and tangy, buttery cheeses. Every texture and every flavor harmonized into something greater than the sum of its parts; a memory. There was no way anyone else could get it to taste so close to what he remembered about his mother's specialty. It was her secret weapon to get the pickiest Grimms to eat their vegetables, and they were obsessed with it.

"Is this my mom's recipe?"

Miguel leaned in, holding his breath.

Daniel put down his fork, his throat tight with emotion. "Can I give you a hug, please?"

Miguel put a hand over his chest, then met Daniel in a quick side-hug. "The official Grimm stamp of approval." He relaxed his posture. "I was afraid to tell you I was making it, because I didn't want to raise your expectations. I attempt this every now and then, but I've never felt like it comes close to your mother's."

Daniel took another bite, and it nearly prickled his eyes with tears. "It's exactly like hers. And I can't even get a peanut butter sandwich to taste the way she did it. Aunt Cass comes close, though."

The pang of guilt poked at Daniel's chest again. He hated thinking about his aunt eating dinner alone tonight. Sure, she'd always been fine with it when Daniel was at Logan's or Macy's, but this time he was *here*, and he'd lied about it.

He'd make it up to her somehow. He'd give her extra help at the café or cook her dinner. But right now, he needed this time.

"Food always tastes better when someone else makes it," Miguel said. "Especially family."

"When's the last time someone made you food?" Daniel asked.

Miguel dropped his chin to his chest. "Hmm. It was probably when Jan brought in some brownies for Halloween."

"The mean lady at the desk?"

"She's actually quite sweet," Miguel said.

Daniel didn't think that counted as someone cooking for him. It made him even more sad for Miguel than he'd been for Aunt Cass. Here was a man with a spacious home, but he had no one to share it with. Here was a man with a billion trinkets, but no photographs framed in the house. Here was a man who only kept two bowls in his cupboard, and who rarely had the opportunity to enjoy someone else's cooking.

Here was a man blessed with kindness and charisma, but seemingly cursed with loneliness.

"I brought something for you." Daniel pulled his photographs out of his pocket. "You probably already have copies, but…"

Miguel shook the pictures into his hand, and a soft laugh escaped under his breath. "The wedding photos. I'll be darned."

The gleam in his eyes suggested that Miguel hadn't seen these photos in ages, but Daniel knew them well. A beachside ceremony. A raspberry wedding cake and a chocolate fountain. Barefoot dances and ear-to-ear grins. His parents had looked so young…immortal, even. Aunt Cass's hair had been longer, her cheeks fuller. In one, she blew bubbles at the camera. In another, she had even been dancing with Miguel, bright-eyed and cheerful. Daniel wondered if maybe their drama started as a romance.

Miguel flipped through the photos one by one, locked in some private memory. "Thank you, Danny. What a blast from the past. Their wedding was a shining memory in my life."

Miguel picked up his bowl and stirred his macaroni. "I always kept people at arm's length before I met your parents. Those two were different. They always made me feel included, from the day I met your father until the day—" He swallowed and cleared his throat. "The point is, there is no one else like them. It's special to be sitting here with you today and to know that my best friends' son is thriving."

Dorian jumped up on Daniel's shoulders, his fur soft and full against his neck. "Miguel," he said, "I'm not exactly thriving. I, uh… When you asked me about school, there was something I didn't tell you. I got suspended from school last week, and I kinda stopped going. I'm gonna do my spring semester online—I'm not giving up—but I can't go back to Costa Linda High."

Miguel rested his elbows on his knees. "What happened?"

Daniel steepled his fingers and took a deep breath. "There's this guy, Billy Schubert, in my English class. Total dick, honestly… pardon my French."

Miguel waved a dismissive hand.

"He's been in school with me forever," Daniel continued. "Devil-may-care, boots-on-the-desk sort of guy. He lives to get a reaction out of other people, and this time, I fell for it. We had to do this stupid rhetorical argument paper and present it in class. A bunch of people talked about vaccines or abortion laws. My friend Macy argued that a hot dog qualifies as a taco. But Billy Schubert decided to argue that my family was murdered, and he presented it while I sat in the middle of the classroom."

Miguel's eyebrows leapt up his forehead. "You're kidding."

"I wish," Daniel said. "The teacher let him go on. Mrs. Golden. She keeps a rosary inside her desk because she thinks I'm cursed."

Miguel shook his head and swore under his breath, his jaw tense.

"So I stood up and uh, spoke some French," Daniel continued. "And may have given some to the principal, too. He defended Mrs. Golden and Billy, of course, then went on some rant about how I'm a troubled teenager. Maybe that part was right, I don't really know."

"Listen to me." Miguel leaned in. "You have been through more than anyone should have had to cope with at such a young age. And I'm not gonna spin some yarn about how it was meant to be or how there's beauty in that. Nobody has the right to tell you what it's like to walk in your shoes."

The tension left Daniel's shoulders, and a feeling of warmth bloomed within. Miguel didn't look down on him after all.

"You have a bright light. And I'm not just telling you what you want to hear or what I remember about the kid with the bandages. You have this fire about you—like candlelight. It's quiet and it's contained, but it's also fierce and it can light up any dark room. And despite every storm life has thrown at you, that candle still burns. Don't let it go out too soon, Daniel. And don't ever feel like you're letting your parents down." He waved one of the wedding photos in his hand. "I promise they'd be overwhelmingly proud of the young man you've become. And for whatever it's worth, I am, too."

Daniel swallowed a lump in his throat. "Man, I don't even know what to say. Thank you."

"Say no more," Miguel said. "Have some pasta. We might as well eat it all, because if I send you home with leftovers, your aunt will catch on."

And she totally would. Her *auntuition* would trace the macaroni right back to Miguel.

Daniel took a deep breath, tapping his fork against his bowl. "So, is it too early to ask what happened between you two?"

Miguel picked up his tea, a thin crease appearing on his forehead. "Ah. I suppose I did just open that can of worms."

Daniel looked down. "I asked her about you, and I felt like I had set the café on fire with your name. You confirmed it yourself; she doesn't want me to talk to you." He swallowed. "What's going on there?"

"Ayy…" Miguel sipped his tea. "It's a very complicated story, Daniel. Believe me when I say, I would like nothing more than to tell you one day, but today simply isn't that day. It would ruin a good thing."

"But why?" Daniel asked. "Do you think I'll be mad at you, too, or something? Honestly, you're awesome. And I can't think of anything horrible enough that it would destroy my image of you. Isn't it better to rip off the Band-Aid and say whatever it is?"

"That's kind of you." Miguel twisted his ring around his finger. "Is it a total copout to suggest that you wouldn't believe me in the first place? Because that is another layer. And you wouldn't believe your aunt if she told you, either. That's at least one reason she won't tell you herself."

Daniel rubbed the back of his neck. "Well, when I was at the cemetery, I noticed how someone left some *pan de muerto* for my family. Bread of the dead."

Miguel nodded. "Mm-hmm. I know it well."

"Did you leave it there?"

"I did not," Miguel said simply.

"Huh." Daniel wondered if he would ever figure out who left the bread at the grave. It hadn't been Aunt Cass, either. "Anyway, I was looking at that bread, and I had a moment where I was thinking about a perfect world. I think about alternate universes all the time. Like, what if Aunt Cass never opened Queen of Cups? What if I were four inches taller? What if we were all on the Costa Linda Bridge even two minutes earlier, and everyone survived?"

Miguel frowned and looked back down at one of the wedding photos. The *I do* one.

"Not that I was wishing upon a loaf of bread or something," Daniel said, "but I almost believed that the *pan de muerto* would guide my family back to visit. Even for a minute or two."

Miguel tilted his head to the side.

"So then you show up on that hill a few minutes later." Daniel leaned in. "You of all people. Somebody who knows my family better than anyone else in my life, besides Aunt Cass. And now I'm in your house, talking about them and eating my mom's mac and cheese."

"And you think the *pan de muerto* summoned me?" Miguel asked.

"Of course not," Daniel said. "But it's cool, right? How we reconnected on the ten-year anniversary? I'm starting to think maybe sometimes the universe listens and makes things happen. *Sometimes.* And if it brought me here, then I could believe almost anything you ever told me."

"Almost." Miguel arched a brow and raised a finger. "That's the key word."

Daniel's shoulders deflated.

"The important thing is that you're here," Miguel said. "Let's lay the details to rest for now and have some more macaroni. I have more photos around here I'd be glad to show you, too."

The message was clear. There would be no answers tonight, possibly ever.

But maybe that was okay.

Daniel had stumbled on a friend. A godfather and a mentor. An extension of his family.

He wanted to keep developing this for what it was. Friends didn't march in and demand answers to questions nobody was ready to entertain.

So what if Aunt Cass wasn't a fan?

His parents were, and that was enough.

Daniel excused himself for more food. Dorian followed him downstairs, slinking around his ankles, and Daniel looked at the ocean of keys that lined the stairway. There were silver ones and bronze ones, winged ones, and some made of wood. One was shaped like an anchor, another like a scythe, and yet another had a bejeweled skull at its head. There must've been enough keys to open every door in Costa Linda.

Past lives, he thought.

Daniel's phone buzzed, and he did a double take when he saw his sister's name.

Hi. Heard from Z.
We need to meet.

INSOMNIA

(a difficulty falling or staying asleep)

Subject: Re: Dinner

November 10 at 7:46 a.m.

From: mhmortiz@hopehaven.com

To: dannyboygrimm@clusd.org

Dear Danny,

I've been informed that it's archaic and 'boomerish' to write emails in this age. I didn't think a text message would suffice today, and I don't have much trust in carrier pigeons anymore. Long story.

Your dad used to believe that when you have something difficult to say, you should say it in person. When you have something nice to say, you should write it down. That way, the receiver can read it whenever they want, and the words live on.

With that said, I wanted to thank you for sharing a meal with me on Friday. As I mentioned numerous times, you're a lot like your parents, and at the same time, you're unique. There is no doubt in my mind that they would be proud to see the man you've become, and I'm honored that you gave me that privilege.

I feel terrible that I couldn't answer your question, and I hope that this didn't spoil a good evening. Please know that I would never intentionally cause you harm. My silence on this matter is strictly for your own good.

Anyway, Thanksgiving is coming up soon. You probably have plans already, which is great. But if you'd like to share another meal around that time, be in touch. You have my number and my email address now, and you know where I live. In fact, any time you'd like to have some dinner, crash in my library, celebrate something, vent about something, or whatever it is that godfathers and godsons do, I'd be honored to play that role in your life. That is, if you want.

However, if you have reservations about staying in contact, I will also respect that and politely step aside.

In the meantime, I dug up some more photos and thought I'd send them your way.

Take good care,
Miguel

P.S.: For what it's worth, Dorian's a fan of you. You wanna cat-sit sometime?

Miguel H. Mortiz, M.D. | He/Him/His
Emergency Doctor, Hope Haven Medical Center
225 Hospital Dr., Costa Linda, CA, 94070
Email: mhmortiz@hopehaven.com | <u>Visit Us Online</u>
"Live as if you were to die tomorrow; learn as if you were to live forever." – Mahatma Gandhi

Subject: Re: Re: Dinner
November 11 at 11:29 p.m.
From: Daniel Grimm
To: Dr. Miguel H. Mortiz

Hey Miguel,

I still use email all the time, so 'ok boomer.' :P

Friday was awesome. Thanks again. You made me feel a lot better about the whole school thing, and I hope there are many cool memories to come. Totally down to hang with Dorian any time. The only thing is, apparently, Aunt Cass is allergic to cats…I don't know how I never knew this, but I came home covered in cat hair and she sneezed her entire lungs out. I had to lie and pretend my friend Logan got a cat, but his mom is lowkey allergic, too. It's whatev. I'll figure it out.

Katie and her husband are coming to town for Thanksgiving dinner, but if I can have TWO dinners? Omg. Let's do it. I'll bring whatever you need. Tbh, I'll probably end up buying it pre-made at the store, but it will be pre-made with love.

Daniel Grimm

Subject: Re: Re: Re: Dinner
November 11 at 11:35 p.m.
From: mhmortiz@hopehaven.com
To: dannyboygrimm@clusd.org

Great! I'll text you about dinner plans. Glad you get to see your sister soon.

I'm sorry about Cassandra's allergies… if you're serious about watching Dorian, I'll leave you a spare key. And a lint roller. Maybe some Claritin.

Off to bed, youngling. Tut tut.

Miguel

Subject: Re: Re: Re: Re: Dinner
November 11 at 11:38 p.m.
From: Daniel Grimm
To: Dr. Miguel H. Mortiz

"Youngling?" "Tut tut?" Wow.
   What are YOU still doing up?

   Danny

Subject: Re: Re: Re: Re: Re: Dinner
November 11 at 11:41 p.m.
From: mhmortiz@hopehaven.com
To: dannyboygrimm

Ain't no rest for the wicked.

   Ciao, my friend.
   Miguel

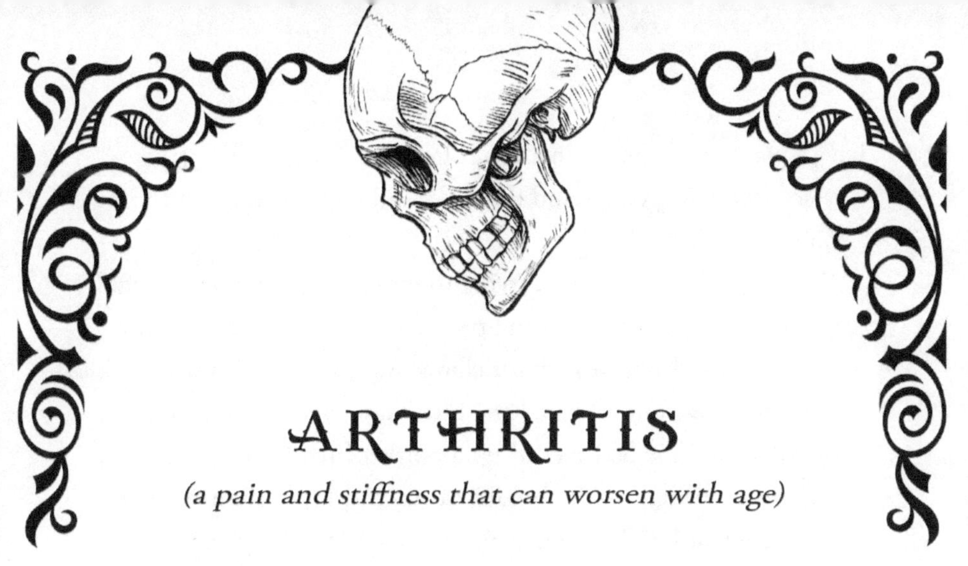

ARTHRITIS

(a pain and stiffness that can worsen with age)

Near the end of November, the smell of buttered honey rolls, roasted chicken, and creamy mashed potatoes filled Aunt Cass's home. She even let Daniel help with the stuffing, even though he'd been on fruit salad duty for years. Logan took that honor this year, and Macy brought a few bottles of sparkling cider.

And Katherine Grimm-Scott arrived with three different pies, her husband Justin, and a full baby bump.

Aunt Cass barely stopped grinning.

"So," she said at the dinner table, "I don't want to paint this holiday with sunshine and rainbows, but before we dig in, I see a lot to be thankful for right now. Should we share a few words?"

The group murmured their agreement.

"I'll start off." Aunt Cass extended her hands toward Daniel. "Daniel, I want to thank you for not burning the stuffing, and for all your help painting the living room this month."

Macy chimed in with an applause of snaps. "The living room looks awesome."

Aunt Cass smiled. "Thank you, Macy and Logan, for being such wonderful friends to my nephew, and for being a part of our family. I adore you both, and I hope that even after your graduation and whatever comes next in your lives, you'll continue to know that you have a place in my home and in our hearts."

Macy stood, jogged around the table, and hugged Aunt Cass from behind.

"Dang, Aunt Cass, are you trying to make me cry or something?" Logan picked up his glass. "Can I try some of that wine, by the way?"

Daniel nudged Logan with his elbow. Aunt Cass let Daniel drink wine sometimes, but he hated the bitter taste and the way it made his head swim. She had picked up a bottle of red for dinner, but it had gone unopened. Katie couldn't drink, and Justin didn't want to.

Aunt Cass bit her lip. "You're not driving home, are you?"

"I was thinking I could maybe stay here tonight?"

"Of course, you can." Aunt Cass pinched her fingers together. "Just a little bit, okay? And if your mom asks about it, I'm looking the other way."

"Deal." Logan picked up the bottle, looking like he'd just struck gold. He offered some to Macy, but she shook her head.

Aunt Cass continued her rounds. "Katie, Justin, grandniece-to-be: Thank you for coming and spending a weekend with me. It is so beautiful to picture the family you'll become. Just like I told the kids, you will always have a home here whenever you need it."

"Oh, Aunt Cass," Katie said, "this is *amazing*, and I want to raise my glass to you for all you've done for me, Daniel, and Zeke. I can't speak for Zeke, but I think I speak for Daniel as well, when I say that you are Superwoman, and we love you very much."

Daniel picked up his cider. "Yes. I couldn't have said it better."

Aunt Cass waved the comment away. "Oh, stop, you two."

"You may not have raised me," Justin said, "but I'll raise my glass to this wonderful meal and the home you opened to us for the weekend. I always love visiting you, and the angel Katie grew up to become speaks volumes about your influence."

Aunt Cass dabbed the corner of her eye with a napkin. "Thank you, Justin. Thank you *all* for having dinner with me tonight. It's so nice to get some family together, and I cannot wait to meet that li'l pumpkin. Here's to family."

The group clinked their glasses together, and Daniel downed some of his sweet and bubbly cider.

"Who's next?" Aunt Cass said. "Logan?"

"Me?" Logan took a breath. "Dang, how am I supposed to follow that?"

"Just speak from the heart," Katie offered.

"That wine oughta loosen your tongue soon," Justin said with a grin.

Logan chuckled. "Ugh, let's see. Well…I was gonna wait to say anything until I decided on something…" he sighed, "but maybe this is a good time to tell you all that I got into Harvard."

"Yes!" Daniel drummed his feet against the floor, and applause and cheers rang across the table. "Dude, I told you! You were all nervous about it."

"Congratulations," Katie said.

"That's the least surprising thing I've ever heard." Aunt Cass rested her fist under her chin. "Gosh, I'm so proud of you, kiddo. You keep drinking that wine! Tomorrow, I'm gonna bake you a cake. Any kind you want. We'll celebrate."

"Heck yeah, we are," Macy said. "Why didn't you tell us sooner? What are we gonna do?"

Logan shook his head. "Nothing." He pursed his lips. "Honestly. Nothing special."

"Dude, it's *Harvard*," Daniel said. "This is a big deal for you."

"Nope," Logan said. "Things are changing too quickly. I haven't made up my mind yet, but I have these cool offers and I don't know if I'm gonna stay in Costa Linda. When it comes to celebrating, I just wanna hang out and play video games with y'all. This is how I want to remember things. No big gestures, just lowkey, everyday memories with my best friends."

Daniel had understood a while back that these times were running thin. The weight just hadn't hit him the same way it hit Logan. Daniel was used to the brevity of beautiful things. Seasons ended. Aunt Cass's Aztec mochas were finite. So were lives.

"So yeah," Logan said. "Thank you all for putting up with me for all these years…enabling me with my podcast, sharing your food, and letting me crash on your couch and stuff."

Daniel threw his arm around his friend and pulled him into a buddy hug. "I love ya, man."

Logan cleared his throat, his eyes glossy. "This is too sappy. I'm done. Mace, you go."

Macy snickered and covered her mouth with a fist. "I'd like to say thanks to the wine in Logan's system. This is the most emotion I've ever seen from him, and I think he's *already* buzzed. Lightweight."

"Am not," Logan muttered.

"You are," Macy mouthed.

Logan shook his head. "Danny, I'm passing it to you instead."

Daniel thought for a minute. "Gah, why is it my turn?" He rubbed the back of his neck. "Y'all said all the good stuff already. This has been a hard year…it's been a weird month, actually. I can't even describe it all."

Daniel had visited Miguel one more time since they first connected. They'd set up the fire pit in his backyard, mixed a pot of hot chocolate, and then enjoyed it with toasted marshmallows. Miguel even played his harmonica. He played a few songs Daniel had never heard before—some with a rock edge, others sad, sweet, and folksy, but all beautiful and complex.

They didn't talk every day. After all, Miguel's grueling hospital hours were the opposite of Daniel's ample free time. But they exchanged a few emails, the occasional text, and Daniel felt they had built a real bond.

He'd stopped thinking about the big secret Miguel and Aunt Cass were keeping. He tried not to think about the fact that Katie had specifically come to town to blow it all open—at least, to present her theory. The chilling part? She'd refused to say anything over a text, a phone call, or even a video chat. It had to be in person…after dinner.

Logan kept telling Daniel that his 'Spider-Sense' was buzzing. Apparently, while he didn't believe in tarot, he certainly believed in comic books.

"Say one day you do solve your mystery," Logan had said. "Then what could you do? Even if I ever figured out what happened to the DiLegnos or the Fernweh Express, what could I ever do with that information?"

"Probably sleep better, for one thing."

"Or not," Logan had said. "Look, I get it. Miguel sounds awesome. Coming from someone who grew up without a dad myself, I would be thrilled to find a Miguel. But personally? I think everyone has their secrets, and you should stop knocking on this door, Danny Boy. You may not be able to close it again."

Macy's bangles rang as she waved a hand in front of Daniel's face, bringing him back to the dinner table. "Are you done, or do you have more to say?"

Daniel blinked. "Oh, I'm sorry. I zoned out. I guess what I really want to say thanks for is family—the family I get to share my name with…and the family I found."

"Aww!" Katie said.

"That's beautiful, Daniel," Aunt Cass said. "There's a lot of love in this room."

"If we keep this up, we won't need to eat anything sweet tonight," Justin said.

Katie groaned. "Pardon my husband." She tapped the side of her head. "Whatever part of the brain makes dad jokes, well…the baby woke it up."

Chuckles filled the dining room.

"It's science, babe," Justin said. "That's how I'm gonna become a great father."

"And maybe a single one," Katie deadpanned.

"Dang!" Macy pointed across the table. "Shots fired. Is this the part where we start the roast?"

Katie and Justin wrinkled their noses at each other.

Aunt Cass grinned. "No drama at the dinner table, at least, not tonight."

"So Daniel," Logan said, "speaking of dads and found family, what's Miguel doing for Thanksgiving?"

The world froze on its axis.

A sharp silence cut through the conversation.

Macy cleared her throat and looked at her plate.

Daniel looked from his best friend to his aunt, assessing the damage as alarms blared in his veins.

Logan clamped both hands over his mouth as if trying to force the words back down his throat.

Aunt Cass swiveled around slowly, revealing a look of pain and disbelief.

"Did I miss something?" Justin asked.

Katie put down her fork.

"I'm sorry, Logan," Aunt Cass said. "What was that name?"

Macy bit her lip, a lock of her curly hair brushing her cheek. Logan slowly removed his hands from his mouth, but the damage was already done. Between Daniel's dagger-eyed stare and the look of guilt on Logan's face, there was no finagling the story.

Daniel tried anyway. "It's a guy from school—"

"I asked Logan," Aunt Cass said tersely.

Daniel saw the lump in Logan's throat do a slow maneuver. "Yeah," he said as calmly as possible. "It's a friend from—"

"Don't insult my intelligence," Aunt Cass said.

Logan looked up at Daniel with a haunted, apologetic look.

"Aunt Cass," Daniel whispered, "I can explain."

Aunt Cass stood, her eyes full of tears.

Logan and Macy looked at each other.

"This is really good stuffing," Justin said.

When Aunt Cass spoke, she started off calmly, her voice carefully controlled. "I was *crystal*-clear with you." She paused. "There has been *one thing* in ten years that I've explicitly forbidden you from doing, and that was to stay away from Miguel."

Daniel's stomach tightened. He wasn't hungry anymore. "I know you did, and—"

"And did I leave *any* room for interpretation? Because you have no idea what you started. I mean, what the hell, Daniel? How long have you been keeping this secret from me?" By the end, Aunt Cass was shouting.

"Oh, I'm keeping secrets?" Daniel got to his feet. "That's awesome, Aunt Cass. That's *fascinating*. Let's have a conversation about how *I'm* the one keeping secrets from my family."

Aunt Cass tossed her napkin onto her plate and jabbed a dagger of a finger toward Daniel. "Not here." She grabbed her keys off the kitchen counter, fumbled with them, and marched for the front door. "Start saying your goodbyes. Next week, we start packing. We're leaving Costa Linda."

Daniel released something between a sharp breath and a laugh. "Are you serious right now? You don't mean that. What about the café?"

"I've never been more serious about a damn thing in my life." Aunt Cass opened the door.

"Aunt Cass, wait," Katie said. "Stay. Please. Let's talk this out. For once in our lives, let's have a real conversation about this!"

Aunt Cass looked over her shoulder, her gaze cold. "I have nothing to say."

The door slammed behind her.

Silence blanketed the home, and everyone looked at Daniel.

"Daniel…" Tears sprang to Macy's eyes.

"You should probably go home." Daniel pushed his plate away. "So much for a happy Thanksgiving."

Logan grabbed Daniel's shoulder.

Daniel shook off Logan's grip. "Don't touch me."

"Bro, I can't even tell you how sorry I am. Honestly. It just slipped out."

"Did it?" Daniel wondered if that was true. Regardless of the intentions, the impact still burned. "Well, in honor of Thanksgiving, *thanks*. Have a nice life, Logan."

Logan swallowed. "So we're done? Just like that? After all we've been through together, and—"

"Just leave it alone, Logan." Macy stood and pushed in her chair, a mascara-clouded tear spilling down her cheek. "I'll drive us home."

Katie reached over and grabbed Daniel's hand, though he didn't shake her away. "Let's go somewhere and talk, okay?" she said. "Justin, looks like the kitchen is yours. Do you mind?"

Justin picked up a dinner roll. "I don't understand what just happened." He put his thumb through the center, then tossed the bread aside. "Do you need anything?"

"Just a little space. We'll bring you back an ice cream. The baby wants Moo Factory," Katie said, "and there's something my brother needs to hear."

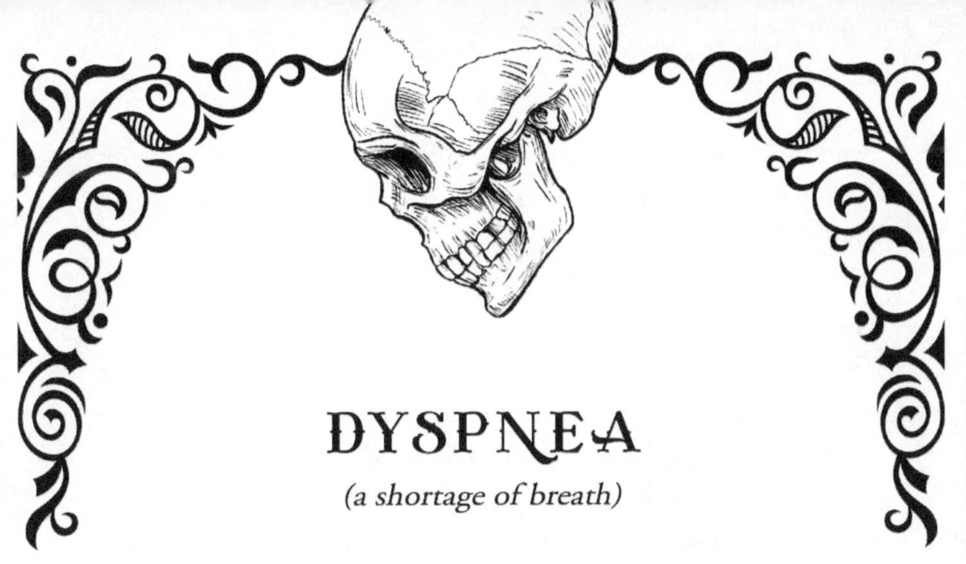

DYSPNEA

(a shortage of breath)

The roads were clear, and the drive was short. Even the Grimm Memorial Bridge didn't twinkle with its usual traffic. But the Moo Factory parking lot glowed like a beacon in the dark. Daniel pulled in and shut off the car.

"Of course this place is open on Thanksgiving," he muttered. He wondered where Aunt Cass stormed off to when everything else was closed.

Katie flashed some sarcastic jazz hands. "America, right?"

Daniel chuckled under his breath and unbuckled his seatbelt. "I mean, I do kinda want some ice cream."

"Wait." Katie grabbed his hand, then pointed to the ice cream shop. "We're not here for the ice cream. We'll go in and get some in a minute, but first, we need to talk in here."

Daniel's heart responded with a leap against his chest. "Okay."

"I know you have questions," Katie said. "It was important to me that we have this conversation as privately as possible, and I'm sorry we didn't have it before…before the drama tonight. I cannot risk a leaky text message, a bugged phone, or the wrong person listening inside the Moo Factory."

Through the window, Daniel could see two workers with their spotted hats behind the Moo Factory counter. They were alone, and they looked bored out of their minds, backs hunched and arms swinging. Katie's warning settled in, and Daniel swallowed. "A bugged phone?"

"Listen for a minute," Katie said. "What I'm about to tell you is not set in stone. Take it with a grain of salt here, and obviously, I expect that this will stay between us. However, I have a strong intuition, and…whether or not I'm right about the details, I'm damn certain that Miguel is not who he says he is."

Daniel reached for the locks on the door and flipped all four, his fingers going cold. His mind slowly filled with static. "I'm…I'm sorry, what?"

"Our godfather's a charming man on the surface," Katie said. "A charismatic angel. Kind. Personalizes every conversation and every thoughtful gesture. Makes you feel like you're the most important person in the world. Am I right so far?"

Daniel thought about the mac and cheese. The emails. The invitation to use his library. Every word of affirmation and act of kindness. "Yeah," he said. "Spot-on."

"Mm-hmm," Katie said. "The thing is, I keep up with a lot of true crime, and I know that *all* the stories start this way—with a person you would trust with your life. A kind, wonderful individual who couldn't possibly have skeletons in their closet. The football coach who went above and beyond for his players. The charming neighbor. The doting godfather. It never starts with a creep. That's why it always works."

"Why what always works?" Daniel adjusted the rearview mirror and glanced around. "Do you know something about him?"

"I don't want to freak you out or anything," Katie said, "but it's what I don't know about him that squicks me out. It's the fact that *nobody* seems to be able to find a goddamn thing about him. His whole existence is a ghost story. It has *Strange Universe* written all over it. Let me tell you why."

Logan would've been beside himself to know Katie listened to his podcast. Daniel almost cracked a smile. Then he remembered Logan just ruined his life, and his throat tightened.

"Until tonight, Aunt Cass didn't know you were talking to Miguel," Katie said, and Daniel nodded. "She's shady about him, isn't she? She doesn't bring him up, she doesn't acknowledge his existence, and if you even *think* his name, she invokes her *auntuition* and locks up like a bank." Katie turned an imaginary key at the corner of her lips. "Obviously, something happened between the two of them. Do you remember the last day he came around?"

"It's blurry," Daniel said. "But that's because it was nothing special or eventful. I'm pretty sure Zeke and I walked to the corner store for like, a candy bar or something. We came back, and Miguel came out of the house and told us he'd see us later, and that was kind of the end of it."

"Okay, now let me tell you what *I* saw, because I remember it clearly." Katie rolled her shoulders. "So, I come home from work one day, and Aunt Cass's car is there. Miguel's, too. The front door is locked. I open up with my key, and the screen door is also locked. That's the first weird thing. Aunt Cass never locked that screen door when one of us was out, because she knew it only opened from the inside. So I figure maybe she slipped up this one time, and I decide to ring the doorbell. Five minutes, Daniel. I stand there for five minutes, ringing the doorbell and calling for Miguel and Aunt Cass, but no one comes for me. Remember, I was yelling through a screen."

Daniel shifted behind the steering wheel. "That's…weird."

"Oh, it gets worse. Anyway, I start to panic and think maybe something went wrong in there. So, I take my clippers and I shredded a little hole in the screen to let myself in. I'm storming around that house like a banshee, and I'm calling their names, checking every possible room. Bathrooms. Showers. Closets. At one point, I started flinging the cupboards open, which just felt stupid. And the house was dead silent. To this day, the aura in the house from that moment…I-I just can't shake it. It's stuck in here." She rubbed her temples and looked out the window.

"Where were they?" Daniel asked.

"That's the thing," Katie said. "I still don't know. My eyes saw them come out of the *pantry*."

"The…pantry?"

"I know. My mind tells me that's impossible because that was one of the places I looked. Three times, I stood there, staring at the frickin' Cheerios, trying to come up with a better idea. You know Aunt Cass's pantry."

"Yeah," Daniel said. "That was my hide and seek spot. But I barely fit, even when I was a kid."

Katie put her face in her hands and shook her hair around. "There's no way that's possible, right? I keep telling myself that my mind was playing tricks on me, but the rest was crystal-clear. I remember Aunt Cass screaming at Miguel."

"*Screaming?*" The feeling in Daniel's gut was clawing at him now. "What was she saying?"

"She was hysterical. It scared me so bad, Daniel, that I hid around the corner. I barely understood most of what she was saying. But what I remember are the words, *You broke us.*"

"*You broke us.*" Daniel dug his thumbs into his palms. "Wh-what does that mean?"

"We have to fill in the blanks ourselves," Katie said, "because, as you know, Aunt Cass never said a word about it again. She looked downright terrified of Miguel, and the whole time, he was chill as a cucumber. A little hurt, maybe. But they were not on the same page about whatever conversation they were having. They weren't even in the same book."

Daniel watched his breath frost the window, obscuring his view of the parking lot.

"He left about a minute later," Katie said, "and he must've crossed paths with you and Zeke on your way back in from the corner store, and said goodbye. Aunt Cass went to her room, I went to mine, and I never said a word about the incident again."

Daniel scrubbed his fingers over his temples. "Um…you don't think that maybe Miguel and Aunt Cass were having some sort of relationship or something? There's a wedding photo—"

"Where they're dancing," Katie finished. "Yes, I've seen that."

"Yeah," Daniel said. "I keep coming back to that, and it's not like it would've started the apocalypse if they were catching feelings. Why would they hide it?"

"I want it to be that simple, Daniel. I really do. And I can't disprove it or anything, but remember, I was like seventeen or eighteen then. I was dating Luke Stone at the time, feeling a little boy-crazy and developing my radar for these things, but when it came to Miguel and Aunt Cass? Absolutely zero vibes." She made an 'O' with her fingers. "Unless they were experts at hiding it, which would be pointless. Aunt Cass knew we adored Miguel. If they were having a thing, none of us would've opposed them. We probably would've cheered for them. I don't know. I just don't think that's the answer."

Daniel couldn't help but recall Macy's tarot cards. The Tower. Unclear intentions. An upheaval. Her reading had been correct. This tower was drenched in mystery.

"As you know, Miguel pretty much ghosted the family after that, and I knew Aunt Cass was never going to talk about what happened. So I carried this memory around for a while, and over the years, I started to get a feeling with a capital F. There was this itch I couldn't shake. Like I said, I watch a lot of true crime. I don't trust people, and that keeps me alive. That's why a few years back, I hired a private detective to investigate Miguel."

"Oh?"

"Yes. Detective Charleston Fitch. I know, his name makes him sound like he walked out of one of those black and white movies, and whatever you're picturing, that's exactly how he looked. Anyway, I paid good money to have him do a deep dive into Miguel's life. It dawned on me over the years that we didn't know anything about where he was born, what his childhood was like, where he went to college, that sort of thing. Right?"

That fit. Miguel's house was mostly trinkets. Coins. Keys. Books. No photos, no documents, no signs of any past.

"So, Charleston Fitch follows Miguel around Costa Linda for about three weeks. He sits in an undercover van and watches him eat breakfast, drive to and from work, spoil his cat, and do the laundry. At one point, Fitch even goes in and poses as hospital staff for a while. It's all very cloak-and-dagger, CIA-type stuff. And then, three weeks later, I sit down to meet with him and go over his report. Do you want to know what he found?"

Daniel's throat was parched. "*Do* I wanna know?"

"Absolutely nothing. And I mean, nothing. This big-money detective couldn't even find a record of where and when Miguel had passed his medical exam. I mean, the Hope Haven website says one thing, but there's no proof anywhere else. Fitch called the universities, but they didn't cooperate because of FERPA or whatever. He kept hitting roadblocks everywhere, and Hope Haven was all like, *hm, shrug*." Katie paused. "That's a problem. I had half a mind to call up every news station in Costa Linda and tell them to run a story on the hospital. Had Miguel been a patient, sure, I know about HIPAA and all that confidentiality fun. But people deserve to know who their doctors are. *I* wanna know who's delivering my baby. Right?"

"I agree," Daniel said. "I see why that's shady."

"Oh, and get ready for the punchline. The day after my sit-down with Fitch, he's killed. Guess how? Surprise, surprise—a *semi-truck* hits him head-on, and the media looks the other way." Katie jerked a thumb over her shoulder.

Daniel's heart plummeted into his hips. It was a chilling coincidence. A semi-truck killed the Grimms. Aunt Cass claimed Miguel broke the family. A detective went snooping and died in a similar manner. Miguel circled *all* the edges. "You don't think that—"

"I think Miguel is some sort of hitman," Katie said bluntly. "With Mom and Dad being employed by the government, who knows? Someone could've ordered an 'accident.' I think Aunt Cass caught wind of Miguel's connections, and he intimidated her into silence. And when he found my detective sniffing around, he took him out, too. I know this is all morbid and I can't prove anything, but it smells like fish to me. If I'm wrong, I'll eat crow. But if I'm right, well, who would ever suspect a doctor as a mobster? There's zero proof."

Daniel leaned his head on the steering wheel, a headache simmering to a boil. He didn't even want the ice cream anymore. Nothing could be cold enough to numb his betrayal. "No," he moaned. "No. It can't be true."

"Zeke told me I'm reaching," Katie said, "and maybe that's fair. But even if I'm way off about the mob ties, we know Miguel is hiding something massive. We saw how Aunt Cass stormed off tonight. She's obviously afraid of him if she wants to leave this place. I'm not gonna tell you how to live your life, Danny. I haven't been around enough to earn that right, and you're an adult now. But I think leaving might be the answer. You have a niece on the way. Talk Aunt Cass into moving closer to us. Or go see the world. Go literally anywhere. But don't chain yourself to Costa Linda. I think it's cursed. It reeks of death. And if you stay here, then here's my two cents: In honor of Charleston Fitch and the family that loved you, you should probably stay away from Miguel."

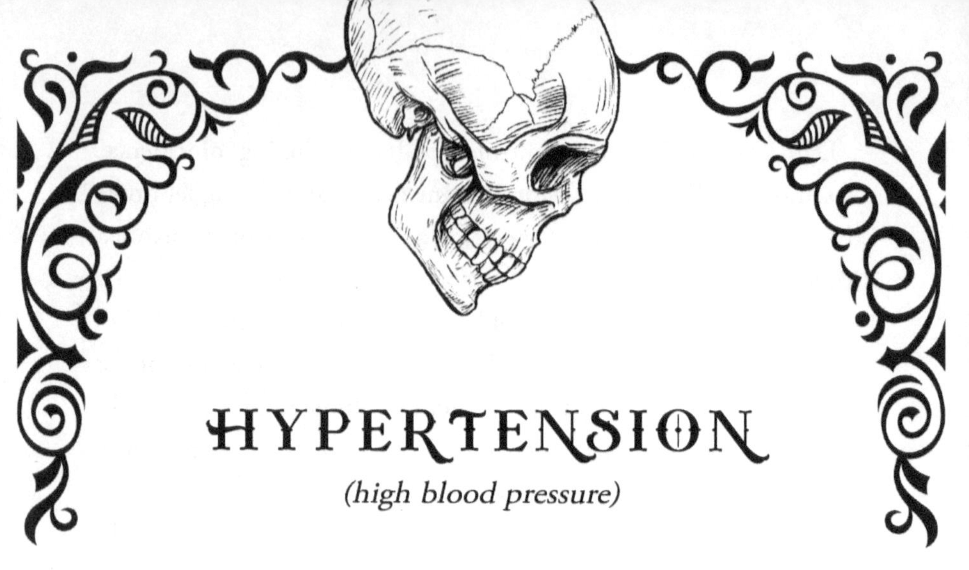

HYPERTENSION

(high blood pressure)

Katie and Justin left Costa Linda the next morning, and Aunt Cass may as well have followed. For three days, her cold shoulder chilled the house. Daniel could've used one hand to count the words she spoke to him since she found out about Miguel. She continued to make dinner for two, but she'd wrap Daniel's portion and put it away without announcing that it was ready. Daniel tried to smooth things over with a card and a flower bouquet, but to no avail. He decided it was fine, and that he wasn't even sorry in the first place.

Then there was Logan. He'd come to pick up his car the same day Katie left, and then blasted Daniel with a storm of text messages.

I swear I didn't mean to ruin things. I honestly think it was the wine. Apparently I am a lightweight. Fresh start?

Buddy.

Come on, Danny, can you please just say something?

Man, I'm so f'ing sorry that I can't even sleep.

Macy followed with pleas for Daniel to hear him out. Daniel at least responded to her. She never meant to get caught in the middle.

MACY: **Danny can you please make up with Logan? Honestly he's getting really whiny and annoying, and I can't take it much longer.**

DANIEL: **Screenshot this for him and tell him I said to leave you alone. It's petty af to bring you into this.**

MACY: **Like what you're doing by asking me to screen this? Tell him yourself, please.**

DANIEL: **I blocked his number already, and I'm not unblocking it. We're done.**

MACY: **No. I'm sorry, but I refuse to believe that. You were too close to let something like this come between you. Lowkey he's actually taking this REALLY hard. I've never seen him this way, and that's affecting ME, tbh.**

DANIEL: **I'm sorry, Mace. I don't want this to affect the friendship you and I have, but you're not gonna change my mind about Logan.**

Then Macy sent Daniel a screenshot directly from her conversation with Logan.

I guess that's how it goes, then, Mace. And honestly, I'm not even mad at him. I'm gutted. Danny's the brother I never had, and I would never do anything to hurt him this way.

Daniel stopped responding. Logan's intentions didn't matter; he ruined things, anyway.

Now Daniel needed to know if Miguel had done the same.

He needed to know if Katie's theory was right.

So, Daniel called his godfather and demanded one more meeting. He told Miguel how Logan had blown open the icy doors of purgatory with a single name, and how Aunt Cass was hellbent on leaving Costa Linda. And he needed to know if the fallout was worth it.

Miguel had been warm and understanding, and he offered up his library if the tension in the house became too thick. As for the answers Daniel needed, Miguel could only make vague promises.

And Daniel was done settling.

He drove over, and Miguel opened the front door before Daniel's feet even grazed the entryway.

His godfather looked tired, eyes tinged with red and hair slightly disheveled. He wore a long-sleeved T-shirt and jogging pants, and he clutched a steaming mug of coffee. He nodded softly. "Come in."

Daniel entered without a word or a hug.

Miguel closed the door behind them and gestured to the kitchen. "There's coffee in the pot. Chorizo and eggs on the stove…warm tortillas. Help yourself."

"No, thank you." Daniel sat by the fireplace and unzipped his hoodie. He hated himself a little. The smoky aroma of breakfast made his mouth water. He'd scarfed down a yogurt before he left home, and it wasn't enough to hold his appetite. But today was a day for business, and Miguel needed to know it.

Dorian crept out of the shadows and nuzzled Daniel's ankle. For once, Daniel didn't feel like returning the cat's affection, so he recoiled and shooed Dorian away.

He thought back to his conversation with Katie. *I think he's some sort of hitman.* If she was right, then Miguel had crafted the perfect mask. Nobody would ever suspect a harmonica-playing, cat-loving, breakfast-champing doctor to orchestrate murders. Of course, that would've made him even more dangerous.

As Miguel pulled up his chair, Daniel kept his fingers inches from his phone and a constant pulse on the door. Just in case.

"Well." Miguel drummed his fingers against his mug—another ad for Hope Haven and how you could count on them, *for life!* "I'm sad to hear that you and Cassandra are leaving Costa Linda. And I'm certainly not happy to hear that our friendship has come between you two. That was never my intention. I can only hope that with distance from this place and a little time, that'll change. Unfortunately, I also know from experience that time doesn't heal all wounds."

"What about the truth?" Daniel asked, feeling bold. "Will that help?"

Miguel leaned forward, elbows on his knees, and took a breath. "Maybe you should just come out with whatever you think you know. You have a theory of your own about why Cassandra is mad at me. Don't you?"

"I do," Daniel said. It may not have been his own theory, but he had resolved to keep Katie's name out of it.

"And the only reason you would be so obsessed with it is because you believe it has something to do with your family's deaths," Miguel said. "Is that fair to assume?"

"It's fact, isn't it?" Daniel said. "I know what Aunt Cass told you the last day we saw you. She told you that you broke our family, and she hasn't forgiven you in ten years. You can't smooth it over with an apology. Obviously, this isn't some petty family drama, so you tell me. *Did* it have to do with my family's deaths?"

Miguel stared at his mug, a faraway look in his eyes as he twisted his wooden ring. "Yes."

It was a simple word with all the staccato of a gunshot, the impact so real that a dull pain spidered through Daniel's chest. His fingers reached toward his heart.

Point for Katie's theory.

Daniel didn't know if he was ready to ask the next question, but he had already come so far. "Does Aunt Cass have a right to be angry?"

Miguel's shoulders drooped. He put the mug down and worked his jaws. "It's only natural, Danny. Of course she would be angry for what she knows."

"But is she *right* to be angry? With *you*, specifically?" Daniel asked more forcefully.

"That's not my place to say, Daniel!" Miguel threw his hands up, his voice suddenly husky with emotion. Tears pooled in his eyes. "I don't blame Cassandra for her anger. Never once have I felt that she was wrong. People curse my name every day, and I bear it. It's part of the job."

"But you weren't even my parents' doctor!" Daniel said. "I thought you were their best friend. And maybe I don't know what you really were to them, but if you can't give me an answer, then I don't know what you are to *me*. I don't know who you are at all. I don't know where you grew up, how old you are, how you got into medicine…" Daniel's breaths became shorter and heavier. He should've come here with a plan. Instead, he was digging himself a grave. He stood, fists clenched.

Dorian jumped into Miguel's lap. Miguel sat still and stared into the plume steaming from his coffee. For the first time Daniel had ever seen, a wayward tear glided down his godfather's cheek.

"Say something!" Daniel said. "What did you do to them, Miguel? Didn't they mean anything to you?"

"They meant *everything* to me!" Miguel pounded the table, sending ripples through his drink. Dorian jumped down and bounded out of the room.

Daniel flinched, stumbling back toward the door. "You keep away from me, man."

Miguel looked wounded. "And now you're afraid…" he whispered, "like everyone else."

"Oh, shut up. Everyone loves you. They love you because you sell them these lies—this fake personality you threw together to gain respect. I'm calling you out," Daniel said. "I don't know what you did, but I'm gonna find out. We're done, Miguel. And when I find the evidence, you're done, too."

"Do you honestly think I *hurt* them, Danny? Is that the core of your theory? That I'm some boss mafioso playing doctor?"

Daniel reached for the doorknob. "Tell me it's not true, then. You already said you had something to do with it. Tell me you didn't kill them."

Miguel brushed his tears away and held up a finger. "Wait right there, please. I need to show you something."

Miguel selected a key from his wall and retreated upstairs. Daniel had a thought to leave. What if Miguel was going for a gun or an axe or something awful? But something stopped Daniel from leaving. This was the moment he'd been waiting for. *Miguel is not a hitman,* he told himself. *He's not going to hurt me.*

And if he does, then at least I'll see my family soon.

Miguel returned a minute later with a black safe slightly bigger than a shoebox, then set it down.

When he opened it, Daniel's breath hitched.

"Come." Miguel crooked a finger. "Take a look."

Daniel gazed into the safe's shallow depths. Another key, gnarled and skeletal, dangled from a silky black ribbon. Miguel slipped the ribbon over his neck, exposing the rest of the contents—a row of thick wax cylinders.

"What am I looking at?" Daniel asked.

"I've been keeping all these candles in this safe since the day the flames went out," Miguel said. "There's a special place where they're supposed to be stored, but for ten years, I've kept them here. With me." He picked one up with both hands, then held it out to Daniel. "Be careful with this. It's heavier than you'd think, but also more delicate."

"Candles?" Daniel took it from Miguel. His godfather wasn't joking about its weight. Daniel could've used it as a dumbbell. It had been partially burnt, the wick blackened, and the sides encrusted with pearly rivulets of molten wax.

Miguel picked up another candle, cradled it in his hands, and stared at it like a newborn. "These are precious to me. All the flames went out on the same day." He sniffled. "And I couldn't protect them."

Daniel rolled his candle between his palms. "Miguel, why are you showing me these? What do they have to do with the conversation we were having?"

Miguel gestured to the safe. "Count them."

There was one in Miguel's hands. One in Daniel's. Eight more in the safe.

Ten candles. All previously lit.

People always said the Grimms died with plenty of light left in them—that their flames were extinguished too soon. Nobody knew the metaphor like Daniel. He swallowed a lump in his throat. "What were these for?"

Miguel drew in a deep breath. "Life, Danny."

Daniel shook his head. "I don't follow."

Miguel gently tilted the candle in Daniel's hand, revealing a gold engraving on the bottom of the wax. In beautiful letters was the name **GRIMM, JONATHAN F.**

Dad.

Then Miguel showed the engraving on his own candle. **GRIMM-LANGLEY, HOPE M.**

Mom.

Daniel's heart paused for a beat. "Are these from their funeral?"

"What if I told you there's one candle for every life that's ever existed?" Miguel asked. "And when that life begins, the flame ignites, and it's preserved carefully in a place called The Archive. As long as the candle burns, life continues. I was deeply heartbroken when these ones went out. For what it's worth, they burned brighter than most candles I've ever seen."

"Stop," Daniel said. "You expect me to believe my family's lives were tied to these…magic candles?"

"It's true," Miguel said. "You have one, too. Every caveman from early history has a candle in The Archive. So does every greedy king, burdened queen, and noble prince. Every town crier. Every President of the United States. Every movie star. Every doctor. Every kind person, every cruel, every bright mind, every dark heart. The only thing they've all had in common is that the candle only burns once, and once it goes out…" Miguel snapped his fingers, "then that's it."

Daniel set down his father's candle. He rubbed his face so hard his eyelids drooped, and he saw black. "God. And here I thought you respected me enough to be honest. This is the best you've got?

A fairy tale?"

"Do I have a reason to spin some outrageous lie that you won't believe in the first place?" Miguel asked. "Look, I don't expect this to make you feel any better. I told you from the start that you wouldn't believe me."

Daniel leaned back in his chair. "Fine. I'll play along until your story cracks. You have this magic 'archive' filled with billions of candles. And you took ten and stored them in a safe. Why?"

"These are the only candles I've ever moved out of The Archive, and that's because of what your family meant to me. I mourn them. Your family treated me like a human being. And for that, I loved them."

"They *treated you like a human being*," Daniel repeated. "So what? The rest of the world is out to get you? Or you're not a human? What are you, then? A vampire?"

"I'm…" Miguel rolled his shoulders. "Let's not label it. This is exactly what I wanted to avoid. I don't want you to think of me differently. But in the end, yes, my responsibility is humans. All of them."

"Because their lives are tied to magical candles," Daniel droned. "In your archive. And once a flame goes out, the person…"

"Moves on," Miguel said gently. "To the next phase of existence."

"Then you're…the god of death? The goddamn Grim Reaper?"

This would've been an excellent time for Miguel to give up the ruse. He'd had his fun. However, the longer Miguel sat in silence, curling his toes and failing to deny Daniel's statement, the more Daniel's stomach roiled. He understood why Aunt Cass hated this man; Miguel had obviously patronized her with this same elaborate lie.

Diagnosis: Delusional.

"Godfather Death." Daniel rolled his eyes. "Unbelievable. You're sick in the head. How are you even a doctor? They should take your license away."

"Your parents knew," Miguel said quietly. "They knew who I am."

"Great, bring them into this! Defile their memory. Can you be any cheaper? If you believe all this…" Daniel held Dad's candle inches from Miguel's face. "Then you light these up. Bring them back. Let them tell me themselves. That's the only way I could ever believe something like this."

Miguel didn't flinch, but Daniel suspected the heartbreak in his godfather's face would haunt him forever.

"Come on." Daniel's voice cracked and sharp tears pricked his eyes. "Do it. Take them back and light them. Now." Was this a new wave of old grief over his family? Anger at his godfather? Anger because Miguel would lie so blatantly, or anger because if all of this was true, it would hurt even more?

Miguel's reply rose barely above a whisper, "I can't, Danny. It won't work here, and the consequences would be catastrophic."

That's when the first tears spilled. Daniel scrubbed them away with the back of his hand. A sliver of him longed to believe that Miguel's magical candles represented life. That if the flames could be extinguished, then they could also burn anew. That somehow, he could make a bargain with Miguel to resurrect his family. He *was* a doctor, after all. Couldn't he fix anything?

"If you'd like," Miguel said softly, "I can show you The Archive."

A chill rolled down Daniel's spine. He was either about to discover that his godfather was truly, dangerously delusional, or that he was Death himself. Whichever version rang true, would it be wise to follow this man into some mysterious nether? Presumably in a dingy cellar under the house? This was where true crime specials always took their dark turns.

Doctor Death, they'd call this man, like some diabolical comic book villain. And one day they'd make a horror movie out of the whole story, and the world would call Daniel a fool for following Doctor Death into the basement.

But Daniel's life was no horror movie. He'd never needed anybody's pity, charity, or warnings. And Miguel Mortiz was not a monster.

Daniel's parents trusted him; they treated him like family. Miguel had come to treat Daniel with that same trust and respect. It was time, once and for all, to find out if that trust was well-earned.

"Okay," Daniel said.

"I do have a condition." Miguel packed the candles back into the safe and locked it. "You must promise me that this will remain a secret for the rest of your days."

Daniel wondered if Aunt Cass had once made this promise.

"Assuming any of this is real," Daniel said, "who would believe me in the first place?"

Miguel gave him a sad smile. "Your word, Danny?"

"My word," Daniel muttered.

His godfather handed him the safe. Then he took the ribboned key off his neck and stood, releasing Dorian into the shadows of the house. "Then come along, my friend. It's time for me to return these candles to their shelves."

SYNESTHESIA

(a crossing of senses)

Miguel stood in front of the library door and took the black ribbon off his neck. He ran his thumb along the skull etched into the top of his key. Daniel had a hard time believing its crooked, uneven teeth would fit the basic lock on the library door, but so far, it was the least outlandish detail of Miguel's story. It was also the last detail standing between him and confirmation of Miguel's tale.

"Still have the safe with you?" Miguel looked over his shoulder.

"Yeah." Sweat coated Daniel's fingertips. He couldn't believe the safe's contents used to be his family's source of life. The thought alone added twenty pounds.

"I need to warn you about something." Miguel's brows drew together as he fidgeted with the key. "Your brain has settled into a framework for what it knows as reality. When I open this door, your mind will code this Archive as a foreign stimulus, like a parasite invading your body. You may feel woozy, nauseous, or short of breath. But the mind is elastic and resilient; it'll stretch. We're going to take a few minutes to breathe while your brain writes a new 'map' for you. I promise, I'll be right beside you the whole time."

"You make it sound like *The Matrix* or something."

Even though Daniel had been expecting a chuckle, Miguel remained solemn. "This is quite the rabbit hole, Danny. It merits a warning."

"I can handle it."

"Yes, I do believe you can. But if it becomes too much for you at any point, let me know. I'll lock the door behind me, and we'll forget about everything." Miguel took his key, and to Daniel's surprise, the jagged teeth slid into the keyhole with a satisfying *zip*. "Take a deep breath and count to three with me."

Miguel turned the key and moved one hand to the knob and the other to Daniel's back. Daniel imagined a stethoscope between his shoulder blades. *Big breath in.*

Daniel inhaled.

"One," Miguel counted.

The daylight under the crack of the door fizzled, then flashed a rosy shade of orange.

What the hell?

"Two."

Miguel turned the knob, and a cool breeze curled around Daniel's ankles.

"Three."

Miguel opened the door.

Daniel's first glimpse of The Archive was a dagger to the mind. He stumbled. His lungs betrayed him. Where he had expected the cozy library, a bright, infinite labyrinth stretched before him. The floor twisted away, and he nearly dropped the safe. *No way,* his mind screamed. *Not possible. This doesn't compute.*

Miguel eclipsed Daniel's view and caught him by the elbow. "Breathe with me! I promise this will pass."

Daniel attempted to mirror his godfather, who led him through another deep breath. When Daniel exhaled, the breath was shaky and strobe-like. A cold sensation rushed through his cheeks. "Miguel, what's going on…?"

Miguel grasped both shoulders. "Stay with me, Danny. It's okay.

Look right here at my nose." Daniel obeyed, and Miguel's face rippled and swelled before his eyes. His voice sounded distant, like he was speaking through a wall, even though he was inches away. "Look. Nothing about this will harm you. Let's take this one step at a time. Tell me what you smell."

Daniel closed his eyes and focused on the cool air entering his nose. "There's a lot," he said. "But not all at once. When you opened the door, I smelled coffee. And then it was like fresh laundry." He sniffed. "And now it's…hair gel? Specifically, the kind Victor used to wear."

"That's good, Danny." Miguel nodded. "I'm not at all surprised. Focus on those scents. You know what I smell?"

The vertigo churned in Daniel's brain. "You don't smell the same thing I do?"

"Smell is one of the most powerful senses, and it's deeply wired to your memory. In The Archive, you smell the memories that you associate with people you love. And now?" Miguel tipped his chin up and sniffed the air. "I smell macaroni and cheese."

As soon as his godfather invoked the food, the lush aroma of cheesy pasta filled Daniel's lungs—as real as if it were finishing in the crock-pot—spinach, artichokes, and all. Daniel took a big whiff, and his ears opened. Miguel's breath rose and fell clearly in Daniel's ears now. "Oh, my god. That's my mom's recipe again."

"Isn't it something?" Miguel chuckled. "Okay. What can you hear?"

Daniel steeled his grip on the safe, then rubbed his forehead. The floor stopped swirling underneath him.

The faint crackle of flames popped in his ears. A light wind whispered to him, and for a split-second, he swore he could hear his mother's voice.

"It's like I'm in a cabin or something," Daniel said. "Like there's a fireplace going. Just a little wind. And…a grandfather clock?"

"Yes," Miguel said. "Those are the nature sounds of The Archive…

At any given time, there are nearly eight billion candles burning at once, one for every human alive on the planet today."

No wonder some lives are so short, Daniel thought. *There are all these tiny open flames in a windy room.* If he coughed wrong, could he extinguish a candle and kill somebody by accident? Then there was the opposite problem—didn't eight billion candles pose a major fire hazard in one space?

How wasn't the room cooking him like a marshmallow?

"Don't worry. Everything is well protected. You'll see." Daniel felt like Miguel had been reading his mind. "Now, what are you feeling?"

Gradually, Daniel's vision settled. His gut stopped writhing in his body. Miguel no longer rippled like he was made of water. His grip was strong on Daniel's shoulders. The floor firmly supported his feet, and the safe stayed in his grip. He was in the *here* and the *now.* He exhaled comfortably. "I think I'm okay," he said. "I feel a lot more grounded now. This is all a lot to take in, but…I've got it."

"Yes, you do. I told you, the mind is resilient. Of course, it's a lot to take in. All of this is. But I've got you, and you'll settle in soon." Miguel squeezed Daniel's shoulders. "Would you like to see the inside?"

Daniel nodded, and his breath settled into a natural, even rhythm.

Miguel side-stepped out of Daniel's path, revealing the gargantuan labyrinth again. There was no ceiling and no end that Daniel could see on the sides. Instead, a pink, twilit sky surrounded them. A small staircase descended into rolling grass. They were outside, and somehow, *not.*

Dark, multi-layered shelves stretched out in infinite columns and rows. The arrangement reminded Daniel somewhat of a library. Only instead of books, this one held a massive collection of candles, which lined the shelves as far as the eye could see.

"Wow," Daniel breathed.

It was real. It was all real.

"Welcome to The Archive. Every human story is bound here, every life recorded in wax, every death marked by the absence of flame." Miguel gestured ahead. "As you can imagine, this is only the tiniest fraction. It goes on endlessly. Shall we walk?"

Daniel walked past Miguel and descended the first step. "This is wild."

"I'll be right behind you," Miguel said, and the door clicked shut behind them.

There were only ten steps before Daniel's feet grazed grass. The shelves towered over him in every direction, and when he looked back, there was an infinite number behind him, too. The doorway he'd stepped through wasn't connected to a wall. It was just *there*, hovering in the middle of space. After Miguel descended, the door—and the stairs—disintegrated like smoke breaking in the wind.

Daniel's heart quickened. "Are we trapped in here?"

"No. If I have the key, I can make a door anywhere, in or out. It'll take us right back." He looped his ribbon around his neck.

Anywhere, in or out. Daniel considered Katie's story about Aunt Cass, Miguel, and the pantry.

Once upon a time, Aunt Cass had been here, too.

Miguel turned in a slow circle and gestured around him. "Take a look. Don't be shy."

Daniel approached a row of shelves. A layer of glass protected the candles behind it. He'd been holding his breath, afraid of extinguishing a flame by accident. Seeing the glass, he released that breath and took a step closer. Miguel stood behind him in the reflection, hands in his pockets.

Thick ivory candles melted into individual dishes, each one forming its own unique pattern as the wax cascaded down the side. Some candles looked new, barely starting to hollow into thin, shiny pools at their centers. Others had grown short and stout, surrounded by gobs of wax that might've melted decades ago. And every one of them had a name engraved on a small plaque.

"Do they…" Daniel started, but the question felt too big to finish.

"They all start the same way." Miguel held his hands parallel to the ground, one palm hovering about a foot over the other. "About this high and maybe as big around as your leg." He reached down and swatted one of his calves. "The rate of melt isn't the same for everyone, though. Neither is the flame."

"So how is this all organized?" Daniel asked. "Alphabetical? Chronological? Dewey decimal?"

"Still working on that," Miguel admitted. "I had a team of librarians in here once. Couldn't keep up. Nearly 400,000 new candles are forged every day."

Daniel read one of the plaques.

STORM, NIRAYA.

"This is a *life*?" He rubbed the goosebumps on his arms. "That little flame?"

"Yes, it is," Miguel said. "Somehow, this one reminds me of your mother. Curious about the world, with a bit of a feisty streak. Brave. Bold. Intensely passionate. The type of person who could stare me in the eyes without flinching."

Daniel processed Miguel's words about his mother. They made him feel warm, and the scent of pancakes drifted through the air. "You got all of that from a candle?" he asked. "Do you know everybody this well?"

Miguel chuckled. "It's an imperfect science. I've never met Ms. Storm. But I will one day, in time."

As if on cue, the rich, deep toll of a grandfather clock sounded somewhere in the distance—the kind of sound that his bones heard as much as his ears did.

"Do you meet everyone when they die, then?" Daniel asked. "Because I don't understand how you'd have time for that."

Miguel gestured at the rosy sky. "It used to be easy for you to believe in a man who could visit every home in the world in one night, with the guidance of a red-nosed reindeer. You used to leave him gingersnaps and a glass of milk. Did you understand how that worked?"

"Oh, come on." Daniel rolled his eyes. "You get why that's different."

"Okay, do you understand quantum physics?"

This question reminded him of Logan, and Daniel waved the thought away. "Not one bit."

"But you believe it's a real, measurable science, like emergency medicine. Sometimes you can believe a thing without understanding it at all." Miguel shrugged with his hands. "Or not. Either way, yes, I do see everyone eventually."

Daniel rubbed his forehead. "Whew. That's a doozy, but okay."

Miguel led Daniel down a corridor of shelves, his walk slow and leisurely. "You must have more questions than you can possibly keep track of. But I also don't want to overwhelm you."

Daniel pinched the bridge of his nose and laughed. "It's a little too late for that."

He probably had enough questions to light every candle in The Archive.

How long had Miguel been Death?

How old did that make him, exactly?

Did he do all this alone?

Did he *enjoy* doing it?

What had he seen over the years?

What was still to come?

"Okay, here's one. Why are you…you?" Daniel asked. "You're like an actual person."

"That's a fair question." Miguel crouched down and let a small spider crawl from a blade of grass onto his finger. He rotated his hand around and watched the bug weave around his fingers. "It's important to me to step out every few decades or so, and *live*. Meet people, enjoy the mac and cheese, work a job, do laundry, pay bills, keep up with the music."

"But why?"

Miguel released the spider back into the grass, stretched, and laced his fingers behind his head. "Perspective. To understand. I wanted to know why some people cling to life so dearly when it's time for them to depart, and others throw it away. And, it's fascinating being among the people. So, I walk among them, try to blend in, and I observe." Miguel flashed a sad smile at his collection. "It does often grow lonely down here. It's nice to be among the humans."

Daniel processed this, and he wanted to hug Miguel. That was one of the saddest things he'd ever heard. If he was Death, had he ever really had a friend in the world?

He considered Charleston Fitch, his sister's detective. No wonder the investigation had thrown him so many dead ends. He had essentially been chasing a god.

The two men turned a corner around one of the shelves.

"So why become a doctor?"

Miguel worked his jaws back and forth. "It's funny. Patients ask me that every day, and the answer I've memorized is that I enjoy helping people. That is true, but now that *you* ask, as someone who knows all *this* now…I guess maybe it's for my conscience, too." He frowned. "It puts me in a good position to ease the pain of it all."

"You mean your patients' pain, or your own?" Daniel asked.

Miguel crossed his arms. "Yes."

"I guess what I'm trying to understand is that I've never thought of Death as some charismatic godfather-doctor-type figure." He looked Miguel up and down. About five-foot-nine. Thick wavy hair. Bright eyes. "You're supposed to be a walking skeleton in a black hood with a scythe. An evil dude."

At this, Miguel laughed out loud, and he had to take a breath and clutch his stomach. "For one thing, I've never *been* a godfather-doctor-type figure before. And that's what makes you special, Danny.

I've never had a godson until I met your family. Now, that skeleton thing…" Another laugh slipped through. "Someone came up with that around the fourteenth century. I confess I was a little offended at the time. But hey, check this out."

Miguel rolled his right sleeve all the way up to his shoulder. In a single shade of black ink, a tarot card followed the curves of his upper arm.

"What?" Daniel's jaw dropped, and he stepped forward for a closer look. "You got it tattooed on your arm?!"

Miguel nodded proudly and pointed out the features. The Grim Reaper stood on a grassy hill with a glistening scythe draped over his shoulder. At his feet lay a gravestone with the letters *R.I.P.* carved into the surface. A single wilted daisy drooped in front of the grave, and a pale moon hung over the scene.

"Dang, Miguel, you rebel!" Daniel exclaimed. "My friend Macy would flip out."

"My reputation grew on me." Miguel chuckled. "I got the ink as a little joke, but it also grounds my empathy for the living. The skeleton thing was when I came to understand how deeply people feared me. Remember what was happening in Europe then?"

Daniel studied the reaper on Miguel's shoulder. *The fourteenth century…* "It was the Black Plague, wasn't it?"

"The Plague," Miguel confirmed. "Candles were blinking out left and right down here, like dying stars. It was dreadful."

Bare, blackened candles sat on every shelf. Some looked so *young*— so recent. Daniel would've guessed they were brand-new had the wicks not been darkened. This gave him another chill. "I'm glad I was born when I was," he said. "It must be easier now, right? With all the advancements in medicine and technology and all that? The candles probably burn longer and longer every century, right?"

"Mostly." Miguel rolled down his sleeve and smoothed out the wrinkles. "Longer, yes. Are things easier…? That's debatable. I've had a front-row seat to all the leaps in communication and medicine and transportation, but I also see the planet growing thirsty. Societies are growing hungry. And behind all the screens, people are losing empathy. They doubt their own beauty and the value of their lives. They're losing comfort. Even with so many lives woven together, people grow lonely. And I wish I could fix that." They came to a crossroads between the shelves, and Miguel paused, considering the twilit horizon. "Maybe that's why I really became a doctor."

Daniel's eyes darted to a candle that confused him. At one point, he saw the bright flame go out with a light puff of smoke. Then, as suddenly as it went out, the flame returned, brighter and stronger than ever. This happened a few more times, and Daniel took a step closer and read the plaque.

ROSAS, DIEGO J.

"What's happening?" Daniel asked. "Is this guy dying?"

Miguel investigated the window. He didn't look as concerned as Daniel felt. "Mr. Rosas is having a momentary brush with death. It'll pass. I'm sure you know one can be 'clinically dead' for a certain amount of time, then find their way back to the surface." He brushed a finger over the glass. "Be easy, my friend. You still have a long and fascinating life ahead of you."

The candle stopped wavering, and the flame returned to a consistent, enduring burn.

It took Daniel a second to realize Miguel was talking to the candle, and not directly to him. Watching him 'read' the wicks and reveal the details of their lives, a new and terrifying question sparked in Daniel's mind.

Where's my candle?

He was tempted to ask—to know how much life was left in his wick. How strongly did it burn? What sorts of patterns did the wax make when it melted down the sides?

But on the other hand, what if there was less wick left than he expected? What if his candle was down to a little stub, sure to burn out any day? Would there be any power in knowing this?

Would Miguel even show Daniel his candle if he asked?

He thought about the possibilities and scenarios. If the candle was still tall and long, and he knew without a doubt that he'd live for sixty more years, would it change the *way* he lived? And would changing his lifestyle change the candle? Could he extend his life somehow? Miguel had told him all about the Plague—a time when candles kept going out like rain—and how now, candles burned longer than they used to. That meant that on some level, the burn *could* be controlled. Didn't it?

Miguel put a hand on Daniel's shoulder. "You're going quiet on me. How are you doing?"

"I'm fine," Daniel said. "Just taking it all in, that's all."

"Would you like me to take the safe off your hands?" Miguel asked. "Your family's shelf is close by."

Daniel passed the safe back to Miguel, then wiped the sweat off his palms. "I'm sorry for the way I treated you earlier. I'm…I'm thankful you showed me all of this."

Miguel's gaze softened. "I know this changes everything for you, but it changes nothing between us. I promise you that. Your parents trusted me to be your godfather, and whether that means you need a mentor, a brother, or a friend, I am more than honored to serve in that role."

"One more question for now," Daniel said. "You told me earlier that my parents *knew*. Was that true? I mean, did my parents know who you were when they asked you to be my godfather?"

"They knew," Miguel said. "They've been here before, and so has your Aunt Cass."

Of course.

Finally, those pieces fit.

You broke us, Aunt Cass had said.

She cast him out. She forbade Daniel from seeing Miguel because she *knew*. She knew Miguel was Death, and in her eyes, that made him dangerous…responsible for the end of the Grimms.

Or at minimum, complicit.

And was she wrong?

The key to The Archive made Dr. Miguel Mortiz the most powerful man in the world: the god of death. He was responsible for all these candles. Every life had a corresponding flame—one that could only be lit once, and once it went out, that was it. He felt that this was equal and fair.

But Miguel was an imperfect god with a broken system. Some flames still went out too soon. Good people died young. Evil men lived long, healthy lives.

Miguel may not have been the assassin Katie suspected him to be, but in some ways, he was the most prolific hitman in the world.

The grandfather clock chimed again somewhere in the distance, and Daniel thought he could make out the pointed silhouette of a tower drenched in fog and candle smoke. It was his upheaval—the warning Macy had given him.

Miguel stopped in front of an empty shelf and set the case on the ground. "Here we are."

He opened the case, revealing the pearly candles, and the names danced through Daniel's mind.

Jonathan. Hope.

Nancy. Alexander. Victor. Samuel. Monica. Ruthie. Bobby. Elena.

Logan had warned Daniel about chasing this thread, believing it would lead nowhere, but here he was.

Say one day you solve your mystery, Logan had said. *Then what could you do?*

This wasn't one of Logan's unsolved mysteries. As it turned out, maybe there was a *lot* one could do.

Daniel's hand dropped into his pocket, where his father's phoenix lighter rested against his thigh.

This place could be the answer.

Miguel had said the consequences would be catastrophic if a candle was lit again.

But he never said it wouldn't work.

The very thought seemed to darken the skies of The Archive. Miguel would be furious. The damage to their friendship would be colossal. Irreversible.

Miguel tipped his head back and sniffed the air, his brows squishing together. "Something's wrong."

The clock bellowed again.

The breeze nipped a little harder, like darts on Daniel's ears.

The nostalgic smells that enveloped him before…? They were fading, eclipsed by the metallic scent of diesel fuel and the noxious stink of sulfur.

But how terrible could the consequences be?

Maybe the Perfect Universe wasn't another world away, after all.

The doorway sat in Daniel's pocket, and it didn't require quantum physics or a multiverse.

It only required a spark.

PART TWO

"The boundaries which divide Life from Death
are at best shadowy and vague.
Who shall say where the one ends, and where the other begins?"

EDGAR ALLAN POE

"The report of my death was an exaggeration."

MARK TWAIN

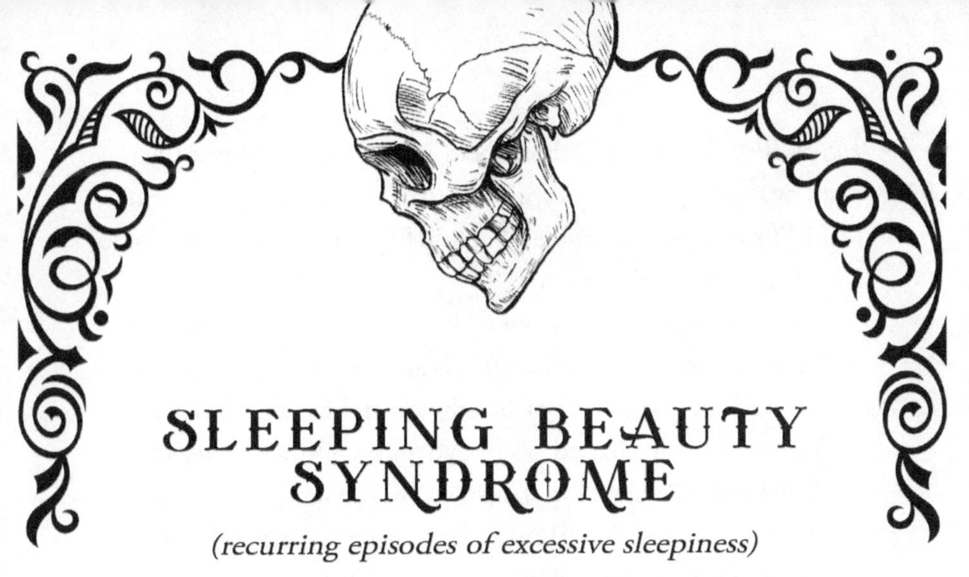

SLEEPING BEAUTY SYNDROME

(recurring episodes of excessive sleepiness)

Ten bright flames nibbled on a row of candle wicks.

The silky, colorful rivulets of wax dripped down the sides, hardened, and told tales in their patterns. The warmth licked Daniel's cheeks from afar, and his heart soared.

Today was a new beginning.

"I'm sorry, kiddo, I swear I had more candles lying around here somewhere." Aunt Cass cut the lights, and the candlelight cast a dreamy orange glow on her face. "We're gonna pretend you're turning ten again today. And for the record, I wouldn't mind if you stayed young forever."

"No, it's fitting," Macy said, her eyes dazzling. "Danny's still pretty much a ten-year-old."

Aunt Cass smirked. "Don't I know it? He still has the *taste buds* of a ten-year-old, that's for sure."

"Okay, let's hurry up and sing." Logan pounded both fists on the table as he chanted, "Logie want dat *cake!*"

Daniel arched an eyebrow. "*I'm* ten?"

"Ugh." Aunt Cass and Macy exchanged a knowing look. "And one, two, three."

Aunt Cass, Macy, and Logan spouted their goofy rendition of

Happy Birthday, where each of them gave Daniel a different name, and Logan filled the spaces with *cha-cha-chas*. For nineteen seconds, Daniel focused on the candles, because he never knew where else to look during the birthday song.

"*And many more!*" Macy crooned into an imaginary microphone.

Daniel sucked in a deep lungful of air, held it for a second, and shot it back out in a laser of breath. All the flames vanished in a blink, leaving only charred wicks and thin coils of smoke. Daniel reddened at the drizzle of applause crackling from his loved ones.

"Shucks, y'all," he said. "Thanks for spending my birthday with me."

"Thanks for being born sixteen years ago," Logan said.

Sixteen? A foreign buzz tapped on the back of Daniel's mind, but he registered this as fact and moved on.

Aunt Cass turned on the lights and rummaged through the kitchen drawers.

"So what'd ya wish for?" Logan leaned on the table. "Hmm? C'mon, tell me, bro. Tell me."

"Stop." Macy rammed an elbow into Logan's side. "You're gonna make him jinx his one perfect wish."

"Baloney," Logan said. "Speak it into the universe; give it power."

Daniel plucked a candle off the cake and sucked the buttercream frosting off the wax. "Don't worry, Mace. It already failed." He chucked the wet candle at Logan's face, where it popped him in the cheek and landed on the floor. "Logan's still ugly and annoying as fuck."

Aunt Cass coughed theatrically and shut the drawers, the knives jangling within.

"Hell," Daniel corrected. "Sorry, Aunt Cass."

"That mouth's gonna get you in trouble at school." Aunt Cass returned to the kitchen table with a large knife. She swept an arm around Logan's shoulder and squeezed him tight. "But not here. In this house, just be nice to Logan, my favorite fucking nephew."

Logan tilted his head with an angelic, toothy grin. *Ding!*

Macy drew in a sharp breath. "Damn, that just happened! Somebody call an ambulance because shots were *fired!*" Macy aimed two finger guns at Daniel, blew on them, then extended a fist to Aunt Cass. "I give you props, Aunt Cass. That was cool."

Daniel narrowed his eyes. "I see how it is."

Aunt Cass pounded Macy's fist. "I was sixteen and spicy once." She stuck her chin in the air. "And I still got it."

Logan clutched the table in a fit of laughter. "Oh my god, I love it here."

"And I hate all of you." Daniel made a heart shape with his fingers. "So much. Worst birthday ever."

"You love us," Macy said. "You're literally obsessed with us. What would you do without us in your life?"

"I'd have more cake to myself," Daniel muttered.

"Well, since it's your cake, you get the honor of cutting it and serving us!" Aunt Cass kissed Daniel on the forehead, then handed him the knife. "Happy birthday, Danny Boy."

Daniel rolled up his sleeves with a chuckle. "Alright, how big a piece does everyone want?"

"Just a little piece for me." Macy held two fingers about an inch apart. "I'm just kidding. Don't skimp. Give me a good one."

The first cut revealed three layers of lush golden cake, spongy against the knife. Aunt Cass had made it from scratch, including the frosting. She cracked open a frosty tub of rocky road ice cream and readied a scoop.

"Just a thought…" Logan said. "It's easier if you take the candles off first."

Daniel froze.

Wait a minute.

He considered the candles. The embers and the wax were fully cooled, and smoke no longer curled from the wicks.

The knife trembled in Daniel's fingers.

Aunt Cass dipped the ice cream scoop into the tub, her brows drawing together. "What's up, kiddo?"

Daniel's throat felt like sandpaper. "I blew out the candles."

Aunt Cass, Logan, and Macy stared at him, unblinking.

"Yes, you did," Aunt Cass said slowly. "And?"

Daniel let go of the knife. "That's not a good thing, Aunt Cass! I wasn't supposed to do that! Oh, my god…" He clawed at his pockets. Phone. Pocket lint. A paperclip. "Where's my lighter?"

"Buddy? You want a do-over of your wish or something?" Logan looked at Macy. "Did I seriously jinx the first one? He didn't even tell me what it was."

"I'm serious!" Tears pricked Daniel's eyes. He tore the cushion off his chair, flipped a napkin, and ransacked anything that could've concealed his lighter.

"Here." Aunt Cass ditched the scoop, letting it sink into the ice cream, and she grabbed the long-necked torch lighter from the top of the fridge. She snapped on a tiny flame. "We can have a do-over. It's okay."

"It's too late," Daniel whispered.

"No, no, it's not too late. We'll make our own rules." Aunt Cass swirled the lighter over the cake like a magic wand, but the wicks wouldn't ignite; instead, they repelled the flame like oil in water. She tried again. "That's weird. Why won't they light up?"

Daniel knew why. He was never supposed to blow out the candles in the first place.

Ten candles.

Ten lives that could've been saved.

And he extinguished them all in a single breath.

Daniel woke up drenched in sweat.

He sat up and caught his breath, relieved to return to a bed he knew, to sunlight in the cracks of the window, to the smell of Aunt Cass's breakfast warming downstairs.

To home.

The whole night had been plagued by nightmares. Every time Daniel thought he'd woken up freshly grounded, a new layer of hell strangled the places he knew.

On one level, Costa Linda High School's hallways fed into the Grimm Memorial Bridge. The dull simmer of hallway gossip flared into the deafening roar of a semi-truck charging him head-on.

On the next level, Daniel sat in the dreary silence of Hope Haven Medical Center's lobby. A practitioner called his name. He followed through a set of mint-green double-doors, and into the ashy weeds of the Crystal Gate Cemetery, which was burning.

On another level, Aunt Cass's café—The Queen of Cups—shriveled in flames that swelled from a single candle.

Daniel swung his feet over the side of the bed and leaned forward, hugging himself. He tried to convince himself that The Archive was the first layer of the dream—an infinite nexus at the center of life, death, space, and time. The idea was fantastical.

Miguel is Death.

There are billions of candles that represent billions of lives.

And yet, The Archive had been so real. Daniel had felt the soft grass under his feet. He remembered the cool breeze and cotton candy sky. His bones heard the haunting bellow of a distant grandfather clock. His heart remembered the nostalgic scents of his family members.

But the nightmares began somewhere in that labyrinth.

He didn't remember leaving.

And that meant this had to be another layer.

Daniel picked up his phone.

Good morning, Danny Boy. Today is December 1. Seize the day.

Macy had taught Daniel about lucid dreams once. If this were one of them, he would know, because the text on his phone would change. He put the phone down, glanced around the room, and then picked it up again.

Good morning, Danny Boy. Today is December 1. Seize the day.

Daniel closed his eyes and exhaled. He'd finally broken through the web of nightmares.

The dark side of waking up was that he'd broken through all the dreams, too. His sixteenth birthday had actually been a joy from start to finish. The Costa Linda Fair had been in town, and Logan and Macy joined Aunt Cass and Daniel for thrill rides, hypnosis, and funnel cake. Now, the memory had taken on a wistful aura.

Logan and Macy would eventually come around, or so Daniel had hoped. But for the past few days, Aunt Cass remained cold and distant. Daniel wasn't even sure he could enjoy the pancakes he smelled.

What was Aunt Cass even doing home? She should've been at the café. Maybe she'd already closed up for good and cemented her plans to abandon Costa Linda. Daniel didn't expect it to happen so soon—actually, he half-expected her to change her mind. She had never told him where she planned to go. Dallas could've been a logical choice, where she could be close to Katie and the baby. But maybe she'd pull a fast one and whisk them to Phoenix instead, where Zeke had replanted his roots.

On the one hand, Daniel couldn't wait to escape this place.

On the other, if he and Aunt Cass moved away with this chasm in their relationship, that wouldn't be a fresh start at all.

He'd be eighteen soon, so maybe he would go his own way. He didn't need to follow Aunt Cass, and she didn't need him, either.

He didn't need pancakes. He needed to shower and go do his own thing today.

Daniel cracked open his bedroom door, surprised to find a fluffy mop in the hall.

When the mop looked up with beady eyes and barked, Daniel leapt back with a yelp.

The mop was actually a Pomeranian, caramel-brown with white feet and a pink tongue hanging out of its mouth.

Aunt Cass had reached a new level of petty; she adopted a dog without saying anything.

"What the hell?" Daniel retreated to his bed. Before he could shut the door, the dog pounced on his lap.

Daniel wanted to be mad. He wanted to shoo the dog away, but the Pomeranian's sloppy kisses forced a laugh. The dog fell in love quickly…and Daniel did, too.

"Oh man, you're a cute little thing, but I don't even know who you are," he said.

The dog wore a green collar, and the tag jingled as the puppy unleashed its energy. The Grimms used to have a Pomeranian that looked exactly like this one, green collar and all. He was the king of the neighborhood, and Daniel's fiercest protector as a boy.

With an iron grip, Daniel steadied the dog and read the tag. When he saw the name, his stomach flipped.

Bowser.

He scooped the dog in one arm and flounced down the stairs. "Okay," he said, "is this supposed to be a peace offering or something? Because I don't know how to feel about this. You didn't think to mention it or to tell me you'd found a dog that looked exactly like our old one? Can we move past the pettiness and talk for once?"

With every step, light music swelled in Daniel's ears, and the smell of pancakes tickled his nostrils. When he reached the bottom of the stairs, the earth tilted beneath him.

A woman stood with her back to Daniel, humming and swaying to an old rock ballad as she washed a spatula in the sink. Her hair fell in a loose bob that resembled Aunt Cass's, but the woman in the kitchen was *not* Aunt Cass.

Maybe the lucid dream tests hadn't been strong enough.

"*Mom?*"

GRIMMOLOGY

(the study of the Grimm family)

When Mom turned around, spatula and dishrag in her hands, time hijacked Daniel's mind. A million thoughts and emotions occupied a single moment.

Mom was every inch the same woman Daniel remembered from his childhood; she hadn't aged a single day. Her smile was full, genuine, and just a little bit crooked. The seven-year-old in Daniel's heart wanted to leap into her arms. The seventeen-year-old knew that he buried her ashes ten years ago, and there was no logical way she could be standing in front of him.

And yet he could smell the zest of the dish soap on her hands. He could taste the pancake batter in the back of his throat. He could feel her warmth, and then, he heard her voice.

"There you are," she said. "Good morning, sweet prince."

"*Mom.*"

Daniel set the squirming Bowser on the floor and raced into his mother's arms. She caught the hug with a joyful laugh and even managed to keep the spatula and the dishrag in her hands. Daniel had no doubt this was real. This level of comfort and warmth had never been replicated in a dream.

The only thing that changed was the fact that his mom was lighter than he remembered. Before, she always appeared larger than life, towering over him. But when she hugged him now, her head fit against his shoulder. She rested it there for a second, then closed her eyes.

"Oh…" Mom breathed. "Well, this is nice. What have I done to deserve such love this morning?"

"Everything." Daniel's voice cracked slightly. "Just being here is everything."

"Aww, how sweet." Mom pulled away and set the spatula down. "Okay, what do you really want?"

"Nothing." Daniel fought the tears back and shook his head. "Nothing ever again. I have everything I could possibly ever want now."

And as long as she was here, Daniel would make sure she never doubted that.

Mom pressed the back of her hand against Daniel's forehead. Droplets of warm dish water trickled into his eyebrows. "Hm. Well, you're not running a fever. You're weird this morning, but I'll take the win!" She cupped his face in both hands, stood on her tiptoes, and kissed him on the forehead. "Eat some breakfast. I put your pancakes aside before your brother could inhale them all. I swear that boy's a Roomba."

Daniel's heart skipped a beat.

She said brother.

My brother.

Mom pushed a steaming plate of pancakes and a sticky syrup bottle across the counter. "Enjoy. I need a shower."

"Wait a sec," Daniel said. "Are you…here for real?"

Mom's brows drew together. "What in the world do you mean? How else would I be here?"

"Are you…staying? You're not leaving anytime soon, are you?"

"Well, we were gonna go see Aunt Cass later if you wanted to join, but that's about it. Why? Did you want me to go somewhere?"

Daniel sat down at the kitchen island.

Reality had shifted under Daniel's feet this morning. Apparently,

Aunt Cass didn't live here anymore. So where was she, and what would a visit to her look like? Would she still give him the cold shoulder?

Mom was here.

Bowser was here.

At least one brother was here.

And Daniel's phone still insisted that it was December 1.

Seize the day.

"No," Daniel said. "I'm just checking. And Mom? Thanks for breakfast."

Mom put a hand over her heart and disappeared up the stairs. "I got you, kid."

Daniel took a bite of his pancakes, closed his eyes, and chewed slowly. They were perfect and melted in his mouth like he remembered. He remembered a conversation he'd had with Miguel. They had agreed, even the simplest foods tasted better when moms made them.

"Oh, c'mon, Rachel!" a voice called from the living room.

Daniel turned his head, following the source of the voice.

A boy about Daniel's age sat on the couch, eyes glued to the TV. He craned his neck and stretched his arms over his head, calmly maneuvering a plate of pancakes from hand to hand while Bowser exhausted himself for a single lick of the plate.

Victor.

Boots on the coffee table. Hair slicked with gel. Victor Grimm hadn't aged a day.

For another moment, Daniel was seven again. He had always looked up to Victor, the tallest of the Grimms in both physical stature and presence in any given room. It was surreal to walk into the living room and see an equal yelling at the TV.

"What are you doing?" Victor whined. "Don't pick the motorcycle guy. He's a schmuck. Tell her, Bowser!"

Victor cut his gaze to Daniel. "What?" He looked at Bowser.

"Somethin' on my face?"

Daniel tightened his grip on his plate. He'd have to play it cool today and dial down his shock. To his mom and Victor, this seemed to be an ordinary morning, and they'd never understand why it was so special.

"Can I join you?" Daniel asked.

Victor swatted the empty cushion next to him. "Attaboy, Dan Torino. Join me. I feel like we haven't caught up in a while, just you and me."

Daniel sat by his brother and used one arm to intercept a Bowser attack. The dog was still hellbent on swiping a pancake, and now he had a fresh target. "It feels like it's been years."

Free from Bowser's wrath, Victor stabbed a forkful of pancake, swirled it around in his syrup, and shoved it in his mouth. "No kidding." He swallowed it whole, then repeated the process. "What is new, brotha?"

"That's a loaded question." The past twenty minutes had been new enough. How could Daniel cover ten years? Had ten years even passed at all for Victor? "Everything and nothing?"

"Everything and nothing." Victor put a fist over his chest. "That's deep. I felt that right here…every word of it."

Daniel grinned. "What's new for you, Victor?"

"Let me tell *you*." Victor muted the TV, then jabbed Daniel in the chest with a ringed pointer finger. "I feel somethin' special today, Danimal. I slept like the dead, and I woke up ready to grab life by the throat."

If somebody were to tie up Victor's hands, he'd go silent. The whole time he spoke, he waved his fork around. With his free hand, he poked Daniel's knees and shoulders, every jab a confirmation that his blustery brother was *real.*

Daniel couldn't remember the last time he'd had a day like Victor was describing. But Victor believed with all his heart that this was going to be the perfect day, and the more he spoke, the more Daniel believed it.

"I love that for you, man," Daniel said. "What are you gonna do today?"

Bowser went still under Daniel's arm, eyes closed and tongue hanging out.

"I'm gonna treat myself. It's a beautiful weekend, so I wanna take a nice long drive to anywhere and listen to my jams on full blast. And then, I wanna go to the beach and think about life." Victor made a fist. "You. Join me. Let's go have ourselves an adventure."

"I thought Mom said we were all gonna go see Aunt Cass later?"

"You do you, Dan the Man. But I can't hear my own thoughts when it's all of us crowdin' around our auntie together. We can always go see her next week."

Daniel's brain latched onto one short part of Victor's speech. *All of us.*

The phrase brought a lump to Daniel's throat. He swallowed it. *All of us.*

Was the whole family around?

He couldn't wait to see them all. He *could* wait a little longer to see Aunt Cass…After all, a little more time and distance would be a good thing for them.

"I'm in, Vic," Daniel said. "Whatever you want to do today, I'm down."

"Attaboy." Victor swallowed his food, then pointed to the empty plate with his fork. "Say, did these pancakes taste funny to you?"

"They were divine," Daniel said. "Where's everyone else, by the way?"

"Who am I, the nanny? I can't keep track of where half of us are anymore. Except the twins; they're about due in five…" Victor glanced at his sports watch. Five seconds ticked by, and then he pointed to the door.

The door swung open with a *boom* before laughter and frantic footsteps poured in. Daniel wrinkled his brows at Victor, astonished at the timing. "How did you—"

"Ice cream! The ice cream truck is coming!"

Two kids thundered into the living room, and Daniel's eyes widened. The last time he'd seen Bobby and Elena—who were the closest siblings in age to him, only a year older—they were eight. They played with many of the same toys and shared similar friends, but they were still "big kids." Now, even though they hadn't aged, he saw how baby-faced they looked.

Bobby and Elena eclipsed the TV screen and broke into a synchronized version of the floss dance, swinging clenched fists as they rocked from side to side. "Ice cream!"

"Ice cream!" Victor roared. "We love an ice cream truck at ten in the morning."

"Yeet!" Bobby threw both hands in the air. "Do you have any money?"

"Who am I? The Monopoly guy?" Victor flicked his palms up. "What's in it for me? Where's the love for your big bro?"

Elena stole a glance at the door. "Hurry, the truck is gonna leave! Daniel, do you have any money?" She snapped out of her dance and grabbed Daniel's sleeve. "I promise, I'll love you forever and ever."

Daniel tousled his sister's hair. "You won't love me, anyway?"

"I will," she pleaded. "But if you buy me ice cream, I'll love you even more. Times a billion."

"That's a really big number," Daniel said.

"And I'm chopped liver." Victor reached into his pocket. "I see how you're trying to buy our love. I see what I'm worth to you…one ice cream. Special."

Bobby's shoulders dipped as if someone had sat on them. "And it's gone. Man, life sucks."

In perfect twin sync, Bobby and Elena dragged their feet toward the door.

"Oh, break my heart," Victor called to them. "Dad's probably gonna come back with ice cream any minute now."

Dad. Daniel's heart smiled.

"But we wanted a Robo-Frog ice cream," Elena whined. "And they don't have those at the store. Only the truck. We never get anything we want."

"Life's hard, then we die," Victor said. "Ain't that right, Danimal?"

A pang of sadness bloomed in Daniel's chest.

He waved Bobby and Elena over, then sat them on the couch. "Come here. Let me tell you something." He rubbed his chin. "Victor's right. Sometimes life sucks, and the universe is cruel. It can take things away from you, like the Robo-Frog ice cream you really wanted. And sometimes that makes us *angry*, for like ten whole years. But if you're patient and kind, and if you ask sweetly, then sometimes the universe gives those things back to you. Sometimes life can be *awesome* and perfect."

Victor raised an eyebrow. "What are *you* talking about?"

"I'm trying to give them a life lesson. Yours was depressing." Daniel put his hands on Bobby and Elena's shoulders. "Hey. Trust me on this."

The twins exchanged a look, then squeezed their eyes shut. "Please, Universe," Bobby said, "bring me a Robo-Frog ice cream. I'll never ask for anything again."

"Just like that," Daniel said. "But then you have to be patient. Just because you asked, doesn't mean you'll get it today. The next time you two see the ice cream truck, you run right back to me and Vic. We'll be ready. Got it?"

"Okay," Elena said glumly, and her twin echoed.

"I love you guys," Daniel said. "Remember that."

"Okay."

Elena and Bobby shuffled away, and Victor reached for the remote. "Check you out, Yoda! Dishing out wisdom for the weasels."

An acute laugh escaped Daniel's lungs as he relaxed on the couch. "Maybe I woke up feeling something different today, too."

Victor rested one ankle on top of the other. "Then that's a sign from the universe. We're gonna have a good day today, Danny Boy, that's for sure. But first, I need to see how this show ends."

"You know none of this is real, right?"

Footsteps on the stairs announced the arrival of Monica Grimm, the middle sister. Daniel's heart soared all over again. As for Monica, she threw Daniel a sleepy, half-hearted wave, then poured herself a glass of orange juice.

"Sup, Mon-Mon." Victor narrowed his eyes at their sister. "What do you mean this isn't real?"

Monica pointed her glass at the TV. "That. It's scripted."

"No, it isn't. Rachel's looking for her true love. It's not scripted."

"Yes, it is. I looked it up. Rachel didn't pick the motorcycle guy. The producers did." She took a long gulp of juice, then wiped her lips. "And they did it specifically to annoy *you*. And I think that's amazing."

Victor scowled. The grimace faded a second later. "You know what? Real or fake, I don't care. Either way, this show is absolute garbage, and I'm obsessed with it." He shook his head. "Friggin' reality TV. Who knows what's real anymore?"

Monica rolled her eyes and retreated upstairs.

A few minutes later, Bowser snapped out of his quick slumber, keen to the jingle of keys in the driveway.

Bobby and Elena thundered back inside like human cyclones.

"Look what Dad found at the store!" Elena cried, her teeth stained a violent shade of green.

"Robo-Frog popsicles!" Bobby shrieked.

"Thank you, universe!" they said in unison.

"That's an interesting nickname for 'Dad,'" a voice said from the doorway, "but hey, I think I'll keep it."

Victor gestured at the door. "And there's the man of the house, folks!"

Daniel raced for the door.

Whether this was a dream or reality, Daniel didn't care. He'd savor it. He'd soak up the lingering taste of pancakes and the sounds of sibling banter. He wished he could seal all of this in a jar to open whenever he wanted.

But he had something stronger and less fragile than a jar.

He had Miguel's secret.

He had The Archive.

I did it.

Daniel remembered the overwhelming urge to light his family's candles. The skies in The Archive had gone dark, and the winds had grown cold. He had reached for his lighter. Miguel had reached for his key and insisted that something wasn't right. The next thing Daniel remembered, he was having nightmares.

But all of those were over.

Now they were dreams.

Real or fake, The Archive had granted the Grimms another shot at life.

And everything was perfect.

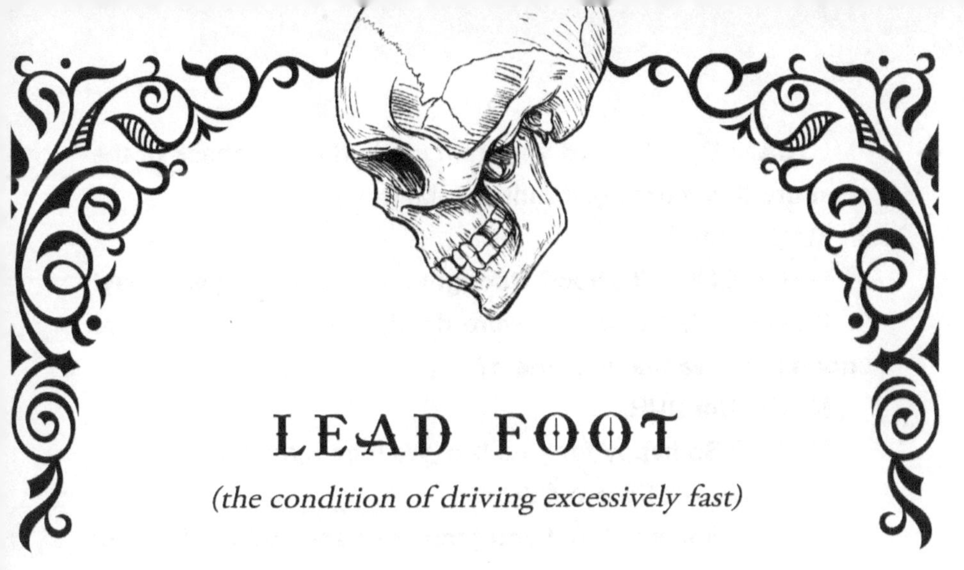

LEAD FOOT

(the condition of driving excessively fast)

Good morning, Danny Boy. Today is December 1. Seize the day.

On a typical day, Daniel's phone wrestled for his attention. Whenever Aunt Cass opened the café, Daniel usually woke up to a good morning text from her. His long-running group chat with Macy and Logan was an emoji-filled record of their friendship, drenched in memes and sarcasm. Lately Miguel had occupied some of that digital space as well.

Today, Daniel's phone had been unnaturally silent.

It was the last thing on his mind, but he'd imagined a slew of notifications might come in. He played some hypothetical conversations in his head.

AUNT CASS: **Hey, your dad just texted me!**

DANIEL: **I can explain.**

AUNT CASS: **No need! The family's alive, after all! Wouldn't ya know? How cool is this?**

DANIEL: **So the Miguel thing…**

AUNT CASS: **What a treat that we have that man in our lives. And what a treat that you fixed everything. Let's bury the hatchet and get some shawarma. All of us. See ya later, kiddo!**

He imagined a separate conversation with Macy and Logan.

LOGAN: **Dude! Heard your fam made the comeback of the century this morning. #CantKeepMeDown**

MACY: !!!!!

MACY: **OMG. Like how? I thought they were dead yesterday!**

DANIEL: **I thought they were dead, too. But nope, they're good now. Wanna meet them?**

MACY: **Um DUH.**

LOGAN: **So happy for you, bro. We'll be right over.**

Then there was Katie and Zeke.

KATIE: **I knew it. I told you there was something off about Miguel.**

DANIEL: **Well yeah, but it turns out he's not a hitman. He's just Death.**

ZEKE: **Oh nice that's way better**

KATIE: **RIP Detective Charleston Fitch. He was never gonna figure that shit out.**

KATIE: **But WHAT omg! You mean the family's back?! Mom and Dad are gonna be grandparents! My bb's gonna have ALL the uncles and aunties!**

ZEKE: **YES. Stop everything and put down the books, Costa Linda. I'm coming home!**

DANIEL: **Woohoo! #GettingTheBandBackTogether**

KATIE: **We need like, a theme song. Keepin' it Grimm, keepin' it Grimm, one day at a time and all on a whim!**

Finally, there was Miguel.

Good morning. Are you proud of yourself?

We need to talk about what you did.

Count the rooms in your aunt's home. You've changed the whole structure.

And you see how none of your siblings have aged? They think you're one of the oldest now. The world thinks they never died. It's about to get strange.

I guess it's all good, though. Just don't do it again.
DANIEL.
Do not ignore me. Remember who I am.
Hey
Dorian needs a cat sitter tonight. You in?

You'd better not tell anyone else about The Archive.

Sweat coated Daniel's forehead. Miguel would come knocking soon, and when he did, there would be a blowout. Daniel didn't want to think about what true anger would look like from such a calm, patient man. There would be a lot of strange conversations ahead, but most of all, he had no idea how to face his godfather again.

One thing was for sure: No one else could ever know about The Archive. The more people who knew about it, the more dangerous it could be. Even the most strong-willed person could wander in and be tempted to do something dark. A breath could extinguish a family. With enough anger and enough resolve, someone could tear The Archive apart and end humanity in one swoop.

As for the fake Miguel from Daniel's imaginary text messages, he had nothing to worry about.

I used The Archive for good *things,* he thought. No one could walk into the Grimm home and think otherwise.

By eleven a.m., Monica, Sam, and Ruthie were locked in an intense video game battle.

The twins had sticky fingers from half-eaten popsicles, and they told Daniel they were going to ask the universe for money now.

Nancy, the oldest sister, sang a song as she prepared Bowser for a bath.

Daniel hugged each sibling, to most of their bemusement. He was almost afraid to leave with Victor—he wanted a guarantee that the family would still be around later.

Only Xander was missing, and Mom made a comment about

how, "That boy always does his own thing. We'll see him when we see him."

"And you'll see us when you see us," Victor said. "As soon as Danny finishes hugging every single human on the planet, we got a bro-date. Please say hi to Aunt Cass and tell her we love her *mucho*. We'll see her another day."

"She knows, hon," Mom said, "but yes, we will make sure to tell her anyway. Also, I just think it's so nice that you two are spending some time together today. Wait a minute. Are you two the same height now? Watch, stand back-to-back."

Daniel and Victor obeyed, their shoulder blades bumping.

"Huh," Mom said. "This feels off to me. One of you had a growth spurt, and I don't know when this happened."

"This is a good thing." Dad threw an arm around Mom's shoulder. "The kids are becoming the adults we always knew they'd be. I'd say we did real good, Mrs. Grimm."

"Yes we did, Mr. Grimm." Mom kissed Dad's cheek.

"'Course you did," Victor said. "'Cause we're angels. We're perfect."

"You're perfect." Daniel hugged his parents and breathed in the scents of lavender, coffee, and well-worn denim.

Dad chuckled and patted Daniel on the back. "Not that I'm not a fan of the extra love today, but what's going on, bud? Did you smack your head and leave Kansas for a while? *And you, and you, and you were there?*"

"Right? I've been trying to find out what he wants," Mom said. "I just saw him hug the twins. He should've been making a cross with his fingers to ward off evil."

Elena stuck out her tongue, tinged with green.

Daniel frowned. "Do I need a reason to be nice?"

"*You* usually do," Mom said. "You're not trying to get Santa's attention before Christmas, are you?"

"No." Daniel put a hand over his heart. "Consider this my Christmas

Carol. I had a bad night's sleep and woke up with a new perspective, how 'bout that?"

"Yeah, God bless us everyone. *Andiamo.*" Victor steered Daniel toward the door. "Who are you, Scrooge? Let's make like the ghosts and disappear. Later, Ma, Pop."

"You two behave yourselves," Mom said.

"Never." Victor flashed Mom an impish grin and closed the door behind them.

An armful of gas station snacks and several songs later, Daniel broke into a fit of laughter that nearly derailed Victor's vocals. Victor barely knew the words to the song on the playlist, but he belted out random syllables for the piano and guitar parts, and any time the word *mama* played, he turned up the car radio and screamed it.

"Man, we should've brought the others along," Victor said. "At least Nancy and Sam. You need at least four people to do this song justice."

"It can be done in three," Daniel said. "I sing this with my friends Logan and Macy all the time. All you need is at least one person with a good falsetto, like Logan, and a few people to harmonize when you get to the part about the little silhouetto of a man."

Victor finished the lyrics.

Daniel blinked and shook his head at his brother. "What the heck, man? So you *do* know the words?"

"Like I know my own name." Victor winked. "You don't learn the words to this song. You're born with them."

"Asshole," Daniel muttered. "I demand a do-over."

Victor laughed. "Hey, I think we did pretty well for two." He rested one hand on his lap, the other tight on the steering wheel. "Man, it's nice hanging out like this. How come we don't do it more often?"

Because you were dead for ten years. Daniel gazed out the window.

Crescent Gate Cemetery wasn't far away. He wished he could peer inside Victor's mind and find out what his brother's inner world looked like. On the surface, he woke up projecting reality TV, relentless optimism, and a love for the beach. But under that, what memories did he carry? Daniel wondered if all the Grimms simply picked up where they left off, like the last ten years were just a skip in the track, and their minds filled in the blanks. They didn't seem shocked that he had aged ten years. Victor had no trouble watching the season finale of a reality show that had mostly aired after his death.

Miguel would have answers, but Daniel didn't need them *that* badly. *Seize the day.*

"I think I know," Victor continued after a long pause. "I'm not that good at the warm fuzzy stuff, Danny. But I feel like maybe I've been distant, or maybe it seems like I don't care. But I want you to know that I love every single one of you derps more than I tell you. If I've ever done anything to make you question that, then I can do better. I *will* do better."

"Victor—"

"Life's too short, you know? It can be extinguished like that." Victor snapped his fingers.

"Tell me about it," Daniel muttered.

He wanted to pry and find out why Victor had chosen to wax poetic about the brevity of life. He also wanted to affirm his brother and tell him he'd always done the best he could…that he knew. He always knew.

But there was a bridge coming up ahead…thousands of feet of metal suspended over a gleaming body of water, and the sight snapped Daniel's mouth shut.

Oh god. Daniel had been on the Grimm Memorial Bridge countless times since the tragedy, but the last time Victor had been on the bridge, he never made it to the other side. Only ten years of secrets, a candle, and a lighter could bring him back.

"Hey, Vic?" Daniel tapped on his brother's arm. "Can we turn back, please?"

Victor frowned. "Turn back? We're already like, halfway there, broda."

Daniel felt like he was breathing through a straw. "I just realized neither of us brought anything to wear to the beach. No towels or anything."

"So?" Victor said. "That's not gonna stop us."

Daniel closed his eyes. He'd have to be more direct. "Victor, I don't want to get on the bridge."

Victor turned down the radio, his brows drawing together. "Why not?"

"Can you please just turn around?"

"You're weirding me out," Victor said. "I thought this was gonna be our day. Now you're afraid of the bridge?"

"Look, I just have a feeling, okay?" Daniel squeezed the handle over the window until his fingers turned white. "Turn the damn car around."

"Nope. That's not what Grimms do, Danimal. We don't turn around when we're afraid. I'll give you two choices. We can pull over and think about this, and in the end, we're still going across the bridge. Or…" Victor grabbed the volume dial, "I can turn the music up, you can grab my friggin' hand if you need to, and we can power through this thing together."

Daniel swallowed the lump in his throat. What if Victor was doomed to repeat his death today? What if the bridge was their personal curse, and Daniel's was to live through it time and time again?

Victor drove through the next light, then pulled over. "Okay. How 'bout you start by telling me what's up. Where is this coming from?"

Daniel repeated his deep breaths. "I don't know how to explain it."

Victor pointed to a sign ahead:

Costa Linda Bridge

Est. 1941
Main Span 4000 Feet
*Here we connect yesterday's memories
to tomorrow's promises.*

And Daniel's heart responded with a kick. The last time he had passed this sign, it announced the Grimm Memorial Bridge, which had stolen his tomorrows and left him with only yesterdays.

Something big had shifted.

Maybe the candles had burned the accident out of the history books.

But nothing could burn the collision out of his memory.

"This bad boy's been standing for almost a hundred years," Victor said. "And I've been driving for, like, one or two or something."

A semi-truck surged past them in the left lane. Then an arsenal of trucks plowed across the bridge. Daniel scrubbed his eyelids with the palms of his hands.

"It's not your driving I'm worried about," Daniel said.

"Oh, I see," Victor said. "It's the rest of them. So what are we doing on the road at all, Danny? I don't mean to get all morbid, but we could bite the dust *anywhere*. I don't see how the bridge is more dangerous than any other place. If anything, wouldn't most people be even more careful crossing the bridge?"

"You would think," Daniel said. "But let's just say I had a really intense nightmare about it once. And don't you dare laugh about it, because you don't know what it was like."

Victor's hands slid to the bottom of the steering wheel, and he tapped his thumbs against it. "A nightmare, huh?"

"Yeah."

Victor put the gearshift into park. "We'll sit here until you're ready, alright?"

Daniel focused on the hum of the car, his pulse roaring in his ears. "I saw you all die, Vic."

Victor's eyebrows leapt up to his forehead.

"A semi-truck lost control…crushed more than half the family. I was one of the only survivors. I saw ten years of my life go by without you all. They talked about you all the time and turned you into some media sensation, but every single one of you was just a statistic. And they called me the Grimm Reaper…in my dream."

Victor scratched his elbow. "Jesus, Danny."

"I know." Daniel played with his seatbelt. "Can you not say anything to the others about this? I didn't even want to tell you, but getting close to the bridge just freaked me out."

"It's between you and me," Victor said. "But you're awake now, and we're good. We're gonna cross this bridge, and you're gonna know that we have the power. We're the Brothers Grimm, Danimal. To hell with the nightmares. As a matter of fact, to hell with death itself! Am I right?"

Daniel relaxed his shoulders. "Yeah. To hell with death."

"My guy!" Victor cheered. "Just lay off the horror movies before bed. We're gonna be fine. Now take a breath, turn up the radio, and let's cross this bridge."

Daniel turned the volume up. An electric guitar droned like a UFO, swelled and swallowed his thoughts.

"Oh, hell yeah," Victor said.

As a cowbell smacked a jaunty beat, Victor seized the gearshift, merged back into traffic, and rolled down the window. Then with two hands firm on the wheel, he gunned the motor. The wind raked through his hair.

Daniel's pulse skyrocketed until it nearly matched the beat kicked off the edgy rock anthem.

His brother bopped his head to the music, nailing every word about the cold kisses of vampires. "Sing, Danny! Put your window down! It's a beautiful day!"

The bridge's rails soared beside him, its curves swelling like a sea monster's spine. Rays of sunlight skipped across the water below while joggers trotted past the cars, some of their footsteps pounding in perfect sync with the song. Finally, Daniel lowered his window and welcomed the whoosh of the morning wind on his cheeks.

"I can't hear you!" Victor cupped an ear with one hand.

Daniel settled into the beat, bounced his shoulders, and sang the chorus with his brother.

"There we go!" Victor said. "That's the way."

At the end of the song, they emerged on the other side of Costa Linda, and Daniel had to admit the crossing had been three minutes of pure joy.

Victor turned the music back down and extended a fist bump. "See? That's how it's done."

"That's how it's *done!*" Daniel echoed.

"How you feelin'?" Victor asked. "Because I feel young and alive and untouchable."

Daniel grinned.

Maybe we finally are, he thought. *We really could have it all now.* "I feel free."

"Attaboy. Now let's hit the beach."

Thirty minutes later, their toes were in the sand. A dull ache trickled through Daniel's face, and all he could do was laugh.

"We did not prepare for this at all," he said. "No towels. No sunscreen. No swim trunks."

"No care." Victor cracked a smile, his eyes firmly shut. Easy for him to say. Victor never got sunburned in his life.

"No care until we get sand all over your car seats?"

"That sounds like a tomorrow problem, my dude," Victor said. "Who am I, Mr. Clean?"

"Yes."

Victor swiped a clod of sand onto Daniel's jeans.

Daniel chuckled. Cleanliness used to be one of Victor's quirks—a pristine bedroom, ironed clothes, and an immaculate car were the keys to his happiness. Not to mention he usually showered twice a day and always smelled like body wash and hair gel. It was strange to see him melting into the sand without a care in the world.

"By the way, don't look now," Victor said, "but the man in the fedora's been staring at us since we got here."

"Man in a fedora?" Daniel repeated.

"He's on your seven o'clock." Clearly, Victor had some sort of radar, because Daniel hadn't seen him turn around since they arrived. "I know I'm sexy, but damn, I haven't even taken my shirt off yet."

Daniel scoffed. "You're ridiculous." He sat up and peeled off his T-shirt, careful not to scrape the fabric against his sunburned face. Then he snuck a peek over his shoulder and tossed the shirt with his shoes. A man in a brown fedora sat on one of the walls, buried in a paperback and munching on a bag of churros while a pair of seagulls circled overhead. "He's not even looking at us. He's reading."

"I can feel his eyes on my scalp like a billion ants." Victor smacked the back of his head. "Say, you think I can rock a fedora like his?"

Daniel folded his arms under his head and laughed. "You do you, bro. Wear what you want. If you love it, it'll love you back."

"That was such a Dad thing to say," Victor said. "All wise."

That was a compliment Daniel wanted to put in his pocket for later.

"Hey, Danny," Victor said. "There's something on my mind right now. Bear with me for a second. Before you woke up today…what's the last thing you remember? Don't think. Rapid fire."

Candles.

Miguel looking up at the dark skies of The Archive. *Something's wrong.*

The phoenix lighter.

Daniel swallowed.

"I told you not to think," Victor said. "Just the first thing that comes to mind. Go.”

“Why?” Daniel said.

“Just curious.”

Daniel rolled onto his elbow. “Nah, you brought it up. What’s on your mind?”

“Oh, I dunno.” Victor sat up and started drawing in the sand with his fingers. “Okay. You know how I told you I woke up all renewed and shit? That wasn’t exactly a lie, but the rest of the truth is that something feels sorta funny today. It’s like there’s a hole in…in time, or like, my memory.”

Daniel’s fingers went cold. He plunged them into the sand to warm them up. “A hole in your memory?”

“I don’t know how else to explain it. It’s almost like I can feel somebody crawling around in my brain, trying to write a fantasy book in the gaps. Is that a thing?”

“I’m not sure I’m following,” Daniel said. “What do you mean?”

Victor sighed. “Okay. You know how the baby on *The Simpsons* has been a baby for like, a bajillion years?”

“No,” Daniel said. “I mean, yeah, but I don’t see how that’s relevant.”

“I guess I just feel like the world changed overnight. *You* changed, but I’m still the baby from *The Simpsons*. I feel like I just stayed seventeen forever.”

“How have I changed?”

“I can’t put my finger on it, Danny. Maybe I feel stuck in life. I’m sorry. I thought maybe you’d understand, but…I’m not making sense.”

“I’m listening. I hear you.” Internally, Daniel’s pulse was building. He didn’t like that Victor was feeling this way. It felt like a gray omen, and he needed to pull Victor out of his thoughts. “Hey, if you’re feeling stuck, then let’s unstick you. Let’s do what you said this morning. Let’s seize the day.”

“Seize the day,” Victor said glumly. “How dare you use my spells against me.”

"Sucks, doesn't it?"

"You're the worst." Victor nudged Daniel, then erased his sand doodles. "I'm gonna go ask Mr. Fedora where he got his hat. That's how I'm gonna seize the day; I'm gonna get a cool-ass hat."

"Good luck." Daniel cocked his head to the side. "He looks a little busy at the moment."

Victor turned around, and the two brothers watched Mr. Fedora fling his book into the sand and sprint after the wayward seagulls, who had stolen both his hat and his churro. Instead of flying away, the two birds taunted him on webbed feet.

"*Stop! Thieves!*" the man cried, arms flailing at his sides.

Daniel and Victor laughed until their stomachs hurt.

They spent most of the afternoon splitting churros, vacuuming the sand out of the car and their clothes, and visiting the mall for no reason. The fedora man became a recurring joke of the day. At the mall, they saw a man chasing his toddler through the food court, and Victor declared, "Stop! Thieves!" And then they exploded into laughter all over again.

When they returned home, Dad was grilling chicken and Mom was warming tortillas on the stove. A rich tomatillo sauce simmered in a pot. Ruthie commented that Daniel's sunburn made him look like a Martian, and Sam insisted that Daniel had always looked like a Martian.

It had been a near-perfect day. Victor said nothing more about his fuzzy memories or the strange feeling he brought up at the beach, but Daniel couldn't stop thinking about it. He knew he'd have to keep a pulse on this moving forward.

It's probably nothing, he told himself. After a good laugh and some time soaking his feet in the ocean, Victor seemed fine.

Everything would be fine. Perfect, actually. Nothing would derail this new reality.

Not even the midnight-blue sedan pulling into the driveway.

FOOD COMA

(a sleepiness that follows a large meal)

Anxiety fogged Daniel's lungs. He stood at the window and watched the god of death step out of his car. Miguel wore shades, a felt coat, crisp jeans, boots, and a casual smile on his face as he grabbed a pie from his passenger seat.

No, Daniel thought. Death was coming to dinner, and that could only mean one thing…He was coming to collect the Grimms. *What do I do? We have to get out of here. I have to turn Miguel away.*

"Miguel's here?" Sam's eyes brightened as he looked up from his laptop. "Sweet!"

"I didn't know he was coming." Daniel's pulse quickened. "Sam, tell everyone to hide."

"Hide?" Sam closed his computer. "Why do we need to hide?"

"Just do it. I'm serious."

"Oh. I think I understand." Sam winked, then cupped his hands over his mouth. "Hey all, come with me!" He beckoned Elena and Bobby to follow him upstairs, and Ruthie followed. Nancy and Victor dragged a whiteboard and an easel into the living room, and Monica remained on the couch.

Daniel flapped his hands at his siblings. "Guys, go with Sam."

Then he took a deep breath, grasped the doorknob, and went outside. He straightened his back and marched up to Miguel, who was hunched over, digging through his back seat.

"Miguel."

Miguel grinned when he saw Daniel. "Ah, Danny!" He opened his arms. "Do I get a hug?"

Daniel stiffened. This was not the greeting he expected. He'd imagined fire and brimstone and scarlet-eyed fury. Miguel's buddy-buddy demeanor had to be a calculated act—a tactic to bring Daniel's guard down before he pounced with a scythe. "Why are you here?"

Miguel lowered his arms, a soft frown on his face. "I've come to dinner. Tonight's game night, bud."

"Um—"

"Hey, you mind taking this pie in?" Miguel offered Daniel the dessert. "That's cherry, by the way. I have to grab the rest of this stuff from the back seat. By the way, you look like you're in some pain." He waved a palm over his face. "Did you get burned?"

"I did," Daniel said.

Miguel clucked his tongue, then ducked back into the car. He tugged out a cardboard box packed with gift bags, then shut the door with his knee.

Daniel's confusion deepened. *Presents?* "Um, should we talk or something?"

"We should eat!" Miguel smacked his lips and sauntered toward the door, his footsteps crisp on the pavement.

Daniel followed, dumbfounded and resentful of the pie's sweet, delectable scent under his nose.

When they entered the house, the air was thick with silence and the smell of grilled chicken.

Everyone had hidden like Daniel wanted, but some hid better than others. Monica's bare toes protruded under the window curtain, and Miguel pretended not to notice.

"I suppose it's just me and you, Danny," Miguel said. "Shall we eat this delicious pie all by ourselves?"

That's when the Grimms stormed out of their hiding places. Most of them filed downstairs, Bobby carrying Bowser under his arm.

"*Surprise!*" the Grimms cried in unison.

Miguel recoiled and clutched his chest, pretending to be startled. "Oh, what a treat." His eyes brightened as he set the box of gifts on the dining room table. He put his hands on his hips and looked at each of the Grimms one by one. "Feels like ages, and at the same time, it feels like only yesterday."

Victor bulldozed his way through the family and hugged Miguel. "You," he boomed. "C'mere, you!"

Miguel wheezed as Victor lifted him a few inches off the ground. "Hello, Victor."

The rest of the family rushed Miguel in a group hug as Daniel watched tentatively, still clutching the pie.

"Danny," Monica hissed. "Get in here!"

Daniel set the dessert down and joined the huddle.

"It's good to see you all again," Miguel said.

When he pulled away and removed his sunglasses, he was fighting back tears.

Dinner unfolded with a surreal aura.

The dining room table crackled with banter and jokes. Nancy, Sam, and Victor told tales of their high school woes, and Mom, Dad, and Miguel reminisced over the distant past. Daniel had longed for a night like this for ten years.

But he couldn't help feeling like Miguel was winding a jack-in-the-box, waiting for him to grow comfortable before he unleashed some hidden fury. The anxiety didn't mix well with his food, and as much as he'd missed his parents' cooking, Daniel couldn't clear his plate. In fact, Miguel was the only person at the table who finished his dinner. Mom scolded Bobby for trying to feed Bowser the scraps on his plate, but then she quietly snuck the dog some of her chicken.

After dinner, the Grimms sat divided into two groups, couches angled in the living room.

Elena stood in the middle, and Miguel stood beside her. He spun a dry-erase marker in his fingers and hovered by a board labeled *Hot Tamales* and *Team Awesome*, and his gaze was firmly planted on a pocket watch in his hands.

"Focus now, time's slipping away," Miguel said to Elena. "Thirty seconds left, and this is for the win!"

"*Go!*" Bobby screamed.

"Oh, yeah, huh?" Elena launched into a series of elaborate pantomimes.

"Song!" Nancy cried. "Four words! First word…"

Elena shook her fist.

"You're shaking something. No, pounding, banging…hitting… knocking! Yes! Third word…the roof, the sky, the ceiling, upstairs. Knocking on the roof!"

"*Knockin' on Heaven's Door!*" Bobby shouted.

"Point!" Miguel uncapped the marker and swiped it across the whiteboard. "The Hot Tamales take the win!"

The room exploded into cheers, brags, and affirmations.

Sam narrowed his eyes. "How the fuck do the twins know who Guns N' Roses are?"

"Hey," Dad warned.

Monica threw her hands up. "They don't! They just have that creepy twin-sync thing going on. Can we make a new rule that they can never be on the same team anymore? It's not fair."

"It's not our fault we're the coolest people in this family." Bobby and Elena smacked palms.

"Hey, watch it," Nancy said. "I taught you everything you know about music."

"Now, kids," Mom said. "Remember, the point of family game night is that no matter who wins, we *all* win."

"And the prize is all the fun we had along the way," Dad said. "Right?"

"Yes," Miguel said. "Though I suppose I could dream up a few additional prizes."

He reached into his pocket and handed something to Bobby.

Bobby's eyes lit up, and then he waved a twenty-dollar bill over his head. "Danny, check it out! Remember Elena and I asked the universe to give us some money today?"

Miguel handed another bill to Elena, then reached into his box of gifts. He tossed Bowser a milk bone, and he gave Sam a set of playing cards.

"That's pretty cool, dude," Daniel told Bobby. "I told you it works. What are you gonna buy with it?"

"I don't know yet," Bobby said. "I'm gonna ask the universe for some more."

"Tell the universe what you want, and the universe will deliver." Miguel winked at Daniel. "You've imparted some wise words on your siblings, Danny. We deserve to be rewarded for our hope sometimes. But we would also do well to be careful what we wish for, wouldn't we?"

Daniel tensed. Was this the moment he'd been dreading?

"Bobby," Miguel said, "can you think of any examples of this, my young friend?"

Bobby shrugged. "Well, obviously I shouldn't wish for like, an alligator."

"And why not?"

"Because it would poop all over the house, and I'd probably have to clean up after it."

"Ew!" Elena said. "That's so gross, Bobby."

"You mean *I'd* have to clean up after it," Mom said. "Who do you think kept your betta fish alive for so long?"

"Also, it could eat people," Bobby said. "But I could wish for an alligator with no teeth, and I could promise to clean up after it every day. And Mom and Dad would be happy because I would learn all about responsibility."

"There's no doubt you would." Miguel chuckled. "Very mature reasoning, my friend."

Bobby beamed, looking proud of himself.

"Now, Victor." Miguel reached behind the couch and produced a brown paper bag. "I saw something in the gift shop today, and for some reason, your face called to me."

Victor accepted the paper bag, a smirk spreading across his face. "Aw, come on. What'd you do, Miguel? You shouldn't—"

"I must," Miguel insisted. "Open it."

Victor pulled out the tissue paper and squeezed it into a ball. His eyes crinkled as he pulled out a black fedora and spun it on his finger. "Look at that, Danimal! Tell them the story!"

Daniel cracked a smile, but internally, his stomach writhed. This was a clear message from Miguel: *Even when you think I'm not watching, I am everywhere, and I see everything.*

"We were just laughing at a guy with a fedora earlier," Daniel muttered. "And Victor was talking about how he wanted a hat like that."

"No kidding," Miguel said. "What a fascinating coincidence. For some reason, I thought, how suave would my godson look wearing a hat like this?"

Daniel flashed a sarcastic smile. *Yeah, right. This was not a coincidence.*

"Danny, you didn't tell the whole story," Victor said. "So, two seagulls stole that dumb guy's hat and his churros. He was chasing them all around the beach like, 'Stop! Thieves!' You had to be there. It was hysterical."

"I'm sure it was," Miguel said. "Do you like the hat, Victor?"

"I love it!" Victor tossed it in the air, then popped it on his head. "How do I look?"

"You look handsome!" Mom said. "When I first saw your dad, he was wearing a hat just like that."

Dad ran a hand along his dark stubble. "Gosh, that feels like another lifetime ago." He stuck his thumbs in the air. "But you look sharp, son."

"What about Danny?" Elena said. "Did you get anything for him?"

The corners of Miguel's lips turned up. "I would never forget about Daniel." He stroked his chin. "But I faced a dilemma. What could I possibly gift a young man who has already figured out the secret to getting whatever he wants? Tell the universe what you want, and the universe will deliver. If you can do that, what gift of value could your godfather possibly offer you?"

Daniel shook his head. "Miguel, it's okay. I don't need anything."

Miguel reached into his coat and pulled out a small green bottle. "Perhaps some aloe vera for your face."

Monica chortled, then covered her mouth with both hands.

"Good luck," Sam said. "Danny's face is unfixable."

"Only a few things are unfixable," Miguel said. "Of course, some conditions are best left alone. Chicken pox, for example—mess with them, and there are consequences." He gave Daniel a pointed look.

Daniel's throat tightened.

Miguel uncapped the aloe vera and swiped the cool, tingly gel across Daniel's forehead. "Fortunately, a sunburn can be remedied. But it's a cautionary tale, no?" Miguel moved his fingers down the bridge of Daniel's nose and rubbed the gel into his cheeks. "It's a reminder that, for all the fun you had in the sun, there was a price. It tells you that you're not invincible, and that perhaps you should have been more careful. The sun can do much worse, and it *will*."

Daniel flinched, backing away from Miguel.

"Dang, Miguel," Monica said, her eyes wide behind her glasses, "it's just a sunburn. You don't have to lay into him *that* hard."

"Forgive me. Sometimes I can't take off the doctor hat." Miguel waved a hand over Daniel's face, fanning him, then handed Daniel the bottle of aloe vera. "But Danny knows what I mean." He winked.

Miguel was clearly sending a coded message here—something a little deeper than a smack on the wrist. But they couldn't untangle the layers in front of the family. All Daniel could do was nod and promise to use literal sunscreen in the literal sun.

"My goodness," Miguel said. "Would you look at the time? It's been wonderful as always, but I'd best be on my way. Tomorrow's another day at the hospital, and who knows what it'll bring?"

A chorus of disappointed groans filled the room.

"Come on," Miguel said. "You all know it's never goodbye, right?"

"It's see you later," Ruthie finished.

Miguel aimed a finger gun at Ruthie. "Correct."

"Man," Sam said. "Do you gotta leave?"

"I'm afraid I do." Miguel gave Daniel another pointed look. "Not all good things last forever."

AROMATHERAPY

*(the inhalation of pleasant smells
to promote holistic wellness)*

Daniel sipped his mocha from the hot chocolate vendor.

He hadn't slept much last night, and he was waiting for the caffeine to spark some much-needed energy. Miguel had planted a seed of fear in Daniel's heart, and the vines grew after his godfather went home. Daniel had stayed up in the living room and constructed an elaborate pillow fort with the twins. His worst fear was that if he fell asleep, he'd wake up with nothing again. He thought maybe if he *didn't* sleep, then nothing could change overnight.

He'd woken up in the pillow fort to the rattle of cereal raining into a bowl. The Grimms were still here, and now they were thriving at the Winter Street Fair.

Costa Linda spared no expense bringing winter to the coast.

Carolers on the stage wore matching red sweaters adorned in silver jingle bells. Their jazzy a cappella rendition of *Let it Snow* heralded cannons of fake snow that peppered the streets. The hot chocolate vendor's line never ended, and couples paid money to ride in a carriage pulled by horses with fake antlers.

But all Daniel cared about was one booth: The Grimm Goddesses.

"Check it out." Daniel picked up one of the candles from his sisters' table. "Look at you entrepreneurs!"

The Grimm Goddesses was a collaboration between Nancy, Monica, and Ruthie.

As the oldest, Nancy was the leader, and she handled the money, created the signs, and hyped up her sisters.

Monica crafted the candles. She'd created a few different series, but her favorite centered on Greek gods and goddesses. Persephone was pomegranate and pine, Poseidon was kelp and ocean breeze, and Aphrodite was strawberries and cream.

The candle in Daniel's hand was Ares, a dark red blend. He unscrewed the lid, and strong floral notes punched him in the nostrils.

He coughed and put the candle down. "Flowers?"

"What did you think Ares smelled like?" Monica asked.

"War," Daniel said.

"So, you wanted what? Blood and gunpowder?"

Daniel shrugged. "It would be fitting. I picture Ares as some beefy dude with a braided beard and big sweaty Hulk muscles. So why flowers?"

"Because love is a battlefield," Nancy said. "And all is fair in love and war."

"Also, there is nothing inherently feminine about a flower." Ruthie took off her glasses and cleaned them on her shirt. "Just because he's the god of war doesn't mean he can't smell super beautiful." She tossed her hair and put her glasses back on.

Ruthie created bracelets to accompany Monica's candles. She carefully selected her stones, colors, and materials. Ares was bloodstone, carnelian, and pyrite—strength, courage, and passion.

Daniel's heart swelled with pride. His sisters were living their dreams.

They were *living*.

"I'm still waiting for *you* to make a candle with me," Monica said.

"Me?" Daniel picked up the Dionysus candle, a dark concoction of chocolate cake and red wine.

"Yes, you," Monica said. "I know you have ideas."

A strange thought entered Daniel's mind.

The god of death was part of their family. He played charades with them, brought them gifts, dined with them, and nurtured their dreams. So did the god of lightning, the goddess of beauty, and the god of war walk among mortals, too? Did Aphrodite play saleswoman at Ulta Beauty?

"Where's Hades?" Daniel asked.

Monica and Ruthie exchanged grimaces. "We haven't figured him out yet."

Neither have I, Daniel thought. "Oh?"

"Maybe you can help. See, look," Monica said. "Don't judge, but if I try to create my own Hades, then this is what I see. I'm picturing a bad boy. A denim vest with all the spikes, black studs in his ears, guyliner, rocker cowboy boots made out of like, a sea serpent, and a Metallica T-shirt. And a guy like that *must* smell like leather and danger."

Daniel covered his mouth to hide his smile. He'd seen Miguel in cowboy boots before, but they didn't invoke heavy metal or dragons; instead, they invoked airport-friendly comfort. This was the only detail Monica had even come close to pinning down.

"I see you smiling." Monica put her hands on her hips. "I told you not to judge!"

"I'm not judging! It's just that you clearly gave this a lot of thought," Daniel said. "What do you need my help for?"

"Because I disagree," Ruthie said. "Hades is a quiet, beautiful, emo sadboi in the graveyard. He's mysterious, but he's also vulnerable and writes poetry on his hand on the city bus. He plays acoustic guitar, and he has a cute little black cat who is his best friend. They watch sunsets together and then they curl up with some little snacks and watch Tim Burton movies. I can see the guyliner, maybe the earrings, but I think he smells like the woods and the fog and a pile of books." She rested her chin on her fist, a dreamy look in her eyes.

Ruthie had gotten half a detail correct, too. Daniel wondered how little Dorian Gray was doing.

"I'm not taking sides." Nancy put her hands in front of her. "You have to settle it, Danny."

"Who's right?" Monica asked.

Daniel smirked. "I have my own idea."

"Better than ours? Let's hear it!"

"What if Hades is just like an everyday dude?" Daniel gestured to the street fair crowd. "That bald guy making the french fries. Or that woman pushing the stroller. Or her baby. Or the hot chocolate guy."

Nancy put down her hot chocolate and made a face. "I don't like that thought."

"But that'd be interesting, right?"

Ruthie cringed. "Why?"

"Why not?"

"But what would he smell like?" Monica asked. "That's the point."

Ruthie tugged on Monica's sleeve. "I dare you to go smell the baby."

"Try rain, spice, and cedarwood." Daniel shrugged. "Just an experiment."

Monica stroked her chin. "Hmm. We shall test your theory. Hades as an everyday person. We could tell that story in a candle...."

Ruthie mirrored Monica. "But I still want black sadboi beads for the bracelet." She reached into her box of beads and got to work. "Thank you, Danny."

"Of course." Daniel pointed to the candles. "Hey, can I have one of these?"

Monica rubbed her thumb and forefingers together. "Sure. You got some *dinero*?"

Daniel hunched his shoulders. "What? No family discounts?"

"You'll cough up the dough just like every other customer! Goddesses gotta eat, too, you know." Monica put a hand over her stomach. "Speaking of eating...Dad?"

"What?" A few tables away, Dad spun away from the smooth cutting boards he'd been admiring.

Monica batted her eyelashes. "Do you think that maybe we can have some yum-yums soon?"

"I don't know. Are you buying?" Dad asked.

"No."

Dad chuckled. "Alright, what do you want?"

"I want nachos. No, wait…I want pizza. No, actually, I want nachos. And no icky jalapenos."

"I want *lots* of jalapenos," Ruthie said, and Nancy echoed her.

Dad tapped Daniel on the shoulder. "Wanna walk with me, champ? Help me carry food?"

Daniel stepped away from the table. "I got you."

"We'll be back." Dad flashed his fingers at the booth as if to wave some good vibes at the girls.

Nancy made a catching motion, then put her hand to her heart. "Thanks, Dad."

Dad tapped his temple. "Got your orders up here." He beckoned Daniel to follow, and he started up the street at a casual pace. Then he mumbled out the side of his mouth, "Did you get all that, Danny? Who wanted jalapenos?"

"Just get 'em on the side," Daniel said. "At least one of them will change their mind, anyway."

"Smart," Dad said. "That's my guy, always helping us hold things together. The girls probably won't tell you, but I'm sure they appreciated you showing up for them this morning. They look up to you, Danny. They really do."

Daniel looked at his feet. It was strange to be the older brother when he had spent his childhood looking up to *them*—all of them— and he would look up to them forever. "I do my best."

Dad frowned. "And yet, I wonder if something's bothering you lately." He slowed his walk. "I couldn't help but notice you were a little tense last night. Am I making that up?"

"Everything's fine," Daniel said. "Perfect, actually."

"Everything?" Dad pried.

"Yep."

Dad tilted his head.

But is this too good to be true?

"Okay, I just worry sometimes," Daniel said. "There's so much going on, and I can't always keep up. And I feel like I should. Like, where are Mom and the others today? Who's watching Bowser? And I don't think I've seen Xander since…"

"Hey." Dad's tone was gentle, but firm. "Let your mom and me do the worrying. You carry more than enough on your shoulders. If we need more from you, we'll tell you. But trust that the world and the family won't fall apart if you stop and take a breath once in a while."

Daniel looked his dad in the eyes. It was like looking in a mirror, or perhaps, into his own future.

"You're still young, kid," Dad said. "If you wanna help us out, live your life. Oh, and maybe keep an eye out for something your mom might like from the vendors. Deal?"

Daniel managed a nod. "Deal. I'm good, Dad."

"Okay. You're good." Dad let go of Daniel's shoulders, then pointed two fingers at his eyes. "But I'm watching you."

I'm watching you. Aunt Cass always said that when she was worried about Daniel.

"Hey, Dad," Daniel said. "How's Aunt Cass, by the way?"

"I think you should ask her yourself, bud," Dad said. "For what it's worth, I believe she's very happy, and I know she's proud of you. You two always had a special relationship. I've always been proud of that."

"Yeah," Daniel said. "That makes me feel better."

"Good," Dad said. "When'd you get taller than me, by the way? Your mom and I were talking about this. Seems like last time we were here, you couldn't *wait* for a picture with Santa and Mrs. Claus.

Now, all my kids think they're too cool."

As if on cue, a toddler's scream pierced the air. Daniel watched a photographer snap a picture of a grizzled Santa suppressing a wince while the toddler wailed on his lap. Behind the beard, Santa looked an awful lot like Mr. Jerricks.

Daniel couldn't blame the kid for crying.

"I bet Vic would still take a Santa photo," Daniel said. The idea made him chuckle…Victor being at least a head taller than Santa, sitting on his lap anyway, and hamming it up for the camera.

"You know, you're probably right," Dad said with a grin. "Gosh, all my kids are *taller* than the big guy, too. That's new. Man, I swear you grew overnight."

Daniel pinched two fingers together. "I think maybe you just shrank."

"Yeah, my waistband would like a word." Dad hooked a thumb into his belt loop. "Don't ever get old."

"Hey," Daniel said. "You're gonna live forever."

"With my cholesterol?" Dad grinned. "I'll keep dreamin'."

"Alright," Daniel said. "How 'bout if you hang in there until you're a hundred and twelve?"

"I don't know if I want that, bud." Dad winced, doubled over, and put a hand on his lower back. Daniel wasn't sure if his dad was exaggerating, joking, or expressing real pain. "Getting old is a pain in the ass. One day you feel all young and spry and hip…immortal, even. The next day, you're like *The Walking Dead*, all mangled and jaded and tormenting people who have had more coffee than you. After thirty, sometimes you even blink wrong and pull a muscle. We can't all be Keanu Reeves."

Daniel chuckled. *That* was a candle Daniel would be interested in visiting in The Archive. "Well, that guy's made of different stuff. Vampire blood, tears from the fountain of youth, angel wings, or whatever."

Dad adjusted his sunglasses. "That sounds like a book we need to get Sam to write."

"Well," Daniel said, "for the record, *I* still think you're young and spry."

"I noticed you didn't say hip," Dad said.

Daniel smirked. "Two out of three isn't bad."

Dad clutched his chest. "The sass!"

"Sorry, Dad. Truth hurts sometimes."

"Ain't that somethin'," Dad said.

And then Daniel picked out a familiar face in the crowd: a tall guy with mousy hair down to his shoulders, shoving golden bits of funnel cake into his mouth. The powdered sugar assaulted his black hoodie.

"Logan!" Daniel said.

But Logan was too far away and too invested in his snack.

Dad put a hand over his brows to shield the sun. "You see one of your buddies out there?"

"Maybe," Daniel said. *As in, maybe we're still buddies in this life.*

"Go hang out." Dad tipped his head to the side. "I've got the food. I can carry it back for the girls."

Daniel bounced on the balls of his feet. "Are you sure?"

"Sure, sure." Dad waved a hand to shoo Daniel away. "Fly. We'll see you back at the booth later."

Daniel made his way through the crowd, thinking about how he was going to fix things with his friend. The conversation felt impossible, but he had to try.

"Logan!"

Logan looked up, a blank expression on his face before his eyes registered a spark. "Oh, hey! Sorry, man, you caught me just like, goin' to town on this cake." He dusted his hand on his jeans, then extended it. "I'd offer you some, but my fingers were *all* up in this thing right now, and I was licking them and…now I am shaking your hand."

Daniel scoffed. They'd already swapped a fair share of spit

handshakes before, and this one wasn't about to make him squirm. At least Logan hadn't given him the cold shoulder. "It's good to see you."

"Yeah, man, likewise," Logan said. "Just taking a walk to clear my head today. The street food's always a bonus, right?"

Daniel thought for a minute. This didn't feel like the place to explain that he was here with his dad and his siblings, who Logan knew to be dead. "Hey," he said, "I just wanted to apologize about Thanksgiving, and hopefully start repairing things. I know I said some things I didn't mean—"

"What *do* you mean?" Logan said. "What happened on Thanksgiving?"

Daniel opened his mouth to explain, but Logan interjected right away, "Wait, isn't that Macy over there?" He set his funnel cake on a bench and cupped his hands to his mouth. "Macy!"

Macy looked up from a display of butterfly wind chimes, then waved as she walked over.

The circle was complete.

Daniel had his family.

Daniel had his friends, and they seemed chipper and unfazed by the Thanksgiving fiasco. Life was kind of beautiful.

"Hey," Macy said. "How's it going?"

"Man, it's so good to see you two," Daniel said. "I feel like I have so much to catch you up on, and I've been wanting to reach out, but I don't know where to start."

Logan scratched his head.

"Yeah?" Macy said. "Well, that's cool. It must be meant to be, then. You're Logan and Daniel, right? Did you two come together?"

Daniel's brows scrunched at the *Logan and Daniel* question.

"Nah," Logan said. "We just met up right now, and then I saw you over there and I thought it was funny. This is like a whole English class reunion."

An English class reunion? Really?

"It totally is," Macy said. "I'm actually here with Billy right now, so it's an even bigger reunion."

Daniel felt the blood rush to his ears.

Billy.

"Billy, Billy…" Logan rubbed his chin.

"You're here with Billy Schubert?" Daniel said, a tingle spreading through his chest.

"Oh, Schubes!" Logan snapped his fingers. "Yeah, I know him as Schubes. The funny guy!"

Macy cringed. "Don't encourage him. He's not that funny."

Something was off. It was one thing for Macy and Logan to hit *reset* with Daniel, but they were also acting like they'd never spoken to each other in their lives. English class was the smallest thing they'd ever had in common, and hating Billy Schubert was another.

Daniel's blood boiled when Billy Schubert swooped in with a carton of seasoned fries and an impish grin on his face. When he put a hand on Macy's back and kissed her lips, Daniel's veins blackened. He wanted to slug Billy. How dare he sweep in and invade Macy's personal space uninvited?

Then something chilled him all over again.

Macy stood on her tiptoes, and she kissed Billy back.

What?

"Got your fries, babe," Billy said. "The nacho line was too long."

What? Babe?

"Bless. Thanks, love." Macy grabbed a fry and popped it into her mouth. "Check it out. It's Logan and Daniel from English."

Billy threw a "sup" nod—a quick uptick of the chin—and stuck out his hand. "What up, bros?"

Logan shook Billy's hand. "'Sup, Schubes?"

Daniel crossed his arms. There was no way in hell he was going to shake that hand. How could Macy do this? How could *Logan*, for that matter? They knew Billy had made Daniel's school life miserable for years. One little fight, and suddenly, Macy and Logan pretended they'd never met Daniel? *Kissing* Billy and eating street food with him?

After a few seconds, Billy retracted his hand and stuck it in his pocket. "Okay, then." He held out his plate. "Anyone want some fries?"

"I think I'll pass," Daniel said.

"Okay?" Billy narrowed his eyes. "That's cool, too. You don't have to eat fries."

An awkward, heavy pause hovered between them. Daniel finally looked at Macy and asked, "What's this about?"

Macy frowned. "What's what about?"

"This. You two!" Daniel pointed at the space between Macy and Billy, where their elbows brushed against each other. He turned to Logan. "And you! I wanted to work things out with you guys, but this is petty. *An English class reunion?* Is that all I ever was to you? Just some guy who sat behind you in school?"

Logan's posture loosened, his gaze elusive. "Uh—"

"Seriously, it's one thing to act like we've never spoken before, but then you go and replace me with *Billy?*"

Billy aimed a palm at Daniel. "Whoa, buddy. It doesn't need to be like this between us. Whatever feelings you have for Macy—"

"That's not it," Daniel said. "It's just that I know how you are and how you treat people, and I won't stand around while you walk all over her. All you've ever done is torment me all my life, and I'm not having it anymore. I'm done."

"I've been tormenting you?" Billy's brows squished together. "Uh, can you be more specific? I honestly don't feel like I've done jack shit to you, man."

Daniel scoffed. He really wanted to walk out as the bigger person in this confrontation. "Whatever. Tell yourself whatever you need to sleep at night, but leave Macy out of it. She doesn't need you."

"And what? You're the thing she needs?" Billy said. "Because this is a classic case of *snooze, you lose,* bro. You seem like a cool guy, but I mean, I got to her first."

"Okay, nope. I'm shutting this down." Macy spun her finger in a circle. "You two don't get to speak for me. Ever. Daniel, a word, please?" She grabbed his sleeve and pulled him aside. Logan jammed his hands into his pockets and bounced on the balls of his feet. Daniel could feel Billy's dumbstruck gaze drilling into the back of his head.

Macy pulled Daniel away from the tents and onto the side street. The copper roof of Garney Plaza peeked over the streets. Daniel thought about taking a walk to Queen of Cups to see if Aunt Cass was there.

"Now." Macy put her hands on her hips. "What is *with* you? What was that all about?"

Daniel spread his arms. "What's with me? What's with you? You and Logan are acting like you don't even know who I am, and that's the most hurtful part of this. After all we've been through, do I mean nothing to you?"

"I asked you a question first," Macy said. "Don't spin it around. Daniel, that was totally uncalled for back there. I don't know who you think you are, but I don't need you *or* Billy to speak for me."

"I get that," Daniel said. "And I'm sorry. But oh my god, Macy, *Billy Schubert?* We hate that guy!"

"*You* hate that guy, apparently." Macy rolled her eyes. "And again, you don't get to speak for me. You literally just apologized, and then you did it again. I'm going to date whoever I want, and Billy is a sweet guy. Whatever you have against him, that has nothing to do with what I have with him. And from what I've seen, Billy has only ever tried to be nice to you. He tries, and then you go all Mr. Hyde on him. And anyway, who I date is none of your business."

"I kind of think it is," Daniel said. "We've been best friends since I don't know when—me, you, and Logan. We've done everything together for years. And I would *never* date someone who treated you like dirt."

"Date whoever you want!" Macy said. "That's the point. And I know this sounds awful, but you're just some guy from my English class."

Daniel felt his shoulders grow heavy. "That's all I am now?"

"I mean, I barely know you, and I barely know Logan. I don't know where you got this idea that we've done everything together for years."

"Because we *have,* Mace!" Daniel said.

Macy's breath quickened. "Don't call me Mace. Only my close friends can do that. And lastly, Billy is a good guy, and we're happy together. I'm sorry if that bothers you for some weird reason, but I need you to accept it and move on, okay? Can we be done with this conversation now? Forever?"

Daniel threw his hands up. There was no use arguing with someone who didn't want to be spoken to. What a way to find out Macy and Logan had thrown the friendship away. They didn't want to know him anymore. They'd moved on.

He crossed his arms and leaned back against the wall, nodding at the ground. "Yeah," he muttered. "We can be done. Forever."

Macy sighed, rolled her shoulders, and massaged her temples as she made her way back toward the crowd.

Daniel slumped down against the wall, pulled his knees up to his chest, and buried his head in them.

She'd practically ghosted him. He wasn't sure how to articulate the pain of it—only that he felt it in almost every bone of his body. Daniel was always sure Macy and Logan would be his "forever crew," the deep center of his circle that would endure through every era of his life. Long after college, regardless of where they all went, they'd be celebrating career moves. They'd make toasts at each other's weddings. Maybe they'd all play bridge a few times a year when they grew old, and maybe they'd have grandchildren who would be the best of friends. He knew these were big dreams, and honestly, he would've been happy if only a sliver of them came true. Only now, it was clear their friendship hadn't even survived high school.

No, none of this is her, he told himself. *I did this.* Daniel brought back his family and woke up in a different life. In a world where the Grimms were alive and well; in a world where Billy had never become his enemy. But on the flip side of the coin, Macy and Logan had never become his friends, and now Daniel had pushed them all away.

This was supposed to be the *Perfect* Universe.

At least Macy seemed happy.

Daniel would accept the consequences if his friends were happy and healthy.

"I'm sorry, Mace," he whispered.

At that moment, Macy stumbled. Her foot slipped as if she'd been caught on something, and then she paused and looked around. She seemed confused, and her body swayed from side to side as she rubbed her arms.

"Macy?" Daniel called. "Are you alright?"

And his breath left his lungs when she collapsed on the ground.

Daniel sprang up and ran to her side. "Oh, god, Macy." She was unconscious, her skin was three shades lighter, and her face was matted with sweat. He took a knee and grabbed her shoulder. "Help," he cried. "Dammit, somebody *help*!"

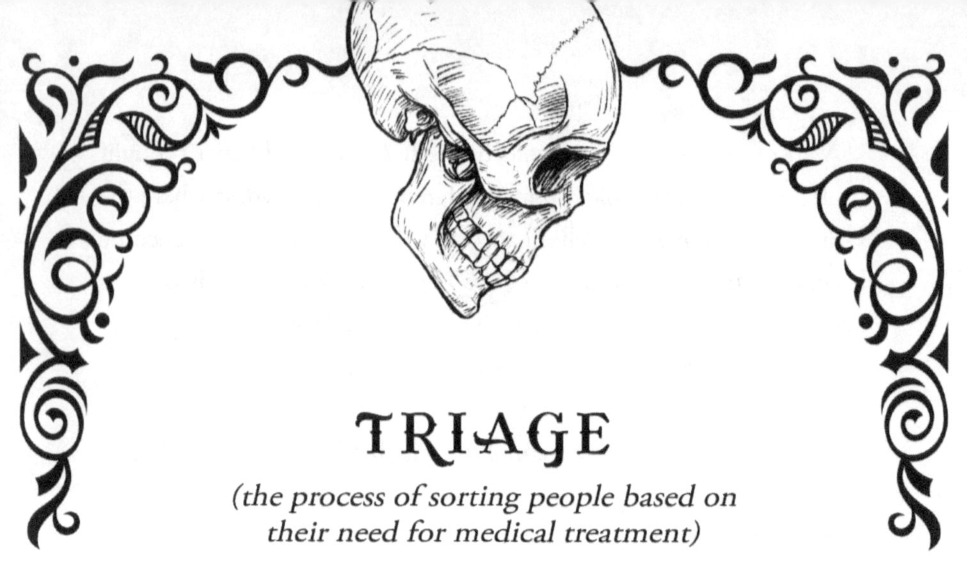

TRIAGE

(the process of sorting people based on
their need for medical treatment)

An ambulance sped Macy and Billy away after she fainted. The whole scene had been a zoo. Strangers had crowded them, wondering what had happened to her, and some even pointed the finger at Daniel.

"I saw her sneak off with him a few minutes before it happened! He did something to her!"

Billy stared daggers at Daniel as he hunched over Macy. "What the hell did you do, Grimm?"

"I didn't do anything!" Daniel insisted. But his mind screamed, *But what if I did? I overwhelmed her, and she fainted. Was this me?*

Logan stood back with his mouth agape. "She was just fine and then…"

When the medics loaded Macy onto a stretcher, Daniel insisted on riding with her. But they would only take one passenger, and they chose Billy when he told them he was her boyfriend.

Dad agreed to drive Daniel to Hope Haven, but he had hesitated at first. "You can't be taking up space in E.R., bud. It wouldn't be appropriate. Do you even know this girl that well? You never mentioned her."

"I saw her go down," Daniel said. "She's…Please. I need to be there."

Dad arranged for Mom to pick up the Grimm Goddesses after the street fair, and he reluctantly drove Daniel to the hospital.

Billy sat in the waiting room, his hair disheveled and his hands pale. He looked up at Daniel with eyes full of venom and growled, "You shouldn't be here."

Dad put a hand on Daniel's back as if to ward off any retorts, then aimed a palm at Billy. "I imagine this was a stressful day for you, and I'm sorry." He guided Daniel to the far side of the waiting room. "We'll stay out of your hair."

Billy muttered something unintelligible, crossed his arms, and slumped down in his chair.

Billy and Daniel's previous encounters had all been based on the Grimms' deaths. And here was Jonathan Grimm himself, alive and well, expressing his condolences to Billy over a medical emergency. And Billy didn't bat an eye about it. The complexities of this so-called Perfect Universe fractured Daniel's mind.

You wrote a whole essay about my dad's death, and now you're breathing his air.

This was a universe Daniel barely knew.

Maybe this was what Miguel had warned him about.

Dad put an arm around Daniel's shoulder. "Tell me what you're feeling."

Daniel looked up at the TV. "She fainted out of nowhere. It happened so fast, and it was like..." *Like a truck swerving into the wrong lane on a bridge.* "I just wish I understood what happened."

"Hopefully, the doctor can shed some light on things and make sure she gets out of here quickly. Do you know her well?"

Billy cut his gaze across the waiting room, and Daniel's knee bounced.

He knew Macy had three sisters and a brother, and she was fiercely close to her parents. So why weren't any of them in the waiting room for her? Did Billy even bother calling?

He knew her favorite animal had always been a platypus because she thought they were funny.

He knew she hated an unsolved mystery, and if she were in his shoes today, she'd pursue the truth.

And Daniel understood that his protectiveness must've resembled jealousy to her and Billy, and for that, Daniel understood Billy's anger. The thing was, he had always considered Macy as a sister in a life where he lost his own.

"I do know her well," Daniel said, sounding more confident than he felt.

He passed the time watching some syndicated sitcom on the lobby TV. The main plot involved a teenager getting her driving permit and wreaking havoc on her dad's mental health, along with the neighbor's mailbox. The B-plot had to do with her younger brother and his friend trying to scam the Tooth Fairy with Tic-Tacs. By the end, the girl had gained her independence and strengthened her bond with her dad, and she learned how to repair a mailbox. The boy had learned a valuable lesson about honesty, and he even got to pocket a few bucks.

Six episodes came and went. The characters grew through comic book conventions, Halloween hijinks, science fair scuffles, kissing crises, and a bottle episode about a blackout.

Daniel kneaded his eyelids. The lobby had its own ever-shifting cast of characters, whose stay averaged about twenty-two minutes, and whose problems would hopefully be resolved by the time they left. Couples flipped through magazines and kids played with blocks, and one woman took a nap on the floor. Another man brought a monkey into the lobby, explaining that it had devoured some banana-flavored lip balm. He spent ten minutes arguing with the receptionists that he didn't have time to take the monkey to the vet, and that the monkey deserved human care because it was just as smart as humans.

At one point, Billy got up and paced around to stretch his legs.

He looked like hell—eyes bloodshot and hair all puffed out. Daniel had never seen Billy care about anything, and he found himself wondering if Billy really *was* different in this life. And at the peak of Daniel's exhaustion, he could've sworn he saw Mr. Fedora from the beach limp out with crutches, a foot cast, and no hat.

Logan showed up a little bit later, breathless and sweaty. By way of greeting, he sat across from Daniel, caught his breath, and jerked his thumb at the door. "I just saw a monkey in the parking lot."

"You missed it." Daniel chuckled. "There was a whole drama about that."

Then Dad and Logan exchanged a glance, and for Daniel, time stopped.

Daniel couldn't imagine the cosmic horror of seeing the formerly dead in a hospital waiting room. He hadn't found the words to explain the situation to Logan yet.

But Logan extended a fist, cool and casual, and said, "Oh, hey, are you Daniel's dad? I'm Logan. I have English with this guy."

He couldn't have sounded more casual if he was asking for the time.

Dad bumped Logan's knuckles. "Logan, it's nice to meet you. I'm Jon." Then he cast a pointed glance at Daniel. "See, I'm hip. I do fist bumps."

Logan cracked a smile, then leaned back as if he hadn't just brushed knuckles with the formerly dead.

This was confirmation that Logan remembered nothing. This was a different world. On one hand, Daniel was somewhat relieved he didn't have to explain the rest. On the other hand, Logan's ignorance made Daniel feel lonely. He couldn't understand Daniel's joy or share the mystery of what this new life held.

"How's Macy?" Logan asked. "Any news yet?"

"Not yet," Daniel said. "It's been...a while."

"Oh." Logan ran his hands through his hair and blew a raspberry. "Hey, uh, while we're both here, can we go talk for a minute? Just you and me?"

"Sure." Daniel bobbed his head once, then nudged his dad. "We're gonna take a walk. Come get us if they come out with any updates?"

"I've got you, champ." Dad picked up a travel magazine and rifled through the pages.

Daniel and Logan walked down a bright, sleepy corridor to the cafeteria, and they grabbed a table.

Daniel waited for Logan to drop the façade—to ask why he had just shaken hands with Jonathan Grimm, to lose his mind. But Logan simply stretched his legs on the booth seat and looked up at the ceiling. "Hospitals always drain my soul a little bit." He picked up the saltshaker and absentmindedly spun it around on the table. "You ever go to Costa Linda General? I hate that place."

"Me, too," Daniel said. "It smells bad, and they have those weird paintings—"

"Oh my god, the ones with all the holes in them?" Logan flinched, then made a gagging face. "Dude, I will puke up my entire life just thinking about those."

Daniel laughed. "I always thought that was just me."

"Nope. It's a thing," Logan said. "So, today was kind of wild."

"Yeah," Daniel said. "It'll mean a lot to Macy that you cared enough to show up." He wondered if Macy would feel the same about his presence.

"Maybe." Logan scrunched his mouth to the side. "We don't know each other that well. And that's kinda what I wanted to talk to you about…So, you know how you were talking to me at the street fair about Thanksgiving and patching things up or whatever? I've been thinking a lot about that."

"Yeah," Daniel said. "I have a lot to explain, man. And a lot to apologize for."

"Don't take this the wrong way, but, um…" Logan put down the saltshaker. "What the hell did you mean by that?"

Daniel's posture slackened and his hands hung limp under the table. "Do you *really* not know?"

"I don't know anything about you. Honestly, I was shocked that you came up to me at the street fair. You seem chill and all, but we've never exactly been like this." Logan crossed two fingers. "So when you talked about patching things up, I didn't understand what you meant. We never had anything to fix. I know I sound like a jerk, and that's not what I'm trying to be; I just want to understand."

The statement stung, but Daniel wasn't surprised. The signs were everywhere. Logan remembered nothing. Perhaps this was an opportunity to understand what Logan did know.

"Logan," Daniel said, "what *did* you do on Thanksgiving?"

His friend shrugged. "I had dinner at home with my mom and Grandpa Weston. Just the three of us."

Daniel lifted his head. *Grandpa Weston?*

How?

Daniel's stomach hardened.

Somehow, he had replaced Logan's memories of Thanksgiving night, and possibly erased their entire friendship.

But Logan had his grandfather back.

The bittersweetness…

Lighting the candles had brought back some of their loved ones, too?

Because Daniel could live with that.

Logan had enjoyed another meal with his grandfather.

His friends were *happy*.

And Daniel wasn't the Grimm Reaper anymore.

"I'm happy you got to spend Thanksgiving with your mom and your grandpa. Truly."

"Yeah," Logan said. "Me, too. It's hard to know how much time I have left with my grandpa. He had a stroke a while back…*barely* survived. So I try not to take these times for granted. We need to enjoy these moments while we have them, right?"

Daniel nodded. "Sure. Yeah, I get that."

"Case and point: Macy," Logan said. "It sucks what happened to her. We feel all young and mighty, but even our days are numbered. Pretty scary to think about. You think she'll be okay?"

"I think she will be," Daniel said. "At least I know she's in good hands. My godfather's one of the doctors in the E.R. Dr. Mortiz."

And if it wasn't Macy's time, Miguel wouldn't let her die. Daniel wondered what her candle looked like. *Please let it be strong. Healthy. With lots of life left in it.*

"Oh, no way?" Logan scrunched his brows. "Hey, why do I feel like I know that name? Have we talked about him before?"

Daniel thought for a minute. *Yeah. And then you had too much wine, and you told Aunt Cass about him.* "Maybe in passing," he said. "Miguel's cool, though. He was kind of a rock for me for a while."

"Yeah?" Logan said. "How so?"

"Just…with family stuff. You know how it can be."

"Oh, I know it," Logan said. "We all need to lean on someone sometimes, especially on days like today. Mine's my grandpa. And I don't know what happened with you and Macy or whatever, but if you ever need to talk or anything, I'm up for that."

"Thanks." Daniel flashed a sad half-smile. "Likewise."

Logan stood, stretched, and drummed his fingers on his thighs. "So, what *did* you think I did on Thanksgiving? I'm still trying to understand what you meant."

"Never mind," Daniel said. "I think I had an entirely different person in mind."

Logan narrowed his eyes and rubbed his chin. "Hmm. You're a strange dude, Grimm. You know that?"

"So I've been told."

"I bet you get that a lot," Logan said. "But that's kind of cool, in an interesting way. I don't believe in things like past lives and fate or whatever, but in another life, I bet we might've been good friends."

Daniel looked at his lap. "I'm sure."

"You mind if I go catch up with Schubes? I feel like someone should check on him."

"Go for it," Daniel muttered. It bugged him to no end that Logan had a brotherly nickname for Daniel's least favorite person—and no record of the friendship they had spent years developing. But the concern for Billy was peak Logan Thane. He came here to check on *everyone*. "I'm gonna chill here for a while. Make sure you take care of you, too, man."

They shook hands.

Logan walked away, hands in his pockets and looking up at the world.

Daniel's throat felt thick, like it had been stuffed with cotton.

He sat in the cafeteria and collected his thoughts. He needed to know what else had unraveled when he lit the candles, but he also didn't *want* to know. For now, he'd hold on to what he brought back. He'd make up for lost time with his family, and he'd smooth the creases and go on as planned.

Shortly after Daniel returned to the waiting room, Miguel entered in his white coat. Daniel felt like this was sitcom luck. Hope Haven had 250 physicians. Of *course* fate would bring Macy to Miguel, for better or worse.

Miguel gave Daniel and Dad a curt nod, then beckoned them over. Billy and Logan took the cue to follow.

"Oh, Miguel," Dad said, "I'm so glad it's you. There are no better hands in this hospital."

Miguel nodded again, this time to convey gratitude.

Billy looked Miguel up and down. "You're Macy's doctor?" He jerked a thumb at Daniel. "I don't want him hearing whatever you're about to say. It's none of his business."

Daniel shot Billy a death glare. "You can eat sh—"

"You must be Billy." Miguel shook Billy's hand. "Yes, I'm Dr.

Mortiz. I've been running the initial care on Macy today. She has given me permission to share some details with whoever came for her, which happens to include Daniel. I'm glad she has friends who care for her."

"So she's conscious?" Logan asked. "If she gave you permission to share, then she's okay."

"She is conscious," Miguel confirmed.

"Well, is she okay?" Daniel asked. "Where is she? What happened to her?"

Miguel worked his jaws, then put his fingertips together. "I'm gonna get to the point."

Daniel steeled himself.

"Macy experienced a myocardial infarction today," Miguel said.

The floor swelled under Daniel's feet.

There was no way he'd heard that correctly. Absolutely no way. Dad caught his shoulder and pulled him in, steadying him.

Logan's mouth hung open, and he brought a palm to his chin.

Billy blinked a few times. "What does that mean?"

"It means Macy had a heart attack," Miguel said gently.

"No shit, Sherlock, I know what it means," Billy snapped. "But what does it *mean*? How did she have a heart attack? She's eighteen, she's healthy. She was just fine, and I don't think you're telling me the truth because there was nothing wrong—"

Daniel rolled his shoulders. "Will you shut up and let him talk already?"

Billy drew in a hot breath and made a fist at his side. "I just don't understand what happened. Can you figure that out so you can make her better?"

"We already have a team working on it." Miguel looked at Daniel, Logan, Billy, and Dad in turn. "She's in coronary care, and they'll be doing all they can to aid her recovery. As I said, she's conscious now. After she gets some rest, they'll start letting in visitors. She'll be here for at least two days while they watch over her."

Dad rubbed his chin. "I noticed her parents aren't here. Have they been informed of all this? Does she have anyone coming for her?"

"She'll be cared for, Jon," Miguel said.

"I know she's in good hands," Dad said. "But if there's anything we can do, I'm sure—"

"She doesn't need your family, understand?" Billy said.

Logan grabbed Billy's shoulder. "Whoa, dude, take a breath."

Billy shrugged Logan off, his breath heavy and bull-like. "No, I'm serious." He stuck a finger in his face. "I don't know what you did today, Grimm, but I know it was your fault."

"Billy," Dad said. "I know this is stressful. Take a breath, please."

Billy lowered his finger, but he didn't step back.

Daniel stared back at Billy in cold defiance.

"Keep *away* from us," Billy said. "I mean it. You scare the hell out of me."

LYCANTHROPY

*(the condition of being forced to
transform into a werewolf)*

Glimpses of Macy flickered through Daniel's mind during the ride home.

He had wanted to stay behind and talk to Miguel, but Miguel was in full doctor mode. Daniel was bewildered by Miguel's ability to wear three different mantles—the warm cloak of the godfather, the pristine white coat of the doctor, and the shadowy veil of death. Unfortunately, none of the three had time for Daniel's questions.

What happened to Logan? What happened to his grandpa?

Are you going to take Macy away from me?

To quell his worries, Daniel fidgeted with his lighter.

"And why do you have my lighter?" Dad asked. "I was looking for that this morning."

Daniel's fingers froze.

Dad leaned over and sniffed Daniel's shoulder, his gaze careful on the road. "You're not smoking cigarettes, are you?"

"No," Daniel said quickly. "I, um…" He shook his head, his mind too thick to concoct a reason other than *I inherited this when you died.* "I don't know. I'm sorry. I should've asked. It's like a fidget toy for me. I like the feel of the little…" He flicked the spark wheel, then shut the cap and offered the lighter back to his father. "Here."

Dad reached for it, closed his fingers halfway, then shook his head. "No." A smile warmed his face. "Why don't you hold on to that for me?"

A soft lump lodged itself in Daniel's throat. Somehow, it meant more to have Dad *give* him the lighter. "You mean that?"

Dad nodded. "It was gonna be yours one day, anyway."

Daniel stared at his reflection in the cap, again seeing his future—his father. "Thank you."

"You're welcome. Just don't…" Dad mimed flicking a cigarette, grunting and making a dopey face. "And be careful. It's not a toy—not that I need to lecture you about playing with fire. You're smarter than I used to be. Did I ever tell you about the time I set the palm tree on fire?"

Daniel grinned. "What? When?"

"When I was in middle school." Dad smirked as he hit his blinker. "I was, uh…playing with matches. It was summer, and everything was dry. I thought I had put one out, and I threw it over my shoulder, and this palm tree *lit up.* Woosh. So, Aunt Cass and I each grabbed a little Dixie cup, running back and forth from the bathroom sink, filling it with water, and trying to put out this burning palm tree."

"You never told me that!" Daniel said. "Dad, you rebel. Did you put it out?"

Dad scoffed. "Heck no. The fire department did. And then they gave me and Aunt Cass the lecture of our lives. Man, I was sobbing, convinced I was going to prison at thirteen. Your grandma and grandpa had some words for us, too. Oh, but Aunt Cass? All she could talk about for a *week* were the good-looking firemen." He chuckled and rubbed his chin. "Oh, those were simpler times… simpler times, Danny."

Daniel pictured a young Dad and Aunt Cass brewing shenanigans together—the thorns in his grandparents' sides.

"Now I get to pay for my mistakes by cleaning up after Bobby and

Elena." Dad pointed at the lighter, his expression suddenly grave. "Swear to me, you'll never let either of them near that thing."

"Oh, god no." Daniel shuddered and pocketed the lighter. Bobby, plus Elena, plus fire equaled the apocalypse.

Dad pulled the car into the driveway and parked. "I know today was tough for you," he said. "And hopefully everything will work out for your friend's health. You okay?"

Daniel nodded. He didn't want to talk about Macy anymore. But he did want to be with his family. "I'll be fine."

"Okay," Dad said. "I'm watching you."

"I'm not gonna burn down a palm tree."

"Too far, kid."

They went into the house, but they stopped in their tracks.

"What in the *Amazon*?" Dad said.

From the floor to the ceiling, every inch of the living room was drenched in jungle decorations. Vines dripped from the banisters and the light fixtures while leaves covered the kitchen counter. Inflatable trees lined the walls, and coconuts littered the floor. A stream of blue butcher paper ran across the living room floor, and someone had drawn fish all over it.

"Who did all this?" Dad massaged his cheekbones. "And who's planning to clean it up?"

The house was stone silent.

A desk sat in front of the door, and someone had left a handwritten note.

Dad picked it up and read the contents, the mask of despair slowly melting away.

"What's going on?" Daniel asked.

Dad cracked a grin and handed the sheet of paper to Daniel. "You've been issued a challenge."

Daniel took the paper. Sam's jagged handwriting spidered across the page.

Hello, DANIEL.

We are monsters, and we are hiding in the jungle. We could be anywhere. We could be right behind you. One of us is definitely NOT in the hunter's camp (your bedroom). You must hunt all of us before we eat your heart. (Please locate the Robo-Frog sticker under this note and place it on your chest. This is now your heart.)

The rules are simple: All of us will attempt to steal your heart. If any of us succeed, we win and you lose. At least you get a really cool sniper gun (In the sink. Please locate the sad, dollar store water pistol, pre-loaded for your immediate pleasure, convenience, and false hope.). If you shoot one of us, that monster is now extinct. Shoot all of us to win.

You cannot cover your heart. You cannot touch us. You can only snipe us. You can also run, but you will not get far. We are fast and we are sneaky AF. We are already watching you. We can smell your fear and you are hopelessly outnumbered.

You cannot stop what is coming.

Your downfall is inevitable.

Hugs!

<3

The Monsters Grimm

Daniel flipped over the paper and confronted a hastily sketched emoji, tongue out and eyes closed.

The tension of the day evaporated from Daniel's body. His siblings were playing a game with him.

"Wait." He picked up the green sticker on the table. "I have questions!

Who else is playing?"

Dad's phone buzzed, and he read the notification. "One of the monsters just texted me. They said, *Nobody is playing. It is a hunt. Put your heart on your chest, hunter.*"

Bowser's tag tinkled as he trotted into the living room, tongue wagging. He wore a tiny safari hat and black booties. He pawed at Daniel's leg, and Daniel recoiled. "Is Bowser one of the monsters?"

Dad's phone buzzed again. "*No.*"

Daniel scratched Bowser's back. "Do I get a partner?"

Buzz. "*Also no.* Okay, I'm no longer here. Good luck." Dad stepped over a pile of leaves, stumbled a bit, and made a beeline for his room, muttering, "Still doing my time for that palm tree…"

Daniel grabbed the water pistol from the sink. It was a cheap toy with a leaky bottom and a weak range. A test squirt reminded him that the stream didn't even reach the length of his pinky.

He rolled his shoulders and shook out his wrists. He'd have to think like his siblings to win their game. Luckily, he shared their DNA.

Daniel peeled the sticker off its backing and slapped it over his heart. He patted it twice for good measure, but the edges still curled like a wilted daisy.

He crept out of his shoes and held his breath, listening for footsteps in the house.

Bowser tilted his head, and his tag jingled.

Daniel put a finger to his lips and shooed Bowser away. "You're gonna give me away," he mouthed.

Bowser let out a muffled, resigned bark, then trotted up the stairs.

Daniel started with the guest bathroom. His siblings had planned this with diabolical intensity. He didn't want to expose himself in the middle of an open floor, but if he got too close to the walls, the plastic vines would whisper. If he looked up, he'd step on leaves and sound a crackling alarm for his siblings. If he looked at the floor, he became vulnerable. If he wasted too much time, the leaky pistol would run out of water, which already carved a steady rivulet on his forearm.

Daniel picked up speed and his socks slipped on the bathroom tile. He pointed his water gun forward, leaned back, and threw open the shower curtain. He squirted into the dark, then turned on the light.

None of his siblings hid behind the curtain, but a toothless plush alligator sat in the bathtub.

An alligator. Daniel shook his head. The universe fulfilled a wish from the twins again.

Daniel refilled the water gun and scoped out the living room. He didn't bother stepping over the paper river. He hoped the crinkling sound would lure one of his siblings out from behind the couch or one of the nearby rooms. He held his breath, feeling exposed and vulnerable and ready to shoot.

But no one attacked.

"I'm in the middle of the living room!" Daniel called. "I'm open."

The silence lingered.

Daniel turned in a circle, his finger loose on the trigger. "Come out and face me! You can't hide from me forever. Marco?"

Upstairs, Bowser woofed.

"Cowards!" Daniel charged, ruffling paper and plastic in his trail. He bounded up the staircase and toward his bedroom.

Another note had been taped on his door, this time written in Ruthie's cute, curvy handwriting:

Hunter's Camp—

There are definitely no beasts here. :) :)

Daniel pressed his ear to the door but only heard his heartbeat.

He cracked it open and peeked into the dark, but only the void stared back.

He inched it open a little more, and then all at once.

When he flicked the light on, he stared into an empty room. A smile spread across his face. "Y'all aren't sneaky."

Daniel lowered himself to the ground and lifted his bedspread, posing his water gun to shoot into the dark. There was a time when Bobby and Elena used to take turns hiding under the bed and grabbing Daniel's feet, blasting his heart rate halfway to hell. Daniel had been so traumatized that Mom and Dad had to knock the legs off his bed so the twins couldn't fit anymore.

"*Get him!*" Victor roared from behind.

Footsteps pounded into the room as streams of lukewarm water pelted Daniel from head to toe.

"We've got you cornered!" Bobby said.

Daniel rolled over and fired at his stampeding siblings—Victor, Sam, Bobby, Ruthie, Monica, Nancy, and Elena. They wielded Super Soakers as big as their legs, and their streams were infinite. The pressure made little dimples in his clothes, while the water from his gun simply oozed out of the top and rained down on his face. He didn't manage to squirt a single person except for himself.

"No!" Daniel screamed, laughter pouring from his chest. "Stop! You can't gang up on me like this! This is unfair on so many levels! Stop it!"

"Do you yield?" Bobby asked.

"Never!" Daniel pumped the trigger until the gun only fizzed droplets of water and puffs of air. Then he dropped it at his side and threw up his hands. "Okay, I yield!"

"You yield?" Ruthie asked in her best Evil Queen impression. "Then surrender your heart!" *Surrendah yaw hawt.*

Sam lowered his gun. "Wait. Where is your heart? Dude, did you not read the letter? I put so much work into that."

Daniel looked down at his hoodie, five shades darker where the water had soaked him, but there was no sticker. "I put it on. I swear."

Elena bent over and picked something up by the door. "I got it!" She held the curled sticker proudly in the air, an enormous grin on her face as she jumped up and down in a circle. "I got the hunter's heart! I got the hunter's heart! You lose!"

Daniel tilted his head back on the floor, catching his breath. Bowser trotted in and licked his face, and then Nancy threw a towel over Daniel's head. Daniel sat up and ran the towel over his hair. "That was fun," he said. "Unfair, but fun. Man, I was doomed from the start."

"It would've been more fun if you did better," Sam said. "We told you we weren't in your bedroom, and that made it easy to corner you when you came in here, anyway. Did you think we were *lion*?"

Monica crossed her arms and sneered at Sam. "Boo! Zero out of ten. Go away and think about what you've done."

Daniel chuckled.

Sam winked. "Danny thinks I'm funny."

Daniel tossed his water gun onto the bed. "So, what's with the jungle in the house?"

"We wanted to know if you'll have a sleepover in the living room with us," Elena said. "We're gonna play games and watch movies."

"On a Sunday?" Daniel asked. "Why?"

"I dunno," Elena said. "Because we want you to. But if you don't want to, then—"

"Yes." Daniel cherished the innocence. They wanted to bond with him, and he would never deny that chance. "I would love to hang out with you. Can I, uh…put on some dry clothes first? Or are you all just gonna blast me again?"

Victor shooed the others toward the door. "Clear out, weasels. Give the man his space. What are we, sardines in a can?"

"Asked the dude who *smells* like one," Sam said.

"Ha," Victor said. "Hilarious. I'm hysterical."

When everyone else left the room, Victor and Nancy both stayed behind and shut the door.

"You okay?" Nancy asked. "I know you had a rough day."

Daniel cradled his forehead. "It's nothing compared to the day Macy had." He blew out a breath. "Did you all at least have a good sales day at the booth?"

"Meh," Nancy said. "We didn't stay too much longer. We knew

our brother needed us."

Victor flexed a fist. "Can I pop Billy Schubert in the face? Give him a little sandwich?"

"No," Daniel said. "Please don't pop Billy Schubert in the face."

"I don't like that guy," Victor said simply. "I don't know why; I just don't."

"I don't like him, either," Daniel said. "But don't be a bully, Vic. He had just as bad a day as I did, and my stress has nothing to do with him. I'm just worried about Macy, that's all."

Victor pursed his lips. "I'm not too good at this, but if you do wanna talk about it, you know…we're here and stuff."

Daniel nodded. "I know. I appreciate it."

"I'm sorry about everything." Nancy shook her water gun. "Was the game too much?"

"Time with my family was exactly what I needed," Daniel said. "It means a lot that you all wanted to cheer me up. I don't wanna help clean up the jungle, though."

"Man," Victor said, "we were gonna make you clean it all. Since you lost."

"Jerk." Daniel puffed out his chest, put on a husky voice, and said, *"Who am I, Mr. Clean?"*

Victor narrowed his eyes. "What is that? Is that supposed to be me? I don't sound like that."

"Yeah, you do," Nancy said.

"No, I don't."

"Yeah, you do!" Elena called from downstairs.

Victor thumped Daniel on the forehead. "You all are the worst. I'm going to bed. Good night, Dan Torino."

"You're not coming downstairs with us?"

Victor shook his head. "I wanna, but I'm gonna go lay down in my room. I think I might be coming down with something."

"Flu?" Nancy asked.

"I dunno. It's not too bad," Victor said. "Just like my mind's a little foggy, and I can't taste anything these days. I feel like my head's stuffed with straw. Should try to sleep it off and not push myself too hard."

"Sleep it off," Daniel said. "And then tomorrow will be a better day for all of us, yeah?"

"Better believe it, bro."

Daniel believed it.

Macy would get the treatment and care she needed at Hope Haven. She would go home feeling fine and happy, and over time, he'd develop a new friendship with her and Logan…maybe an even stronger one. Daniel didn't even care if Billy came with the territory. If he gave Billy a chance and tolerated him long enough, maybe they could put their drama aside.

The day hadn't been perfect, but for now, this universe still sang to him. His sisters were creating crafts and flourishing. His siblings were inventing elaborate games, and Daniel was having water gun fights and sleepovers with them. They were laughing and building memories.

They put on a movie downstairs, but they didn't pay attention to it.

They played a game about crossing the Amazon River, and by the end of it, the blue butcher paper was a wrinkled mess.

Then they all grabbed sleeping bags and pillows, and Sam read the first chapter of his book aloud—a space fantasy he called *Silver, Spells, and Stardust*. Each character had echoes of one of the Grimms. Vic'Zor was the master of charisma and love; Nan'Dree was a cool, even-keeled sorceress who healed wounds through the power of music. There was a pair of droids named Rob-3 and E-L3N4, who were equipped with lasers, whistles, radar, and they dispensed popsicles at will. There was one named Dan'Grell, who wielded fire, and Sham'Yule was a sort of bard who told all their stories.

By the time Sam finished reading, Monica was asleep.

"Can you keep going?" Daniel asked. "I want to know what

happens to the space wizards."

"There is more," Sam said with a dramatic gleam in his eye. "But that is for another day…in another time…in another galaxy." He snapped his binder shut. "Or maybe tomorrow. I'm kinda tired. You really liked it, though?"

"Every word," Daniel said.

Sam passed Daniel the binder. "You can read it if you want. I'm a little nervous, but maybe you can give me some feedback?"

Daniel took the binder, chunky with hole-punched sheets of paper bathed in red ink. Nancy had even designed him a book cover—a council of wizards standing around a spaceship. Daniel ran a finger over the binder. These were the contents of his brother's mind—his heart and soul.

"I would love nothing more, Sam," Daniel said.

"Can I read it after him?" Ruthie asked.

"And me?" Bobby asked.

Sam reddened and pulled his sleeping bag up to his face. "Maybe." He yawned and bunched up his pillow. "Yeah. Just remember, it's still a work in progress."

He drifted to sleep a few minutes later, and Daniel waved Bobby and Elena to his sides. "Here. Let's read it together." And he began to narrate. "*Her name was Ruth Zora Kal'Ifer, and she was a master of diversion. Hand her a moon rock, a screw, and an empty packet of food paste, and she would concoct a game that bound all the players to her spell. One night, during a game of dice, she accidentally enchanted a bounty hunter, and he forgot his quest…*"

Two chapters later, Ruthie was snoring, and Daniel realized he was the only one still awake. His muscles were tight with exhaustion, but his mind buzzed like a cloud of bees. He stood up, did some light cleaning, and turned out the lights. He left the TV humming in the background. Some of this siblings snored like jungle animals, and the twins had never looked more peaceful. Daniel watched their breaths rise and fall, strong and healthy, and he slid into his sleeping bag.

This may not be the Perfect Universe, he told himself. *But I can get used to this.*

He had just entered a soft, quiet dream before an ear-splitting scream pierced the night.

NIGHT TERRORS

*(feelings of great fear experienced on
suddenly waking in the night)*

The scream ripped Daniel out of his sleep and sent shockwaves through his blood.

He sprang out of his sleeping bag and nearly tripped over one of his brothers.

Daniel grabbed his sister's shoulder and shook her. "Elena!" he said. "Elena, wake up! You're having a nightmare. It's okay."

Elena startled awake and sucked in a shaky breath that cut off her screams. She looked around the room, eyes wide and confused.

"*Hey*," Daniel whispered. "Look at me."

She locked eyes with him, and a glimmer of recognition softened her gaze. She blinked, sat up, and pressed her hands over her eyelids. "Danny, it was so scary…"

"Elena," Daniel said softly, "it was just a dream."

Light flooded the room, and then Bobby stirred in his sleeping bag. Mom and Victor entered the living room in their pajamas, their eyes red with sleep.

"What happened?" Mom asked.

"Elena had a nightmare," Daniel said. "I've got it, Mom."

"Aww." Mom took a knee and tucked a lock of hair behind Elena's ear. She pressed the back of her hand to Elena's forehead. "Are you okay, baby?"

Elena tucked her sleeping bag tight against her chest. "I'm okay."

Mom tapped Victor's ankle. "Vic, go make us some tea, please."

Victor nodded and dragged his feet to the kitchen.

Daniel remembered nights when Mom and Dad would sit with him after a bad dream. On the worst nights, he'd dream of the monsters from Sam's video games and Monica's horror movies. Daniel's hauntings had all been grotesque and fantastical until the incident on the bridge—that's when the monsters stopped chasing him. Nightmares became a single memory replaying in infinite loops, and Aunt Cass became the protector when he'd wake in the night. He'd lost count of how many nights she soothed him back to sleep with cocoa and a late-night story. He also lost track of when he'd stopped waking her and started fighting the nightmares alone. He only knew that they never went away. He was willing to bet that was true for Aunt Cass, too.

"It felt real," Elena said.

"They always do," Daniel said. "Wanna talk about it?"

Elena pulled her knees against her chest. "We were going on a trip," she said. "And I was in the car with Dad and Bobby and Sam."

Daniel's fingers went cold. He focused on the familiar sounds of tea prep in the kitchen—the clamor of the cabinet door, the tearing of paper and shaking of a tea packet, the *whoosh* of water spilling from the faucet into a pot.

"And then we got on the bridge and there was this huge truck coming, and it went like this." Elena drew a sharp curve in the air. "It was gonna hit us, and Dad got scared and he was honking… and then I woke up."

Victor looked up from the teapot on the stove and cut his gaze to Daniel. It hadn't been long ago that Daniel had described the same scene to his brother, then sworn him to secrecy.

No, he thought. *My sister did not have a dream about the day she died. It's just an ugly coincidence. There was something in the movie we were watching. It's a common thing to dream about.*

"I think I had the same nightmare," Bobby croaked. His hair was matted with sweat.

No, Daniel thought again. *It's just twin sync…the power of suggestion.*

"I did, too," Ruthie said. "I was in the big van with Vic, Nancy, Xander, and Monica. And Mom was driving."

Daniel's swallowed the bile that crept up his throat. Victor hadn't taken his eyes off him.

"Hey, kids." Mom sat cross-legged between Bobby and Elena's sleeping bags. "Let's think this out. Dreams are just like movies your brain makes in your sleep. Sometimes they're nice, and sometimes they're not so nice. But the main thing to remember is that they can't hurt you. You're safe here in the house, we're not going anywhere, and you're all gonna be okay."

"How did we all have the same dream?" Ruthie asked. "That's creepy."

Victor came around and passed out mugs of chamomile tea. He handed a World's Best Mom mug to Daniel. There was suspicion in Victor's gaze when they made eye contact.

Daniel clutched the mug and inhaled, allowing the steam to loosen his muscles.

"Brains are weird," Mom said, "and so are dreams. But I think you can use something you learned from Danny and Miguel. Before you go to bed, tell the universe you want a good dream."

"I did." Elena frowned. "And I still had a nightmare."

"Well, then maybe it's trying to tell you something, sweetheart," Mom said. "And I don't know what that would be, because it sounds like a pretty awful dream, but we're all gonna be okay." She stroked Elena's hair. "Try to get some more sleep, okay?"

Elena made a face at her tea. "I don't think I can sleep."

"Why don't you read a book for a little bit?" Mom pointed at Elena's mug. "And that's sleepy-time tea. I know you don't love it, but it'll help you feel all nice and relaxed again."

Daniel shut his eyes.

Mom was wrong.

Elena and Bobby's shared nightmare wasn't trying to tell them anything. *What if this is a message for me?* he thought. *They're being haunted by their own deaths.*

And for the first time since he greeted Bowser and the aroma of pancakes outside his bedroom door, Daniel's stomach prickled with the fleeting thought that maybe he had made a mistake in The Archive.

SENIORITIS

*(an affliction of students in their final year of school,
characterized by a decline in motivation)*

Monday morning hit like a sock full of bricks.

Apparently when he lit the candles, Daniel had also put a defibrillator to his flatlining education. Dad had woken him up and told him to get ready for school.

"I don't go to school anymore," Daniel mumbled.

Dad tossed his newspaper down on Daniel's face. "Yeah, nice try, champ. Scoot."

Faucets gurgled and cereal bowls clanked, and Mom rummaged through her purse. Sam had hogged one of the showers, sparking sibling outrage. This was a true Grimm Monday. Daniel might've loved it if he didn't have to go back to Costa Linda High.

"Taking the Grimmlings." Dad gave Mom a peck on the lips as Ruthie, Bobby, and Elena filed out of the house. "Love you."

"Love you *mas*! Did the kids get their lunches?"

Ruthie made a U-turn back into the house and collected a paper bag from the fridge. All three of the youngest had springs in their steps, countering the rough night they'd just had.

Daniel still hadn't shaken the night out of his head. Between Logan's memories, Macy's incident, and the Grimms' nightmares, this was not the Perfect Universe. At first it felt like a sitcom, like a laugh track could interrupt him at any minute. But something ugly chewed on the back of his mind—a feeling of foreboding, like all the good was seconds away from imploding underneath him.

Daniel changed his clothes, brushed his teeth, and put on shoes. Then he threw together a text to Miguel.

Can we meet?

Miguel's reply came in quickly.

MIGUEL: **Busy. Stop by hospital after school.**

DANIEL: **Urgent.**

MIGUEL: **After school.**

Daniel growled under his breath. Even Miguel wouldn't bail him out of class.

Daniel grabbed a muffin on the way out the door. He beelined for his car, but Nancy honked at him and rolled down the window of her sedan. "Hello? Where are you going? I'm driving today."

Sam stuck his head out the passenger window and jerked a thumb behind him. "Get in loser, we're going to hell…I mean, school."

Daniel yawned and scooted into the backseat. A pale, lean boy with large ears sat behind Nancy, staring out the window and resting his chin on his palm.

"Xander!" Daniel threw an arm around his brother. "How have you been? I've barely seen you."

Xander faced Daniel and raised a brow. "Alive."

"How vague of you," Nancy muttered.

There was something about Xander's gaze and tone that made Daniel flinch. He pulled his arm back and buckled his seatbelt. Xander went back to staring out the window.

Nancy backed out of the driveway. "So I guess Vic's got the house to himself today."

"Is he still not feeling well?" Daniel asked.

Nancy shook her head in sync with the cactus air freshener dangling from her rearview mirror. "I think he's spreading whatever he has, too. I couldn't even taste my muffin. It was like water."

"Ugh, you too?" Sam puckered his lips. "I thought it was just me."

"You, too?" Nancy glanced in the rearview mirror. "What about you, Xander?"

Xander nodded, his fist against his temple.

"Daniel?" Sam asked.

Daniel popped some of the muffin into his mouth, the blueberries bright and juicy. "I mean, I did feel a little sick to my stomach last night."

Because my siblings had a dream about the semi that killed them.

"Then why are we going to school?" Sam asked. "Let's ditch."

"We have finals," Nancy said. "I have stupid calc and effing econ today."

Great, Daniel thought. *My first day back at school and I have finals I didn't study for.* He couldn't even say what classes he had. Did he even have the same schedule?

"Self-care comes first," Sam said. "Victor knows."

"Victor has a bunch of easy electives. How hard can woodshop be?"

"Says the band queen. And remember when you took ceramics?" Sam asked. "Your turtle had like, seven legs."

Nancy cupped a hand to her ear. "I'm sorry. Did I just hear you say you'd like to walk the rest of the way?"

"Nah, I'm good." Sam smiled sweetly and tilted his head. "Did I ever tell you what a beautiful turtle you created?"

Nancy tossed her hair. "Aw, you're so nice."

Returning to Costa Linda High felt a bit like trying on someone else's tiny shoes, then realizing they had wheels. Daniel had never exactly felt comfortable in these halls in the first place, and now he was in a world he barely knew. The siblings split off and went in separate directions. Nancy disappeared with a girl Daniel had never seen before, Sam disappeared with a whole crowd, and Xander just disappeared.

Something about his demeanor had worried Daniel. Xander had

always been the most pensive and introverted Grimm, but in the car, he had been downright distant…even broody. Daniel wondered if maybe Xander had been having nightmares, too.

Before classes, Daniel used to meet Macy and Logan at a picnic table near the football field. They'd eat their breakfast and catch up on everything and nothing. Instinctively, Daniel gravitated toward that table, only to find it occupied. *Of course,* Daniel thought. Macy would still be in the hospital, and even if he could find Logan, their friendship was colored in shades of gray. They were practically strangers.

Daniel took an empty bench and considered the field. He could've sworn it used to be greener. Football was the pride and joy of Costa Linda High. Administration invested in keeping the field fresh year-round, the smell of grass always thick in the air. Today, the grass looked patchy and worn with the dull color of an onion.

Daniel texted Miguel again. **Can you at least tell me how Macy's doing?**

Suddenly Miguel wasn't so quick to answer anymore.

The bell rang and Daniel headed for his first class, silently praying he didn't have a government final.

The universe delivered, but not in the way Daniel expected.

He walked into his classroom. Instead of the usual U.S. President prints, enormous Constitution, and the poster containing lyrics to an old-school song about a bill on Capitol Hill, Shakespeare quotes lined the walls.

His bland, mustached government teacher had been replaced by a woman with raven hair and dark lipstick, and she was scrawling on the board. She met Daniel's eyes and gave him a quizzical look. "Can I help you find someone?"

Daniel read the board.

Why do you think Orpheus turned to look at Eurydice?

Daniel didn't know who either of those people were, but they probably had nothing to do with the American government system.

"Um," Daniel said, "this isn't U.S. Government."

The teacher shook her head slowly, eyebrows high and disapproving.

Daniel wriggled his way out while more students piled in, and he did a double take at the room number. He knew he used to have government here—room twenty-three—across from the perpetually empty and vandalized snack machine. If this wasn't his classroom, then he had no idea where to go.

The bell rang again, and Daniel found himself alone in one of the dizzying, infinite halls of Costa Linda High. He pressed his fingers to his temples. This was not the problem he wanted to tackle today.

I don't have time for this.

Daniel beelined for the door—the light at the end of the tunnel. Maybe he could get out, take a bus home, and check on Victor. Or hunker down at the Hope Haven cafeteria and wait for Miguel's schedule to clear up. Anywhere but here.

The soft squeak of rubber wheels echoed behind him. Daniel heard the squelch of a mop hitting the tile, and he kept his pace. The janitors usually minded their business and looked the other way. They had enough messes to clean up without tangling themselves in students' sticky dramas.

"Excuse me," a voice said. "Where's your pass?"

Dammit.

Daniel spun on his heel. While the janitor mopped the floor, a hall monitor had turned the corner and decided to pounce. Daniel gave the hall monitor his brightest, cheesiest grin. "Left my homework in my car."

The hall monitor crossed his arms. "You think I don't hear that every day?"

Daniel pointed his thumb behind him and took slow steps backward. "It's like a science thing. Highly combustible. If I don't get it out of the sun, it's gonna…I gotta…Wait a second." His eyes cut to the janitor behind the hall monitor. Daniel recognized the man's cleft chin, chiseled jawline, and hardened cheekbones. "I know you. Since when do you work here?"

The janitor blinked a few times, turned away, and grabbed his mop. "Since always."

"I feel like I see you everywhere else these days," Daniel said. "Didn't I see you at the beach?"

Stop! Thieves!

Victor had been so certain the guy was watching them.

"You were also at the hospital. What happened to your cast? Where did it go?"

The janitor dragged his mop over a black sticky wad on the floor. "I must have one of those faces. I get that a lot." He waved Daniel along and shook his head at the hall monitor. "Let 'im pass. He has a science project in his car."

The hall monitor flapped his clipboard. "He's obviously lying!"

The janitor glared, eyes cold and hard. "Let him pass."

Daniel saluted the janitor and the hall monitor, and he forgot all about him.

But when Daniel turned around, another familiar face barred his path.

Mrs. Golden.

Daniel's heart sank.

She carried a walkie-talkie on her hip and a tablet under her arm. And when they locked eyes, Mrs. Golden brightened. "Good morning, Danny." She gave him a polite nod. "Fancy seeing one of my favorite students. How are you?"

Daniel's knees locked. *Favorite?* What was possessing her?

"Uh, fine," he said.

Mrs. Golden tilted her head. "How are Mr. and Mrs. Grimm? Doing good?"

There was a time when she would've corrected him on that same phrasing: *You mean doing well, Daniel?*

Dead or alive, Daniel never wanted to hear his parents' names in Mrs. Golden's mouth again. And apparently all of Costa Linda knew they were alive. It was like they had never left.

"They're…also fine," Daniel said.

"Please tell them I said hello," Mrs. Golden said. "So where are you off to in the middle of class? Don't you have any finals right now?"

Daniel looked at Mrs. Golden's lanyard. Her smiling face beamed from the photo on her ID. Her expression used to be sour, and *English Department* used to be printed under the Costa Linda logo. Now in fading ink, the ID read *Principal*.

Daniel skipped a breath. "Um, where's Mr. Jerricks?"

Mrs. Golden's smile melted away. Her eyes misted up, and she fanned herself with her hand. "Oh, don't make me sad, dear. Exams must be scrambling your brain. How 'bout if you come get some water from the teacher's lounge and then I'll write you a pass back to class?"

Beads of sweat bubbled up on Daniel's forehead. He didn't want water, a pass, or another second of Mrs. Golden's attention.

A door opened nearby, and a boy named Travis Holiday burst from the room with a goofy grin and a carton of eggs in his hand.

There were only two things Daniel knew about Travis Holiday: that he had a taste for theatrics and mischief, and that he was a heck of a baseball pitcher.

Travis Holiday gave Mrs. Golden an impish grin, cupped his free hand to his mouth, and yelled, "Anarchy!"

And then he decked the halls with shells and egg yolks. Lockers, floors, ceiling tiles, water fountains, and Mrs. Golden's sandals were all targets.

Mrs. Golden's face reddened as she shook an egg from her foot. *This* was the way Daniel remembered her. "In all my life!" she trilled. "Mr. Holiday, you stop that right this instant!"

"Nope!"

Mrs. Golden started running as more doors opened in the hall.

Teachers and students popped out to see the commotion. Before Mrs. Golden could contain the madness, students were stampeding from the rooms.

Elaborate paper airplanes soared in the halls, rock music poured from the intercom, and the fire alarm screamed over it. The ceiling sprinklers popped on and sprayed the high school.

Daniel looked up and opened his arms to the indoor rain, grinning from ear to ear. He couldn't believe his luck. He seized his opening and left the chaos behind him.

The universe had come through once again, and Daniel did not envy the janitor.

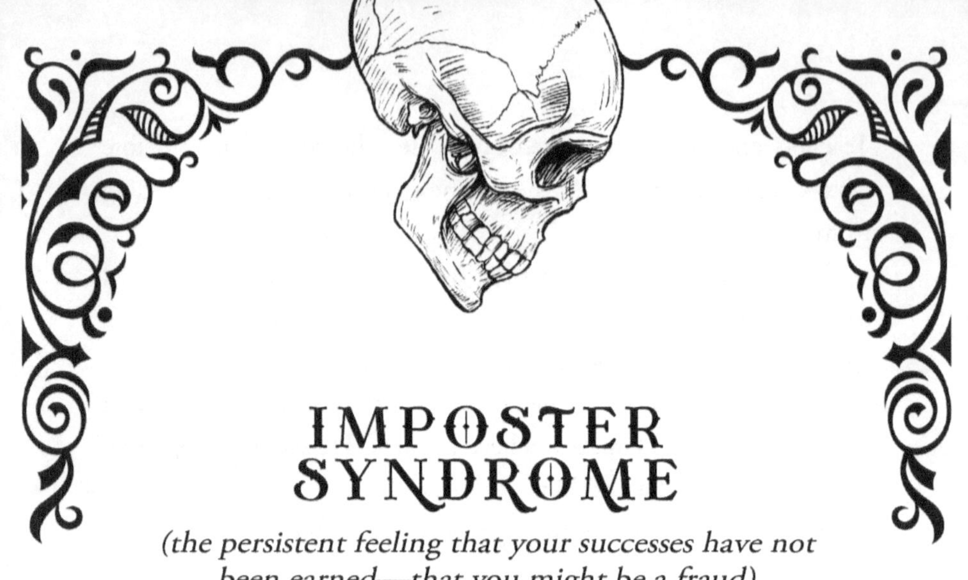

IMPOSTER SYNDROME

*(the persistent feeling that your successes have not
been earned—that you might be a fraud)*

Miguel's Hope Haven office was simple—a separate world from the whimsy of his home library. A tidy desk, a modest bookshelf, a whiteboard, and a window with a view of the hospital courtyard.

"So you just couldn't wait until after school." Miguel handed Daniel a mug of tea, and the clean smell of hospital soap drifted from his hands.

Daniel clutched his tea. This was the first time he'd had Miguel to himself since The Archive. He'd been dreading this moment, yet he couldn't ignore it any longer. "How could I?"

Miguel raised a brow. "It's high time we had a talk, isn't it?"

Daniel ran a hand through his hair. "This is torture, man." He stood and paced the office. "I've been waiting for you to rip into me."

"And yet you've come to me." Miguel took a seat and rested his chin on his fist, looking satisfied. "Why?"

Daniel's shoulders slumped, and he tilted his head back. "Did I do a bad thing, Miguel?"

Miguel made a broad gesture. "You tell me. What gives you that idea?"

"Well, I barely recognize my high school." Daniel paced again. "My English teacher is my principal now, and apparently, she *loves* me, and I don't know where Jerricks went." He took a breath. "I woke up the other day thinking life was a sitcom—all I needed was a laugh track—but it's been up and down. Things feel off. One minute Victor's on top of the world, and the next, he's going off about having fake memories. Then Macy got hurt, and on top of that, she and Logan don't even know who I am."

Speaking the pain out loud gave it new power. He wondered if he'd go the rest of his life carrying memories that didn't exist for Logan and Macy. A few years of birthday parties, inside jokes, laughter and tears lived in his bones, but for Logan and Macy, it all evanesced.

"Worst of all," Daniel said, "something's not right with them, Miguel. My family, I mean. They're having nightmares and complaining that food doesn't taste right, and this morning, Xander…" He flinched. *What was that with Xander?*

Miguel shrugged out of his white coat and hung it by the door. "I'm sorry."

Daniel paused. "I just realized you never texted me back about Macy. Is she going to be okay?"

Miguel said nothing.

"*Miguel?*"

After a long pause, Miguel stood and held his hands about a foot apart. "Not so long ago, Macy Sterling's candle looked like *this.* Bright and full, with plenty of wick and plenty of wax." He took one hand away and spread his thumb and forefinger in a C-shape. "Today, her candle looks more like this."

Daniel took a step back, his breath quickening. "Wait, w-why? Why did it go down that much?"

Miguel twisted his ring. "Because you went to The Archive and played dominos with reality. I told you there would be dire consequences for lighting candles, Danny. Perhaps I should have been more specific."

"What does that mean?"

"It means you went too far," Miguel said. "There's a storm of dark energy brewing in The Archive right now. I told you all lives were recorded in wax, but you went in there and started changing them. You raised the dead. This storm is moving through the library and changing all the lives connected to you, and it will ripple."

Miguel picked up a black marker and scribbled Daniel's name on his whiteboard. "I've just written something on a slate." He picked up a green marker and drew a squiggle. "Now I'm writing over it. Your name is still there, but that green line is cutting through the black. That's what's happening to the candles. Every drop of wax tells a story. *I was born in Costa Linda. I have a cat. I like to play piano.* This storm carves through those wax patterns and writes new ones."

"I-I don't understand."

"Look at your family," Miguel said. "You lit their wicks at the precise moment they were fated to die, and for the past ten years, yours just kept burning. You've aged; your story has continued. But your family has not aged; they picked up exactly where they left off. The Archive then had to readjust. The twins are now the youngest in the family, the Costa Linda Bridge is no longer a memorial, and you're still in school. The ripples are monumental, Daniel. You played God, and there are consequences."

Daniel massaged his jawbones, his mind reeling. "Is that why Logan thinks he had Thanksgiving dinner with his grandpa? I never lit his grandpa's candle."

"You're in for a few more shocks, then," Miguel said. "The storm doesn't just alter lives...it can also light flames in its path. Weston Thane lives."

Daniel swallowed. "But that's a good thing, isn't it? I mean, Logan has his favorite person back. He loved his grandpa."

"One problem, Danny." Miguel held up a finger. "The opposite is happening, too. The same storm that can flicker candles back to life is also blowing them out. I'm sure you were wondering why Macy's family hasn't been to see her in the hospital."

A lump lodged itself in Daniel's throat. *No. Don't tell me.*

Miguel put his fingertips together. "It's because all she has left is her oldest sister."

Daniel turned away, clawing at his hair. "Please tell me you aren't serious."

"I am not that cruel."

"Fuck!" Daniel slammed a fist against Miguel's counter. "No! Why, Miguel? They had nothing to do with this!"

"Neither did Billy Schubert," Miguel said simply. "But thanks to the 'storm' in The Archive, Billy's time is coming. Quite quickly, I might add."

"*Billy?*" Daniel asked. "No…No, Miguel. I-I don't want that."

"You seem to be having a difficult time with this," Miguel said. "I'm curious. Isn't Billy the young man you once referred to as, and I quote, 'a dick'?"

"Yes," Daniel said. "But that doesn't mean I would ever wish for him to die."

"He would've died, eventually." Miguel pulled out his phone and started typing something.

"Are you seriously texting?" Daniel said. "Miguel, you have to stop this! Billy, Macy, Macy's family…I can't have that on my hands. I didn't want this for them."

"I'm not done." Miguel handed Daniel his phone. "Read on."

The phone trembled in Daniel's fingers. The man in the photo had more hair and a thinner mustache than Daniel had ever seen him with, but he knew the face. He scrolled down and read the blurb.

Carl Henry Jerricks was born to Stan and Joan Jerricks in San Antonio, TX on September 13, 1964. It was there that he met the love of his life, Fran.

Carl and Fran moved to Costa Linda in 1994, where Carl began a legendary career in teaching. He spent fifteen years teaching math in the Costa Linda Unified School District. In this short time, he was a three-time recipient of the prestigious Golden Apple Award, which is more times than any recipient has been honored. Under his tenure as the principal, Costa Linda High School was consistently rated an A+ school by the California Educational Foundation. Carl often referred to his students as "his kids," and he was fiercely passionate about their success.

He is survived by his wife Fran, sister Patricia, and three sons, Jerome, Anthony, and Carl Jr.

Daniel's mind lurched. This was an obituary.

Mr. Jerricks was dead.

"Anaphylactic shock," Miguel said. "Wasp sting. But at least you have your family back, right? At least Logan has his grandfather. You've cracked the code! You've bested me. In seventeen years, you learned all there is to know about life and death—more than me. Congratulations."

Daniel wished Miguel would've just started shouting at him. The sarcastic undertone cut deep, yet it was mild in comparison to the emotional cocktail within.

"Miguel." Daniel marched up to his godfather and put his hands together. "I am *begging* you to let me back into The Archive. Let me fix this."

"No." Miguel sipped his tea and looked down at his boots. "I'm sorry, Danny, but that's not something I'm going to do for you. Respectfully, enough damage has been done. There is absolutely nothing you can do except wait this out."

"Is there anything I can do to save just one of them?" Daniel asked.

"Can't we make like a bargain or give Macy what's left of my candle or…I don't know. How much more damage is that storm gonna do?"

"It's tough to predict."

Daniel put a hand over his stomach. "Why aren't you furious with me?"

"As a matter of fact, I'm livid," Miguel said calmly. "But what good does it do for me to lecture you? You came in here asking if you've done a bad thing, so now you tell me. Do you believe you've done a *good* thing for your family? Do you believe they're happy here?"

Daniel's lips parted. The 'yes' clung to his throat, refusing to come out.

When he traced it all back, nobody had finished a single meal since they returned. The twins had been leaving melted Robo-Frog popsicles all over the counters. Victor scarfed down his pancakes, then told Daniel they tasted like water.

Ruthie, Bobby, and Elena had dreamed of every detail of the bridge, right down to who had been riding in each car.

Daniel pinched the bridge of his nose.

"Do you remember when I had a talk with Bobby about wishing for an alligator?" Miguel asked.

Daniel looked back up.

"Teeth or no teeth," Miguel continued, "your family would be just fine if you adopted an alligator. It would bring you joy, the twins would learn responsibility, and you'd make plenty of memories. But you know, ultimately, it's a bad idea, right? Not because it would be a danger to you, but because it wouldn't be fair to the *alligator*."

Daniel sipped his tea, averting Miguel's gaze.

"Do you see the damage now?" Miguel said. "You've yanked your family in from the next world over, and they simply cannot thrive here. They do not belong here anymore, and despite the jazz hands and the punch lines, they will not be happy."

Tears spilled down Daniel's cheeks. "I really thought I'd fixed everything.”

“Death isn’t something you fix.” Miguel locked eyes with Daniel. “Listen to me. I’m going to tell you this as Miguel, as Dr. Mortiz, and as Death himself.”

Tears blurred Daniel’s vision.

Miguel put his hands on Daniel’s shoulders. “You *cannot* fix everything. I have learned this a thousand times over. I can’t fix every patient; I can’t heal your emotional pain. We cannot raise the dead. This is a broken world, Danny. You can’t fix everything that’s wrong with it. You’ll keep trying, and that’s because you still *care*. But sometimes, the only thing you can work on is your pain.” Miguel tapped Daniel’s chest. “I have learned this, too, even as Death.”

Daniel scrubbed a sleeve over his tears. “How does *Death* learn a lesson like that?”

“That’s a story I’ve never shared, Danny.” Miguel returned to his seat. “But I’m going to tell you. After all, we share something in common now.”

Daniel sniffled. After all he’d just learned—after all he’d done—he couldn’t believe Miguel still trusted him.

“This is not the first time someone has caused a storm in The Archive,” Miguel said.

Daniel sat across from Miguel, facing the window. Clouds were building outside, darkening the courtyard. “How did the last one happen?” He wondered if maybe Aunt Cass was the cause, or his parents—someone else who knew Miguel’s secret. *What if I was dead once?* Daniel wondered. *And Aunt Cass lit my candle? Would I even know?* He shuddered. He hated the thought. “Was it someone I know?”

“Yes.” Miguel pursed his lips. “It was me.”

Daniel’s jaw dropped.

Miguel nodded. “You’re surprised. Remember how we talked about the pestilence in Europe?”

Daniel recalled the haunted look on Miguel’s face when he referred to the fourteenth century. He'd tattooed the skeletal Grim Reaper on his upper arm as both a tongue-in-cheek joke and a dreary reminder of how much people feared Death, both uppercase and lower.

Candles were blinking out left and right, he'd said.

When the pieces clicked, Daniel's breath hitched.

"*You* caused the Black Plague?"

"Medically speaking, it was Yersinia pestis—bacteria had a way of getting around through the rats and the fleas and…" Miguel drummed his fingers on his lap, and that dark expression returned. "But yes. If you peel back the layers, I started the plague. It began with a single flame. It was arrogance, it was folly, it was…the worst mistake I ever made. I could not fix it, and I will bear that for all of eternity."

Daniel couldn't believe his ears. Miguel had just shared one of the biggest secrets in history with him. It was such a human thing to share, yet the implications were massive. Miguel was flawed. He'd been tempted before, and he'd made a mistake that caused one of the darkest eras in history. No wonder he'd been so compassionate toward Daniel—he'd been bearing the same guilt for centuries. Daniel was grateful for Miguel's candor, and at the same time, he was horrified at himself.

Did I just cause a plague?

"Oh my god," Daniel gasped. "Did I—"

"No," Miguel said quickly. "Not yet, at least. Things could get bad, but I have a plan. There is a failsafe for this, but I have to catch it before the storm gets out of hand. It's not going to be easy, but it must be done."

"What can I do?" Daniel leaned forward. "Anything you need, Miguel. I'll do it. Please."

"No," Miguel said. "You've done enough, Danny. I know I just lectured you about how we can't fix everything, but The Archive is my responsibility, and I am equally at fault. I'm going to set things right and clean this up."

"By *cleaning it up*," Daniel said, "does that mean you can bring Macy's family back? And she can live?"

"Perhaps," Miguel said. "If I'm quick, I can repair most of the damage. I'll do my very best to do right by Macy, and the Schubert kid, too. On that, you have my word. But I'm only going to say this once, Danny: What you've done in the Archive must never, ever… *ever* happen again."

"Never," Daniel said. "I swear it. Can you at least tell me what you're about to do? Is it dangerous?"

Miguel gave Daniel a sad smile. "You don't need the details, Danny. I will be going to The Archive and doing this alone. There's only one thing you can do right now, and it's a boon. I hate to say that you brought it on yourself, but, well…"

Daniel swallowed.

"You have to prepare yourself to say goodbye to your family a second time."

A fresh stream of tears carved their way down Daniel's cheeks, tracing the salty paths of the ones that had already dried. "I knew they couldn't stay."

Deep down, Daniel had known for a while that this couldn't last. His family was the alligator. It didn't matter how well they were fed or how much they were loved, they didn't belong here, and he couldn't bear to think of them suffering for his comfort. Daniel would've cut out his heart for a few minutes with them, and he'd stolen a few days.

"I'm sorry, Danny," Miguel said.

"I *just* got them back," Daniel whispered.

It wasn't an argument, and Miguel nodded because he understood.

"No one gets to decide when their loved ones depart," Miguel said. "You have the opportunity to decide how you'll remember them, and how you'll move forward. Recognize that this is also a gift."

Daniel said nothing.

"Every night," Miguel said, "I hear people whisper their bargains into the wind. I listen to them curse my name; I count their tears. You have stolen a *generous* amount of time to hug your loved ones again. This is more than anyone has ever been allowed."

Daniel looked up at Miguel's clock, and the second hand's speed almost seemed to double in front of him. *Tick. Tick. Tick. Tick. Ticktickticktick.* He thought of the haunting bellows of the grandfather clock in The Archive. Even Death's domain was bound by time. "How long do I have?"

Miguel cut a glance at his watch. "A couple of hours? *Maybe* the rest of the day? It's not good for anyone if I wait any longer. They could start remembering, and Macy could get worse. The storm could spread deeper into The Archive, and I will not have another plague on my hands." Miguel shuddered, then straightened. "I recommend you go home and enjoy this night, because tonight, I will be sending them home."

Daniel brushed away the last of his tears and swallowed the lump in his throat. *Home.* So they had a place to go. There was something for them beyond The Archive. One day he'd have to ask about it, but today, all he could focus on was *now*.

"Will they feel anything?" he asked. "I mean…will it hurt them?"

"No," Miguel said. "It'll be as peaceful as going to sleep."

This was Daniel's only comfort.

It won't be painless for me, he thought.

Miguel gave Daniel a sympathetic smile. "When this is all over," he said, "we'll celebrate their lives. We'll live every day the way they'd want us to."

Maybe it was time to make amends with Aunt Cass. Her life and memories had probably changed in big ways, but she would want to be around for one more night with the Grimms. There was no way he could share the context with her, but he owed it to her to invite her.

"What can I do for you, Danny?" Miguel asked.

Daniel tried to swallow the lump in his throat, but it wouldn't budge. It clung there and strangled his next words. "Can you stop taking people away from me?"

Miguel looked wounded by Daniel's words. "I am deeply sorry for the many burdens I have placed on you at such a young age." He stared into his mug, his fingers tightening around the handle. "You're strong enough to carry them, but that doesn't mean you deserve them. Just know that you don't have to carry them alone. I know it may not feel like it, but you have never been alone. And from now until long after the day when your turn comes, I can promise that you never *will* be."

My turn. Daniel's spine tingled.

He wished he could believe Miguel's promise, but it echoed with empty space. Even with the Grimms alive, Daniel had been alone most of the day. He wanted to hate his godfather, to reduce The Archive to ashes and the lingering scents of its ghosts. All his life, he'd been waiting to flip Death the bird. But Miguel's chest wasn't quite as hollow as his promises.

Daniel couldn't hate the man—not entirely—even as he knew he'd be journeying home to prepare his goodbyes…again.

Alone.

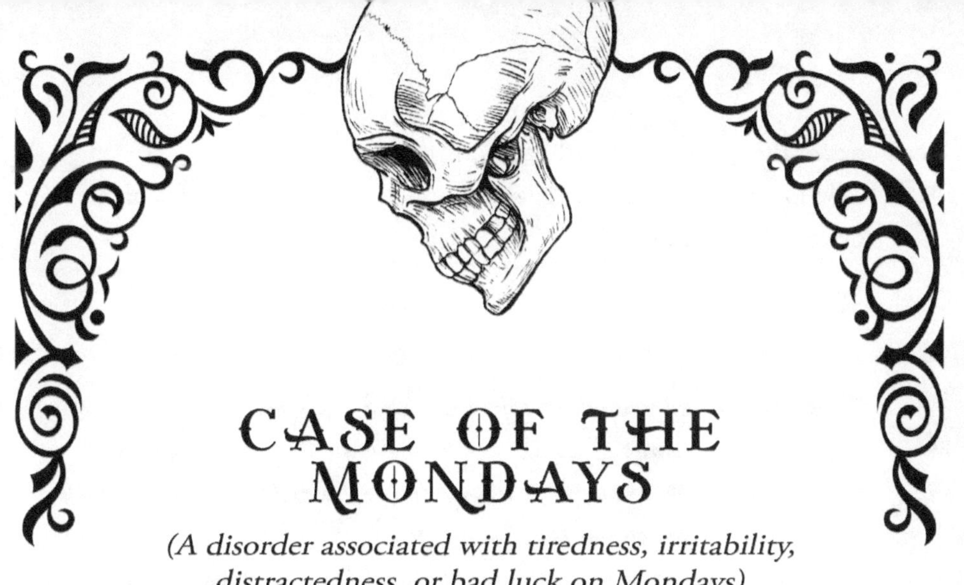

CASE OF THE MONDAYS

(A disorder associated with tiredness, irritability, distractedness, or bad luck on Mondays)

Daniel's grief counselor, Dr. Barnes, once gave him a project he never completed.

She wanted him to write letters to his family. She suggested he needed to say a proper goodbye.

"What's the point if they'll never see them?" Daniel had asked. "Who's gonna deliver them? The mailman?"

Dr. Barnes suggested slipping the messages into balloons, then releasing them at the beach as a symbolic delivery. Daniel knew the balloons would eventually pop and pollute the ocean, which would've upset Ruthie. For that matter, Daniel was still warring with himself on the idea of Heaven, and a symbolic sky delivery didn't resonate with him.

"No one ever has to see the letters," Dr. Barnes said gently. "Not even me. These are for you. If you'd like, maybe you can imagine how they'd respond to you."

Daniel started each letter many times.

He tried writing one to the whole family, which was overwhelming.

He tried writing one to each person, which felt pointless.

She also suggested writing to the truck driver, and that was simply out of the question. Daniel had nothing to say to that man.

So finally, Daniel wrote a letter to himself, which he kept on a flash drive in his sock drawer.

Dear Daniel,

I wanted to tell you what a jerk I think you are.

Dr. Barnes says I can't really heal until I start to love myself. But right now, and using Victor's words, I just think you're kind of a schmuck.

I'm mad because you were ungrateful for the time you had with your family. Your best friend, Logan, is an only child. He always says he wishes he had brothers and sisters...you had ten. Well, you still have two, but you spent your childhood wishing they would all go away. They gave you everything you ever asked for. But when they took too long in the bathroom, or they took the last pizza slice, you got mad. It doesn't matter that you were only seven; you were still stupid.

I'm having trouble writing to my family because I don't see the point. Aunt Cass tells me that if I'm quiet, they'll talk to me, but that's just one of those things people say when they don't know what to say. The one I hate the most is, "They're in a better place." Aunt Cass hates that one, too. Anyway, telling me to listen makes it worse because I've been doing that all along. All I ever hear is silence. They're never going to answer me. They're never coming back.

If I could go back, this is what I'd do.

I'd give them lots of hugs, and if they kiss me on the forehead, I won't wipe it away.

I'd stop complaining about seven-hour car rides on vacation, even if Nancy just wants to listen to obnoxious classical music or Bobby wants to play I Spy for like three hours.

Daniel read this every night until he eventually memorized it.

And after he visited Miguel at Hope Haven, Daniel read the letter in his head. He spent his bus ride wondering how he could possibly say goodbye to his family now that he had the chance.

He was going to need some help.

He took a deep breath, searched *Katherine Grimm* in his phone contacts, and pushed the call button.

The phone rang three times, and Daniel ran through a script in his head. There was a strong chance The Archive had affected her. He'd find out what she knew, what she remembered, and what her life looked like now. He'd check in on Justin and the baby.

Daniel was not prepared for a random man to answer the phone.

"Auto Mob, this is Jim."

Daniel blinked a few times, his breath shallow.

Auto Mob? Jim?

He took the phone away from his ear and double-checked the name. It definitely said *Katherine Grimm* on the screen.

"Hello?" Jim prompted.

"Um," Daniel said, "Hi. I'm looking for Katie Grimm?"

A pause lingered before Jim answered, "Who's this?"

"This is Daniel, her brother. Is she there?"

"Wait, back it up, hoss. *Who* you callin' for? *Cade?*"

"No. Katherine Grimm—Katie. Kate. She might go by any one of those names. She's had this same phone number for years. Look, is she not there right now?"

A husky sigh clouded the receiver. "Just a minute."

Daniel heard Jim's muffled speech in the background. "There ain't no Katie hangin' 'round today, is there?…I don't know. Some guy?… Well, hell if I know…"

Daniel hung his head, his fingers tight on the phone. The storm had erased his sister's number, just like it had erased his friendships with Macy and Logan.

Finally, Jim from Auto Mob spoke again, an irritated bite in his voice. "Sir, there ain't no *Katelyn Grimm* here. No Kate. No Katie. No Kathleen. This is an auto shop!"

"What about Justin?" Daniel said. "Please. Is there a Justin Scott working today?"

"Christ," Jim growled.

And the line went dead.

Daniel looked at his blank screen, his jaw tense and his breath hot. He couldn't wait to leave Auto Mob a scalding review.

Then he had a chilling thought…

What if he hadn't just erased his sister's number?

What if he had erased his sister's *life?*

Macy didn't have a family.

Mr. Jerricks was dead.

Daniel's actions in The Archive hadn't just made ripples; they'd made waves.

His heart slammed against his chest. How else could he find Katie? She stayed far away from social media. He didn't have an email address for her. He didn't have Justin's number.

Please be okay, he thought.

He dialed Zeke's number next and put the phone to his ear.

It rang once.

Pick up, Zeke. Please pick up.

It rang again, and time stretched like a rubber band.

Come on.

Daniel's foot bounced under the seat.

After one more ring, Zeke's voice thundered in Daniel's ear. "What up?"

Daniel let out a full breath, and his shoulders deflated. *Thank you.*

"This is Zeke. You have *not* reached me, and I can't take your call right now. Feel free to leave me a message, and maybe I'll get back to you as soon as I can. But honestly, you should probably just text me. Thanks."

As much as Daniel hoped he'd get to talk to Zeke, his familiar voice was a hug for the soul. For a minute, it was enough.

The beep sounded, and Daniel looked up as if for divine inspiration. Where to begin?

"Hey Z. Um, it's Danny. Look. I don't know how to explain in a voicemail, but there's a lot going on lately." He paused. "That's an understatement. The thing is, I need you. If you or Katie could please call me when you get a chance, that would mean more than you'd know. Or you can text me. I prefer that, too, but…I just needed to hear your voice. Bye."

He ended the call, and the feeling of dread returned with a deeper chill.

Just because Zeke still had the same number and a voicemail box, didn't mean he was alive.

No. Daniel shoved the thought to the back of his mind. *You're catastrophizing. Miguel would not have let things get that bad.*

Daniel tapped his phone against his lap. Miguel didn't deserve the blame. None of this was his fault.

Daniel decided to try one more number.

It was time to repair the relationship with Aunt Cass.

His finger hovered over the call button on his phone.

If she picks up, where do I begin?

If she doesn't pick up, what does that mean?

Finally, Daniel shut his eyes, jabbed the button, and asked the universe for some love.

Not Aunt Cass. Don't you mess with Aunt Cass. Or Katie and Zeke. Please. Let them all be okay. Even if all of this goes away tomorrow… don't put me in a world without my aunt. Don't you do that to me.

"Come on," he whispered.

The phone didn't even ring once.

We're sorry. The number you have dialed has been changed or disconnected. Please hang up and try your party again.

"Dammit!" Daniel cried. "Why?"

The bus driver cut him a startled gaze in the rearview mirror.

This was starting to feel ugly, stomach-clenching. Katie used to call this a Feeling with a capital F. He wondered if it always felt like knives in the gut. How much physical pain was she in when she hired Charleston Fitch to follow Miguel?

Daniel bit his lip. He could always go to Queen of Cups and check on Aunt Cass. He could find out for sure.

If I've done something, he thought, *Miguel will fix it. He promised.*

But he also has to take my family away again.

Daniel wished the bus would speed up. The air was growing stuffy, and he was bumping elbows with a stranger in a damp windbreaker. Sometime during the ride, it started to rain, and the smell of wet earth clouded the bus. He wanted to be home. He never should've let Nancy drive him to school today.

When the phone buzzed in his hand, his eyes snapped open. The caller wasn't Zeke, Katie, or Aunt Cass.

Daniel answered, "Victor?"

A clap of thunder drummed outside.

"I need you to come to the cemetery," Victor said, his voice thick and nasally.

Daniel's heart dove into his stomach. Had Victor had figured it out? Had he seen his name on the grave? What would that do to a person's mind? "The cemetery? Why?"

"Just get here."

Daniel hated the snap in his brother's tone.

He pulled the cord to signal the bus to stop. Crescent Gate wasn't too far behind him, but the cemetery was the last place Daniel wanted to spend his last day with his brother. "Victor, it's gonna be a little bit. I'm on the bus. It's raining outside." *I'm running out of time.* "Can't you meet me at home?"

"Just *get here*," Victor repeated. "Look for the big tree on the hill."

The tree on the hill, Daniel thought. *Where all of this started.*

"I'll be waiting for you there," Victor said.

And the call went dead.

WALKING CORPSE SYNDROME

(the belief that you are dead, dying, or don't exist)

Daniel was five years old when Grandma Alba passed away. It was his first experience with death.

He remembered a few details about her passing.

Usually, Mom and Dad were equal forces in a graceful partner dance, and Grandma's death was the first time Daniel had seen Dad stumble. Mom became the true captain of the ship for a while, instructing everyone to give Dad his space while he grieved. Bedtime evolved from a coordinated team effort—music, stories, and tuck-ins—to a strict, regimented, "Off you go. Now." She bustled to distract the kids with coloring books, crafts, and snacks. Zeke and Katie made a game out of "fend for yourself nights," when Mom had been too tired to cook and the Grimms survived on sandwiches, ramen, and pizza. At one point, Daniel remembered telling Mom that she was mean, and Zeke had pulled him into his room for a lecture he never forgot.

On the morning of Grandma Alba's wake, Mom had dressed Daniel in stiff, tight black shoes, a light blue button-down, dark pants, and a tie. It was the first time he'd ever worn anything formal, and he despised it. He fought his mom until she nearly left the room in tears.

"You are getting on my last nerve, young man," she said. "All you've been doing lately is misbehaving. Do you not understand that your grandmother is dead now? *Dead.* That means she's never coming back. How would you feel if that was me or your father?"

Miguel swooped into the room in a dark suit and put a hand on Mom's shoulder. "I've got him. Go do your thing."

Mom massaged her temples and gave Miguel a weak smile. "Thank you," she whispered.

Miguel took a knee. "Here. Let's straighten this tie, bud. You don't like wearing this, do you?"

Daniel pouted. "It's uncomfy. And so are my shoes. I wanna wear my other shoes."

Miguel fidgeted with his own tie, shiny and dark like his hair. "Well, you look sharp…like James Bond. You ever watch James Bond?"

Daniel made a face. "He's boring."

His godfather cracked a sideways grin. "I can respect that. But you know who loved James Bond? Your grandmother. I think she'd be happy to see how nice you look today."

"Mom said she's never coming back," Daniel said. "She can't even see me. So why do I have to look nice?"

"That's an excellent question." Miguel smoothed a wrinkle on Daniel's sleeve. "When you're older, I think you'll remember today, and all the times you had with your grandmother. She loved you, you know. You'll feel good remembering that you looked handsome for her funeral." He grabbed both of their neckties and put the ends together. "Besides, isn't it kind of fun that we match a little bit?"

Daniel pinched the end of Miguel's tie, the linen cool and soft against his fingers. His grandma had a blanket that felt similar.

At the wake, Daniel saw the casket at the front of the room—creamy white, tipped with gold. From the back, he could see a puff of Grandma Alba's thick, silver curls, but the thought of getting any closer made his limbs feel like spaghetti. Katie told him there was nothing to be afraid of, and that Grandma would just look like she was sleeping.

When Katie and Zeke finally convinced Daniel to walk up to the casket with them, he felt they had lied. She did look like she was sleeping, but she also looked different. She looked smaller somehow, younger. She almost looked like a movie star with how they'd fixed her hair and makeup. Someone had also tucked a wooden spoon under her cold, manicured hands, and Daniel didn't understand why.

He remembered dreamlike piano renditions of Johnny Cash songs.

He remembered Aunt Cass's face streaked with mascara as she delivered the eulogy.

He remembered how Dad didn't cry until the end.

He remembered Miguel, calm and cool in the back row, with a serene smile on his face.

Mom's words hadn't hit until a little later. Grandma Alba would never wake up. She'd never make her famous bourbon pineapple upside down cake again. Daniel would never fall asleep watching cartoons on her couch. If he got sick, she wouldn't rub Vicks on his chest anymore.

The fear doused him all over again when they buried her. He'd never been at a cemetery. He only knew Victor, Sam, and Monica were obsessed with a black and white movie where corpses clawed their way out of their graves and terrorized the living. Daniel squeezed Monica's hand through the whole burial.

"Relax, Danny, they are *not* gonna get up," Monica whispered. "Not right now."

Zeke shot Monica his darkest glare, which usually terrified everybody but her.

Twelve years later, Daniel's fear of the cemetery redoubled. Where he'd once found a numb sense of acceptance, now he feared the unknown. He tore through the rain to get to Crescent Gate, wondering what he'd find when he arrived.

Had Victor found his grave?

Were there new graves, courtesy of The Archive?

He knew there was something *off* about the layout, like a spot-the-difference photo. Here was a fresh patch of grass where a bevel once lay. Here was a new memorial dated seven years back. The idea twisted Daniel's brain into knots, but he only cared about one thing.

The memorial he'd wept at so many times was gone. Instead, the grass was untouched, where thriving daisies drank the rain.

He counted ten flowers.

And on top of the hill, Victor Grimm sat on the bench by the barren sycamore.

But Victor wasn't alone; he was with Xander. They both looked like they had jumped into a pool with all their clothes on. The rain had slowed to a drizzle, and water dripped from the sycamore onto Victor's fedora.

Daniel waded up the hill, the grass slick with rainwater, and he sat between his brothers. It didn't matter that the Grimm monument wasn't at the bottom of the hill. This was the only time he'd ever sit here with Victor and Xander. He wanted to remember how it felt to sit in silence with them—between Xander's pensive calm and Victor's carefree bluster.

Victor was the one to break the silence. "Hey."

Daniel narrowed his eyes. "Hey?" he asked. "What are we doing here, guys?"

Victor pointed at Xander. "Ask him. Don't ask me how I knew he was here. But he's been sitting like this all day." He reached across Daniel's lap and snapped his fingers in front of Xander's face. "Hello? Earth to Alexander Grimm? Our brother's here."

Xander didn't even flinch. "I can see that, Victor. Hello, Daniel."

"Hey there." Daniel leaned forward, resting his elbows on his knees. "You didn't even finish the school day, huh?"

"Did you?" Xander asked simply.

Daniel decided not to answer, and instead, he gestured out to the graves. "Are we admiring the scenery or something?"

Xander nodded. It was the first time he'd moved since Daniel sat down. "It *is* a lovely view." He put his fingers over his heart. "It makes me feel a certain way."

Daniel bit his lip. "Could you elaborate?"

Victor took off his hat and rubbed his forehead. "Aw, brother, here we go."

Xander tilted his head to the side. "It's odd. You're likely to feel alarmed, but…I feel peace here."

"Peace?" Daniel repeated. "Don't you usually go to the library for peace? Or the park?"

"Sure," Xander said. "But it's different here. I feel like I belong here."

Victor rubbed his arms. "Who are you, Tim Burton? You're giving me the chills, man."

Xander turned to Victor. "You can't feel it?"

Victor spun his hat on his finger, a faraway look in his eyes. "I dunno what you mean."

"Xander," Daniel said, "you've been coming here every day, haven't you? This is where you've been disappearing to."

Xander gestured at the ground, his feet firmly planted on the grass. "I woke up the other day, and I felt it calling to me. I don't know if I'm a knight or a rook or a pawn, but this is my box. It feels wrong when I'm *not* here."

"I feel like this is weird," Victor said. "I don't think you should hang out in the cemetery. You want peace? Let's go do some hot yoga or something. Let's put on ocean sounds and drink tea. At home."

"Is it really that strange to you, brother?" Xander asked. "You feel something. You found me here. I never told you where I was."

"Danny, talk some sense into this kid." Victor massaged his eyelids. "I wanna get out of here."

"Vic," Xander said gently. "That's not why you called him."

"Yes, it is," Victor said. "I want you to snap out of your *Night of the Living Dead* phase and come home with me."

"No," Xander said. "Tell me honestly that you don't feel what I feel. Tell Daniel what we were talking about before he got here."

Victor turned away. "Xander, I'm tired, man. I'm stuffy, I have a headache, and I wanna go home. Whatever I started saying, it's probably the fever talking."

"We'll go home after you ask Daniel your question."

A crow settled on the barren sycamore, rattling the branches and startling Daniel. He stood and considered his brothers. "Vic," he said. "What's going on?"

Victor shook his head, saying nothing.

Xander turned to Victor. "You already know the answer, don't you?"

Daniel threw up his hands. "Will you two stop beating around the bush? Guys, I'm not having a good day. This isn't how I want to spend my time with you. Can we get out of the cemetery and go play Jenga or something?"

Daniel turned to leave, but Xander caught his wrist. His grip was gentle, but his fingers were cold. He was always the brother with the frostiest gaze—always seeming to look right through something with his stare.

"Tell me what happened on the bridge."

Bile prickled Daniel's throat.

"What do you mean?"

"Don't play dumb." Xander tightened his grip on Daniel's wrist. "And don't you *lie* to us, Daniel. Don't do that to me, because I would never lie to you. I respect your intelligence too much."

Daniel looked at Xander's stony fingers. Victor was pacing, rubbing his hands together and muttering something about how this wasn't what he wanted.

Xander's words stung. Daniel wasn't sure if it would hurt more to keep lying—to keep pretending he knew nothing—or to drop the truth. He didn't want to say anything at all. If this were really the Perfect Universe, then he could distract his brother with a one-liner or a slapstick bit. *Don't be a goofus, Xander! It's all water under the bridge! Let's go home!* Roll credits.

Suddenly, he understood how Miguel must've felt when Daniel stormed into his home demanding answers about his family… about death. Now Daniel was on the receiving end of an impossible question, and he couldn't divert it with mac and cheese and iced tea.

"You were always smarter than me," Daniel said. "Tell me what you think you know."

Xander relaxed his grip before he let go entirely. "At first, I thought maybe I was sick or losing my mind. Cotard's syndrome…the delusion that you're dead."

"You read too much," Victor muttered.

"Well, I don't have Cotard's syndrome," Xander continued. "I've given this a lot of thought. I loved my life, Danny. And death made it meaningful—*beautiful,* even. The thing is…I don't know how it happened or why I'm here, but I do know that you did something, and that Vic and I do not belong here."

Victor stopped pacing, removed his hat, and placed it against his heart. "The nightmares? The cloudy memories? Your overwhelming sappiness?" He looked at the ground. "Is Xander wrong, Danny?"

Daniel's mouth dried like a bone. "Xander…Victor…" Daniel said. "I—"

"I know we can't stay much longer," Xander said.

"Xander. Jesus, man." Victor sat back down and cradled his hat in his hands. "Don't upset him."

Don't upset him.

Victor had already figured it out somehow.

"Am I correct in assuming we only have tonight?" Xander asked.

Tears sprang to Daniel's eyes, which were already dry from crying in Miguel's office. "I…"

"You don't owe me an explanation," Xander said. "I need you to accept what's going to happen. But sooner or later, the rest of them will figure out what happened to us, and they will not be as blasé as we are."

"I am not blasé!" Victor threw his hands up, and his hat tumbled to the ground. "Xan, we're *dead*. We're literally sitting in our final resting place, and there isn't even a grave to mark it. Everything sucks, man. How can you sit there all chill, like some six-foot brooding Yoda?"

"Yoda, I am not." Xander finally cracked a grin that showed his teeth. "I am making sense of the worst thing that ever happened to us. I'm trying to make friends with death, dear brother."

"Who are you, Edgar Allan Poe?" Victor beat the mud off his hat.

Daniel sat between his brothers again, pain blossoming in his gut. "I am so sorry about all of this. I'm sorry to both of you. All I wanted was…"

Victor scrubbed a tear from his eyes and buried his head in his hands.

"You know what?" Daniel wrapped his arms around his brothers. "It doesn't really matter what I want. What do you two want?"

Victor shook with a silent sob. "I wanna stay."

"Vic." Daniel leaned against his brother's shoulder. "God, there's nothing I want more for you. I want the extra time with you…with all of you. But this can't be good for you, right?"

"I mean, I just have too much not done," Victor said. "I put on a big, blustery ego, and I take swings at the world. But by now you must've figured out that I'm *terrified* of dying."

"We've been dead for ten years." Xander pounded a fist into his palm, suddenly more animated. "Think about it, Victor. It has not been that bad."

Victor tilted his head, thinking for a minute. "No, it really hasn't, actually. I know." He rubbed his chin. "But I've got too much life left unlived!"

"We all did." Xander pointed into the distance, where a woman sat cross-legged in front of a grave. She looked like she had stepped out of a time machine, wearing a long gray petticoat with lace and frills, her hair in ringlets. She wore black boots with short heels, and beaded bracelets adorned her wrists. They reminded Daniel of the Grimm Goddesses' projects. "You see that woman?"

Daniel saw the woman walking the coast sometimes. She only wore dark colors, but her umbrella was a rich rainbow tapestry. Every color of the rainbow danced on the canopy, but due to her outfits, people called her The Gray Lady.

"She grieves," Xander said. "She walks miles and miles every day for those she's lost—that story isn't mine to tell. But you can see her hanging on in her own way."

Victor gently kicked a rock under the bench. "I didn't want to become president or put my name in flashing lights. All I ever wanted was, like…Like, I saw myself standing at the end of the aisle with someone. I wanted butterflies in my guts, and I wanted to profess my undying love. And then I wanted to make schmaltzy toasts at everyone else's weddings and become uncle of the year. And one of you was gonna be a billionaire and buy a ritzy mansion, and we were all gonna have epic murder mystery parties there. That's what I wanted."

"Nothing terribly specific, I see," Xander said.

"Nah."

"I would've loved that for you, Victor." Daniel would've loved some more beach days, laughing about the seagulls, and watching Victor become uncle of the year one day. Sam and the others would give him a run for his money, though. Any Grimm baby would be lucky to grow up with Sam's stories, the twins' energy, Xander's realism, and Victor's zest for life while the sisters would pour in Nancy's love of music, Monica's fight, Ruthie's creativity.

It was a crime that Katie's baby would never get to meet them.

"Think harder, Vic," Xander said. "Do you remember Katie and Justin's wedding? Because we were there."

"You were at Katie's wedding?" Daniel choked on his breath. *In the true universe, before I lit the candles?* Katie married Justin long after she moved away from Costa Linda. Daniel and Aunt Cass were there, and so was Zeke.

Victor rubbed his chin, squinting as he tried to piece together

Xander's words. Finally, his eyes lit up. "Oh my god, yes!" he cried. "Yes, it's coming back to me now. Of course we were at Katie's wedding. All of us were." He put his hands up and mapped out the ceremony in the air. "Nancy was up there with Aunt Cass and the bridesmaids. Most of us sat up front. Zeke walked her down the aisle and gave her away, but…"

"But then Dad whispered something in her ear as he walked behind them," Xander finished.

"Yeah." Victor nodded. "Dad was so stinkin' proud to see them walking together."

"And he likes that Justin guy," Xander said. "We all do. He seems like good people."

Daniel replayed the ceremony in his mind. Katie had been crying most of the week and talking about how much she'd wanted her whole family there. He remembered her wiping tears from her eyes on the way down the aisle, until about halfway down, when she took a breath, smiled to herself, and began to walk a little taller. By the time she got to the altar, she was glowing, and Justin was crying instead. Daniel couldn't remember Justin's vows to Katie—only that he joked quite a bit and got some "awws" and chuckles from the audience. As for Katie's vows to Justin, Daniel had heard them multiple times.

"There are three things I have learned for sure in life. The first thing I learned was that you can never trust tomorrow—the cruelties of life taught me that. The second is that, in times of darkness, love is the only way forward—my Aunt Cass and my brothers taught me that. I know that somehow, my mom and dad are smiling at us right now, and that every single one of my siblings would have adored you. The third thing, my love, shouldn't make any sense at all. That is because it goes directly against the first thing, yet somehow, it is still true. You have taught me that, no matter how dark the night, morning always follows. I have no delusions of living in a perfect universe where night never comes. I know that love will challenge us in ways we cannot imagine, and we will face many nights together. But Justin Scott, there is no one I would rather face the night with, and I trust you with *all* my tomorrows. You are my heart. You are my family. You are my morning."

When Daniel pictured the ceremony with his whole family present, a knot bloomed in his throat.

"You know, the reception was my favorite part," Victor said. "And Danny Boy, I saw you dancing. You were dressed, looking studly as hell. I was like, *damn*. Who are you, James Bond?"

"I am not James Bond." Daniel massaged his face, grinning between his fingers.

"Well, you clean up good," Victor said. "Because the Brothers Grimm are a bunch of sexy beasts. All of us."

"*Ow!*" Xander hooted. "Damn right we are."

"And we're a couple of real weirdos too, you know that?" Victor continued. "We could be literally anywhere else on the planet right now. But here we are, a couple o' boys in the graveyard, waxing poetic in the fog."

"You told me to come here!" Daniel said.

Xander shrugged. "I'm quite content."

Victor stared into the distance, his hands in his pockets. "Yeah," he said. "After all this time…me, too. It *does* kinda feel like we've been doing this for ages, doesn't it?"

"Sitting in the graveyard?"

"Yeah, but no. I'm talking about following Danimal around." Victor whapped the heel of his hand against Daniel's forehead.

"Sure," Xander said, a hint of a smile on his face.

"Then I think I'm gonna be okay with this," Victor said. "Yeah. I know I will. As long as Danny Boy knows I've got his back, I'll be okay."

"Stop it. I'm sick of crying," Daniel sniffled.

"Tell us you're going to be okay," Xander said.

Daniel considered the patch of grass where the Grimm family

memorial once stood, and where it would soon stand again.

A strange sense of peace settled in like a balm over the pain.

He'd bear it and grow from it every day. And maybe he wouldn't really be alone.

When you're ready, Miguel, Daniel thought, *I will be, too. I can do this. Somehow.*

"Guys," Daniel said, "I'm gonna be okay. I don't want you to go away again, but—"

"We never left," Xander said.

Daniel took a deep breath. "But I know you'll be at peace now. And the rest of us can be, too. You're our strength. You're *my* strength."

"Then there's one thing I want to do with my time," Victor said. "I want to go visit our dear auntie."

Daniel took in a cleansing breath. He'd been ready to give Aunt Cass a hug so tight it would melt all the ice from their last interaction. When he didn't know what to say, a hug was a strong place to start.

"Will you join me?" Victor asked.

"Man," Daniel said, "I'd love nothing more."

"Hang on." Victor crouched, grasped a daisy by the root, and tugged it out of the ground. "I didn't have time to stop and get her flowers, so this'll have to do. She's got a wild heart, anyway."

Daniel wrinkled his brows. "I feel weird about you pulling flowers out of the cemetery grass."

Victor flicked some damp soil off the daisy. "Apparently, they're ours. This is my bedroom now, isn't it? When we cross over again, maybe I can ask my neighbors, the…" he read the next headstone as he plucked another flower, "O'Haras. I hope they're chill."

Daniel wondered if he should arrive with a gift as well, but he had never thought of Aunt Cass as a flower enthusiast. She had a gardening phase once, but it didn't last. Once, she brought home a tiny potted succulent no bigger than her palm. She obsessed over it for a day or two, then swore off plants entirely.

"Here." Victor held one of the flowers out to Daniel. "You can give this one to her."

Daniel wrinkled his nose as he accepted the daisy. "I don't think she cares about flowers."

"I think she cares that we care." Victor walked, and his brothers followed. "And FYI, Danny, when I go back underground, I'll accept any and all offerings. You can bring me flowers; I'm man enough to love 'em. Or you can bring me some of that delicious *pan de muerto*. Or money. You can write me a letter. You can bring me a cold beer when you're old enough…or sneaky enough. We can do a *cheers*."

Daniel forced a wan smile. This had never come up on the mental list of things he'd wanted to do with his family. "I'm not gonna drink in a graveyard, Vic."

"What Victor's trying to say," Xander said, "is that we'll happily accept your time and your thoughts whenever you can spare them."

"That's not what I was trying to say at all." Victor smirked. "Nah. I'm just kidding, Danny. You never have to bring any of us a thing. We know ya love us. I just feel better picking the flowers for Aunt Cass because I'll do anything to make up for lost time."

"Hear, hear," Xander muttered.

Victor slowed his walk. "I didn't tell her I love her as often as I should've. It's a regret I carry. A daisy isn't much, but it's what I have today. The thing is…" Victor raised his chin and his flower to the sky. "Dear Aunt Cass, you deserved the whole world and more."

Then Victor took a knee and laid his daisy on the nearest grave.

And the world twisted beneath Daniel's feet as he read the headstone, a polished bevel made of morning rose granite.

CASSANDRA A. GRIMM

1977 - 2016

QUEEN OF CUPS

QUEEN OF OUR HEARTS

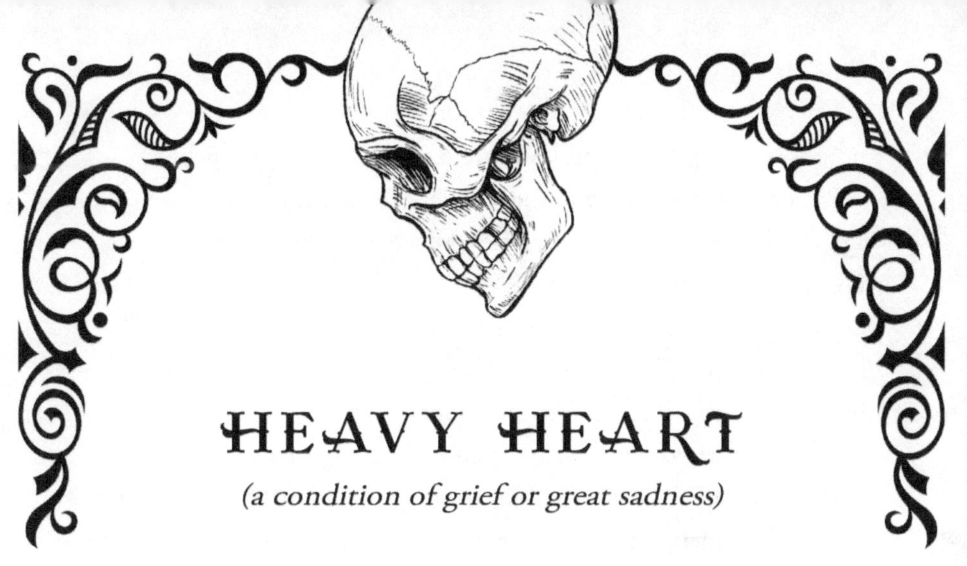

HEAVY HEART

(a condition of grief or great sadness)

Daniel had always heard that hindsight was 20/20. The more he sifted through the details, the more he realized he shouldn't have been surprised by Aunt Cass's grave. Unfortunately, clarity didn't soothe the burn.

In addition to the disconnected phone number, there had been something *off* with the way his family had talked about Aunt Cass the past few days. When Daniel had asked Dad about her, he'd been vague. *I think you should ask her yourself.*

People had been telling Daniel something similar about his parents for ten years. *Talk to them. Listen. Write them letters.*

There was also Dad's wistful memory of the burning palm tree, especially when he talked about Aunt Cass gushing over the fire department. *Simpler times, Danny…simpler times.*

Daniel's knees became weak.

"I'm glad we came, just the three of us," Victor said. "Can't hear myself think when it's all of us together. I need quiet time with her."

Daniel collapsed onto the thick, damp grass, pulled his knees to his chest, and circled them with his arms.

She always had my back, Daniel thought. *Since the very beginning.* He thought about her phone showdown with Mrs. Golden, her Aztec mochas, her hugs. Her notes in the lunchboxes, and her love for his friends, treating Macy and Logan like her own niece and nephew.

For every time she'd stood in Daniel's corner, ready to square off against the world, he thought of several where he hadn't been in hers. He thought of the times he didn't help her at Queen of Cups. He thought of how she wanted to paint the house—how she could've hired someone. She just wanted to spend time with Daniel, and instead, he lied to her and left her alone.

All she ever asked of me was to stay away from Miguel, Daniel thought.

He couldn't decide who had been wrong. Connecting with Miguel had been wonderful. Daniel never would have changed that in a million years. But now he understood the consequences—not of disobeying Aunt Cass, but of prying too hard. He had forced open a door that was never meant to be opened. He couldn't blame Aunt Cass, and he couldn't even blame Miguel. They had both tried to protect Daniel.

He rested the daisy next to Victor's, the roots exposed and hungry for soil. He traced Aunt Cass's name with his finger, the stone slick with cold humidity.

"I'm sorry," he whispered. "This is all my fault."

"Hey, whoa," Victor said. "There's no need to blame yourself."

"There is, Victor," Daniel said. "There is. The same accident that brought you back is the same thing that put Aunt Cass in the ground. She's not supposed to be there."

Victor insisted that Daniel was wrong—that over the years, he had never given himself the proper space to grieve. "You never let yourself feel it, Danny. Denial's a powerful thing, and we've all been there. But man, this is real now. You gotta face this, and you gotta stop blaming yourself. You gotta let us in and talk about it."

As for Xander, he'd been quiet, and Daniel wondered if he *knew.* Xander had been the first to realize the truth about his life and death, and he figured it out almost supernaturally. What else did he know? Had he ever "haunted" Aunt Cass in recent years, and remembered it?

Furthermore, did Miguel know about Aunt Cass's death?

That should've been the first thing he told me, Daniel thought, clenching his fists. *He should've said something.*

He'll fix this. That's why he didn't say anything. He was sparing my feelings while he was planning to undo this. Tomorrow I'll wake up, and Aunt Cass will be there, and my family will be at peace, and all of this will be done.

But…what if it isn't?

Daniel touched two fingers to his lips, then pressed them to the grave. A ladybug scuttled over the edge and onto Daniel's finger. He released it onto the grass and dried his eyes. "I love you, Aunt Cass," he said. "We'll make this right. I promise."

And then the ground lurched beneath him.

Daniel didn't know where the pulse came from, but it was strong enough to shake the sycamore branches on the hill…a single *boom*.

With that pulse, something ugly happened. A wave of rot rippled through the cemetery. Daniel felt the grass dry up and crumble under his feet—one minute, a vibrant green, and the next, khaki-brown and thirsty. He could almost hear the moisture leaving the ground with a sickening *creak*.

A pigeon plummeted from the sky and into the barren branches of a rosebush.

He turned in a circle. From the flowers on the graves to the butterflies in the bushes, death and rot had gripped every inch of the cemetery, dusting the ground. Even the pink glow of twilight couldn't restore the beauty.

"What the hell was that?" Victor asked. "I didn't like that."

Daniel scrubbed a thumb over his lighter. He didn't like it, either, and he had no doubt it was connected to Miguel.

Was Miguel already in The Archive, hatching whatever plan he had up his sleeve? Because this felt like an act of the classic Grim Reaper—wiping out all the flora of the cemetery and sucking the life from the air.

It's all gonna be okay, he told himself. *Maybe it just has to get worse before it gets better. It'll go away by morning.*

Daniel realized maybe there was something he feared more than losing his family a second time, and that was letting them hang on too long. After all he'd seen, he *wanted* Miguel to succeed.

He'd never considered the possibility that his godfather could fail.

"Hold out your hand."

Daniel sat at the dining room table with Ruthie and Elena, and he did as he was told.

Ruthie tied the bracelet she was making and slipped it over Daniel's wrist. The elastic contracted, and the beads snapped together in a satisfying crackle. Most were burnt orange, and every fourth bead was shiny silver. As soon as she put it on Daniel, she set to work on another one with the same colors. "How does it feel?"

Daniel shook his wrist, and the bracelet hung on. "Perfect fit," he said. "What are the stones?"

"Jasper and hematite. It's supposed to attract positivity and good energy. I'm making one for everyone, because today felt weird." She looked under the table, where Bowser rested with his eyes closed and his head on his outstretched paws. She gave him a pet with her bare foot. "Even King Bowser feels it, huh? Poor little prince. I think he's sick."

Daniel looked around the house. Everyone was doing their own thing. Mom and Dad were watching TV in the living room with Victor—another one of his spicy reality shows. Sam and Bobby were lying on their stomachs playing a card game. Monica and Nancy were up in their rooms, and Xander was reading a book. He appeared to be somewhere in the middle, and Daniel wondered if he would ever get to finish it.

On one hand, Daniel wanted to gather everyone together, make a grand I-love-you speech, and insist that they play a round of charades. On the other hand, this was the closest thing to a normal night at the Grimm house, and maybe that was what everyone needed. He knew he wouldn't be able to make a big speech without crying or freaking the family out, especially the twins.

So, he'd let them go on doing what they loved. He'd let them be in the moment. He'd join them as they let him, and he'd say his piece. He just hoped that Miguel would keep his word and send them off peacefully.

Jasper and hematite. Daniel ran a finger over one of the silver beads, cool to the touch. Ruthie looked so focused and peaceful when she was beading. She played pop music at a low volume from her phone, and she hummed along as she strung her beads, one by one.

"Thank you for this, Ruthie," Daniel said. "I really love it."

"No problem!" Ruthie pushed her box of beads to the middle of the table. She had organized her box by color, creating a sort of rainbow effect. "Wanna make some with me?"

Daniel picked up a handful of cool silver beads and let them drip between his fingers. "Do I have to know what all of them mean?"

"Hmm, no," Ruthie said. "Sometimes I just look at the colors and then I make whatever I want."

"That's what I do." Elena strung a green bead onto an elastic band. Then she held up one wrist and showed off a bracelet made of chaos—all the colors clashed and created a dissonant effect that hurt Daniel's eyes when he stared too long. "It's relaxing."

Daniel chuckled. Chaos represented Elena well. "You're pretty good at that."

"What are you gonna make?" Ruthie asked.

Daniel stroked his chin and thought for a minute. Then he picked up a black bead and some twine. "I'll figure it out as I go, I guess."

"Yay!" Ruthie smiled, then counted out fifteen orange beads and piled them in front of her. "Monica and Nancy have a present for you, by the way. It's from me, too."

"Really?" Daniel picked up another bead. "Why do I get a present?"

"We just felt like it." Ruthie cupped her hands to her mouth and called for Monica and Nancy. "Do you have the thing?"

Nancy came down with a white bag stuffed with gold tissue paper. "*I* have the thing."

Monica followed. "Daniel Grimm, the Grimm Goddesses present thee with this boon." She winked and added, "Family discount."

"Careful, it's fragile." Nancy set the bag on the table, then took a step back and clasped her hands together. "Okay! Open it."

"You all are too nice." Suddenly, Daniel had wished he'd brought something for them. Anything. He pulled out the tissue paper and unwrapped two red candles. He took the lid off one of them and inhaled the scent of roses.

"Ares and his flowers!" Daniel laughed. "What are these for?"

"Well, we knew you wanted one," Monica said. "And after everything that happened at the street fair, we thought we'd bring you an Ares one so you can remember to be strong."

Nancy sat at the table and picked up one of the candles. "I always loved candles," she said. "I wonder if I got that from Grandma Alba. She always had her prayer candles and her citrus candles and the ones with the crackling wooden wicks. They were so soothing. I used to think they were magic—like she could light a candle and fix any problem in the world."

Daniel gave her a weak smile. "I did, too."

"And maybe it can't, but it can definitely make us feel better sometimes."

"We gave you two so you can also give one to your friend in the hospital," Monica said, "if you want. That way she can be strong, too. Tell her it's from you, not from us."

Daniel turned the candle in his hands, tracing the rim of the glass with his fingertip. "I don't think Macy's gonna want to see me."

"You'll give it to her when she's ready," Nancy said. "Or maybe you can have a friend pass it on. She can't stay mad at you for long. Who could?"

Daniel fidgeted with his bracelet-in-progress. "I've made mistakes. Some big ones, to say the least."

"Dude, join the club," Monica said. "It's called being human."

"We've all been there," Nancy added.

"But I mean, like *epic* mistakes," Daniel said. "The kind that someone else has to fix for me. I thought I was doing a good thing, and it just ended up hurting people. I *know* you haven't done anything that stupid."

Mom got off the couch and made her way to the table. "This is a Mom job," she said. "Danny, is this about Aunt Cass?"

Daniel looked down. "Yeah."

It was a half-truth. There was also Macy and Billy and Mr. Jerricks, not to mention the family he was about to lose for the second time. Aunt Cass's grave represented them all today—the sum of his errors.

"She knew you loved her," Mom said.

He'd missed so many opportunities to say *I love you* in life. It was a guilt that nagged him every day.

"How can I know that?" he said. "How do you know that?"

"Because it's in everything you do," Mom said. "I've seen how you interact with your siblings. I used to see you with Aunt Cass. I've seen you with Miguel. I'm sure your friend Macy knows you love her, too."

Daniel drummed his fingers on his lap.

"You don't believe me." Mom tipped Daniel's chin up with her finger. "And you need to, Daniel. I really need you to believe this."

"And…and if one of us died tomorrow…" Daniel swallowed, "would you know? Would you know I love you?"

"Of course, sweetheart," Mom said. "I know that with *every* bone in my body."

"We all show love a little differently," Dad said. "We know."

The girls had their candles and their music and their beads. Sam had his stories and the twins had chaos. Mom and Dad had their words. Xander radiated tough love. When Victor went somewhere or spent his time with someone, he was fully in the moment, and he didn't hold back.

Mom kissed Daniel's forehead. "We will always love you, no matter what. Just remember that."

"Yeah, even though you're *weird*," Monica added. "By the way, I think I'm gonna model the Hades candle after you, because you're like a combination of my idea and Ruthie's idea. Kinda moody, kinda weird. But hey, this whole family's weird."

"Fuck yeah we are," Sam said.

"*Hey*," Dad warned. "For the last time, not in front of the kids!"

"We're not kids," Bobby said.

It broke Daniel's heart that he'd never get to know what Bobby and Elena would be like as adults. He wondered if they would've always had their twin sync and their energy.

He wondered how Sam planned to end his story, and if it ever would've seen a wider audience.

He wondered how Victor would've enjoyed being uncle of the year, or how many candles Monica would sell throughout her lifetime.

He wondered if Ruthie would always maintain her love for beading, and what other passions she'd develop.

He wondered if Xander would've opened up a little more, but he was grateful for the time they'd shared today.

He wondered if Nancy would've ever become a CEO or a famous musician. She had the drive and the diplomacy to do whatever she wanted.

But sometimes the universe said no to things. The twins confessed they had asked the universe to bring back Aunt Cass. The irony was that if Miguel succeeded in The Archive, the twins would get their wish yet again, but they would never know it.

Wherever they went, he hoped they would never stop believing in magic.

Daniel considered his Ares candle—fresh, new, and smooth—and imagined what his Archive candle looked like. He wondered if anyone *ever* died without leaving something unsaid or undone. Maybe every candle looked a little messy when the flame went out.

And maybe there was some uncanny beauty in that mess, and the history of it all, and the impermanence of the flame. A part of the candle would still endure.

The clock struck ten, and Daniel grew uneasy. Miguel had never given him an exact time, or an idea of what the transition would look like. Would they simply blink out of existence at midnight? Would Daniel just go to bed and wake up in another version of his reality?

He wasn't sure he wanted to be awake when they left. He wanted to *choose* his last moment. He wanted to choose the goodbye—something he didn't get to do the first time, and something very few people ever got to do.

Daniel stood and stretched his arms over his head. Then he looked around the room. "Fam," he said. "I think I'll be going to bed now."

Bobby looked at his watch. "All *early*?" He made a face. "Don't be boring. We can sleep when we're dead."

Daniel turned away. *Do not make this hard.* "I'm pretty tired, Bobby."

There were some kinds of *tired* no sleep could satisfy.

"You don't have to look all sad about it." Bobby threw down a card and announced that he'd beaten Sam at their game. He looked back at Daniel and shooed him off. "Okay. Bye. Why are you just standing there?"

"I'm just thinking."

Elena put her beads down. "I think I know." She got up and walked over to Daniel. "You had the same nightmare we did, huh?"

Daniel twisted his bracelet around his wrist. "I did," he said. "I've had it probably a hundred times by now."

"Maybe the bracelet will help," Ruthie said.

"Yeah…" Daniel murmured. "Maybe it will."

"So why do you wanna go to bed?" Elena asked.

Under the table, Bowser shifted in his sleep, rolled over, and stretched out his paws before his breaths settled back into a deep rise and fall. He had never looked more comfortable.

Daniel looked around at his family. "Because most nights I get to dream of you."

"D'aww," Sam said.

Nancy put a hand over her heart. "That was so sweet! Daniel!"

Across the room, Victor and Xander sat in silence, each in their own private thoughts. Victor winked, and Xander rocked in his chair, arms folded and eyes closed. For a second, he looked like he had survived deep into his thirties—all at once rougher, softer, depleted, yet full.

Monica rolled her eyes and stood. "This is too many feelings for me. I'm gonna go get changed."

"That was sweet, Daniel," Mom said. "And I think we should *all* be getting to bed so we can be well-rested and healthy in the morning. You too, Bobby. You can stay up when school's out and tire your chaotic heart out all you want."

"And then it's gonna be Christmas!" Bobby threw his hands up. "New stuff!"

"Not the point, sir," Dad said. "Go put your pajamas on."

Victor sprang up from the couch. "C'mon, weasels. Let's make it more fun with a song. Ready? And one, two, three! *So long, farewell, a something say good night…*Meh, I'm kidding. Who are we, the Brady Bunch?"

"Wrong fictional family," Nancy said. "Wrong words, too. It's *auf wiedersehen.*"

Victor spun his hat on his finger, then gently set it down on the coffee table and gave it a soft pat. "That's what I said, isn't it?"

Nancy grinned. "Sure, Vic."

"Well," Victor took another look around the room, and his gaze lingered on Daniel, "it's been a lot of fun, hasn't it?"

"The most," Daniel said.

"Until we meet again? In the morning, obviously?"

"You'll know where to find me," Xander said.

Daniel opened his arms for a hug. "Can we all get a group hug before bed? Please?"

"Has Bobby showered yet?" Nancy wrinkled her nose. "I'm totally just kidding. I think a group hug would be nice."

Dad turned off the TV and exchanged a look with Mom. "They kids are awfully sentimental tonight, aren't they?"

"I know," Mom said as she gathered the Grimms in a circle. "Aren't they beautiful, Jon?"

Yeah, Mom. Daniel closed his eyes and held on to the warmth, crystallizing a memory. *We got it from you.*

CHARLEY HORSE

*(a sudden and painful cramp, often occurring
in the middle of the night)*

Daniel spent the night on the living room couch, wrapped in the sights, smells, and artifacts of the most lived-in place from the Grimms' brief return. He had one of Mom's favorite blankets draped over him, the smell of lavender baked into the fabric. The Ares candle crackled in the night, spewing its floral scent and bathing the living room in a soft glow. Daniel had lit it with Dad's lighter, which he nestled in the crook of Victor's hat. He wore Ruthie's beads on his right wrist.

On the coffee table, Sam's wizard story sat unfinished in his black binder. Xander's novel sat on top of the binder, and a black ribbon hung like a lazy tongue between the pages, about halfway through the book.

Would all this simply disappear with the rest of the family? Every trace of them gone, every story unfinished?

Did anyone's life ever end like most books did, where every character found fulfillment and purpose, said their goodbyes, and resolved every element of the plot?

Maybe everyone left something behind—an upcoming holiday, a story they wanted to tell, a place they wanted to explore. Not even a second chance resolved the story of the Grimms. Daniel's only comfort was that they'd had some fun along the way. They'd created, they'd laughed, they'd loved, and they'd dreamed.

Daniel blew out the Ares candle and soaked the room in darkness.

Sleep arrived more gently and easily than he thought it would, but it didn't stay. It visited, twirled him around, and woke him up, spinning away. The dreams were random, and they didn't sync with his conscious thoughts. There was a circus tent filled with soaring paper cranes. There was a pallid goblin eating some fruit from a dying tree. At one point, he saw a hotel valet parking a gray horse at Queen of Cups. He remembered jazzy, big band music and cocktail party chatter, and he wasn't sure which dream that fit into.

And every time Daniel woke up, he'd steal a dreary glance at his surroundings. Victor's hat was still there. The beads were still on his wrist. Mom's blanket still smelled like lavender.

Then he fell right back to sleep and tumbled into a new, nonsensical dream.

The cycle continued until he heard the dissonant bellow of a grandfather clock.

Daniel couldn't tell if the chime had been part of the dream, or if it had sounded in the real world, but it had been so startling that it pierced the fragments of his sleep like a javelin. He sat up, coated in a thin film of sweat. A dull violet glow seeped through the blinds, signaling the first rays of dawn.

He pressed his palms over his eyes. He massaged the sleep out of them and stole a glance at the clock.

It was early morning.

Everything was still in place. The binder. The hat. The candle.

And yet, things didn't feel quite right. The buzz of the uncanny trembled in the air.

Miguel had told Daniel that he only had the rest of the night with his family, that things would be different in the morning. He would've checked in when he was done.

Aunt Cass would already be in the kitchen whipping up breakfast and preparing to open the café. Her house would be smaller again. All the extra rooms would fall away, and the Grimms would once again just be memories.

Daniel's heart crawled up into his throat.

If something had happened to Miguel, then the implications were terrifying. People would keep dying. The dead would walk, haunt themselves, and grieve their own lives until they turned into walking skeletons. A plague would blaze through the world, and Daniel would be responsible for *all* of it.

He thought about the dying grass at the cemetery—all the falling birds, and the weeds siphoning the life from Crescent Gate.

That had been the beginning of something, hadn't it?

What if Miguel had been harmed somehow?

Daniel tip-toed to the front door and silently cracked it open. As the door opened wider, so did his eyes.

The bushes, the trees, and all the grass in the neighborhood had turned charcoal gray, and particles of dust hovered like spores in the air.

Ashen vines crawled up the side of the house, caging it in weeds.

Obsidian clouds swallowed the first rays of dawn.

A pack of rats scampered into the storm drain down the street. Daniel had never seen live rats in Costa Linda before, but there were seven of them hurrying into the neighborhood's underbelly. It almost looked like they were running toward something…or *from* something.

Daniel considered his last moments in The Archive—how the skies blackened, and the smell of sulfur overpowered every pleasant scent in the air. How Miguel had looked up and said, *Something's wrong.*

Daniel was ready to retreat inside when a slender gray cat appeared in the driveway, eyes glowing like jewels in the shadows.

The cat looked at him, purred, and went up to him with no hesitation.

"Dorian," Daniel whispered. "What the hell? What are you doing all the way over here?"

Dorian meowed, pawed at Daniel's leg, and bounded back to the end of the driveway.

There was no sign of Miguel or his car anywhere—the cat had come alone.

"You're so far from home," Daniel said. "How did you know how to find me?"

More importantly…*why* did Miguel's cat feel the need to find Daniel?

Dorian meowed more insistently and ran into the street. For a second, Daniel thought Dorian was leaving, but then the cat turned again, made eye contact, and tilted its head. The next meow was more of a whine than anything else, long and steeped in pain.

Shit.

At least he knew why the rats were running, but this was not a good omen.

Miguel was in trouble. And if something had gone wrong, then Daniel didn't have the first clue how to fix it.

But there were layers to Miguel.

If Death was in trouble, who was equipped to help him? Daniel didn't necessarily *want* to help him. Death had robbed him many times, and even though Daniel was growing to understand Death, they would never be best friends. Death didn't need Daniel's help; Death didn't *want* Daniel's help.

He'd explicitly told Daniel never to meddle again.

If Dr. Mortiz was in trouble at the hospital, intervening with Dr. Mortiz's job would be disastrous. He had a whole team ready to support him; there were people who made a living in medicine.

But first and foremost, Miguel was Daniel's godfather, mentor, and a man who simply wanted to understand what it meant to live and to love among humans. He was a friend of the Grimms.

That was the man Daniel owed his debts to.

He would start there, even if he didn't know how.

Daniel slipped back into the house, stumbled into some jeans and a hoodie, and collected a backpack. He put Sam's binder in it and some mementos, like Ruthie's beads and Victor's hat. He wrapped Macy's candle in Mom's blanket. Daniel didn't know what was coming or how long he would be gone, but he felt like he would need some comfort wherever he was going.

I can't keep you all here, he thought. *But I can always keep you with me.*

He picked up his lighter and stared into his reflection in the metal.

This thing caused me an awful lot of trouble.

I shouldn't even take this with me.

Daniel thought of his dad's story and how the fire department having to extinguish his burning tree. Dad had made his own mistakes in life…but they could be fixed, even if the tree was never the same again. There were lectures and lessons, and then life went on. Hopefully, he never set another tree on fire.

He kissed the lighter and put it in his pocket. "We'll keep the lid on you this time," he whispered.

Finally, Daniel grabbed his shoes, went outside, and closed the door. He wouldn't look back. He wouldn't say goodbye again. He'd forge ahead, and he'd grieve again when it was all over.

Daniel stooped down, snapped his fingers, and beckoned the cat into his arms. "I've got you, Dorian. Let's get you home."

The drive to Miguel's told a tale of a dying world.

The same weeds that covered Daniel's house sprouted around every corner. They clawed their way out of the cracks in the sidewalks and seized the streetlights. They grasped swing sets and curled around the Costa Linda Light Rail stops. The river had turned a sickly shade of gray-blue, and vines ascended the bridge. Dorian meowed in the passenger seat.

"I *know*," Daniel said. "It's okay. We'll be there in a minute."

Daniel's unease deepened with every mile. He cycled through the radio stations, mostly finding talk shows and commercials.

"Stay away from First and Castle. We have a collision holding up traffic over there. Take Grant if you're on your way to work. Other than that, the streets are clear on this bizarrely dreary morning in Costa Linda. This has been your TraffiCam morning report. Stay—"

"—perfect gift for your loved ones this holiday season? Why not surprise them with tickets to Yule-O-Ween at the Chateau Theater next Friday? We've got all kinds of frightful, delightful guests lined up, door prizes—"

"—sure to talk to your doctor about whether this is right for you. Side effects include dizziness, high blood pressure—"

"—still investigating the cause of death."

Daniel switched off the radio and finished the drive in silence.

When he arrived at Miguel's, the dark sedan glistened in his yard. Daniel phoned him, but the call went straight to voicemail. He let Dorian out of the car, and the cat bounded to the front door.

Daniel followed and rang the doorbell. "Miguel?"

When no one answered after about a minute, his stomach squirmed.

Now he knew how Katie must've felt the day she came home to find the car parked and the house empty.

Daniel thought of when he wrote an English paper on *The Picture of Dorian Gray*. That was the first time he'd learned about the literary present. *You should always write in present tense,* she said. *Because Dorian Gray is* always *sitting for his portrait. He is* always *selling his soul for eternal youth. He is* always *attending Sibyl Vane's show.*

And in ghost stories, spirits haunted the sites where they died by repeating their deaths in infinite loops. Maybe literature, potent memories, and flashbulb events became ghosts, too. Like broken records, some histories seemed to repeat themselves.

Miguel's history felt like one of those loops.

Daniel let himself in with the key Miguel had made him. Dorian ran inside and disappeared into the shadows, and the knot tightened in Daniel's stomach. He didn't even need to venture beyond the front door to know everything was wrong.

Keys were strewn about the house. An ocean of them sprayed every surface, from the floors to the fireplace. They used to line the walls and shelves in neat shadowboxes, but now, broken glass glittered on the edges of the floors, and some of the shadowboxes lie tipped on their faces. The kitchen cupboards were wide open.

Daniel took a cautious step, and glass crackled under his shoe. "Miguel?" he called.

A guttural cough sounded upstairs, and a thin crack of light spilled onto the staircase. Someone had left Miguel's library open. Miguel had always kept that door closed, presumably because he often used the same door to access The Archive.

Daniel closed the front door behind him and pocketed the key, then he crept up the stairs.

He pushed the library door open, and he froze.

A man sat on Miguel's leather couch, and the scent of coffee and cigarettes hung thick in the air. The man was tall and gaunt, his eyes sunken in as if someone had pressed them deep into his skull. Daniel recognized the man's cleft chin, though he was paler and chalkier today—almost the color of bone. A tablet, a cup of coffee, and a pack of cigarettes all rested on the table in front of him.

The man looked up and tipped his fedora. "Morning."

Daniel recoiled and assessed the room. "Where's Miguel?"

The man held up a hand and winced as if he'd pulled a muscle. "Easy. It's six-thirty in the morning, and I haven't finished my coffee yet. Give me a minute before you start with the questions."

"You're the guy who's been following me around," Daniel said. "Why are you here?"

The man sipped his coffee. "Guess we're diving in." He reached for an unlit cigarette and tucked it behind his ear. Between the long, dark coat, the fedora, and the tobacco habit, the man looked like he belonged in a 1920s detective movie. "I haven't been following *you*, necessarily. I've been following a jigsaw puzzle, and you just happen to appear on all the edges. How 'bout you join me for a few minutes and help me fill in the middle? Then I'll disappear."

When he pulled out a badge and an ID, Daniel's blood flushed cold.

No fucking way.

"You're looking for Miguel Mortiz. I suppose today, our interests intersect." The man extended his hand. "What do you say we start fresh, go grab a skillet or some waffles, and make this nice and comfortable? My name is Charleston Fitch."

Daniel backed up and stumbled into a bookshelf.

I brought back the detective Katie hired to look for Miguel.

And somehow, Fitch still retained his pursuit of the truth, whether Katie still wanted it in this life or not.

Fitch retracted his hand. "Cat got your tongue?"

Daniel shook his head. "No. Um…look, man, whatever you have for me right now, I just don't have time for it. Can we do this some other day?"

"I'm afraid time is of the essence, and it is quickly slipping away." Fitch gestured to the empty space on the couch. "Sit."

Daniel bit the inside of his cheek, feeling the throb of his heartbeat.

"Don't you have to read me Miranda rights or something? Do I have the right to remain silent?"

Fitch chuckled. "Well, you're not under arrest, though you might find it in your best interest to cooperate with me." He tapped on his tablet. "I have access to information that will interest you greatly."

Daniel considered the tablet. This was the same detective who failed to deliver any substantial information to Katie when she hired him—he'd kept hitting dead ends. Fitch wasn't about to find anything Miguel didn't want the world to know. But the ransacked living room told a strange tale—and Daniel didn't like the aura of it. "Tell me what you know."

"Here's how we're gonna do this," Fitch said. "This game is called quid pro quo. I'm gonna ask you some questions. You play ball with me, then I tell you what *I* know. You hold back or start lying to me? Well, I'm gonna know it. My bullshit detector?" He made a circle with his thumb and forefinger, then let out a whistle. "It's top-notch. That's what they pay me for."

"Good," Daniel said. "Because you're not nearly as conspicuous as you think you are. I hope they don't pay you to be sneaky."

Fitch held his hands in front of him as if to shield himself from the comment. "I get my job done. So…breakfast?"

"No, thank you," Daniel said. "We can do this right here. Time is of the essence, right?"

"Smart." Fitch plucked the cigarette from behind his ear, produced a lighter, and cupped the light in his hands. "I can't smoke in a restaurant, and everything I eat seems to taste like shit these days." He tipped his finger toward his pack of cigarettes. "Would you like one?"

"No," Daniel said. "Look, I don't think Miguel would appreciate you smoking in here."

"I think that's the least of his worries."

"You already broke into his house," Daniel said.

"That makes two of us."

"I had a key. And the smoke bothers *me*."

"Fair enough. We'll have it your way." Fitch flicked his cigarette into his coffee and replaced it with a stylus. "Now, can we move onto my questions?"

Daniel sat down.

"Dandy. This will be as painless as you let it be." Fitch maneuvered his stylus around his tablet and shifted on the couch. "So, let's start with a warm-up round. What's your name, kid?"

"All this time you've been following me, and you haven't learned my name yet?"

"Disclaimer: I already know the answers to most of these questions. Don't screw this up, Daniel."

A chill worked its way down Daniel's spine. There was something eerie and uncanny about hearing his name come from Fitch's mouth.

Fitch cleared his throat. "So. Birthday?"

"March twenty-seventh," Daniel muttered.

"A fellow Aries man." Fitch smirked. "Never really believed in that zodiac nonsense. Muddies the water and gets tangled with our view of the facts. But maybe there's some truth to it, eh? It fits *you*, for one thing. Stubborn. Impulsive. Argumentative. Intense. I've been called all that and worse."

Macy used to say *brave, ambitious, enthusiastic, and free.* Daniel wanted to bite back, but that only would've proved Fitch's point. So instead, Daniel said nothing.

"Occupation?" Fitch asked.

"I'm a student."

"Of course. Not the star, I noted. You ever turn in that 'science project' you left in your car?" Fitch winked, then waved the comment away. "A rhetorical question, of course. Is playing hooky a habit for you?"

"School hasn't exactly been my priority," Daniel said.

"Why?" Fitch reached for his coffee, remembered the cigarette butt floating on the surface, and retreated. "You're not interested in college? You seem bright to me. You haven't picked out a career… thought about where you want to be in five years?"

Daniel buried a hand in his hair. "Man, half the time I'm just trying to get through the day. I've had a lot going on."

Fitch's eyes brightened. "And I respect every word of that. I'd be fascinated to learn more."

Daniel clenched his jaw. His answer blew the door wide open for Fitch to dig deeper.

"The warm-up round is over. We're gonna get into the weeds now and unpack all those things you have going on." Fitch tapped on his screen and rotated his tablet for Daniel to see. "Can you confirm that this is Miguel Mortiz?"

Daniel glanced at the photo on the screen—the one from his basic internet searches about a month ago. Miguel beamed back at him in full reverent doctor mode, white coat and all.

"Yeah," Daniel said.

"Great." Fitch crossed one leg over the other. "Tell me about Mr. Mortiz. Who is he to you? What's the relation?"

"*Dr.* Mortiz…" Daniel said, "is my godfather."

Fitch took his tablet back and scribbled something. "So if I told you that Dr. Mortiz—your godfather—is at the center of my investigation, what would you think?"

"I'd be curious to know why," Daniel said. "Has he done something?"

Fitch shrugged. "You tell me. Should I believe he's done something?"

"I mean, you're here. But for the record, Miguel wouldn't hurt a fly." Daniel knew this from experience. When he really thought about it, he had never seen the god of death kill a fly before. He usually opened a window and shooed them outside.

"That seems to be true." Fitch studied his notes. "Every indication I've had is that Dr. Mortiz is the cat's pajamas. He has excellent reviews from his patients; they say he's compassionate, competent, even funny. He's won a Latinos in Medicine award. He has a sterling reputation, and quite the track record. Furthermore, you seem to care for the man."

Daniel rotated his shoulders, working out the stiffness. "Yes. And?"

"And yet I've been doing this for a while." Fitch rested his chin on his fist. "And the *only* thing I've learned for sure is that everybody's got a shadow. Would you agree?"

That was a tricky question to answer. A *yes* cracked the door open even further, and Daniel was determined to steer Fitch away from Miguel's truth. But a *no* would've been suspiciously elusive. "Sure," he said. "I guess I can see that."

"So," Fitch said, "what's his shadow? You said he's your godfather.

I gather you're close if you're bringing his cat home."

Daniel's leg bounced under the table. "I mean, it's complicated, but yeah, we get along fairly well."

"Why's it complicated?"

Because he's literally Death.

"Because family is always complicated," Daniel said. "You're the one who said everyone has a shadow. Happy families have drama, too."

"Of course," Fitch said. "What does drama look like in your family?"

Daniel winced. "That's personal, and it has nothing to do with your investigation."

"Sure it does," Fitch said. "Everything's connected. I respect that this is touchy, and it's not necessarily pleasant, but this is my job. I told you that you need to cooperate if you wanna know what *I* know."

Daniel curled his fingers into the leather seat.

"Maybe I'll start. Quid pro quo, right?" Fitch put down his tablet and tapped his chest with both hands. "I'm goin' through a divorce. Now you're too young to understand heartbreak, but it's a vile thing, kid. Barbara and I lost our daughter some time ago. Ivy was supposed to finish high school. She liked to dance. She wanted to go to culinary school one day. She was funny, and she liked dinosaurs, and she knew every word to most songs on the radio."

Daniel relaxed his posture.

"Having a kid changes your world, but losing one sets it on fire. Barbara and I coped in different ways. We each walked out of the flames a little harder, scarred, but tough. But the marriage…? That was engulfed beyond repair." Fitch put his fingertips together and studied Daniel. "So. Family drama."

"I'm sorry," Daniel said. "I can't imagine what it was like to lose your daughter or to go through a divorce. But you're wrong about one thing."

Fitch nodded, an invitation for Daniel to continue.

"I do know what heartbreak's like," Daniel said. "It might not be the same for me, and I may not have been in your shoes, but I do know heartbreak. And I'm tired of people minimizing it."

Fitch tipped his hat as if to yield an apology. "Noted. No disrespect intended." He picked up his tablet again. "I did read up on the death of your aunt, Cassandra Grimm. Terrible. You have my deepest condolences."

"Thanks," Daniel muttered. Something about Fitch made Daniel's bones want to crawl out of his skin. He wished Fitch was lying about his daughter to bring Daniel's guard down, but Daniel believed every word. He hated that they had found common ground.

"In *my* grief," Fitch said, "I buried myself in my work. I became obsessed with the truth. Other people's misery distracted me from my own. But in your grief, I gather that you turned to Dr. Mortiz. I'm wondering if you can tell me a little bit more about him."

Daniel leaned back, snapping his guard back up. "What do you wanna know?"

"Anything. What got him into medicine? When he leaves work, what does he like to do for fun? I assure you, no detail is too small."

"I don't know where to start."

Fitch gestured absently around the room, a sarcastic bite in his tone. "What's his favorite color, for starters?"

"I actually don't know that. But…Miguel once told me the same thing a lot of people say when they go into medicine. He wanted to help people, and I genuinely believe that's true. I have never seen my godfather demonstrate anything but amazing care for the people around him. When I was a little boy, my grandma died from kidney failure. It was incredibly difficult for my dad. My mom picked up a lot of the slack, but she couldn't be everywhere at once. Miguel stepped up in a lot of ways. Emotional support. Cooking. Babysitting. All that stuff. I had forgotten about that for a long time, but it's just one example of who he is. My best friend, Macy, had a heart attack the other day, and I almost lost my marbles. When I saw that Miguel was running the initial care on her, I knew she was in good hands."

Fitch rested his fingers against his temple, squinting at Daniel and processing the story. "Mm-hmm," he said. "Let's chat about Macy, then. You say she's your best friend."

"Yes. One of them."

"Do you think Ms. Sterling has the same regard for you?" Fitch asked. "And let me preface that with the insight that I've been to see her. I visited her yesterday."

Daniel scooted to the front of his seat.

"Key witnesses had seen you talking to Ms. Sterling only moments before she collapsed near Garney Plaza. I wanted to get her side of the story. What do you think she told me?"

"I have no idea," Daniel said.

"Guess."

Daniel slammed a fist against the table. The burst had come out of nowhere, but it was clear Fitch was getting under his skin—asking questions he already knew the answers to, just to make Daniel squirm. And Daniel *had* to play along.

Fitch didn't even jump. "There was no call for that. It was a simple question."

Daniel rubbed his brow. "I don't think Macy's a huge fan of me right now. Probably feels like she doesn't even know me anymore. I was upset to see her at the fair with Billy Schubert, and no, it wasn't jealousy, because I know that's your next question. I have no romantic feelings toward Macy whatsoever. I consider her almost like a sister, and Billy's just kind of a jerk. I told her all that, and she went down a few minutes later."

"I see," Fitch said. "Well, she did confirm just about all of that with me, with one discrepancy. Don't sell yourself short, kid. She thinks highly of you."

Daniel did a double-take. "Really?"

"Her exact words were, 'I don't always understand Danny, but I believe he would do anything for someone he cares about.' You seem surprised to hear that. I suppose I would be too after a slight altercation." Fitch sighed and scrolled through his notes. "Okay. So when you were ditching school yesterday, where were you off to in such a hurry?"

"I was visiting Miguel," Daniel said. "Just needed some guidance."

"I see," Fitch said. "Well, as far as I'm aware, that was the last time he was seen. We're approaching twenty-four hours…not yet concerning in my book, but curious, to be sure. Where else did you go yesterday?"

Daniel's heart skipped a beat. *Definitely concerning. Miguel, where the hell are you?*

"I went to the cemetery to visit Aunt Cass," Daniel said. "And then I went home."

"Busy day," Fitch said. "The cemetery, huh? You were feeling sentimental? Pondering death in the middle of the day?"

Daniel rolled his eyes. "Is there a right time to grieve?"

"I'm merely observing. I know how it can hit very suddenly," Fitch said. "Around what time did you go home?"

"Between six-thirty and seven-thirty?" Daniel said. "Rough estimate."

"Interesting." Fitch tapped the stylus against his lip. "Something else happened at about six p.m. last night. You tell me you're not fond of William Schubert. Well, I'll have you know that he's dead. He was found unresponsive in the swimming pool at the Coronado Palms last night."

Daniel's heart dropped into his stomach. "No way. That can't be true. It wasn't supposed to be yesterday!"

"Oh?" Fitch's eyes brightened. "And when was it *supposed* to be? Did you have his death marked on a calendar somewhere?"

"Of course not!" Daniel said. "Do you think I had something to do with it? Is that what you're getting at?"

"I'm saying you, too, have a shadow." Fitch held up a hand and started ticking off names on his fingers. "Macy Sterling. Billy Schubert. Now you're breaking into Miguel Mortiz's home, and conveniently, he's missing."

Daniel leaned back, exasperated.

"This isn't a great look for you, kid." Fitch took off his hat and scratched his head. "This investigation started with Dr. Mortiz. But apparently, it doesn't surprise you to know that much of my interest has shifted toward *you*. I've gotta tell ya, you fascinate me. You interest me almost as much as the good doctor does."

Daniel stood, his breath hot in his lungs. "You know what?" he said. "I have been completely honest. I'm tired, and I want to know where Miguel is. It's your turn. Tell me what you know."

"Okay. You've been nice, kid, and a deal's a deal. I'm gonna show you something." Fitch tapped on his tablet and slid it over to Daniel. "A video."

Daniel gasped.

Aunt Cass sat frozen in the center of the screen, visible from the shoulders up. She wore the forest-green turtleneck she'd had on during Thanksgiving dinner. She was at Queen of Cups, but the lights were dim.

"Found this video stuck in the cloud," Fitch said. "It appears to feature Cassandra Grimm recording a message for her niece on Thanksgiving night. Now you and I both know this should be impossible for several reasons, not the least of which being that Cassandra is dead. I'd like you to view this. Then, perhaps you can help me make sense of it."

Daniel covered his mouth. He was about to see and hear Aunt Cass for himself again, but what was she about to say?

Fitch stood and smoothed the wrinkles in his pants. "I'll step out and give you a moment with this. I'll return in ten minutes. The video is about that long."

When Fitch closed the door behind him, the stench of cigarettes lingered. It would probably haunt Miguel's library forever.

Daniel braced himself.

Then he hit play.

ALICE IN WONDERLAND SYNDROME

*(a condition that distorts one's perception
of their body or the world)*

I need you to listen to me very carefully.

I don't even know if this is going to work, but if it reaches you, I need to say something right off the bat. You're not dreaming, you're not drunk, and you're not losing your mind. I am also not some sentient A.I; I am perfectly lucid right now, and I assume you are, too. This is me…Aunt Cass. It's about a quarter to seven…a little after dinner on Thanksgiving of 2022, and I'm sitting here at the café, just processing my thoughts.

At this point the audio registered a distant tap on glass, and Aunt Cass looked up and flapped her hand. "Sorry, I'm closed now!" She stepped out of the frame for a few seconds, and Daniel heard the *whoosh* of curtains on the rails. Aunt Cass returned to the camera, scrubbed her eyelids with her palms, and sighed.

Jesus.

Sorry. Where was I?

Katie, I have something to tell you.

Growing up, you were different than most girls. You loved your fairy tales, but you didn't love them for the same reason your friends did. When everyone wanted to go dance at the ball, you just wanted to talk to the birds. I think that's why we always had such a strong relationship, because I was the same kind of gal. I'd find myself thinking about the prince sometimes, and I knew he was a good dancer. I kept him at arm's length, anyway.

It's not that I didn't believe in these stories, but when your father died and I lost so many of my nieces and nephews, and your mom, who became like my best friend…I, um…I came to understand that I had been protecting myself all along.

We've protected ourselves because we knew something. We've known that all the velvety, shimmering fairy tales were originally told in the shadows. We know the spell book was written in blood. We suspected Prince Charming had some skeletons in his closet. We were both strong enough to face them, but neither of us were going to cut off our toes to make the shoe fit. I never wanted to move into a castle built on the backs of the poor, especially when I was perfectly happy running the apothecary.

Aunt Cass picked up a mug and swished the contents.

The fairy tales are true, Katie. And they're darker than you expected.

Our family is tangled with Death himself.

Literally.

I always thought he would be colder somehow. I never expected I'd dance with him at my brother's wedding. I know how he takes his coffee. I baked him lemon bars when he won an award for Latinos in Medicine. I never thought I'd come to see him like a second brother.

Perhaps you're catching on by now. It's time you knew the truth, Katie. I know you've been looking into Miguel, and the truth is stranger than any explanation you've come up with.

I'll give you the abbreviated version; I just hope you'll take my word.

About nine years ago, Miguel gave me a peek behind the veil.

There's a sort of library beyond, where billions of candles burn. One flame equals one life. Miguel is the keeper of these candles, and when a flame goes out, that person dies. Miguel showed me this place after the accident and… it defies logic. It smells like your dad's hugs, and like fingerpaints, and like after-school swims with your siblings, and like bourbon hitting a hot pan. My mom—your grandma—used to cook with that sometimes, and that's why I use it for pineapple upside down cake.

This library—this Archive…I know how it all sounds. It sounds batshit crazy.

I don't know how to prove it to you; I can only describe what I've seen and what I felt. I've seen Agatha Christie's candle, burnt down to a little ivory stub, no bigger than the tip of my finger. Charlie Chaplin rests just a few rows away, and for some reason, so does Cleopatra, Elvis Presley, and my hairdresser.

When I say it out loud and I stop and think about it, it would all be an easy gimmick, wouldn't it? Take away the Hollywood smoke and mirrors, and it would all just be wax and flame and a name engraved on a plaque. But there's an aura about it. I took one look, and I knew it was real. It's breathtaking, learning once and for all that we're all cosmically intertwined by something so strange and so seemingly arbitrary. But it's all the same thing.

It's the end.

I don't fully know why I'm telling you this.

I suppose I'm just processing.

I've spent ten years reflecting on that day on the bridge. Only love can hurt the way this does, so I bear it. I bear it because I know it's just love hangin' on. It scars and bruises, and it never goes away. I used to go to these group therapy sessions where we'd talk about how there are five stages of grief…and I'd come home, and I'd journal about your siblings. I'd write down feelings, memories…. I used to take you all to those summer superhero movies, and some of you used to dress up, and we'd get through the big buckets of popcorn by the end of the trailers. I still go see all the new ones, you know. Sometimes my imagination is so vivid that I sit there for two hours, and I see your brothers and sisters taking up the whole row with me. I hear them crunching on popcorn and slurping sodas. I see their faces light up through all the plot twists and the fight scenes, and all the while, they're laughing and gasping and cheering and…And when the lights come back on, they all just leave me again like smoke in the wind…and reality drives a knife back into my gut and I realize I can't recall a single detail about the movie.

While we're on the subject, can I make a confession? I really hate baseball. I live for spicy reality shows, stimulating documentaries, and high-concept thrillers. I need escapism. Sports don't do it for me, unless Costa Linda University is playing basketball.

But when I'm flipping through channels, and I stumble on a baseball game? I drop everything. I go to my room and put on a jersey and a cap. I come out and I turn up the volume, I make some popcorn, and I sit and watch the whole thing. I pick the team with the better mascot, and I cheer like there's no tomorrow.

It makes me feel like your mom and dad are there sometimes. It's a ritual for me. We need rituals to keep love alive.

These are the things I do to bear the pain. I've learned that grief isn't linear. Sometimes I'll hear people call it a circle or a spiral or some other arbitrary shape, but none of these truly capture the complexity, not for me at least. In my experience, grief has been a million balloons filled with paint. You start with this beautiful blank canvas filled with possibilities. You have ideas about what it might look like in the end, or you're at least willing to play. Then you scar it with your darts, and all the colors start fighting. They trample each other and they bleed together, and everyone keeps trying to tell you it's a process, but you just don't see the beauty in the mess. And just when you thought you saw something familiar, someone pops another balloon and spills another layer. You thought you were finally numb, but you had forgotten how sharp the darts were.

I've accepted that my family isn't here anymore. I need to recognize that sometimes letting someone go is the best way to protect that love. But it's okay to hold on to their memories, because they stay with you if you do that.

The question I kept coming back to is how Miguel allowed them to die so soon, so coldly, and all at once. And for a time, I accepted that, too. I resisted the urge to light their candles again. There are certain beliefs we hold on to. Your grandmother used to do the pan de muerto and the altars—and yes, I've tried that. We tell ourselves they're all in a better place. We tell ourselves their souls moved on and that they're all watching over us. I think…I think I can agree with this. They give me little signs sometimes, and I do believe they're all at peace. And I've seen that Miguel grieves, too. I can empathize with his plight, and I can accept that nothing lasts forever. Don't get me wrong; this was an incredibly difficult place to get to.

But even in this place of acceptance, I could not allow Miguel to remain in our lives. Regardless of his intentions, he's dangerous. He is the end of all things, and he cannot be bargained with.

Tonight, I found out that Daniel has been visiting him, and we got into a fight. You were there. I always knew something was off…I knew it. I should've listened to my "auntuition."

That kid…he's my world. I love him dearly. Maybe I haven't done a great job of showing him that, or maybe I haven't been as open and vulnerable with you all as I should have. I'm over here trying to be Super Aunt, and I'm not showing him or you or Zeke that I'm grieving, too—every day. I haven't told Danny how much he reminds me of Jon. I haven't told you that you have your mother's grit. I haven't told Zeke that he was my rock. I have your parents' recipes, and I've never offered to make your favorites because I'm terrified of screwing them up and… and I accepted long ago that I will never be enough to fill the gap they left in your lives.

I just don't know what to do.

I can't blame Danny for looking for a father figure. And on a real human level, Miguel could be everything Danny still needs. A father. A brother. A new friend. A mentor. God, how I want that for him. I really do. Selfishly, I don't think anyone will ever care for Danny as much as I do, but…but if anyone could, Miguel would get pretty damn close to the bullseye.

But still, that doesn't change the fact that our family has had enough with Death.

We will not start inviting him to our doorstep again. I reject this with every fiber of my being. You are having a baby girl soon, and that baby deserves the world. You and Justin, and Zeke, and Daniel and his friends…you must live your full lives. If we get too close to Miguel again, then I worry we're going to lose the light we still have.

I'm going to tear down my "apothecary" and leave Costa Linda soon. I will rebuild somewhere else. The safety of my family is the most important thing. Before that, I suppose deep down, I have a secret hope that Miguel will show Daniel The Archive, and he'll do what I couldn't do. At the very least, I wonder what life would look like if everyone came back.

You can't blame me for being curious.

But I also wonder about all the unknowns. I have this feeling there might be consequences. Ripples. I was always told that you shouldn't play with things you don't understand.

I think I know why I'm recording this now.

Katie, all I've shared with you is true.

I'm scheduling this to reach you in about two weeks.

If your life looks different than what I've described, then that means Daniel and Miguel have done something before we could leave Costa Linda. Maybe you have your siblings back. If you do, congratulations. Hold them tight and never let them go. But if something's changed…if you've lost something, then you need to know that it wasn't supposed to be this way. Miguel has the answer, and you can be stronger than I was. You can make sure we don't lose them again. You can bring everyone back together.

Miguel has the key to The Archive. You've probably seen the hundreds of keys in his home. Maybe one of them will let you in, but of course, there's an even bigger possibility that he has the key on him. What I suggest is that you start by searching his library high and low. That's his sanctuary.

Go and see it for yourself.

Decide what you want and if you're willing to risk more ripples. I couldn't do it, but you deserve the truth.

You deserve to make a decision.

This is not a fairy tale, but reality is stranger, and just as dark. So, protect your light, Kate. Protect your family.

Give them all my love.

Then the video ended, and the library went silent.

Daniel sat back and buried a hand in his hair, his feeling boneless while his eyes burned with tears.

What. The fuck.

He stared at the image of Aunt Cass. She was frozen in an earnest and contemplative smile at the end of her video.

"Oh my god," he whispered.

Paint balloons on a canvas.

Daniel had no idea the pain was still so raw for her. She had told him it never went away, but she carried it so gracefully. Then she let her heart bleed open in this video. It felt like something Daniel was never meant to see—like a secret diary, or the writing assignments he never finished from his therapist. She'd never been this vulnerable with him. Had she ever opened up to *anyone* this way in ten years?

But he hadn't exactly been vulnerable with her, either.

And Death had been mourning alone for years.

We all failed each other, Daniel thought. *We brushed Death aside. We hated the idea of him so much that we didn't speak of him. And when he showed up looking for family, we demanded too much of him. We all failed.*

I failed.

Daniel's stomach tumbled in his body.

He had to fix this.

He had to help Miguel finish his plan, whatever it was.

But what the hell was he doing in The Archive? How could Daniel help him, and how could he get in without a key?

And moreover, a formerly dead detective paced outside the library, sifting through Miguel's strange existence and scrutinizing Daniel's every move. Daniel would have to be careful about what came next. The Archive was already in enough danger without Fitch discovering its secrets.

Daniel had to get rid of him somehow…throw him off the trail.

Fitch knocked, then entered without a word. Daniel could feel him reading his posture, his face, and his mind. Then Fitch picked up a random book and leafed through the pages, apparently trying to look more approachable. "Your godfather has a fascinating home, doesn't he?" He shook the book. "You a reader, Daniel?"

Daniel said nothing.

"Well." Fitch tossed the book away. "I guess that's beside the point. So, you've watched the video."

Daniel nodded.

Fitch leaned back against a shelf full of biographies. "Any idea what it all means?"

"Not really," Daniel said. "It's a lot to take in. Honestly, I'm still processing it all, man."

"You know what I've learned in this business?" Fitch asked. "Sometimes it's better to dive in with what you've got and get your gears turning right away. A little processing time is a good thing, kid, but sometimes, you can let the ingredients simmer too long. You can boil an overcomplicated solution, and you miss the simple one in front of your face. The *correct* one."

"What are you saying?"

"I'm saying I want your initial thoughts," Fitch said. "Your aunt… You think that was really her?"

"It can't be," Daniel said.

"She says she's not an A.I.," Fitch said. "Perhaps that's what an A.I. would say, and I've been astonished by the advances lately. Now, for the sake of argument, what if? She looks older than when she was last seen. Does she sync up with your memories of your aunt?"

Daniel stilled. "It's uncanny."

"Real or not, she spins a compelling yarn in this video, yeah?"

"She does," Daniel said. "But it doesn't make any sense to me."

"There's a lot to unpack, isn't there?" Fitch said. "Off the top of my head, she directly states that her brother's dead, along with most of her family. Your family seems very much alive to me. And yet, this is a woman carrying some intense grief. The way she talks, I'm inclined to believe her. Did your aunt have a theater background or something?"

Fitch had stumbled into something Daniel was glad he didn't have to lie about. "Yeah, actually. She used to do improv a long time ago."

"Huh. I was under the impression improv was funny." The detective raised a brow. He picked up his tablet and scanned through the video. "Your name comes up a few times. How'd that make you feel?"

"Confused," Daniel said without missing a beat. "Why would I need a father figure when I have a father already?"

"I think we're getting to the million-dollar question here," Fitch said. "Because, however you spin it, the fact I glean from this video is that Cassandra's views on Dr. Mortiz were complicated. She didn't seem to trust the man, and now he's missing. She directly addresses your sister, Katherine Grimm. You can't shed any light on this?"

"No," Daniel said. *Why don't you call the Auto Mob and ask for her?* "Not at all."

Fitch put a finger against his temple. "How 'bout all this talk about Agatha Christie's candle and whatnot? The *Archive*. I found that striking."

"Striking, yes," Daniel said. "But that's all it is. Aunt Cass loved mysteries. And Elvis. And fairy tales. This was just more improv, man."

"So you don't believe any of it?"

"Not a single word."

Fitch shrugged. "I mean, she seems like an intelligent woman to me—intuitive, resilient. It's not surprising to me that she was a

Cancer." He chuckled, but Daniel didn't laugh with him. "Do you have reason to believe otherwise about her character?"

"With all the love in the world for my aunt, I think intense grief can make us say, believe, or do just about anything. It doesn't care how 'intuitive' or 'resilient' you are."

"Perhaps." Fitch crossed his arms. "Those are wise words. I tend to agree with you. Death fucks us all over in the end, doesn't it? If he really walks among us, then he's probably a smug little bastard."

He's actually very down-to-earth and compassionate, Daniel thought. *Doesn't mean I don't hate him sometimes, but that's family, I guess.* Daniel wasn't about to stumble into one of Fitch's logic traps, though. "Sure."

"Imagine Death thinking he's *fair* with his secret candles and magic flames. What about what we want? Me? I wanna live forever. I don't want to leave any stone unturned, any story unfinished. Most of all, I wanted Ivy to finish high school. I want my daughter back. To hell with the consequences. What about you?"

"I think we should be careful what we wish for," Daniel said.

"Well, you love your family, don't you? Including Miguel?" Fitch said. "You'd, uh…*say, believe, or do just about anything* to protect them?"

"Of course I do," Daniel said. "Of course I would."

"You'd tell me the truth?" Fitch said. "All of it?"

"That's what I've been doing all morning."

"Huh." Fitch adjusted his collar and picked up his tablet. "Well, we've chewed the fat for a bit, haven't we? I've learned a lot from you this morning. I enjoyed our chat, and I thank you for your time."

Relief flooded Daniel's bones. Fitch was finally leaving, and Daniel could do the real work now. When he got into The Archive and fixed his mistakes, Fitch would be one of them. "I'm glad I could help."

Fitch extended a hand, and Daniel shook it. It was cold, firm, and pale, like stone.

When Fitch got to the library door, he looked back at Daniel. "Before I go," he said, "are you quite sure you haven't left anything out?"

"I'm positive," Daniel said. "Maybe I can call you if I think of anything?"

"I'd value that. A lot can change in a short time, you know. And if you want an example, a few days ago, I didn't even believe in astrology." Fitch dropped his hand into his pocket. "But now, I hold the key to Death's door."

Daniel's body went cold. "What do you mean?"

Fitch took a large skeletal key from his pocket, and the room spun under Daniel's feet.

"Let's cut the bullshit," Fitch said. "I know everything, Daniel. I know about your family, your aunt, and your godfather. I know Death walks among us in the body of one Miguel H. Mortiz, and I'm going to hold him accountable for his crimes against humanity— including my own untimely demise. And that of my daughter."

Daniel blinked rapidly, trying to process what Fitch had just revealed. *How? How did he figure it out?*

"Fitch, give me the key," Daniel said. "You don't know what you're doing."

"And you do?" Fitch asked. "A brooding teenager? That's fun, kid. I was going to let you in to say goodbye to your godfather, but seeing as how you've lied to me…well, now I can't trust ya."

Daniel sprang up from the couch. "Fitch!"

In a flash, Fitch drew something from his coat, and Daniel found himself staring at the dark barrel of a gun.

"Ah ah ah!" Fitch said. "Please. I didn't wanna do this—it's not in my nature. But you're gonna sit right back down, and you're gonna stay put."

Daniel's throat tightened. "You cannot do this."

"I must." Fitch cocked the gun, the click heavy and crisp. Sweat trickled down his forehead. "I said sit down."

Daniel swallowed the lump in his throat, then backed up and sank into the couch. He wondered what would happen to his candle if

Fitch shot him. Would the flame go out first, the wick still long and full of potential, and then Daniel would cease to be aware of anything? Would it be the other way?

"I truly don't wanna hurt you, Daniel," Fitch said. "If I'm being honest, I like ya. I also owe you a thank you. Your mistake gave me a second shot at life, and now I can go give one to my daughter, and perhaps even my marriage. You led me to the greatest mystery in the history of the world. So, consider this a favor. I take care of Death, and you get to keep your family. We *all* win."

With one hand still pointing the gun at Daniel, Fitch plugged the key into the lock and turned it. The cracks of light under the door turned purple—many shades deeper than the bright orange and pink twilight Daniel had seen when Miguel opened The Archive for him. The distant rumble of thunder drummed behind the door.

"Don't do this," Daniel said. "We don't win this way. This isn't good for anybody."

"No?" Fitch said. "Who gets to be the judge of that? It's *my* turn. Stay out of my way."

Fitch opened the door, and thick fog poured into the library. Daniel's vision twisted. Apparently, his brain hadn't fully integrated the realities of The Archive into his mind yet.

The fog swallowed Fitch and his gun until he was nothing but a dark silhouette, and he shuffled backward into The Archive, one hand on the doorknob.

"Goodbye, kid," Fitch said, his voice distant and fuzzy.

The door slammed behind him, locked with a harsh click, and the fog evanesced into nothing.

As Daniel's mind cleared, the only sound he heard was Dorian scratching at the other side of the door.

On the other side of the *veil,* Miguel was stuck in The Archive while a storm raged within.

And Charleston Fitch had just waltzed in with a firearm.

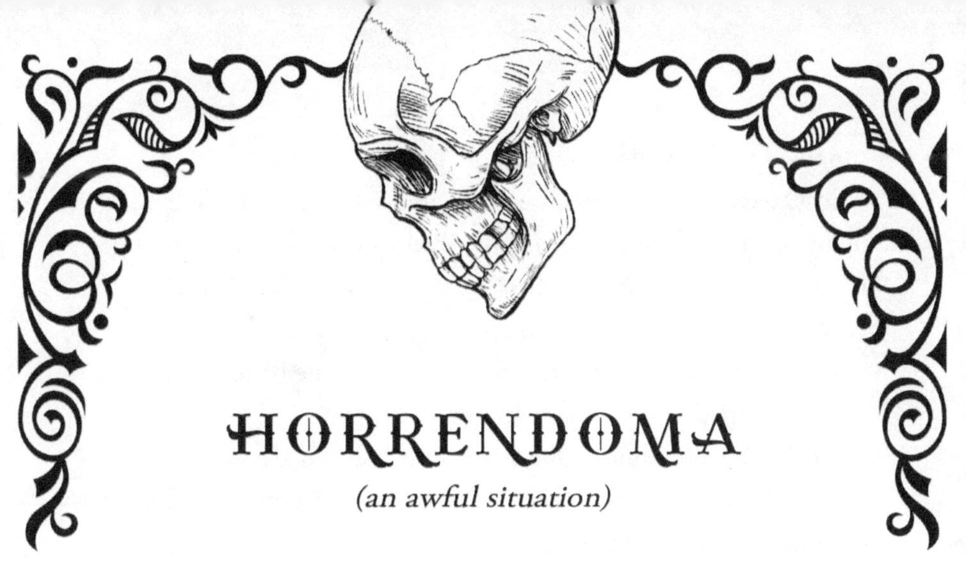

HORRENDOMA

(an awful situation)

Daniel yanked the library door open, desperate for a miracle. Instead of The Archive, all he found was the quiet staircase of Miguel's house, and Dorian Gray lounging on the top step. The cat looked up with an inquisitive meow, and Daniel cursed and slammed a fist against the door pane. Dorian bounded down the stairs and into the shadows.

Daniel had to breach The Archive somehow.

He considered all the keys scattered around the house.

Fitch must've found a duplicate. There was no black ribbon on the one he used to open the door.

Was it possible Miguel kept multiple duplicates in this infinite stash? The most secretive, important vault in the universe had to have multiple keys. What if one tumbled into a garbage disposal or a storm drain? Miguel would've had a plan.

On the other hand, the more copies that existed, the greater the risk.

But risk was Daniel's only hope.

He picked up a silver key and tried it on the library door.

The lock resisted.

Daniel tossed it over his shoulder. He remembered that Miguel's key didn't look like an obvious match for the library. The teeth were jagged and long, and somehow, it slid right into the tiny lock. It was supposed to fit any door.

So Daniel tried hex keys, car keys, and mailbox keys. He tried as many as he could fit in his hands, then discarded them in a large metal bowl. Every now and then, his resolve would build. *This has to be the one. Come on. Tell the universe what you want.*

And then he'd feel foolish and angry, and some of the keys even bent as he tried to force them into the lock.

Finally, Daniel sank to the floor, hopeless and devastated. He'd never be able to try every key in the house, and even if he did, he doubted he'd find the one.

He'd clung so hard to everything that he was about to end up with nothing. The pain was so acute that he *almost* wished Charleston Fitch had shot him. But he would never forget the *click* when Fitch cocked the gun. That sound had sent ice rippling through Daniel's blood. He'd thought that was the end of it, and he wasn't ready.

Think, dammit, think.

Daniel imagined himself in Miguel's shoes—the doctor, the man, the god. *Where would I hide an entrance to the most secret place in the world?*

He pushed himself off the floor, his body feeling like rubber.

Could Miguel have hidden something in a book? A highlighted passage, a secret code, or a hidden compartment cut from the pages?

Daniel surveyed the shelves, and the library seemed to swell and twist around him. Not for the first time, Daniel thought the space was an impossibility. It defied the confines of Miguel's house, infinitely more spacious than the outside had suggested.

Like The Archive, the books didn't seem to be arranged in any particular order. In general, Miguel seemed to keep biographies, historical events, and medical knowledge in the same areas. But Daniel also found an Oscar Wilde biography shelved among a few thrillers. A bread recipe book sat nestled between *The Fellowship of the Ring* and *The Bell Jar*. Agatha Christie's mysteries were scattered throughout, along with several books about plant life.

I saw Agatha Christie's candle, burnt down to a little ivory stub no bigger than the tip of my finger.

Daniel could pour through Miguel's keys and books for the rest of his life, and he felt he'd barely make a dent.

He shuffled down the stairs, where he found Dorian slinking around an empty bowl. When the cat meowed, Daniel rubbed his eyes so hard, dark nebulas swam in his eyelids. "I don't know when he's coming back, Dorian." He grabbed a can of cat food from Miguel's pantry and cracked open the tin. "You're a smart cat. I don't suppose you magically know how to talk, too? Because that'd be convenient right about now."

And moreover, stranger things had happened.

Dorian mowed down his cat food and disappeared into Miguel's bedroom.

The bedroom, Daniel thought. There were few more intimate spaces in a person's private life, raw and unfiltered. He never even went into Aunt Cass's room uninvited. But that also made Miguel's bedroom a strong place to look for clues.

And the room was so…well, *human.* A metal hamper contained a careless pile of laundry. Rubber-coated dumbbells and a Hope Haven coffee mug rested on his nightstand. A Linda Ronstadt record gathered dust on a Victrola while crisp white coats hung in his closet. Sometimes Daniel struggled to understand where Miguel ended and Death began.

Daniel thought of the flash drive in his sock drawer, where he'd stored his scathing letter to himself. It was one of his most private possessions—the kind of thing he'd never want Aunt Cass to see.

He rummaged through Miguel's sock drawer, and guilt gnawed at his gut.

All of this had started because Daniel had pried into something he wasn't meant to know. Aunt Cass had warned him; Miguel had warned him—twice. *Your time in The Archive is done.*

Am I about to make things worse? Daniel froze.

But Fitch's threats echoed in his mind.

No. I need to do this now. It's not for me…it's for Miguel, and for everyone else.

Unfortunately, all the sock drawer revealed was that his godfather had a taste for patterns and prints.

But at the foot of the bed, a laptop blinked on its charging cord.

Bingo.

Daniel opened it up and faced the login screen of Death.

Username: mhmortiz

Password: |

Daniel thought for a minute, chewing on his lip. After a long pause, he typed in *Dorian.*

The username or password is incorrect.

No. This, I can figure out. He cracked his knuckles. *I know Miguel better than anyone does, except for himself.*

Grimm

The loading wheel churned for a few seconds, filling Daniel with false hope.

The username or password is incorrect.

Ah, Daniel thought. He wasn't thinking complex enough. The computer would've wanted more from Miguel. Capitals, numbers, special characters. *I've got this.*

D0ri@n

The username or password is incorrect.

Gr1mm!

The username or password is incorrect.

God, this can't be that hard. Daniel grabbed a pad of sticky notes and scribbled a few ideas, plus different configurations of capitals and other elements he knew the computer would require. He tried different versions of Hope Haven. He tried every member of the

Grimm family. He even tried **Archive**, **Yersinia pestis**, and **Linda Ronstadt**.

The username or password is incorrect.

Before he knew it, Daniel had burned an hour and trashed thirteen yellow sticky notes.

"Dammit!" He slammed the laptop shut and brought a fist down on the cover.

Dorian looked up at him.

"What?" Daniel snapped. "Help me out here. What did you see? How do I get him back, Dorian? Huh?"

The cat let out a long, dramatic meow.

"Help me out or shut up and get out of here."

Dorian stretched and lay down on his paws.

So far Daniel had thousands of keys, thousands of books, and infinite possible passwords to Miguel's laptop.

What was he missing?

More minds.

Daniel took a deep breath, grabbed his phone, and dialed the only person left in the world who might still listen to him. *Please don't be a disconnected number,* he thought. *Come on, come on, come.* He closed his eyes as the phone rang.

"Hello?"

Relief surged through Daniel's veins and he jumped up from the bed. "Oh my god. Logan," he said. "This is Daniel Grimm. Is this a bad time?"

"Oh. Hey, Danny," Logan said. "How's it going? I mean, we're supposed to be taking a final right now, but apparently, they canceled class because…I assume you know about Schubes?"

Billy. Daniel hung his head and tapped the phone against his temple. He'd forgotten about Billy for a minute.

"I heard. It's awful, and I want to talk more about it, but listen," Daniel said. "How much information would you need to hack into a computer?"

Logan faltered a bit. "Uh, are we talking, like, logistical information or moral?"

"Logistical?"

"Logistically I can do anything," Logan said. "I do need some context, though, but not too much. If you're trying to hack the Pentagon or something, then the less I know, the better."

"It's literally life and Death, man, with a capital D," Daniel said. "There are lives on the line."

"Stop right there," Logan said. "*Are* you hacking the government? Because the system's fucked and I'm ready to burn it down, but I'm also trying to go to college and have a future first."

"It's not the government," Daniel said.

"Mafia?" Logan said. "Again, trying to have a future."

"No." Daniel sighed. "Just…I could really use some help right now. I don't know who else to turn to."

Logan paused. "I'm not committing until I know I'm not going to jail or dying. Where are you at?"

"I'll text you the address," Daniel said. "Come over. I'll tell you as much as you want to know. You can stop me at any time, and if you back out, I'll understand. But honestly if you just open this laptop, I will give you anything and everything, Logan. The keys to my car, or I don't know. You name your price, and it's yours."

"Jesus," Logan said. "Well, I can't say I'm not intrigued. I'll stop by and have a look. No hard feelings if I back out?"

"None."

"Okay. How soon do you need me? Do you mind if I, like, eat something first?"

Daniel bit his lip. Every second counted while The Archive was raging. Meanwhile, his stomach was doing the same. When was the last time he'd eaten anything?

He opened Miguel's fridge, slightly disappointed by all the

uncooked vegetables. "Can you bring me something on the way? Address coming."

"Yeah, sure," Logan said. "Dang, now I get *two* favors, huh?"

"Smartass."

"Kidding. See you soon."

The call ended, and after Daniel texted Logan the address, he stood in the center of Miguel's living room. For the first time since he'd run into Fitch, Daniel had a flicker of hope. He had a friend. The tricky part would be explaining everything that led up to this moment. Would Logan even believe it? Daniel had needed hard proof to believe in The Archive, and Logan was even tougher to crack. He enjoyed the occasional conspiracy and strange tale, but only because he was a diehard skeptic determined to find the cracks.

Keys.

Books.

Computer.

Daniel drummed his fingers on Miguel's laptop.

What other secrets do you hold?

About ten minutes later, Daniel flinched when a knock sounded at the front door, as sudden and forceful as a gunshot. He hadn't expected Logan to arrive so soon.

Dorian bounded up the stairs.

"'Ey, Miguel!" a man's voice boomed, but it wasn't Logan's. "Miguel, open the door! I wanna talk to you!"

Daniel thought of the moments when he'd been convinced that Miguel was a mob boss. By the thunderous sounds at the front door, it certainly seemed like Miguel had made his fair share of enemies. Someone was furious, but Daniel couldn't imagine who. A fellow doctor? Another detective?

"Please!" a woman added, and Daniel's heart skipped a beat. So there were at least *two* people outside Miguel's home. "Miguel, we can see your car's home! We know you're in there."

I hate to break the news to you, Daniel thought.

It felt strange to answer someone else's door when they weren't home. People were here on business he wasn't equipped to deal with, and the best he could do was send them on their way. He'd have to keep it simple. *Miguel's not home. I don't know when he'll be back. I'm his godson and…I guess now I'm looking after the cat.*

But it felt even stranger to open the front door and find two people Daniel knew. He knew them well, but he never expected them here.

By the blank looks on their faces, Zeke and Katie Grimm didn't expect to see him, either.

They're okay, Daniel thought. *They're both okay.* Katie's unborn baby appeared to be, too. Daniel closed the gap between them and threw his arms around them.

"Danny?" Zeke breathed.

Daniel couldn't remember the last time he had seen Zeke. It had been multiple years. In that time, Zeke had grown a short beard and he looked like he'd started living at the gym, his shoulders thick enough to serve a buffet on them.

"Hi," Daniel said.

"Danny, what are you doing here?" Katie asked. "I got this bizarre email with a video from Aunt Cass, and that's not possible because she's dead, and she looked *older* than I remember, and she was talking about Miguel. I think I'm losing my mind. I don't know how to explain it, and—"

"Katie, you should take a breath," Daniel said. "You don't have to explain a thing. I've seen the video, too."

"So Miguel's not here?" Katie walked in tentatively.

"Yes, and no." Daniel dry-washed his hands. "My best friend is on his way over. I asked for his help with something, and now that the two of you are here, maybe we can all figure it out together."

"Figure out *what?*" Zeke charged into the house and cupped his hands to his mouth. "Miguel! Get down here!"

"He is not here," Daniel said. "He's…beyond Death's door."

One way or another, Daniel would get into The Archive. He didn't know what he'd find in the middle of the storm, where he'd find Miguel or Charleston Fitch, or even if he'd survive the trip. But Daniel knew one thing for certain.

Miguel's promise had been truthful.

Through all the ups and downs, the sitcom moments and the dramas, Daniel was never alone. Hopefully that promise would be enough.

When I'm afraid to cross the bridge, that's when I need to do it.

Grimms don't run away when we're afraid.

"Death's door," Zeke repeated.

"Yes," Daniel said, "and that's where I need to go. The video's real. And so is everything Aunt Cass said. Can you please sit down? I have a lot to explain."

Maybe Katie, Zeke, and Logan wouldn't stick with him after he told the truth, but it had to be done.

Life was no sitcom. The universe was strange. Daniel wasn't sure the perfect universe even existed. Chasing it had been dangerous— not just for him, but for everyone he loved.

But for those people, Daniel would cross his bridge and put all of this to an end…even if it meant he didn't get to come back from the other side.

PART THREE

"The timing of death, like the ending of a story, gives a changed meaning to what preceded it."

MARY CATHERINE BATESON

"The Citadel ridiculed Sham-Yule for wishing on a fading star. But Sham-Yule knew better than all of them: He was the only one there when the star died. But he wouldn't waste the light it left behind."

FROM *SILVER, SPELLS, AND STARDUST,* THE UNFINISHED NOVEL BY SAMUEL J. GRIMM

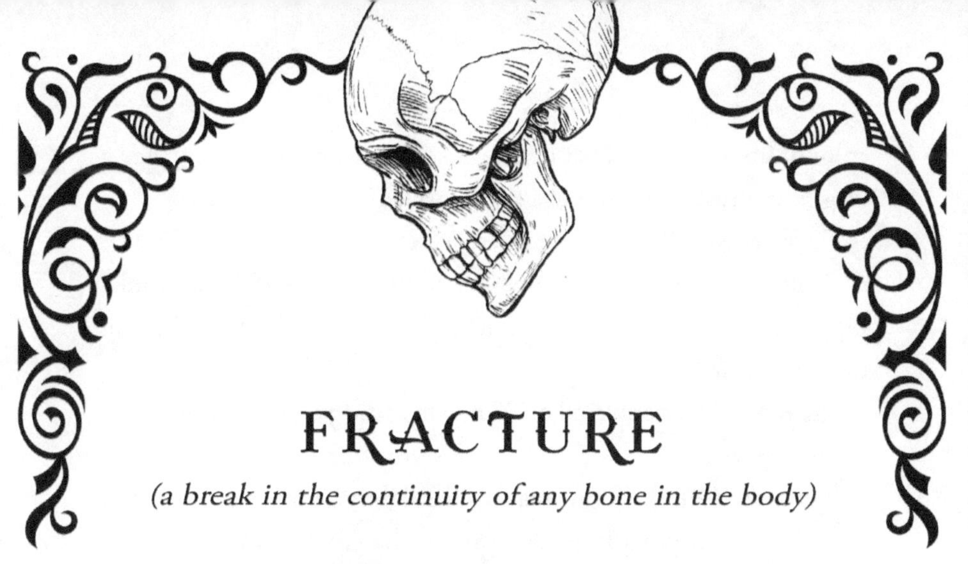

FRACTURE

(a break in the continuity of any bone in the body)

FIVE YEARS AGO

The man swayed on the Grimm Memorial Bridge, watching ribbons of moonlight twinkle and swell in the river below.

Above his head, bridges and pylons twisted into an Escher-like anomaly, and the ground thrummed against his boots. Car horns and motorcycle engines howled in his skull.

He was nine beers deep. He'd been trying to numb it all—the inner and outer noise—but now, even the air itself seemed to bend around him.

The moonlight was his balm. From where he stood, it reminded him of a watercolor painting or a candle flickering in the night. He reached for it, staggering slightly, and his long fingers closed over brisk, empty air. He caught the railing and steadied himself.

"Trying to catch a firefly?" a pleasant voice lilted. "I think you're more likely to catch a cold first."

The man turned, and he nearly leapt out of his skin when he faced the woman behind him. She had come from nowhere. He thought he would've heard the thick heels of her boots against the concrete, or her dress swishing in the wind. Though she was petite and wiry, her presence was large. Her graying hair cascaded down her shoulders in thick ringlets, and dark ribbons and lace—all the color of iron—adorned her dress. Most peculiar of all, she clutched a bright, multicolored umbrella that sparkled over her head.

The forecast called for clear skies.

"Hello." She waved and gave her umbrella a twirl. "It's awfully nippy tonight—much too cold to go swimming. Is that why you came here, sir?"

The man did a double take. "Wh–where did you come from?"

Another time?

"Crescent Gate." The woman spoke lightly and matter-of-factly, as if she were coming from the bank or the grocery store instead of the cemetery.

The man considered that she might have been a beer-induced hallucination, but he had seen her multiple times before. For seven years, he'd spent half his waking hours on the interstate. He made his routes across the Costa Linda Bridge, and she'd march her own parades in the opposite way. He couldn't count the number of times the umbrella stole his attention—a beacon of defiant joy. Rain or shine, she always pointed it in the air.

Out of necessity, the man had developed a rich inner life on the road. Thanks to the long stretches of highway, he'd learned to appreciate—or at least, tolerate—multiple genres of music. He loved silence even more, but too much of it was damning. The highway lull had a way of hypnotizing him if he didn't keep his mind moving. So he'd invent stories about the hidden gems and oddities he'd pass on his routes—the abandoned theme parks, the dubious gas stations and hotels, the waterlogged billboards pointing to nowhere...the woman on the bridge.

America was strange.

People were stranger.

Many times, the man entertained the notion that the woman could be a ghost. He passed her in the same place every time he crossed the bridge. Sometimes she clutched a cup of coffee in her free hand. Other times, it was a gallon of milk or a bag of produce. Most often, she carried flowers.

And the man would think, *What if…? What if she's a spirit?*

He had breakfast at a diner once, and he asked about her. The server knew exactly who he was talking about, and the customers overheard him and chimed in.

"That's The Gray Lady," they said. "She's a local legend. Everyone in Costa Linda knows about her!"

But soon it became apparent that nobody knew anything at all. They could only speculate, and every person had their own tale.

"She's a witch, you know. I think she cursed me once."

"There's more than one of her, and they're all actresses. That's why we see her everywhere."

"Not necessarily actresses; it's a top-secret society of umbrella people. One of them told me herself."

"If it's a secret society, why would she tell you?"

"There is only one Gray Lady, and I *adore* her. She's an icon."

"An icon? I offered her a ride once, and she refused. Not a nice person."

And now, in the man's darkest hour, here she stood. She'd found *him*. She held her umbrella over his head, and she offered him a soft, wrinkled smile.

"Sir, what's your name?" she asked.

The man scowled. "Don't pretend you don't know. You seen my face," the man said. "You know my name. And it don't matter anyhow. I ain't no one."

"I assure you, you are *not* no one." The woman extended her hand. "Tell me your name. There's power in saying it out loud."

"J…siah," the man muttered.

"I'm sorry," the woman said, "I didn't quite catch that."

"*Josiah!*" the man roared.

"Oh. I'm glad to meet you, Josiah," the woman said. "My name is

Linda. Won't you come and sit with me for a few minutes?"

Linda. The name sounded a bell in Josiah's head. She was a person. With a *name.* His mother's name, in fact. He wondered if this was one of those signs from beyond. She was nothing like his mother, but the name had a way of stirring up memories. All at once, he swore he smelled peach cobbler in the wind.

Josiah stumbled, and Linda caught him by the elbow, her grip firm and soothing. "Oh! I've got you." She turned him away from the river and guided him along the bridge. "Easy now. Let's find somewhere safe to sit."

Linda hooked her elbow around his and opened her umbrella, cocooning them both in a canopy of all colors.

She talked to him as they walked, but he was too focused on walking a straight line to process her words. Besides, the bridge traffic didn't relent at night. Every headlight was a dagger to his eyes, every car engine a sonorous roar. Some even honked as they passed by, and Linda simply kept on talking, as if she were in her own little world. He made out little words here and there: *found you, chilly, peckish, walking shoes.*

Before he knew it, he was sitting across from Linda in a bright diner, her umbrella folded up on the table as she studied a menu. A glass of water sat in front of him, the outside dewy with condensation. An eighties pop song played on a neon jukebox.

"I don't know why I bother reading the menu," Linda said. "I always get a grilled cheese. It's my comfort food, and I'm a creature of habit, you know. But perhaps I should be bold tonight. What do you usually like to eat?"

Josiah didn't even remember walking into the diner. It had been a while since he'd had a well-cooked meal; most nights he settled for ramen noodles, TV dinners, or bologna sandwiches. After all, he was a creature of habit, too. He didn't watch TV because he didn't want to see his face on the news. He was too depressed to read or pull the weeds from the backyard, or finish any of the countless house projects he'd started way back when. Most nights all he could do was put on some music and drink, or put on an old movie and drink, or just…drink.

"I think I *will* be bold tonight. I'm feeling breakfast for dinner." Linda shimmied her shoulders and smacked her lips. "What will you have tonight, Josiah? And it's on me, of course."

Josiah could feel the beer sloshing within.

"I'm not hungry," he lied.

Linda raised her hand and waved at the server. "Excuse me? Can you bring us two of the Charlie's Complete Breakfasts?" She made a peace sign with two fingers. "Please and thank you."

The server gave Linda a thumbs up and disappeared into the kitchen.

Josiah scooted toward the end of the booth seat, and Linda caught him by the hand again. "Please stay, dear. One meal."

Josiah jerked his hand away from Linda and rubbed his wrist as if she'd burned him. "I don't need your goddamn charity."

"Of course not." Linda sat up tall and folded her hands in her lap. Josiah remembered the man who complained that Linda wouldn't accept a ride from him. Some people complained she was abrasive and ungrateful, but maybe she was just proud and independent. "But I would really value the opportunity to share a meal with you. It's just breakfast."

The smell of home fries, sizzling bacon, and fried eggs wafted through the diner when the server returned with two full plates. Josiah's stomach bucked. He sank into the seat and put his head in his arms.

"Thank you," Linda said. "Now, may I ask you a question?"

Josiah grunted an ambiguous response.

"Why were you looking at the water like that?"

He lifted his head and scrubbed his hands over his face.

Linda leaned forward and whispered, "Is it because you wanted to die?"

"No," Josiah said. "I wanted to go for a midnight swim."

"Oh, good! You have the presence of mind for sarcasm." Linda grinned, then sipped her water. "I figured as much from the moment I saw you. You kept reaching for the light, like you had lost too much of your own. Wanting to die is nothing to be ashamed of, dear. Many of us have been there." She pointed to Josiah's chest. "But I don't think all the light is gone, you know. I think you still have a lot of it left."

"You don't know jack shit, lady. You ever seen the light go out in someone *else's* eyes?" Josiah put his fingers over his eyelids, trying to vanquish the haunting image that invaded his mind. "Have you?"

"Yes," Linda said, unflinching.

Josiah hadn't planned for a response.

"Three times on the same day," Linda added. "One by one, until I thought I'd lost my very heart. And I was responsible for all three, Josiah—at least, that's what I tell myself. I wasn't the only one driving that day. But if I hadn't gone back for my purse or if I had a faster reaction time, then *maybe* my husband and kids would still be alive."

"Car accident." Josiah shook his head. "Christ. You feel responsible for three deaths? I killed *ten*. Some of them were dead before I got out of the truck, while others died more slowly. Ringing any bells now?"

"I'm sorry. I don't keep up with the news. But let's not play hardship Olympics, Josiah; we all carry pain, and we all lose. It's a pointless game." Linda tapped the handle of her umbrella. "I know it hurts, but I certainly wouldn't want you to lose your light. May I tell you a secret?"

Josiah leaned back, exasperated. "What?"

Linda bit off a corner of her toast, swallowed, then wiped her lips with a napkin. "Would you believe Death talks to me sometimes?"

Josiah looked up, a question in his eyes. She wasn't smiling, averting his gaze, or changing her tone. She believed exactly what she had just told him, as plainly as if she had told him the sky was blue. "You some kind of kook or something?"

Linda waved the comment away. "I know how it sounds, but

he does. And he's a kind, wonderful man…not so different from yourself. I think he's also a bit lonely. It makes me sad sometimes when I think about him, but I'm delighted to know him. He's not the sinister, cold, ghastly type you would expect him to be."

"Yeah?" Josiah pressed his fingers against his temples. "Well, next time you see him, tell him I said he can *shove* it."

Linda frowned. "Now that's not very kind of you," she said. "But I tell him that, too, sometimes. He's used to it. In fact, if you ever told him yourself, he'd probably offer you a lollipop."

"Death would offer me a sucker," Josiah muttered. "Why the hell would he do that?"

"Why not?" Linda said. "Anyway, you and I could be friends if you'd like. Or not. I just don't want you to feel alone anymore."

"I'm never gonna be alone again," Josiah mumbled.

Linda's sad smile told him she knew he didn't mean this positively. Josiah had a shadow that would never leave his heel. He had a demon that rode firmly on his shoulders, its ankles chained together. He had mic-wielding reporters hounding his doorstep and threats teeming in his inbox, bolded and capitalized and written in many languages.

Most damning of all, Josiah had ghosts, and some of them weren't even dead.

"I'm simply stating that I think there's still more light left for you. That's all."

Josiah studied the woman across from him. "Used to think you were a ghost," he said. "I've seen you. Thought you lived on the streets. Now you're buying me dinner. What the hell is your story, anyway?"

"Oh, I'm very much alive," Linda said. "Flesh and bone and everything in between. And I don't live on the streets; I live in a little place about five miles north."

"And what's with…" Josiah gestured to the umbrella, then the dress. "All the walkin'?"

"It's for my family. Every day I walk to Crescent Gate and I sit with them. I carry this umbrella for my kids, and I dress up for my husband. And I tell them about what's been going on." Linda smiled. "It's nothing terribly exciting, I'm afraid. Trips to the grocery store. People I met on my walks. A book I started reading or a recipe I found, things like that. But they listen. They don't care if it's always the same. I don't either, for that matter."

"That's depressing as hell," Josiah said.

Linda shrugged. "I'm not alone, you know. People offer me rides, they stop and talk to me, and I meet interesting people everywhere I go." Her eyes cut to the doors as the diner bell chimed. "There's one of them now, in fact. The timing! Imagine."

A man strode into the diner, and when he caught Linda's eye, they both waved. The man made a beeline for their table. "Ah, dear Linda!"

Josiah felt exposed. No one could ever tell him a single detail about The Gray Lady, and now that he was drunk at her table, suddenly everyone knew her.

Linda stood and hugged the man. He was a full head taller than her, and he wore khaki pants and a light blue button-down.

"Miguel!" she said. "What a happy surprise."

"Likewise, as always," Miguel said.

There was something vaguely familiar about Miguel, like an itch in the back of Josiah's brain. One or two beers fewer, and he might've known where he'd seen the man.

Linda gestured to the booth. "Join me and my friend for breakfast? This is Josiah."

"Josiah…" Miguel tilted his head, "it's you."

The calm voice and the soft gaze snapped the pieces into place, and Josiah scrambled out of the booth. He felt like his bones were trying to get out of his body, and his skin couldn't keep up. He stumbled into the bar counter. Pain exploded through his arm.

Miguel was one of his ghosts…one of the survivors of the wreck on the bridge. Josiah had ruined his life, and he couldn't possibly face the man.

Liquid sloshed around in Josiah's belly as he made his way toward the door. Linda's voice swam in his ears. "Wait, Josiah! Where are you going?"

Anywhere but here.

Somewhere I can't be found. Somewhere even I wouldn't look for me.

Instinctively, his feet pointed back to the Costa Linda Bridge, toward water and the flickering moonlight. But he was tired. He felt heavy inside and out. His knees were like putty.

"Anywhere," he groaned, stumbling up a hill. "Anywhere…but…"

Here.

His knees hit the grass, then the rest of him followed.

He lost a battle against his eyelids as he stared out at the moonlight on the water.

The next time Josiah Retzlaff woke up, he lay in a bed so short, his bare feet dangled over the edge. He still wore last night's jeans with a baby-blue blanket draped over him. Sunlight brightened the unfamiliar room.

His head still felt like it was floating, and his stomach was tight, but as he sat up, the warm smell of steel-cut oatmeal soothed him. It steamed on a tray next to the bed, freshly sliced strawberries forming careful peaks in the center. There was also a steaming cup of tea and a handwritten note. Josiah rolled over and saw his boots neatly parked by the bed.

The panic of unfamiliarity gripped his throat, only to melt away when he picked up the note and read:

Josiah,

Hope you don't mind we put you to bed.

For what it's worth, I forgave you a long time ago. It's what the Grimms would've wanted, and I've certainly made some big mistakes *of my own.*

*   You're in good hands with Linda. She'll take care of you until you're ready to go home. She hasn't driven ever since the accident, but if you're willing, perhaps I could swing by and drive you home after my shift. Linda has my number. If you ever have a rough night again, would you call me?*

*   She was right, you know.*

*   You have a lot of light left in you.*

*   Trust me, your time is not up yet.*

In kindness,
Miguel H. Mortiz

Until that morning, Josiah thought he had been too numb to cry.

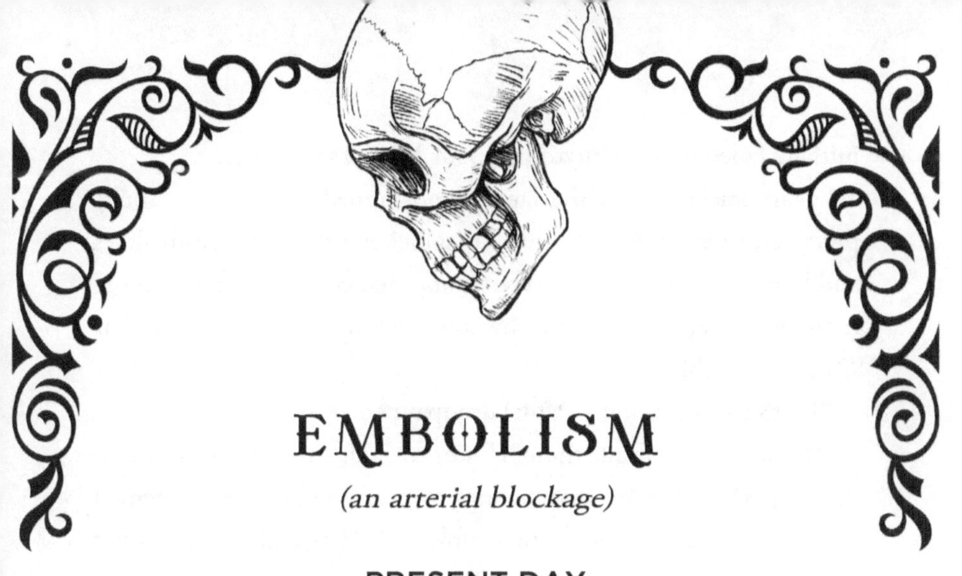

EMBOLISM

(an arterial blockage)

PRESENT DAY

The crackle of flames broke the dreary silence of Dr. Miguel Mortiz's living room. Daniel Grimm put his hands up to the fireplace and rubbed them together. He wasn't alone, but he hadn't heard a word in close to ten minutes.

"Can you please say something?"

Logan Thane crammed the last bite of his breakfast burrito into his mouth and chewed. His face hosted a wave of expressions before he finally smacked his lips and put his fingers together.

"So, to be clear…" Logan drummed his palms on Miguel's shiny black laptop. "You're saying you invited me over here hoping I'd break you into *Death*'s computer. Like, the Grim Reaper himself."

"Yes." Daniel was done treading lightly. "In a nutshell."

Logan raised his eyebrows. "That's chill. That sounds *way* less scary than hacking the government or the mob." He took a sip of his coffee. "I'm going to assume this is code for 'mind your business'? *The less I know, the better* kind of situation?"

"Maybe." Daniel wasn't sure what secrets Miguel's laptop would reveal, if any. If he had a miracle, he'd discover clues about how to open The Archive and what to do when he did. But Miguel wasn't the type to drop breadcrumbs. It was why Charleston Fitch had initially failed to learn anything about Miguel's existence.

Logan cracked open the laptop and tapped some keys. "You're pretty creative, man," he said. "Imagine? A list of our death dates and how we're gonna go? Maybe an app that counts down to the big moment? Since he's a doctor, he could call it like *Time of Death* or *DoA* or something."

"That's almost funny," Daniel deadpanned.

"It's not funny at all, though," Logan said. "You're asking me to hack a personal laptop that belongs to your godfather, who seemed like a decent dude when I met him at the hospital. I'm probably breaking about a dozen privacy laws, especially if I find patient records. I obviously don't believe the whole Grim Reaper thing, but this is kind of shady."

"Fair." Daniel sighed. "Does it mean anything that I believe he'd want us to get into his computer?"

"Respectfully, Danny, I don't know the man—I barely know *you*—so it doesn't mean very much at all." Logan cracked his knuckles. "But okay. I'm gonna do my thing. Give me twenty minutes, and I'll give you more than you ever wanted."

Daniel stood, his ankle popping inside his boot, and he stoked the fire. "How does it all work? How are you gonna get the password?"

"A magician never reveals his secrets."

"You are magic." Daniel chuckled under his breath. "Hey, Logan? Thanks for being here."

"Sure." Logan waved Daniel away. "Bye."

Daniel listened to the drizzle of computer keys behind him while he took the stairs up to Miguel's library. Halfway to the door, the smell of cigarettes and coffee stained the air. His interaction with Charleston Fitch would haunt him forever. He wondered where Fitch was now—if he'd found Miguel, if he was lighting candles or blowing them out, or if The Archive had swallowed him whole.

More importantly, where was Miguel?

Infiltrating The Archive would only be half the battle. If Daniel could breach it, how would he reverse the damage he'd done? How would he help Miguel finish his task?

What would become of Fitch, Aunt Cass, and the Grimms?

And me?

Inside the library, Katie lay on the couch with her knees bent and her feet up on the arm, a stack of books at her side. One book rested against her belly as she read aloud. When she heard Daniel's footsteps, she lowered the book and smiled.

"Hey," Daniel said. "Is *The Scarlet Pimpernel* giving you any ideas on how to get into The Archive?"

"No. I'm just trying to make the baby an early reader."

Daniel flashed a wan smile. "How are you feeling?"

"Oh, I'm living the dream," Katie said. "I'm surrounded by books. This one's making the baby kick. You want to feel? Watch. Put your hands right here. It's okay."

Daniel let Katie guide his hands to a spot on her belly.

He closed his eyes, and Katie held her breath. At first, Daniel felt nothing, but then, something fluttered.

Katie lit up. "She knows you're there."

Daniel laughed. "That was her?"

As if responding to Daniel's voice, three soft drumbeats pulsed against his fingers.

"She can hear you," Katie whispered. "Keep talking."

Daniel found something profound about realizing his sister was carrying life. Death had been following him everywhere—rippling through his universe—and now, a fresh life was blooming before them. "Hey there, weasel," he said, stealing Victor's word. "This is Uncle Danny speaking. I can't wait to meet you. Kick me once if you can hear me!"

The baby went still.

Katie yawned. "Now she's shy."

"Kick me twice if you want me to go away," Daniel said.

Three mighty drumbeats.

"Whoa!" Daniel let go, smiling from ear to ear. "I don't know what three means, but she's gonna be a fighter."

Katie massaged her fists. "Her mom knows krav maga and her dad's a *Mortal Kombat* champion, not to mention that all her aunties and uncles are tough as nails." She bit her lip and shifted her position on the couch. "By the way, Justin thinks I'm at this 'mothers-to-be' retreat with a friend. I didn't tell him I'm here, and you can't, either. He's already in raging papa bear mode these days. I promise to tell him the truth after all this is over."

The truth. Justin would be in for a few shocks.

"So, you believe me about everything?" Daniel asked. "And you don't hate me?"

"I'm processing," Katie said. "I know Aunt Cass almost better than I know myself. And that video she sent me? It's haunting. It's bewildering. In some ways, it's downright terrifying."

Daniel rolled his shoulders to work out the kinks. He had replayed Aunt Cass's video several times in his head.

I need you to listen to me very carefully.

"But I do know that it's real, Danny. I know it in my gut, just like I knew there was something different about Miguel. And was I wrong about him?"

Daniel picked up a key that looked like an anchor at the head. "You thought Miguel was a hitman who killed our family."

"Again, was I wrong?" Katie raised her brow, a bite in her tone.

Daniel discarded the key and ran a hand through his hair. "Katie, Miguel isn't our villain."

"Maybe he's not *your* villain, but Aunt Cass made herself crystal clear. I have a daughter on the way, and she will not grow up in Miguel's shadow." Katie closed her book. "I'm going to say this once. I'm here to help you, I'm here to help Aunt Cass, and I'm here for my daughter's future. But when it comes to Miguel, I could not care less about that man."

Footsteps pounded up the stairs, and Zeke lurched into the library, Dorian cuddled up against his chest. "I friggin' love this cat," he said.

Katie made an X with her fingers. "Keep that thing away from me. I am not a fan."

"That's kind of mean. What did he ever do to you?"

Katie wrinkled her nose.

"Are you working on the keys?" Daniel asked.

Zeke shook his head. "Nope."

"Why? I thought we talked about this," Daniel groaned. "Katie's looking through the books, Logan's working on the password, and you were gonna go through keys. That's what we decided."

Zeke put Dorian down and let the cat run loose. "No. That's what *you* decided. But *I* decided we're not doin' this."

Daniel did a double take. "Excuse me?"

"I said we're not doing this." Zeke made a broad gesture. "This *doors of death* thing. These magic candles. Breaking into our cagey godfather's secret life and messing with things that aren't meant for us. Do I need to be more specific?"

"Zeke…" Katie said.

"Are you serious?" Daniel asked.

"I'm dead serious."

"What about Aunt Cass?" Daniel asked. "You saw the video. Do you not believe any of this, or what?"

Zeke took a seat and jammed his hands into his hoodie pockets. "I believe there's something going on, yeah. None of this feels right, and that's why I'm calling this off. It's dangerous. Aunt Cass said it herself. Whatever Miguel has going on? We're not touching it."

"Stop putting it all on Miguel," Daniel said. "He didn't do all this."

"I know," Zeke said. "*You* did. You stormed into something you didn't understand, and your plan is to do it again? Without all the facts and details? Why do you do these things, Danny? Why would you mess with something so monumentally huge, and not even think to talk to me first?"

"Because you weren't *there*!" Daniel snapped.

Zeke's lips tightened.

"You weren't there," Daniel repeated. "If you had half the memories I'm carrying, you wouldn't be so quick to back out. You would want to do everything in your power to fix it. In your mind, Aunt Cass has been gone for years, and our family's always been here. But all I know is the opposite. I've been hollow for *ten years*, man. I survived. I had my friends and Aunt Cass and the little things I would do just to get through the day. For a while, I had you, too. But then you started keeping to yourself and you went to parties, and at the peak of all our sadness, you *left!* You left and you never came to check on us. I can count our conversations on one hand, Zeke." He held up a palm and flexed his fingers. "Just one."

Zeke opened his mouth. "Danny—"

"No." Daniel lowered his hand. "You left us, and Aunt Cass talked about that all the time. She felt like you weren't happy, and guess what? Now you get to carry that with you. So excuse me for trying to fix my biggest mistake, and excuse me for not telling you all about it before it happened. *You weren't there.*"

"You selfish, childish—"

"Knock it off, you two!" Katie snapped her fingers.

"Then tell him to stop acting like a two-year-old," Zeke said. "He needs to be put in his place!"

"How would Mom and Dad feel about you two snapping at each other like this? Huh?" Katie asked. "How would Aunt Cass feel about it?"

"By all means, keep the jabs coming, bro." Daniel paced in front of his brother. "I guarantee you won't tell me anything I haven't told myself."

"*Stop*," Katie hissed. "This is stressful enough without you two blowing smoke at each other. Do you want me to go into labor on this couch?"

Daniel and Zeke both went dead silent, mirroring each other's wide-eyed expressions.

"Please don't," Daniel said.

"Hell no," Zeke muttered.

Katie flashed a triumphant smile and rubbed her belly.

Zeke took a deep breath, then put a hand on Daniel's shoulder. His tone was softer now. "Okay, here's the thing, bro." He pointed at Katie. "*That* is why we're not doing this. Our sister's due to have a baby any day now, and that child's father isn't here. It's just us. You really want to be responsible for that? For delivering a kid?"

"Of course not," Daniel said.

"Me, neither," Zeke said. "So, we're not opening that door any time soon, Danny. Death can wait. There's a life to take care of first. I'm taking Katie back home first thing in the morning."

"Good," Daniel said. "I don't want her or my niece involved in what's happening. Or you. This is my mess."

"You missed the point," Zeke said. "You're done, too. I can't let you do this with or without us. If you meddle, you can ruin Katie's life. Or the baby's. We owe it to that kid to leave things alone."

"Zeke," Katie said. "I want to help Danny. *For* the baby."

"Help me open the door, and then leave," Daniel said. "I'm not gonna leave it alone. Charleston Fitch is in there, and Miguel's in trouble."

"You can't do anything about that," Zeke said. "We're gonna stop playing with keys. We're gonna stop reading books. We're gonna have some lunch in a bit, and we're gonna have a real conversation about all this. Stress-free. Go tell your buddy to put down Miguel's laptop and head out. He doesn't need to be a part of this, either."

"Too late!" Logan tapped on the library door, then slid in with

Miguel's laptop cradled in his arms. "Hi. Sorry to interrupt at the most awkward moment possible, but…" Logan slapped a sticky note against Daniel's forehead. "There. That's your password."

Daniel checked his watch. "That wasn't even close to twenty minutes. How did you do that?"

"I like to under-commit and over-perform," Logan said with a shrug.

Daniel peeled the sticky note off his forehead and squinted at Logan's chicken scratch. He never would've guessed this password in a million years.

c3V@sc0!_1875.

"Cevasco?" Daniel asked.

Zeke held out his hands. "Let me see?"

"Be my guest." Logan passed Zeke the laptop. "But I should tell you, I don't think—"

Daniel's breath left his body as Zeke raised the computer over his head, then flung it down the stairs.

The machine hit the floor, crackled, fizzled, and burst into several jagged pieces.

Daniel clawed his fingers into his hair. "Zeke, what the hell?"

Logan stared down at the laptop with his lips twisted to the side of his face. "Most people just say thank you, but okay."

"I say we're done." Zeke sauntered down the stairs, hands in his pockets. "End of discussion."

Daniel was at a loss for words. He looked at the dying ruins of Miguel's laptop, and all his hope died with the fading glow of the screen.

He crumpled the sticky note and crammed it into his pocket.

The clock was ticking, and all he had was a password to a dead end.

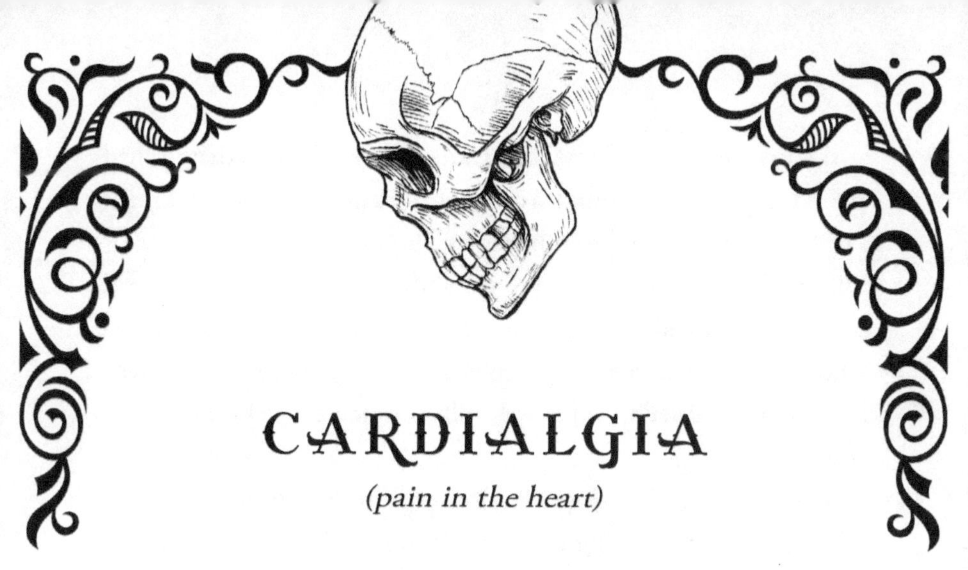

CARDIALGIA

(pain in the heart)

The ruins of Miguel's laptop lay dormant in front of Daniel, an impossible jigsaw puzzle of sharp plastic, cracked glass, and loose metal.

"It's not even a little bit salvageable, is it?" He picked up a piece of hardware that reminded him of a spider. "What the hell does this thing do, anyway?"

"That's an optoisolator." Logan took the hardware and bounced it around in his hand. "I'd explain it to you, but then I'd have to explain about fifty other things. Your brother really jacked this thing up. *Maybe* you could save the hard drive if you took it to the Circuit Sages?" He examined a chip with a disk shape inside. "But it would cost you an offensive amount of cheddar, and it wouldn't be quick."

Daniel tipped his head at the ceiling. Time was what he *didn't* have, and he wasn't in the mood for a trip to Electri-City, which was overpriced and overcrowded. "I don't know where to go from here," he said. "I thought Miguel's laptop could help me out."

Cevasco.

He couldn't believe he had been so far off from guessing Miguel's password. Of all the possible words, who, what, or where was Cevasco?

A hasty internet search pointed him to a locksmithing company in Florida, a professor of Italian cinema, and a rising ketchup brand as the first three hits. Somehow, Daniel doubted his godfather had crafted a password around a faraway locksmith, or a condiment Daniel had never even seen in Miguel's home.

Daniel's thumb hovered over the link to Dante Cevasco's email address. He hoped the password had nothing to do with a cinema scholar, which would only spotlight new avenues of mystery. Maybe he was an old friend? There was still so much Daniel didn't know about Miguel.

"Honestly, man," Logan said, "I don't think you were gonna find much. There was nothing there unless your godfather knew how to hide it. But there isn't much you can hide from me. Just saying. If you think his solitaire record would've helped your cause, then that's cool. Otherwise, I wouldn't even bother going to the Circuit Sages. Just…maybe have your brother save up some money to buy your godfather a new computer. This was a *nice* laptop. RIP."

Sometimes it bewildered Daniel that death could be referenced so casually. Colloquially, laptops and phones didn't lose power for a limited time, they *died. RIP.*

He wished someone like Victor or Nancy was around to cool Zeke's heels. Zeke had always taken his *eldest brother duties* seriously, but his temper had never been this precarious. None of the Grimms would have smashed a laptop like it was nothing.

"You don't have to stay here, you know," Daniel said. "I know it's awkward."

"I just want to understand all this," Logan said. "Selfishly, I'm getting all kinds of ideas for my podcast right now."

"You're still podcasting?" Daniel asked.

"What do you mean, *still?*" Logan asked. "I barely started. I'm only a few episodes in."

"I just wondered if that went away after everything in The Archive," Daniel said. "Macy and I were both there when you started your podcast. You were obsessed with this missing person's case, and something about a train to Switzerland."

"Me, you, and Macy," Logan said. "You're so sure it was always the three of us."

"Because it was," Daniel said. "We were best friends."

"So, what was it you were trying to repair?" Logan asked. "When I ran into you at the street fair, what was all that?"

Daniel chuckled. "You pissed me off. Aunt Cass told me never to contact Miguel, and you and Macy knew I contacted him, anyway. You kept it a secret for a while, until Thanksgiving, when you had a few sips of wine. And you let his name slip, and all hell broke loose." He touched his fingertip to a jagged plastic shard. Looking back, that dinner seemed so petty in the grand scheme of things. "Dinner was a bust. Aunt Cass started giving me the cold shoulder. Katie told me all about this Charleston Fitch she hired to investigate Miguel. I told you to have a nice life and tried to ghost you. And I pried Miguel's secrets out of him, and nothing was ever the same again."

"Huh," Logan said. "So, we were the kind of friends who had secrets and spent holidays together and stuff?"

Daniel tossed the shard aside. "Yeah."

Logan looked away.

"What's up?" Daniel asked.

"I just wish I could remember something like that," Logan said. "We're graduating soon, and it hit me the other day that I don't have…I don't have anything that's gonna last."

"What do you mean?"

"I mean, in ten years, there's gonna be a high school reunion," Logan said. "And I can't think of a single reason why I would go. I don't have any of those relationships that's gonna stick, you know? I'm not trying to be downer or anything, but it's pretty much just me, my mom, and my grandpa. And who knows how much longer he's gonna be around?"

Now it was Daniel's turn to look away. How could he tell Logan that Grandpa Weston wasn't meant to be here in the first place?

"I talked about you on my pod," Logan continued.

"Oh?"

"Yep," Logan said. "I did a whole thing about the Mandela Effect. What do you know about that?"

Daniel looked at his lap, his knee bouncing. "Macy and I got into an argument once. I had been thinking about a movie I saw when I was a kid. I remembered karate and bright, cheesy nineties outfits, and the villain was that guy from Phil vs. the Specters. I thought it was called *Fearless Warriors*, except Macy told me I was remembering it wrong. It was called *Fear the Warriors,* and the villain was Chris D'Agosto from The Vegas Thunderlings. We both dug our heels in, swearing there were hundreds of people who would back us up."

"It's *Fearless Warriors*," Logan said with a smirked. "With Phil Spektor."

"That's what you told us the first time," Daniel said. "You looked it up, and we watched it that night. But we also found internet threads and people at school who remembered it the same way Macy did. Only you don't remember anything about that, do you?"

Logan bit his lip. "I'd be lying if I said I didn't feel an itch right now. It's like when you're packing for a trip and you know you've forgotten something, but you don't know what it is. The funny thing is, Macy and I had a whole conversation about that recently. And we kept coming right back to you. There's something about you, Grimm. I don't know what it is, but it's activating that same part of my brain that swore the Monopoly guy had a monocle."

Daniel wrinkled his brows. "Wait. He doesn't?"

Logan waved Daniel's question away. "I think we should go see her, man."

"Macy?" Daniel asked. "I am *all* for checking in on my best friend. But Logan, I still don't think you understand how urgent this is. I need to get into The Archive *today*."

"I get that," Logan said, "or at least, I'm trying to. I do understand that you're not giving up on this, even though your brother's doing everything he can to stop you. That's about the only thing I understand right now, except that somehow, you have been through *hell*. I don't know if it's lasted for ten years, three days, or a few hours, but you need to take some time to breathe, man. Do you know how much a glass of water weighs?"

Daniel picked up the glass in front of him. "What does that have to do with anything?"

"It depends on how long you have to hold it." Logan took the glass away and set it by the fireplace. "Come on. One hour. You and me. We sit down with Macy, and we clear your head. No Grim Reaper talk, no magic candles. After that, we can dive right back into this."

"Logan—"

"You called on me to help you, and this is what you need," Logan said. "Trust me."

Over the next few minutes, Katie protested the idea of Daniel and Logan leaving the house. "It's disgusting outside," she'd said. And she had been right. Every time Daniel looked out the window, a new set of tangled weeds and blackened vines webbed the ground. Daniel could almost feel the earth thirsting beneath his feet, dry and touched by death.

Then she decided she would join them.

Zeke protested the idea of *Katie* leaving the house, but he yielded almost immediately and decided he would drive them all to Hope Haven.

Daniel wasn't in the mood to spend a single minute in his brother's company, but he had even less energy to argue. The only reason Zeke had yielded was because he thought a trip outside of the house would distract Daniel from his goal. It would do everyone some good if Zeke thought he had won—at least, for the time being.

The ride to the hospital pulsed with tension.

Some of the vines had slithered across the roads, and Zeke would slow the truck to get over or around them. The skies teemed with iron-gray clouds, and lightning flashed beyond the Costa Linda Bridge. Despite the grisly weather and the ominous vines, Costa Linda traffic flowed as if for any other weekday.

"This is your friend we're about to visit?" Zeke asked.

Daniel heard the question but chose not to answer.

"Okay." Zeke cut his eyes to the rearview mirror. "Great. Everything's cool, right? Also, 'Hey, thanks for driving us around in this hell weather, Zeke.' Sure, no problem. You're welcome, by the way."

"I didn't ask you to drive," Daniel snapped. "Logan and I could've handled it." The car bounced with a *whumph* as Zeke ran over a charred-looking vine. Daniel hooked his fingers around the bar that hung over his window.

"Uh-huh," Zeke said simply.

Daniel let go of the bar and dug his fingernails into his palms. *Uh-huh* boiled his blood more than any other response because it was condescending without saying anything at all. There was no good way to respond to it.

Katie reached for the radio controls. "Music?"

"That'd be good." Logan didn't look away from the window. His brows were wrinkled, the mask of a brain working overtime. Daniel imagined Logan's mind like an orchestra. Observers only saw a poised mass of people sitting still, and they heard the output—crisp, clear music. But only the players knew the complexities of synchronizing their breath, their thoughts, and the tiny, precise motions of their fingers, not to mention there could be over a hundred of them working at once.

Similarly, Logan could work derivatives and integrals without breaking a sweat, analyze the plot of a movie playing in the background, and still have fresh wits to crack jokes the whole time.

The stereo buzzed with static, and Daniel wondered if Logan's brain ever did the same thing.

Katie cycled through all the crackling stations before she turned the volume all the way down, sighed, and rested her head against the window.

Zeke reached for his phone. "Here. We can hook up my—"

"No," Katie said. "Just drive. Two hands on the wheel."

Zeke flexed his fingers. "Whatever you say, *Mom*."

A fresh layer of memories stabbed Daniel's chest as Zeke finished the drive in silence.

Maybe families were orchestras, too. When the players were in sync, the music bound their hearts together.

And when they weren't, then everything was just noise.

Hope Haven was different today. Daniel wasn't sure if it was his surly mood, Miguel's absence, or the grim weather, but the hospital didn't radiate its usual warmth. The waiting room was crammed. Half the staff shuffled around in the dregs of sleep, bleary-eyed with coffee cups tight in their hands, while others stormed around with feverish urgency.

Jan, the desk assistant, explained that only three people could visit Macy's room at a time. Zeke held up his hands in resignation and offered to take a walk. "Guess I'm just the chauffeur today," he muttered.

Daniel rolled his eyes.

"Should I go with him?" Katie asked. "Maybe you and your friend need some space."

"You can come." Daniel hoped somehow Macy and Katie would remember each other—that seeing each other's faces could lift some of the fog in their memory. "Let him sulk."

When they entered Macy's room, she was watching a game show, her eyes pink. Daniel thought she might've just woken up until he noticed the sticky film on her cheeks. She had been crying. She looked up at him, turned off the TV, and stared, her lips in a flat line.

Daniel stood, unsure what to do with himself, and gave her an awkward wave. "Hey."

Macy stared until Daniel looked away, and then she turned and smiled at Logan. "Hello again."

"Morning, Mace," Logan said. "I hope you don't mind, but I brought some friends with me this time."

Macy turned to Katie.

"You look familiar…" she said. "Have I met you before?"

A prickle crawled down Daniel's spine. When Logan arrived at Miguel's house, he told Katie the same thing. *Do I know you from somewhere?*

Katie rubbed the back of her neck. "I guess I have one of those faces. I'm Katie, by the way." She pointed a thumb toward the door. "Should I, um…?"

"You're fine." Macy crossed her arms and considered Daniel. "And *you*. Do you have something to tell me?"

Daniel jammed his hands into his pockets, his palms sweaty. Before he entered the room, the desk staff had taken their names and left to ask permission for visitors. He assumed Macy had known he was coming, or that she had had the opportunity to turn him away before he got there. "I just wanted to come and see how you were doing."

Macy arched an eyebrow and gestured around her. "Well? I'm here. Stuck in a hospital bed."

I deserved that. "How are you feeling?" Daniel tried again. "Do you get to go home soon?"

"Do I get to go home soon?" Macy repeated. "Who knows? What's the point? The doctors still can't figure out what happened to my heart. They keep saying it was some kind of anomaly and they're not sure it won't happen again. And on top of that, it's broken now.

My boyfriend is dead. Billy's *dead*." Her voice cracked, and Daniel wondered if this was the first time she had spoken those words aloud.

Daniel's fingers quivered in his pockets. "Macy," he said, "I'm so sorry about Billy."

"Are you, really? That's funny, because the only thing I know for sure about you is that you hated Billy." Her lips slammed shut, fighting back emotion. When she spoke again, her voice came out in a croak. "Did you come to tell me you understand my pain? That you know something about loss or that you can *fix* this somehow?"

"Look, you didn't have to let me in if you didn't want me here." Daniel pinched the bridge of his nose. "Logan, can we go? This was a stupid idea."

"No," Macy said. "I have something else to say to you."

Katie put a gentle hand on Daniel's chest, blocking him from leaving. He thought of Aunt Cass when she would drive him around. Any time she thought she was braking too hard, she would throw an arm in front of Daniel, even though his seatbelt kept him strapped tight.

Macy handed Daniel a business card from the nightstand beside her bed. "I wanted you to know that a detective came to see me yesterday. This was before Billy…" She swallowed. "Before Billy. And the detective was awfully interested in you."

Daniel took the business card, and his fingers twitched. The cardstock was gray matte, with silky black ink, and the design was simple. An odor of tobacco drifted off the paper.

CHARLESTON FITCH
PRIVATE INVESTIGATOR

"I know you didn't do anything to me or to Billy," Macy said. "But this guy seems to feel differently. I got him out of my room, but I don't know if I got him off your back. He didn't give me a good vibe, so…heads up."

Logan looked over Daniel's shoulder. "Charleston Fitch. That's the same guy you told me about?"

Daniel nodded stiffly.

Macy swallowed, her eyes suddenly serious. "He caught up with you?"

"Yeah," Daniel said. "He'd been watching me for a while."

"What happened?" Macy asked.

Daniel passed the business card back to Macy. She tore it in half and flicked the pieces into the trash.

"Danny," Katie said. "I think you should tell her the truth."

How?

Daniel rubbed his eyelids and leaned back against the wall. "Okay. Well, for starters…" Daniel pointed from Macy to Katie, and back again, "you've met before. We all had Thanksgiving dinner together a few weeks ago, and our lives looked different. The three of us were best friends, and I was living with my aunt. And that's just a snapshot of it all."

Macy scoffed, "Best friends, huh?"

"It's true." Daniel drummed his fingers on his elbows. "We celebrated Logan getting into Harvard. You two came with me to the principal's office when Mrs. Golden kicked me out of class. You used to practice tarot readings on me. And I swear, every goddamn day, I think about the last time you did that while the three of us were sitting in Logan's bedroom."

Macy's expression softened, and she drew in a quiet breath. She covered her lips with a fist, trying to hide her surprise. "I gave you a tarot reading?"

"Yep," Daniel said. "Do one for me now if you want. Maybe it'll tell you everything you need to know about me."

Macy swallowed, then sat up in her bed and straightened her posture. "What exactly did I tell you?"

"You knew the things I had been through," Daniel said. "Things I had lost…things no one today would possibly believe, because everything changed. We talked about how my godfather had just come into my life. I trusted you and Logan because I wanted to get to know him, and my aunt forbade me from contacting him. You were the one who encouraged me to follow my heart, but to be careful. I remember The Devil and Death and The Tower showing up. And now that I'm in the middle of the storm, your weather report makes all the sense in the world."

Macy picked at one of her cuticles. "My mother used to call them weather reports," she said softly. "That's where I got that from. She always said you can't stop the weather from coming—"

"But you can bring an umbrella," Daniel finished. "*You* told me that."

A single tear slid down Macy's cheek, and she brushed it away. "Your godfather…that's Miguel, right?"

Daniel nodded. "Dr. Mortiz is my godfather."

"He insisted I call him Miguel."

"I'm not surprised."

"You're lucky. I liked meeting him as my doctor. I'm sure he's an even better godfather." Macy swept a lock of hair away from her eye. "So what happened? Why did you need to be careful?"

"Because he's also Death," Daniel said.

Beside him, Katie pursed her lips. Logan leaned back against the wall, one ankle crossed over the other. Daniel waited for Macy to react—to laugh, scream, or cut him off—but she just tilted her head.

"Did you hear what I just said?" Daniel asked.

Macy took a sip of water. "Yep. Go on."

And Daniel told Macy the rest as simply as he could:

How he had pushed too hard and discovered Miguel's Archive.

How he had lit some of the enchanted candles, changing everything.

How Aunt Cass had recorded a video for Katie.

How Miguel vowed to help Daniel reverse the damage.

How Charleston Fitch had shown up and breached The Archive.

And how time was running out.

Macy was stoic the whole time, her expression unchanging. Daniel had left out the part about her family, or how Billy Schubert used to grate on her nerves.

When Daniel finished, he was out of breath.

Macy bit her thumbnail and shrugged. "Hmm."

Daniel swallowed. "*Hmm*? After all that?"

Macy pulled her pillow against her chest and hunched forward. "I've been keeping a diary of my tarot readings," she said. "There was an entry for the one you mentioned…about The Devil and The Tower and Death, and The Ten of Swords. I didn't remember pulling those, but apparently, I wrote it down that day. For days, I had been pulling cards that told me something was *off*."

Logan wrinkled his brows. Daniel remembered when Logan was in the room during the reading. He'd been an adamant skeptic. "You believe it?"

Macy narrowed her eyes at Daniel, studying him. "I want to. I hated Death for a while, but I knew he wasn't supposed to be scary." She bit her lip. "The thing is, I want to believe my family met someone like Miguel when they died."

"I bet they're so proud of you," Katie said. "I know we don't know each other, but for the record, I thought you looked familiar, too."

"Thank you." Macy squeezed her pillow. "If it's all true, then you need to fix it. You'll do it, right?"

Daniel buried his fingers in his hair. He was relieved that Macy didn't hate him, or fully disbelieve him. It was one of his only comforts now, because the weight of The Archive was tumbling back into his lap. "I don't know how to open the door and get back in. Miguel and Fitch literally had keys." He sighed. "Do you think I could force it open somehow? Like if I can't open a door, then can I knock out a wall or something?"

"That doesn't feel like a good idea," Macy said. "The point of a door is you need to be able to close it again. If you leave it open, the wrong person could get in…or something could get out."

Daniel sank into the chair by Macy's bed, feeling like his heart would just keep traveling through the tiled floor.

"Don't force it," Macy said softly. "Just knock, boo. Cevasco-style."

Daniel perked up, his heart skipping a beat. *Cevasco.* "Wait. What did you just say?"

"Cevasco," Macy said simply. "Sorry, that was an elevated joke. There's this old sculpture of a woman knocking on Death's door. I learned about it in art history one day, and then I saw it circling around on WowFeed a few weeks later. All I remember is the guy who did it was something Cevasco. It's a fun name to say, almost reminded me of Tabasco."

Daniel's eyes widened. He jumped up and grabbed Logan's shoulders. "Cevasco. Wasn't that Miguel's password? Cevasco and then a bunch of numbers?"

Logan blinked. "I don't see how that's gonna do you any good now. Remember how your brother Hulk-smashed the computer?"

"It has to mean something." Daniel bounced on the balls of his feet. "Katie, can you get on your phone and look up the sculptor, Cevasco? Death's door?"

Katie pulled her phone out of her purse and started typing. Macy looked pleased with herself, while Logan remained cool.

"Dude, do you think we're just gonna fly to Italy and start ripping up statues or something? Because, really, I don't recommend it."

"I dunno yet," Daniel said. "Whatever it takes."

"Got it." Katie waved her phone in the air. "This is Pietro Badaracco's tomb in the Staglieno Cemetery in Genoa. Giovanni Battista Cevasco carved a sculpture of Badaracco's wealthy mourning widow knocking on Death's door. Look."

Daniel zoomed into the photo, his heart quickening. A gray woman knocked on a bronze door set with a winged hourglass. She held a wreath, and several symbols embellished the area above the door: a compass, an anchor, some books, a globe, a ship's helm.

"Macy, you're a genius," Daniel said. "I don't know what's gonna happen next, but all of this is for you. You've always been at my side, and it's time for me to do something for you. I'm gonna fix this. Hang in there, okay?"

Macy's brows crinkled. "Did I really help you that much?"

"More than you know." Daniel passed Katie's phone back to her. "Are you ready? We should go find Zeke. Or I don't know, maybe we should leave him here."

Katie gave him a disapproving look. A Mom look.

"Hey," Macy said. "In case you didn't know…I believe in you. And no, I don't remember the way things were, but this is me *now*, and I have a feeling this will all work out."

Outside Macy's room, one of the nurses shouted, "Nancy!" and Daniel felt the name land like a tap on his shoulder. He couldn't believe he'd almost forgotten…

"Before I go…" He unzipped his backpack and removed one of the Ares candles. Nancy, Monica, and Ruthie had insisted that he bring it to Macy in the hospital. Daniel held it for a second. Their fingerprints still lingered on the glass. "I don't know if you're allowed to light this in here, but I wanted to give it to you, anyway."

"Ares." Macy accepted the candle and unscrewed the metal lid. She stared at the ruby-toned wax and breathed in the floral fragrance. Her shoulders relaxed as she exhaled. She closed her eyes, then painted on a smirk. "You know I'm a Pisces, right?"

Daniel rolled his eyes, mirroring her grin. "It's the god of war, Mace. To give you strength."

"Uh, *doi*." Danny couldn't help but notice she didn't correct him for using her nickname.

Macy waved her arms in. Daniel hunched over her bed and met her in a gentle hug. She closed her eyes and squeezed. "I love it," she whispered. "Good luck, Danny. I'll see you soon."

Daniel wasn't sure when he'd become such a hugger, but something about it felt right.

On the way out the door, Logan tapped Daniel's shoulder. "My guy, unless you plan to defile a tomb today, I don't see how this is any sort of breakthrough."

"We're *not* defiling a tomb." Daniel quickened his pace. "We're just going back to the library."

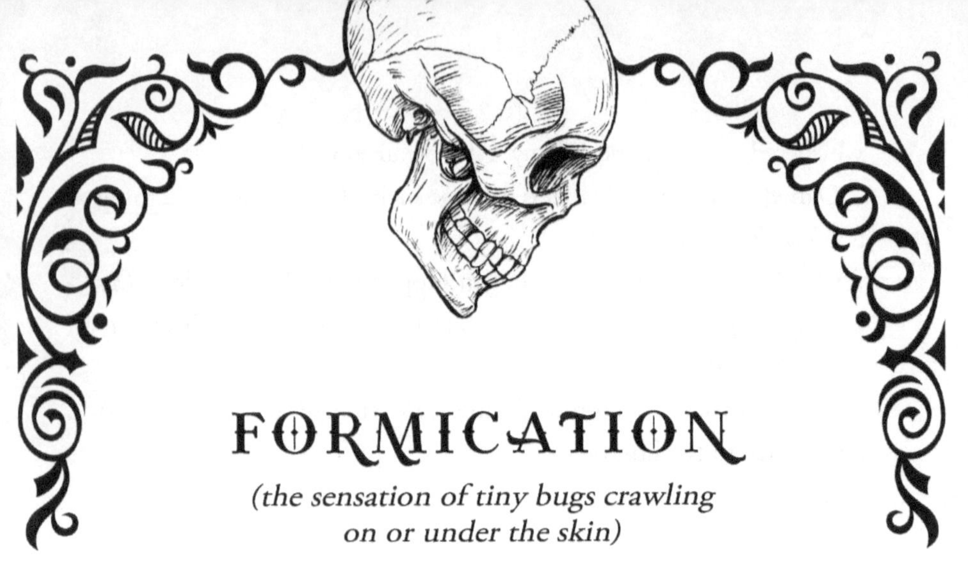

FORMICATION

*(the sensation of tiny bugs crawling
on or under the skin)*

"I *cannot* believe you're still on this." Zeke paced back and forth, his veiny hands buried in his hair. "Look, I thought we had an agreement here."

Daniel scooped a hefty handful of keys out of a mixing bowl and dumped them on the table. Logan spread them out and sifted through them. "I never agreed to anything," Daniel said. "I understand you're not part of this—you can leave in the morning if you want—but yes, I'm still on this."

"And much more optimistic now." Logan enlarged the photo of Cevasco's sculpture on his phone. "What are you thinking?"

"I'm thinking this was Miguel's failsafe." Daniel studied the list he'd made on one of Miguel's notepads. *Miguel wanted me to figure this out in case something happened to him. I'm sure of it now.* "All these symbols on the tomb? I've seen them before. And now I know what they mean. All the sites say the same thing. The wreath is for rebirth and renewal—victory over death. The winged hourglass is about the fleeting nature of time. The compass, anchor, books, globe, and ship's helm are all tributes to Badaracco's occupation as a ship captain. And we're among the books, so it feels like an obvious place to start."

"So we're looking for a key with one of those symbols," Logan said.

"An anchor or a wreath or something?"

"I *know* I saw a key with an anchor on it." Daniel let a handful of keys drip through his fingers.

Katie had been misting the library with rain-scented disinfectant, attempting to ward off the persistent odor of tobacco. She wiped down the couches and sat down.

Zeke slumped down next to her and buried his head in his hands. "Kate," he said. "Why are you encouraging this? Help me understand."

Katie's hand drifted to the contours of her belly. "We've discussed this."

Zeke tilted his head back against the couch and closed his eyes. When he opened them, his eyelids drooped. Daniel had always seen him as the paragon of calm—the natural second dad of the house. And he seemed to maintain order with effortless cool. Was Zeke just a master at hiding the stress until now, or had experience taught Daniel how to find cracks that had always existed?

Zeke and Daniel stared at one another, and neither said a word.

Dorian padded into the room and jumped into Zeke's lap, breaking his eye contact.

Fine. Take his side, then, Daniel thought.

"Found something." Logan shattered the silence.

Daniel whirled around. "What'd you find?"

Logan held up a jagged iron key and passed it to Daniel.

Daniel's heart danced in his chest. The head of the key was a smooth disk about the size of a quarter. One side was encased in a dusty glass lens, creating a sort of dome. Inside the dome, a tiny arrow spun about the center, the tip gently oscillating toward a fixed point. An ornate *N* embellished the top, though time had tarnished it. But there was no doubt that the head of the key was supposed to be a compass.

"Logan, you're the best." Daniel closed the library door and bolted the lock. "I'm gonna give this a try."

He leveled the key against the lock and drove it forward.

He might as well have tried to force his foot into a glove. No matter which way Daniel aligned the key, it didn't fit. He tried a few times, gritting his teeth, while Logan quietly suggested that it probably wasn't that simple. "I *know*." Daniel pounded the side of his fist against the door. "But I thought for a second that it could be."

"Danny," Zeke said, "this is exactly why I didn't want you chasing this. It's hurting you, and to what end?" He took the key and held it up to the light. "I mean, this isn't even a working compass. It might as well be a toy out of a cereal box. Most of Miguel's junk doesn't have meaning."

"The compass doesn't work?" Logan frowned.

"Which way would you say north is?" Zeke paused. "Anyone?"

Daniel looked out the window. He knew the sun rose in the east and set in the west. But the clouds had choked the sun away.

And when Daniel couldn't find the sun, he used the Costa Linda Bridge as a reference. If he knew where the bridge was, he could infer the rest.

He pictured the drive to Miguel's house.

Katie pointed toward the driveway, beating Daniel to the punch. "That's north."

Zeke copied Katie's movement. "That's north? See, I agree." He showed Logan the key, then pointed to the west. "So why's the compass pointing that way?"

"Because it's meaningless," Daniel said. "Point taken. Thank you. Let's just find the anchor one. I know I saw it around here…"

Logan walked around with the key, following the walls. "I don't think it's broken, though," he said. "I think it's just pointing to something in *here*."

Daniel found his bearings and followed his friend. "Something in here?"

Logan slowed his walk and scanned one of the bookcases, pointing the key flat in front of him like a remote control. "Yep. You know how it's all magnetism, right?" He shifted a few steps to the left, then to the right. Daniel watched the compass needle sway, adamantly fixed to the shelf in front of him. "It's something right here."

Daniel scanned the books.

A Global Perspective on Medicine.

Around the World in Eighty Days.

A Wizard of Earthsea.

"I think we're on track." Daniel's heart fluttered. "All these books have to do with the world, or the earth…or a globe."

"Like the symbol on the tomb," Logan said.

Daniel pulled a handful of books off the shelf and stacked them behind him.

Most of Miguel's shelves were made of pristine, glossy wood. But when Daniel moved the books, he noticed that this bookcase was different.

The back was made of a smooth, dark metal.

Daniel grabbed another handful, and Logan helped.

They cleared most of the books before Daniel found the keyhole on the bottom shelf. It was simple and small, perfectly camouflaged against the black metal and the shadow of the shelf above it. Nobody would've seen it unless they were hunting for it. "Bingo."

Logan held out the compass key. "Wanna do the honors?"

Daniel got on his stomach. When he took the key, it felt heavier than before, and his fingers were greased with sweat. It was like having a key to Miguel's car—an instrument that was powerful, dangerous, and fragile all at once.

The lock swallowed the key with a satisfying *zip*, and Daniel turned it to the right until something clicked behind the shelf. Then something *groaned*—the squeal of old gears churning as the floor hummed against Daniel's knees. He sat up, and when he tried to remove the key, the wall pulled it away from him.

The wall was *moving*. The library buzzed as the bookcase slid away into a hidden compartment.

Logan drew in a sharp breath.

Zeke swore, the syllable low and drawn out.

Katie squealed with delight.

And Dorian bounded out of Zeke's lap and pranced into the secret passageway that had just opened in Miguel's wall—a stone spiral staircase descending into darkness.

Daniel clapped a hand to his forehead. "No way!" He let out an exasperated laugh. "I can't believe that worked!"

"Oh my god," Katie said. "This is my childhood fantasy! I used to have dreams about this sort of thing."

"I know you did," Zeke said, "but hold it. You don't know what's down there."

Daniel had lost his fear of the dark long ago. People tended to fear the dark because it concealed the unknown, but Daniel found it comforting. Too much light drew his attention to the hollow, Grimm-shaped spaces in the world. Darkness masked the emptiness so Daniel's mind could fill it.

He leapt to his feet and stepped into the shadows, activating the flashlight on his phone. The musky smell of old books and damp dirt hit his nostrils. He pulled his shirt up to his nose, then steadied himself by putting a hand on the wall. The stairs were steep and narrow, and the descent seemed much deeper than the ground level of Miguel's home. With the darkness thickening, Daniel guessed he was going *underground*.

Logan, Katie, and Zeke called after him, their voices echoing down the stairs.

When they all met him at the bottom, he rolled his eyes.

"You didn't *all* have to follow me."

"I was *not* going to miss the chance to follow a secret bookcase passage," Katie said.

"What if the bookcase seals us in here? Someone has to be able to turn the key again."

Zeke rolled up his sleeves. "Someone has to protect you all."

Daniel shined the flashlight around the musty room, illuminating cobwebs, a small table with a magnifying glass and a pot of ink, and more shelves running from floor to ceiling. "The cat had no problem coming down here. What do you have to protect us from? A couple of black widows, maybe?"

Zeke flinched and danced in a full circle, swiping invisible *somethings* off his bare arms.

"I didn't know you were afraid of spiders." Katie smirked.

Zeke pushed his sleeves back down. "Nah, man, I just felt something tickle me, that's all." He cleared his throat. "So, where are we now? What is this?"

One major difference marked this floor of the library: each book looked like it weighed as much as a car tire. Daniel could've spread his palm across any one of the massive leather spines, and he still wouldn't have covered the full width of the book. From what he could see, none of the volumes had titles. They were simple spines embossed with various icons.

"The restricted section?" Logan joked.

Daniel traced a finger along one of the books, lifting a thick stripe of dust. "But actually, though." He realized in horror that an embossed skull had been raised on the spine of the book he touched. "This feels…forbidden."

"All the books have different symbols," Katie said. "Here's the sun, and a bunch of different phases of the moon, a pair of scales, a crow…This one looks like an origami bird. Pretty much every kind of tarot symbol."

Daniel remembered Miguel's smug response when he'd asked about all the keys once. *Past lives.* Maybe the symbols were a record of Miguel's avatars over the years. Another incarnation. Another key. Another book.

"Ah!" Katie used both hands to tug a book from its shelf, and Zeke rushed to help her. "An anchor."

"Easy." Zeke cradled the book from the bottom, staggering under its weight as he carried the book to the table.

Daniel spotted a lantern on the wall and lit it with his lighter. When the thin veil of firelight rippled through the room, he saw Dorian pawing at a spider web.

Daniel blew a sheet of dust off the tome and wiped down the cover with his sleeve.

"What's it say?" Logan peered over Daniel's shoulder, waving dust out of his face. "*Book of the Dead? Diary of a Grim Reaper? Necronomicon?*"

"Nothing." Daniel studied the blank cover, wondering how old the leather was. A century? Hundreds of years? However long it had been, the leather had aged well. It sported a rich, dark luster, and it was supple to the touch. Bound with multiple layers of twine, the inside pages had darkened over time, the edges jagged and tan.

"Open it up!" Katie grinned.

Daniel cracked open the cover, and a wooden ring rolled out of the binding. He caught it and held it up to the soft light of the lantern. The center glistened with a thin band of silver. "This is Miguel's." He slid it on his finger, and it was a perfect fit, like lock and key. "I always saw him twisting it when he was thinking. We're getting warmer."

He looked at the pages of the book, where someone had handwritten careful notes in black ink. All Daniel could tell was that it wasn't Miguel's handwriting; it slanted to the right and reminded him of a roller coaster—a track constructed with graceful loops and extravagant swipes.

"Is this French?" Logan asked.

"Let me see." Katie moved her pointer finger along the ornate script, silently mouthing the words. Every now and then, a few syllables escaped her breath, and then she would return to silence. "*Cher ami…peste…remedier…*"

Daniel looked at his sister in awe, feeling as though he hardly knew her. "You speak *French*? Since when?"

"*Oui, mon frere.*" Katie nodded proudly. "Justin and I have been using the Parlance app every day since our honeymoon."

"You honeymooned in Paris?" Logan asked. "How original. Sorry…that was jealousy."

"Never been," Katie said. "Costa Rica, actually. But we decided Paris was next on our list, and that we'd bring our kid one day. I don't want to brag, but my daily Parlance streak is flawless."

"*¿Verdad?*" Zeke inquired. "*¿Lo hiciste hoy, hermanita?*"

Katie blanched and muttered something in French. Her tone housed a grit that made Daniel wonder if she was swearing.

"Hey!" A sly grin spread across Logan's face. "I know what *you* just said."

"Can we focus?" Daniel stabbed the parchment with his pointer finger. "Katie, read the book. What does all this mean?"

"I can't translate every word," Katie said. "Parlance only got me so far. But this is somebody's letter to a friend. And they're distressed about an illness. They insist they're working on a cure."

"An illness?" Zeke repeated.

"That's what it says. Sometimes it's referred to as *le fleau*…and from what I understand, *le fleau* has more than one meaning. It's a plague, but it's also *evil*. It's a *curse*."

Daniel stiffened.

Katie turned the page and continued to mouth the words to herself. "They urge the reader to have hope, but also to take caution. The worst is yet to come."

Logan tilted his head and read the signature. "It's signed by *Michel de Nostredame*. Michel de Nostredame. *Dude.* That's Nostradamus!

Right? Nostradamus wrote in this book."

"The prophet?" Daniel asked. "*That* Nostradamus?"

"He wasn't just a 'prophet.' He was a lot of things. But the main thing is that he was one of the guys fighting the plague. He was a doctor." Logan flinched and held his hands up. "Shoot, I don't even feel like we should be touching this."

"You're not gonna get the plague from touching an old *book*," Daniel scoffed.

"I mean, I'm not worthy," Logan said. "This is a crime! This is Nostradamus's five-hundred-year-old handwriting sitting in your godfather's library, and I'm just…like a deeply average, basic-ass dude."

"You are *not* a deeply average, basic-ass dude." Daniel rolled his eyes.

"Unworthy," Logan said. "Put it away."

"No. Go get some medical gloves from Miguel's bedroom or something," Daniel muttered.

"How do we know that's the real Nostradamus's writing?" Zeke asked. "I could spend thirty bucks at Craft Country and forge something like this."

"Do you know enough French?" Katie asked.

"I can build up a Parlance streak; Miguel can do the same."

"Why would Miguel go through all the trouble to forge a letter from Nostradamus and hide it underground? Let alone an entire book of…whatever this is?" Daniel flipped to a random page, the parchment soft against his fingers. "And anyway, it doesn't matter whether it was the real Nostradamus. This is what Miguel wanted me to find."

"How can you be sure?"

"Because I see Miguel's breadcrumbs now."

When Daniel had turned sixteen, he asked Aunt Cass if he could get a tattoo.

"Sure," she'd said casually.

Daniel wrinkled his brows. "Really?"

"You thought I was gonna say no?"

"Well, I guess I just didn't expect it to be that easy. Just like that?"

"Why not? What's wrong with tattoos?" she said. "You'll be the one who has to pay for it, though. If you're willing to put in some time at the café on the weekends, I'll give you a little spending money. Or you can just go get a job. What are you thinking of getting?"

"I have no idea." He'd been thinking about getting something that represented his family, but he didn't feel like talking about that. "Something epic and badass, like a scorpion. Or a wolf howling at the moon or something."

"I mean, you do you," Aunt Cass said. "Just prepare for some pain, and a lot of questions about why. I don't care, personally. But my mom—your grandmother—used to say something about your outer world reflecting your inner world. I think there's something to that. She also used to say if you get tattoos, you're basically scarring yourself. But a scar tells the story of your body; a tattoo tells the story of your heart."

After that, Daniel never got the tattoo. He couldn't have cared less about the pain, but the real agony was trying to choose one design that conveyed a full story.

Then there was Miguel, who had an infinite history, and somehow managed to choose the perfect tattoo. The Grim Reaper on his arm packaged his sense of humor, the weight of his duties and humanity's fear of death, and a memento of one of his most important chapters: the plague in the fourteenth century.

Miguel's clues had guided Daniel back to that chapter: a tome from fourteenth-century France.

"Breadcrumbs, eh?" Zeke said. "Would've been nice of our godfather to tell us he was besties with *Nostradamus*. But I'm sure that's none of our business."

Daniel flipped to a random page—a sort of astrology chart.

When he flipped pages again, his heart skipped a beat.

At the top of the parchment, the words *En cas d'urgence* had been written in ornate, beautiful letters. But the word that caught his eye was smaller: *Archive*. And toward the bottom, someone had sketched what appeared to be a tower.

Daniel tapped Katie's shoulder. "Kate…" He touched the parchment, his heart quickening. "How much of this can you read?"

Katie wrinkled her brows. "The top says, *In case of emergency*." She cleared her throat. "*In case of emergency, you must go to The Archive and rekindle the dying flame at the…colonne du temps*? I can't remember what that means."

Daniel studied the flowing script, different from Nostradamus's right-slanting curls. If he squinted, it looked somewhat like Miguel's chicken scratch. He guessed *chandelle* meant candle, *flamme* meant flame, and *fin* meant ending, finish, or termination.

"*Colonne du temps…*" Katie repeated.

"The temperature of the cologne?" Logan asked. "Does Miguel wear cologne? Maybe we find it in his bathroom, and it needs to be heated just the right amount."

"*Column of Time*," Zeke held up his phone. "That's what *colonne du temps* means."

Daniel shivered. Macy's tarot reading couldn't have been more literal.

"I saw a tower in The Archive," he said. His bones tickled as he thought of the distant silhouette and the dissonant chime of the grandfather clock. He shuddered and rubbed his arms. "And I bet that's where Miguel's going. Somehow, that tower is the heart of The Archive. I think when I lit the candles, I affected the tower."

"So you think Miguel is trying to light a flame at this *Column of Time*," Zeke asked. "Why hasn't he succeeded? What do *you* expect to do that he can't do?"

"I really don't know," Daniel said. "But there is something I learned from all of this."

"Enlighten us," Zeke said.

"For ten years, I've been trying to carry my grief alone," Daniel said. "We all did. I would always go to the cemetery by myself. I tossed up walls in therapy, and I barely talked about my pain. You and Katie left Costa Linda. Even Aunt Cass would sort of hide in her café."

Katie tucked a lock of hair behind her ear.

Zeke looked at his boots.

"We've grown too used to doing things alone, and I'm not going to let Miguel suffer by himself in The Archive. Death may be a god," Daniel said, "but Miguel is our godfather. And right now, he needs my help."

Zeke sighed, closed his eyes, and pulled something out of his pocket. "I picked this up after the hospital." He passed Daniel a new key. "After I heard you talking about anchors and hourglasses and all that."

The head of the key was shaped like a wreath, and it was made of both metal and wood, but there was a hollow groove along the edge where something appeared to be missing. *Victory over death.*

"You had this one in your pocket this whole time?" Daniel asked.

"I didn't know if it would mean anything," Zeke said. "Hell, maybe it doesn't. But just in case it did, then I thought holding on to it was the best I could do to stop you."

Daniel traced the wreath with his thumb. "So why give it to me now?"

"I'm asking myself that same question," Zeke said. "Maybe I've realized I can't pull you away from this. And if I can't stop you, then maybe joining you is an opportunity to finally spend some time together. It's not ideal, but I have to admit, there's something kind of exciting about this. Or at the very least, it's nice. Me, you, Katie, and your friend are working on something together. It's like our sister just said; Aunt Cass would be proud to see it."

"I'm really sad for that laptop, bro." Logan pursed his lips. "That was a nice laptop."

"Yeah, well, Miguel's a doctor. He makes good money."

Daniel raised a brow.

Zeke scoffed and swatted Daniel's elbow. "C'mon. Sometimes I feel like you take me too seriously. I'll buy Miguel a new computer after all this."

Daniel removed Miguel's ring from his finger. "Yeah? Well, let's make sure we actually get through all this first."

He pressed the ring into the groove. It clicked neatly into the center of the wreath like the interlocking pieces of a jigsaw puzzle.

Then a fresh set of teeth sprung out along the key's edges, transforming it entirely.

Daniel's breath froze in his throat.

"What just happened?" Logan asked.

The key cast a silent spell over the room. Daniel couldn't look away from the wreath, the silver tendrils anchoring the ring in place and threading it into a more intricate design.

"This is it," Daniel said. "I'm positive. This is the spare key to The Archive."

"So now what?" Logan asked.

Daniel shrugged, then looked at his brother and sister. "I'm going in and looking for the tower."

The silence thickened. Daniel knew the possibilities. There was a chance that he'd never come out again…that this could be goodbye.

"Don't you mean *we're* going in?" Logan asked.

"Logan—"

"I didn't come all this way for nothing," Logan said. "I'm part of this, too. I want you to remember *I* cracked the password."

"There's a man with a gun in there, Logan."

"Then we'll have to get to the tower before he can get to us," Katie said. "I hope you don't think you're leaving me out of this. I promise I won't break. What if you need my Parlance skills again?"

Daniel took a deep breath. "I can't change your mind, can I?"

"Nope," Katie and Logan said in unison.

"I'm in a nightmare." Zeke pinched the bridge of his nose. "We'll never change her mind. She got her stubbornness from Mom." He put a hand on Daniel's shoulder. "No matter what, we look out for her?"

"We look out for *each other*." Katie gave Logan a pointed look, as if to say *You're family*. "All of us."

"Then I have conditions," Daniel said. "And I won't open the door until you agree. If I get any pushback from any of you, then I'm going alone. End of story."

Zeke looked resigned. He was used to being the leader of the house—Mom and Dad's second-in-command when they weren't around. When they were out, Zeke made the rules. Zeke *enforced* the rules. Zeke was the law.

But Zeke had never been beyond Death's door.

"Let's hear it," Zeke said.

"Number one." Daniel held up a finger. "We stay together. The Archive is huge, so I need to be able to always see you. This isn't a sightseeing adventure; you may not wander off."

"*Someone* doesn't remember wandering off at the zoo when he was four," Katie muttered.

"Second thing…" Daniel held up another finger, ignoring Katie's remark. "No matter what sort of temptation you feel in there, you may not light a candle. You may not blow out a candle. We leave everything exactly the way we found it. Is all of that clear?" He was starting to feel like Mom and Dad before a trip to a grocery store. *Stay where I can see you. Don't touch.*

Katie straightened her back, and for a moment, she looked just like Mom—strong, determined, and wise. "We're with you, Danny." She grabbed his hand. "One hundred percent."

Logan nodded. "I'm with you, too."

"You can't talk about this on your podcast."

"We'll unpack that later," Logan said. "Right now, I'm just here for a friend."

Daniel swiveled his gaze to Zeke. "Bro?"

Zeke massaged his knuckles. "I agree to your conditions," he said. "I'm with you."

Daniel closed his hand over the key, the fringes of the wreath biting into his palm. "Okay. Let's go upstairs and get what we need. Snacks. Water. Use the restroom…"

He snapped some photos of Miguel's book—the diagrams, the letter from Nostradamus, the *en cas de urgence* page. Then he returned it to its shelf, went upstairs, and grabbed his backpack. It had already been stuffed to bulging with belongings from his family—Victor's hat, Monica's candle, Mom's blanket, and some other things—but Daniel managed to cram it with some crackers, bandages, and other essentials. Zeke grabbed one of Miguel's umbrellas and filled a large water bottle. Katie packed some bandages, gauze, and some over-the-counter medicines. Logan grabbed a jacket from Miguel's closet.

And when they were ready with everything they needed, Daniel zipped the wreath key cleanly into the library door.

PYREXIA

(a fever)

During his life, Charleston Fitch had been shot in the leg, stabbed with a pencil, and tasered by a partner.

He'd worked undercover as a rodeo clown, as a stage crew member, and as a river tour guide.

He'd caught thieves, smugglers, and murderers on desert highways, in college laundromats, and in candy-colored toy stores.

He'd even died before, and somehow, he brushed it off.

Fitch thought he'd experienced everything.

Calm seas never made a strong sailor; a calm life didn't make a great detective.

And Fitch was one of the best.

There were two things he was always proud of. The first was that he always stuck with his gut. In the Costa Linda police force, he'd broken up trafficking rings and saved lives; he'd solved impossible cases. Opportunities started knocking on his door, and he knew he could've made a name for himself in the CIA or the FBI.

"Choose the bigger life, detective," recruiters had told him. "Make a difference."

But the truth was, he always felt he did better on his own.

Fitch resented the bureaucracy of it all. The system was built with strings attached…the cold weight of hierarchies and surveillance.

And partnerships came with a vulnerability that had burned him before. He'd been betrayed by more than one kind of partner, and he swore he'd never be fooled a third time.

So Fitch kept his guard up in every aspect of his life. He worked solo, charged his own rates, set his own hours, and he was his own best partner.

Ivy, his daughter, was his second pride and joy. She was his light.

Fitch held on to a mental image of her as he pushed through Death's door—the razor-thin boundary between the world he knew and the beyond, the liminal space between logic and madness.

Stepping into The Archive was a new kind of mind-numbing experience. His feet dragged, and his vision spun as the ground twisted like the floors of a funhouse. The temperature plummeted about thirty degrees. With every step, Fitch retraced touchpoints of his daughter's life.

When he stumbled, he remembered scooping a six-year-old Ivy off the sidewalk the first time she crashed her bike. Her lips were curved into a heartbreaking pout as she reached for him.

When the frigid wind whipped at his cheeks, Ivy was nine, reaching a mittened hand to him for support in the ice-skating rink. Only this time, she was telling him everything he'd once said to her.

Grab on!

Look, get your balance. My hand is right here, and I won't let go.

Steady…okay. Now let's push off with one leg. One baby step. Come on, I've got you. Now move your other leg, and…there! See, we're moving!

Fitch remembered the joy on her face when she realized she could skate.

He also remembered how she toppled over a few seconds later.

The ground rushed up to meet him, gritty and harsh against his chin. Darkness exploded across his eyelids. All the sensation melted from his cheeks, then his fingers.

Dying had felt something like this…like color leaking from the body. Like a light slowly dimming. First there was pain, and then there was nothing.

And then there had been Ivy—sixteen and toughened by life.

Get up, old man. This is a pathetic look for you. Am I supposed to feel sorry, seeing you like this?

Fitch groaned, his lips barely parting.

And inch by inch, he willed life back into his bones. He wiggled a toe, and he summoned the strength to flex an ankle. His ring finger twitched, and an icy sensation traveled through his palms and into his wrists. Then he clawed at the ground, slushy and amorphous in his hands, and heaved himself up into a sitting position.

Snow matted his hair and eyelashes. It soaked his socks, adding weight to all the little threads. Clumps of it clung to his jacket. He spat a rivulet of grit out of his mouth, and when he looked up at the dark sky, a new white flake descended onto his tongue and melted away.

Fitch picked up his fedora, swatted the ice off the brim, and fixed it back on his head. He'd moved to Costa Linda to escape winter, and this certainly wasn't part of the plan.

The Archive was supposed to be a library of lives, not the afterlife. *But it's hell*, he decided.

But it *was* magnificent…after he flexed and blew the life back into his fingertips, massaged the warmth into his toes, and got his heart pumping again, reality settled over him.

Infinite shelves each contained a row of tiny flames…a mosaic of lives burning defiantly against the snowy conditions.

Fitch swiped a film of frost from one of the windows and peered inside. Shanice Thomas's flame danced on the head of a blackened wick, while Enzo DiLegno's had been reduced to little more than a smoldering ember.

A spark flickered in Fitch's bones.

His distrust and independence—his sheer resolve—had paid off. He'd chosen the bigger life.

Had he remained with the police force, they would've kept him on a leash. A partner would've held him back. He never would've discovered this place.

He was intelligent enough to see through the cracks in Miguel Mortiz's facade—to ask the questions that had teeth.

He was bold enough to track him down in his home—to pursue the god of death and find his Archive.

Those were people's histories written in wax. Those were their *lives*.

Fitch had only known fire to destroy beautiful things. He'd watched it reduce sturdy houses to flaky rubble. He'd seen it swallow the fragments of past relationships—letters, Polaroids, and mixtapes. Even when he lit his cigarettes, Fitch knew the lighter was chewing minutes off his life. But the power was in *his* hands every time.

Fitch put his hands up to the glass.

This was the fire of creation. What it stole from the wick, it sculpted in memories.

He'd seen his share of lifeless bodies before, and it was always the eyes that got him—glassy, dull, and unseeing. He'd never paid much attention to that twinkle until he'd seen the ones who lost it.

And looking at these candles, Fitch wondered, *Were these the source of that gleam?*

Katherine Grimm would never know how much she had changed his life.

"I was wondering if you could do some digging on my godfather."

By all counts, her request had been deeply unremarkable. When people hired Fitch to investigate someone, that someone usually wasn't a stranger. It was *family*.

"I think my husband's sneaking around with his boss."

"I think my sister's dating a cult leader."

"I think my son-in-law came here on an alien spacecraft."

Most of the time, their suspicions were wrong, and all Fitch unearthed were embarrassing histories.

By the time Katherine Grimm had reached out, Fitch was dripping with ennui and exhaustion. The money was nothing to complain about, but he wished people would start growing brains and backbones.

Your godfather did not *order a hit on your family. When will people sit down and have some goddamn conversations for once?*

That was what he thought, but what he said was, "Sure thing, kiddo. I aim to serve."

And sure enough, this godfather…this Miguel Mortiz, started as another average Joe case. *He takes his coffee black and averages two cups a day. He buys his groceries at Food King. Here are his receipts.*

Fitch couldn't pinpoint the minute when things started to feel wrong. He only knew that it excited him. Why couldn't he find a birth certificate, or a degree, or any evidence of Miguel's past? A family? Finally, someone with a real shadow.

And now Fitch was *here*, in Death's domain, with a key in his pocket.

Most people only dreamed of finding something this important.

But most people weren't worthy. They would share it with the world and expect glory. They'd want to be touted for unveiling the Fountain of Youth. But Fitch knew that in the wrong hands, the key was an atomic bomb.

There was power in guarding a secret. Because once you shared it, it spread like a virus and diminished your power. He didn't need the glory. All he needed was his daughter.

"Thank you, Katherine Grimm," Fitch whispered, the words rising in a white puff of air against the cold. She would never know what a vault her godfather had been protecting. She'd suspected he was some kind of monster, but she'd failed to recognize that he was a dragon all along…hoarding gold, casting a shadow over the world as he engulfed it in tiny flames.

Fitch followed an aisle of shelves, wiping the frost from the windows. While he trudged through the snow, he mouthed the names to himself.

Vaughn.

Suresh.

Kane.

Cordova.

Zhang.

Rosenfeld.

Fitch froze, then retraced his steps.

The names weren't even arranged alphabetically—not by first name, not by last name.

He turned in a full circle, watching the pinpricks of light extend into infinity. There must have been billions of lives recorded in The Archive. How in the world was Fitch supposed to find *one* if they weren't arranged in order? He could walk for all eternity and never find Ivy Fitch. One candle was a needle in a haystack.

He reached into his coat and produced his lighter and a pack of cigarettes, half empty.

And as he lit his cigarette, he felt the comfortable weight of the gun in his inner pocket.

An idea bloomed in his mind.

He emptied the chamber. Two rounded bullets *clinked* together in his palm. He rolled them around a bit, each one cold and heavy, and he considered his position.

He could work wonders with two bullets and one candle.

And if he couldn't find the candle, then he'd have to get the attention of the god who knew this place—the dragon who ruled the den. He pushed the bullets back into the chamber. When he closed it, it clicked.

If Dr. Mortiz was the dragon, then Charleston Fitch would be the knight.

BRADYKINESIA

(slow movement or reflexes)

The Grimms used to rely on a bit of old folk wisdom about how *the third time's the charm*. Grandma Alba was an avid fan of fairy tales, especially those that followed a "rule of three." She believed in threes with all her heart, and when her family needed comfort, they turned to the mantra like a spell or an old recipe.

Daniel remembered Mom reciting this wisdom for Zeke when he tested for his driver's permit. *"The third time's the charm, Zekey. I swear it."*

Dad recited it for Monica when she poured her second batch of candles. *"You know what your grandma would tell you right now? The third time's the charm, kiddo."*

Aunt Cass recited this to Daniel when she taught him how to bake scones. The first time, they came out too dry. The second time, the flavor was off—more bitter than sweet. The third time, The Queen of Cups herself employed her stamp of approval: The scones were perfect.

And the third time Daniel faced an open door to The Archive, his mind didn't fight. The door opened, the wreath key turned effortlessly in the lock, and his body stood firm as he faced the hidden world. He let out a sigh of relief, then turned to his siblings and his friend.

Zeke had a glazed, hollow look in his eyes.

Katie's eyelids drooped, and her lips parted in a quiet exhale. "I…" she said.

Daniel grabbed Katie's hand. "Take one deep breath in, everyone. In through the nose."

Katie took a rich, full breath, held it, then let it out slowly. She blinked as if coming out of a trance, and a single tear fell from her cheek. "It's so beautiful," she breathed.

"Logan!" Daniel caught his friend by the elbow as his knees buckled. His breath was strobe-like and shaky. "It's okay. This is real, but you won't get hurt here…not if we're careful." Daniel snapped his fingers and gave Logan a gentle shake. "*Logan.* Deep breath in, now. Do it with me."

Ugh, Miguel was so much better at this, Daniel thought as he yanked everyone back to reality. Miguel had been patient, gentle, and calming. Daniel decided he would never possess the bedside manner, no matter how much his younger self liked to play with stethoscopes and bandages.

This was a terrible idea. Daniel had nearly fractured their minds already. There was still the Fitch problem, and they needed to light a flame in the Column of Time. He considered grabbing the key and leaving Logan, Zeke, and Katie behind.

Something cold tickled his nose. He brushed it away with the back of a finger, then saw the brittle fronds of a snowflake melting away. It was *snowing* in The Archive. And as long as the door was open, that snow would spill into the library, too. Daniel had never experienced snow before.

While Daniel assessed the situation, Dorian dashed through the doorway and pounced into a blanket of snow that only exposed his tail.

"Dorian!" Daniel gritted his teeth. If the cat froze to death on this journey, that would be a whole new crisis to explain to his godfather.

The deep, dissonant toll of the grandfather clock lurched in the distance, rumbling books on the library shelves. The sound was even more haunting than before, and Daniel shivered.

The Column of Time.

When the toll faded, Logan gasped as if coming up from water, and Zeke shook his head as if to clear it. Katie pulled her hands away from her ears.

"What is all this?" Logan rasped.

"Come on." Daniel put a hand on Logan's back and guided him through the doorway. "We need to close the door. We'll walk and talk."

He removed the key, took a final fleeting look at Miguel's library, and closed the door behind him.

The doorway vanished, and they stood in an aisle of candles.

Daniel's throat itched when he saw how much The Archive had changed. The sky was darker, and the flames pulsed around him—some snapping on and off like strobe lights, while others blinked out forever. Some candles had been reduced to stubs, but the flames reappeared. A few windows had been broken, icicles climbing up the shelves.

I'm gonna fix this. Daniel picked up Dorian, dusted the snow off his fur, and gestured around him. "This is it," he said. "Remember what we talked about. Don't touch. Don't wander. Are you all still with me?"

Zeke blew into his hands and rubbed them together. Logan peered into one of the bookshelves, where a candle flickered mightily. Katie looked up at the sky, her eyes wide with wonder.

"When Miguel brought me here," Daniel said, "he walked me through the five senses. Do you all feel the snow under you?"

"It's cold as *hell*." Zeke hugged himself. "I don't know how to deal with this level of cold."

Daniel assessed Logan's expressions. He'd been expecting awe, confusion, or wonder, but instead, all he saw was a deep look of pain.

"What's going on, Logan?" Daniel asked.

Logan spun in a slow circle. "It smells like butterscotch in here."

He swallowed. "Why does it smell like my grandpa's truck?"

"This place always smells like a memory," Daniel said, his eyes slamming shut as a pang of guilt stabbed him. "Something that reminds you of someone you miss."

Logan leaned back against one of the glass cases and buried a hand in his hair. "Grandpa," he choked, slumping down. "I remember now. I remember the way things are supposed to be...I remember the day we lost him."

"Man," Daniel said, "I am so sorry I didn't talk to you about this sooner. It's one thing to ask you to wrap your head around this whole place, but your grandfather—"

"I need a moment." Logan stood, clawed a teardrop from his cheek, and stormed away, swearing under his breath.

"Logan!" Daniel said. "Don't—"

"Don't go too far. Stay where I can see you, *whatever*," Logan muttered, the snow crunching under his shoes. "I got it. Just leave me alone for five minutes."

Daniel bit his lip as Logan disappeared around the corner. It hadn't been this tough on Logan the first time he lost Grandpa Weston. At least, he hadn't pushed Daniel away when it happened; in fact, Logan had come to Daniel and Macy when it happened. Logan had been able to say the words Daniel always seemed to swallow before they got past his throat: "*I need you two right now.*"

The three of them had picked up sodas and a bulging bag of dollar cheeseburgers and had driven up to a lookout on Mount Naranja. The moon had been silver and full, and the bridge looked smaller from the lookout, like Daniel could squish it between two fingers. And sitting there with his friends, he felt fuller, stronger. Logan spun incredible stories of his grandfather's life—some he'd even written down—and Macy and Daniel listened, laughed, cried, and marveled at how Logan carried himself in the face of grief.

But grief was never as clear or consistent as it appeared on one particular day, and it was one thing to lose a hero. Losing them twice was a full twist of the knife.

Daniel rubbed his elbows. What if Fitch was around that corner? He could be *anywhere*. The Archive was infinite, but Daniel's luck was limited.

A strangled sob escaped from Katie's throat, and Daniel looked to see her and Zeke in a tight embrace, her head against his shoulder.

Daniel set the cat down and wrapped his arms around his brother and sister. He didn't ask why they were crying.

He knew.

The Archive had awoken their memories.

They remembered everything.

"It was real," Katie whispered. "Aunt Cass's video. All of it was real."

Daniel watched her breath come out in little white wisps that dissipated into the wind like ghosts. "Every word," he said.

"This place smells like her." Katie produced a tissue from her purse. "A minute ago it was Thanksgiving stuffing. And when we first walked in, it was Dad's hugs."

A breeze blew past Daniel's nose, and he caught the aromas of coffee, cream, and spices. He could taste the Aztec mocha on his lips. *Magic wake-up juice.*

In an instant, the scent changed. It was a creamy, fruity popsicle with bubblegum eyes—the kinds the twins left all over the house.

It was buttery pancakes and maple syrup.

It was warm paper, fresh ink, and the punch of Sam's highlighters.

It was the Costa Linda Street Fair—nachos, kettle corn, and the Grimm Goddesses' candles.

It was Xander and Victor sitting in the graveyard—wet grass and faint cologne.

Zeke was the one to break the silence, his voice rough and husky. "You know the way the house always smelled after the New Year parties?"

Time had weathered most of those memories down to pebbles, but fragments hovered from their last New Year's Eve, when Daniel was finally allowed to stay up for the countdown. "Champagne," he said. "Even though most of us only got to have sparkling cider."

Sam and Monica had used fake British accents all night, sipping white sparkling cider and pretending it was champagne.

"This fahncy champagne is quoite strong and bubbly, innit, Mon-Mon?"

"Bobbly, yes, Sahm. Deloightful. But nawt neeeeely strong enoff, dahling."

"Puh-hops we'll orduh something stronguh on Chewsday."

"Yes. Puh-hops Chewsday."

Zeke chuckled to himself. It was the first semblance of a laugh Daniel had heard from him in a while. "Heh. Chewsday," he muttered.

"Chewsday!" Katie clapped her hands to her cheeks. "Oh my gosh, I can't believe I forgot about that."

"Monica and Sam were such clowns. And then Aunt Cass used to lecture Mom and Dad because the Christmas tree was still standing. She said it was bad luck if the tree was still up on New Year's Day." Zeke hugged his knees, and Dorian nuzzled up next to him. "That's what I smell. Pine. Champagne. And a little bit of spicy queso."

"And silly string," Katie said wistfully. "We were all together for that. I wish I had known that would be the last one."

On one of the shelves behind Katie, a candle went out, quick as a breath. A thin plume of smoke coiled above the wick, then broke into nothing.

"You wanna know something?" Daniel asked. "Aunt Cass stopped feeling Christmas the last few years. She tried, mostly for me, I think, and her customers. But I knew she was struggling. She had me decorate the café, but the most we did at home was a tiny plastic tree. And you know what's funny?" He paused. "I don't remember her lecturing Mom and Dad about the tree. Last year we had our little one up until like, February."

A thoughtful silence passed, and Katie wrapped the cord of her hoodie around her finger. "You know, there are probably so many things about our lives that would make more sense if we just started talking about them. So many memories we could unlock."

"None of us have ever been great at that." Zeke scratched his beard. "Talking and feelings have never been my thing."

Katie balled up her tissue and stuffed it in her purse. "Well, we can work on that. Together. Right, Danny?"

Daniel nodded. "We can work on it together."

"It feels good, doesn't it?" Katie said. "Like when you said *Chewsday* and started talking about New Years, I felt them here. It's like they were with us."

Daniel unzipped his backpack and pulled out Victor's hat. He spun it on his finger, flipped it a few times, and rested it on his knee. "I think…I think they always have been." He took out Mom's blanket, shook it open, and draped it over his sister's shoulders. He watched her inhale the lavender scent, her muscles relaxing. "They started to remember some things they shouldn't have been around for. They told me a story about your wedding, Katie."

Katie wrinkled her brows, running her fingers along the blanket's fringe. "My wedding?"

"Xander and Vic. They said the whole family was there. They were at the reception and everything. They love Justin. And they said when you were walking down the aisle—"

"Dad was behind me," Katie whispered.

Daniel nodded.

She closed her eyes and covered her mouth, taking a second to collect her emotions. "I felt him that day. I heard him whisper in my ear."

Dorian's tail swished around like a serpent, and Zeke held him close. "I know the exact moment you're talking about. I was walking you to the altar, and there was this moment where you *stopped*, and I remember this chill going right through me…like *full* body. And I smelled Dad." He swallowed. "I always told myself it was just a draft or my mind being silly. But I think about it every goddamn day."

"And all this time, we never spoke about it," Katie said quietly.

"No," Zeke said. "But today's a start. And it's a beautiful thing, Danny, what you just told us."

Daniel put the hat on and zipped up his backpack. "Maybe we'll start getting together on New Year's again?"

Katie pulled the blanket close. "I'd really like that."

Daniel paced around to get some blood flowing again. "So, what did he tell you? What did Dad say when you were walking down the aisle?"

Katie's lips fluttered, and then she put a hand over her heart. "I think…I think I'm going to keep that one to myself for now," she said. "If that's okay."

"Of course." Daniel traced the felt line around Victor's hat.

He welcomed the promise of sharing more with Katie and Zeke, and learning more from them. But he knew each of them would have their own special moments to keep to themselves. And that was okay.

"While we're talking," Katie said, "I've been thinking a lot about this place. And about Charleston Fitch."

Daniel's lips slammed shut.

"I remember the day I hired him now," Katie said. "And I feel awful about it. I remember that day with Miguel and Aunt Cass… when I came home and saw them come out of the pantry. They were *here*, weren't they?"

"It makes sense. Aunt Cass wanted us to stay away from Miguel because she knew about this place. He showed it to her, and then she blamed him for what happened to our family." Daniel paused. "Do you blame him, too?"

"I don't know," Katie admitted. "I don't think I do, but I don't necessarily forgive him, either. Can you forgive me for hiring Fitch?"

"You didn't know what would happen," Daniel said. "I could've done the same thing. Can you forgive me for messing up The Archive?" He gestured all around him.

Zeke set Dorian on the ground and shook out his limbs. "I can't promise I wouldn't have done the same thing. I won't ask if you forgive *me*, but I'm sorry I tried to stop you, and for all the times I wasn't there for you. I'm sorry for everything, actually."

Daniel shook his head. "No. I lashed out at you earlier. You were always clear about why you left Costa Linda, and it wasn't fair of me to expect you to come around. I never felt like you were leaving me and Aunt Cass behind." He shrugged. "I just missed you. We both did."

"Trust me," Zeke murmured, "there wasn't a whole lot to miss."

Katie's eyes widened. "Why would you say something like that?"

"Because my life hasn't been worth keeping up with. Most people find it impossible to be around me." Zeke sighed. "It's not like I blame them. Danny, you found your friends, and you stuck with Aunt Cass. Katie, you made a career and fell in love. Me? I just took my anger with me and held on to it." He clenched his fists in front of him. When he unclenched, his palms were white. "And it wasn't toward any of you, obviously. It wasn't toward Death, or any higher power. I guess it was a little at myself…and a *lot* at Josiah Retzlaff."

The name prickled Daniel like a wasp.

Katie looked away, and Daniel saw her jaw move.

Zeke furrowed his brows. "What was that look?" he asked. "Both of you."

Daniel reached for Katie's hands and helped her stand up. She rolled her shoulders and clutched her back, wincing.

"I'm gonna go check on Logan." Daniel cleared his throat and marched away.

As he walked, he read the names on The Archive's candles and mouthed them to himself.

It took twelve names to bleach Josiah Retzlaff's from his brain.

He hadn't thought about that name in years.

VEISALGIA

(hangover)

FIVE YEARS AGO

Josiah Retzlaff had a conundrum.

Ever since the accident, the driver's seat of a car made his body feel like a Rubik's cube—every joint tight, every organ twisted and out of place, heart in his throat, and stomach knotted. His mind would hiss with static. He could barely touch a set of keys, let alone a steering wheel. It all seemed to burn his fingers.

The passenger seat made him feel powerless and small. The seat belt became a prison cell—a dagger to his dignity.

He'd grown up in an old-fashioned home. His dad worked in a factory and his mom ran the house, and they'd both instilled Josiah with a bone-deep sense of pride. *Get in the arena and earn every dollar. Take no handouts.* Dirty hands were a badge of honor.

The only solutions Josiah could entertain were to walk, bike, or ride the buses. The problem with the buses was that people knew his face. He could buy a brief semblance of peace with a baseball cap, some sunglasses, and a shave, but some people still had a sixth sense about him. They'd stare, move seats, cross themselves, get off the bus, or curse him entirely. Perhaps he hadn't masked his walk well enough. Perhaps they saw the phantoms sitting on his shoulders.

But nothing made Josiah feel smaller than the passenger seat of Dr.

Miguel Mortiz's sedan.

Where had it all gone wrong? It had only taken a millisecond on the Costa Linda Bridge. Before then, Josiah was *happy*. He wasn't living a thrilling life, at least not in the ways that he used to dream about. There was a time when he longed to be a lawyer. He didn't have an obsession with policies, a thirst to argue, or a calling to defend the innocent. He just figured they made good money, and *maybe* it would be enough for Josiah to see the world.

Driving trucks wasn't so bad. He saw enough. He earned his keep and lived up to his parents' values. He worked hard. People needed their goods, and he was doing the community a service.

He never imagined that, five years later, he'd be sitting with a survivor from a collision he'd caused…and that *that* survivor—a trauma doctor, no less—would be driving him home.

Miguel was a stark reminder of the future Josiah hadn't finished building, and the ones he had destroyed. Josiah didn't want anything from him, but all Miguel wanted to do was give and give and give.

"Feel free to change the radio station."

"You're welcome to adjust the heater if it's too much."

"This water bottle's for you, by the way."

Josiah couldn't even bring himself to curse Linda for phoning Miguel—for *insisting* that he don't walk home in the pouring rain. She'd fixed him breakfast. She'd nursed his hangover. She'd allowed him to shower up. She'd even lent him a change of clothes straight out of her late husband's side of the closet, stuffed with everything from flannels to chinos and well-worn boots.

Josiah looked down at the army-green Henley she'd given him. *Another remnant of the dead,* he thought. It wasn't his style, but it was certainly his size, and Linda had given it over with a joy Josiah couldn't understand.

"Why are you people helping me?" Josiah asked, cutting through the ballad on the radio.

Miguel powered up the windshield wipers and tipped a finger toward the window. "I mean, if you were actually *wanting* to walk in this weather…"

Josiah swallowed his words. He needed to start filtering them more carefully. The worst part was that Miguel's statement didn't come off as a threat, but as an offer—a concern.

What was the catch with this guy? Did he have some sort of Superman complex? Mr. Holier Than Thou running a charity so he could brag and tout his superiority?

"That wasn't an answer." Linda had warded off Josiah's headache with carbs, fluids, and ibuprofen, but the dull pain was crawling back into his temples. "Never mind. I know you. You ain't helping me because you think I deserve it. You're helping me to feel better about yourself."

Miguel scrunched his mouth to the side. "Is that the answer you want to hear?"

"God!" Josiah massaged his temples. "Stop asking me what I want and stop *giving* me things! Told you I don't need no charity, and I don't deserve your help. Tell me how you feel and kick me out of this car already."

Miguel glanced into the rearview mirror, pulled into the next lot, and parked the car. He left the windshield wipers on, the rhythmic squeaks washing away the silence.

"Here's the thing," Miguel said, his voice deep and low. "Your recklessness destroyed a family I loved. You already know that. You demolished a part of me—a piece of my heart I never thought I could feel. There's nothing I can do for *you* that will make *me* feel better. And you certainly don't seem like the type of man who accepts help. So what are we to do about all this pain, hmm? Drown it in cheap beer? Hope the river carries us away?"

Josiah said nothing. His fingers bounced on the door handle, but he couldn't bring himself to pull it.

"You think dying will honor their memory?" Miguel continued. "That won't buy them back."

"I can't *live* with what I *did*!" Josiah slammed a fist down on the glove box, the words bursting from him like cannonballs. How long had they been trapped in his throat? How long had he been trying to swallow them and douse them in alcohol?

And the effects were strange. After the words came out, Josiah inhaled, and it felt like the fullest, cleanest breath he'd taken in years. Freeing the words opened up several passages in his body. They burned cobwebs from his brain. They severed a knot in his chest. They opened his lungs.

Startled and embarrassed, Josiah scrubbed a hot tear away with his sleeve. He could feel Miguel's gaze on him, soft and curious.

"Don't even want to see myself in the mirror," Josiah choked.

Miguel switched off the windshield wipers, leaving only the sounds of steady rain drumming on the windshield and the gentle breath of the heater.

"May I respond to that?" Miguel asked. "Or do you just need to let it out? Because I can listen, too."

Josiah cleared his throat. "You can say what you need to say."

Miguel sipped from his water. "It's more common than you think," he said, "wanting to throw in the towel because you can't even look at yourself. I see it every day. I've been there. But maybe that's when you can let someone *else* see you."

Josiah watched a raindrop slide down the window, first slowly, and then gathering momentum as it sped away.

"The Grimms used to see me when no one else did," Miguel said. "The best way I know how to do right by them is to try to live like they did. They were always helping people, always making the space for people to be who they are, always unlocking the best in others."

Josiah appreciated Miguel's honesty. Maybe he wasn't driving him home to be patronizing or saintly. It wasn't an act of kindness for his ego; it was an act of service for the Grimms. For Josiah, this was still a bitter pill, but he could swallow it. For the Grimms.

"So what about Linda?" Josiah asked. "Why did she help me even when she found out what I did?"

"Because she sees you." Miguel shrugged. "That's just who she is. She can make just about anyone feel at home."

But did she have to invite me to Christmas dinner? Josiah thought. Why would she do that? She must have crossed paths with half the population in Costa Linda over the years. How many did she share holidays with? How many did she clothe and cook dinner for?

"She told me Death talks to her sometimes," Josiah said.

Miguel flashed a sideways smile. "Did she now?"

"That's what she said," Josiah muttered.

"That's fascinating," Miguel said. "Do you believe her?"

"I think it's a load of bull-honky."

"I think it's rare and special to meet anyone who cares what Death has to say. I imagine even he needs someone to see him." Miguel stroked his chin. "Or she. Or they. Who am I to tell Death's story?"

Josiah had never believed in fate or higher powers. There were only actions, consequences, and the occasional spoonful of dumb luck. But if other people found comfort in invoking gods, goddesses, and personifications of life's cruelties, then he could respect their rights. He wouldn't have felt better either way, so he simply let it go.

"How're the rest of them?" Josiah asked.

Miguel wrinkled his brows. "Come again?"

"The ones who survived." Josiah traced his finger along the seatbelt. "There were a few other kids, no?" Three, in fact, plus their aunt. Their faces had been seared into Josiah's mind for ages.

The car freshener swayed back and forth under the rearview mirror, and Miguel watched it with a note of melancholy on his face. "Yeah, there are a few."

Josiah finally opened his water and took a sip. "Can you tell me something about them?"

Miguel thought for a minute. "Well," he said, "I can tell you they're strong. Cassandra, Zeke, Kate, and Danny. There's nothing they can't handle, especially when they're together. I heard this legend once about a flower that can withstand any weather when you plant more than one of them together. Freezing temperatures, droughts, I've even seen photos of them sticking out of the ground after a tornado tried to rip them out. And that's the Grimms...a burst of defiant color in a dying world. I just wish they saw themselves that way."

The idea was a balm on Josiah's soul. He'd wrecked the Grimms' lives, but this man...this Miguel Mortiz saw them thrive. Josiah had to admit Miguel had a grounding sort of presence. He was calm, kind, and genuine. If the Grimms had nothing else, at least they had Miguel.

"You ever tell 'em that?" Josiah asked.

A soft chuckle escaped Miguel's throat. "It's been a while, unfortunately. Cassandra and I are no longer in contact. We had a falling out, and I haven't seen the kids since...I'm not sure when."

Josiah's relief was short-lived.

Miguel's words were a pin to a balloon. He must've seen the disappointment in Josiah's eyes. "It's alright," he said. "It's nobody's fault. It's just the way things end up sometimes."

Josiah recognized the shame in Miguel's eyes. Miguel didn't fully believe his own words. He felt responsible for whatever had driven them apart.

They'd both put down all the bricks they were capable of laying in a day, and Josiah was exhausted. As much as he wanted to know, he couldn't pry anymore. He turned the radio back up as the rain settled to a dull drizzle.

"House is a little farther along," he muttered.

Miguel switched the wipers back on and put the car into gear. "You got it."

They didn't speak for the rest of the drive.

Josiah couldn't stop thinking about Linda and Miguel and the Grimm family. For some reason, he couldn't stop thinking about the rain, either, and how the same weather that nurtured healthy flowers also extinguished powerful flames.

RHINORRHEA

(a runny nose)

PRESENT DAY

Daniel found Logan in an aisle around the corner, sitting against the shelf with his knees tucked against his chest. He didn't say anything when Daniel approached.

"Can I join you now?" Daniel asked.

Logan shoved a pile of snow away from him, then patted the wet patch of grass he'd exposed underneath. Daniel was amazed to see the grass still thriving—healthy emerald blades twinkling in the candlelight. He sat on the patch and didn't say a word.

"I'm about ready to go," Logan said, his voice gravelly. "Sorry I slowed you down."

"You could never slow me down, man." Daniel picked at one of the grass blades. "If anything, I'm the one always holding you back. Now that you know everything, do you hate me?"

"Do I hate you?" Logan echoed. "Damn. That's a bold question. This is, like, a monumental screw up. Off-the-charts nuclear."

"Yeah," Daniel said. "I deserve that."

"But do I *hate* you?" Logan repeated. "God. Haven't we been through everything together?"

Daniel gestured at the sea of candles around them. "Nothing like this."

"This small thing we're dealing with?" Logan scoffed. "This cosmic rabbit hole I followed you into?"

"Logan," Daniel said. "Put the wit aside for a second. We need to get going, and I need your head clear. Tell me what you're thinking and let's work this out."

Logan put his forehead on his knees, the muscles tight in his forearms. "Dammit, Grimm," he whispered. "It's just that people always talk about signs—a tap on the shoulder or whatever. I used to sit in my grandpa's truck after he died, and I tried to put the skepticism aside. I was waiting for the dice to wiggle on the rearview mirror, or to turn on the radio and hear some Johnny Cash song playing. But after a certain point, I realized I couldn't even smell him anymore."

Daniel frowned. "You never told me that before."

"I accepted it. It was logical. You live and you die, and that's it." Logan gestured all around him. "This just cuts even deeper, man. I had another chance with him, and I didn't even get to say goodbye. And if I accept that there's something more out there, then it's like the universe turned its back on me. I have to accept that maybe my grandpa exists somewhere else, and that he's ignoring me."

Daniel spun Victor's hat on his finger. "My brother and sister were just telling me about how they felt our dad's presence at Katie's wedding. She could hear him whispering in her ear, and Zeke felt this chill walking her down the aisle. Me? I was there the whole time, but I didn't feel a thing. Come to think of it, I've never felt any of them before. I've had moments, just like you sitting in your grandpa's truck, waiting for a tap on the shoulder that never came. You've always been skeptical. I think I've always been jealous."

"That's why Macy brings out the best in us," Logan said. "She's always known there's more."

More, Daniel thought. A tiny word for a thousand pinpricks of candlelight. A tiny word for the infinite mysteries Miguel had carved open in the cemetery that day. Fate. Gods. Lives beyond life. Daniel wished Macy were there to help him compress it all into something as simple as the word *more*—something that could fit on a tarot card. She would've figured the *whole* thing out by now.

"I still don't fully know what happens to someone after they die," Daniel said. "But I do think when this is over, we'll know how to find the signs. You told me a story about how you couldn't feel your grandpa anymore. But what I've heard was about ten different things he changed for you. Butterscotch, fuzzy dice, and Johnny Cash, just to name a few."

"Johnny Cash," Logan muttered. He'd always said he despised country music, but Macy and Daniel had caught Logan listening to Johnny Cash multiple times.

"I'm sorry again about everything," Daniel said. "Miguel was wrong to trust me with any of this."

"If I were Death, would I trust you with this place? Would I ever choose you?" Logan shook his head and made an X with his arms. "Hell no."

"Okay, I got it, thank you," Daniel said.

Logan rolled his eyes. "But I *guess* I'm glad I chose you to be my best friend."

Daniel chuckled. "Then I guess thank you." He pulled his friend into a sideways shoulder hug, and they leaned against each other for a few seconds. Daniel savored the warmth, a repellent against the snow's wintery bite. But they didn't have time to rest. He clapped Logan's shoulder. "You good to keep going?"

Logan held up a thumb.

The grandfather clock tolled, and a smattering of candlelight blinked away. Snow lurched from the tops of the shelves, showering the ground.

Daniel and Logan separated, and a chill raced through Daniel's body as he looked for the source of the toll. The tower.

"What the *hell* is that sound?" Logan rubbed his arms. "It's like the bells of the underworld."

"It's the tower." Daniel jogged to the end of the aisle and peered around the corner. He only had to take a few more steps before a view of the horizon opened before him. The sky bled dark clouds, a funnel of which was swirling in the distance.

Below the twisting nebula, a spire stood against the sky.

The last time Daniel had been in The Archive, the tower was a little more than a hazy silhouette. This time, he was close enough to make out the shape: a tall, rounded column, smoke lightly oozing from the top.

"I never noticed last time…" he breathed.

"Noticed what?" Logan asked.

Daniel's fingers dropped into his pocket, where his father's lighter rested dutifully against his thigh. He brushed the phoenix, then left the lighter alone. "How much it looks like a giant candle."

A crack of lightning cleaved the sky, and Daniel smelled car exhaust and funeral lilies. His stomach bucked.

"Your godfather has poetic taste, man. Downright *theatrical*." Logan let out a long whistle. "A place like that just *screams* booby traps to me. Boulders and snakes and poison-tipped arrows."

"I doubt it," Daniel said. "I don't think there's ever been any reason for that before. No one's supposed to know this place exists. But if I'm wrong and it's rigged? Well, I've already come this far. You can still leave, you know."

"Meh. We've been through worse, right?" Logan said. "AP Language and Comp?"

"Too soon." Daniel bit his lip. "I'm getting a prickle in my stomach, Logan. I'm going in that tower either way, but I don't know if I'm ready for whatever's in there. I'm doubly sure I don't want my sister going in."

"Dude, tell me about it. If you told me you wanted to turn around right now and go to the movies or something, I'd be down." Logan paused, flicking a snowflake off his shoulder. "But I also know you, and I know you're gonna finish this. You say it's for Miguel, and for everyone who got swept up in this, but this also has to be a little bit for you. This is taking your grief by the horns, Danny, and that's badass. We have grief to deal with, too. So, when you're ready, I vote we go get Zeke and Katie, and we make tracks."

Daniel tightened the straps on his backpack. A sharp gust of wind nipped at his ears. He hoped there would be some warmth ahead inside the giant candle. "Let's go. Hopefully, Zeke and Katie didn't wander off."

He marched into the snow. They'd press on, and if they didn't stop, they'd reach the tower's base in no time. Whatever came next, they'd figure it out together.

Daniel had only taken a few steps when a crisp, hellish staccato split the air.

He froze.

A gunshot.

ARRHYTHMIA

(an irregular rhythm or rate of the heartbeat)

atie. Zeke. Miguel.

Daniel's mind and heart galloped in tandem. His legs struggled to keep up as he searched for the source of the gunshot. The icy air clawed at his face, driving icicles into his lungs.

Was it a blessing or a curse that he hadn't heard anyone scream before the shot?

If anyone was screaming now, the chaotic buzz of his thoughts crashed against the sound waves. If Zeke, Katie, or Miguel had been hurt…

"Fitch!" Daniel cried, his throat raw. "Katie? Zeke? Miguel?"

He raced past candles, some igniting while others expired. Sometimes Daniel would double back, stumbling to make sure an extinguished candle didn't bear Zeke's or Katie's name. All the candlelight seemed to blur together in a hellish mosaic. The scent of gasoline, lightly tinged with stale coffee grounds, punched his throat.

Please be safe, please be safe, please be safe.

Daniel emerged in an intersection between the aisles, cupped his hands to his mouth, and leaned back. "*Fitch!* Show yourself!"

He found the detective five aisles down, a gray shadow in the snow.

Fitch was pacing and muttering to himself, swinging the gun in his hand.

He was alone.

"Fitch!" Daniel approached, rested his hands on his legs, and caught his breath. "Fitch, what the hell did you do?"

Logan caught up to Daniel, breathless and pale, and tugged on his shoulder. "Danny," he rasped, "please think about this."

Fitch drew his brows together and took a curious step toward Daniel. "*You*," he whispered. "Why are you here?"

Daniel shrugged off Logan's grip, then took a step sideways to shield his friend. "You knew I'd follow you in here, man. Now, where are they? Miguel, my brother, my sister? I heard the gunshot. What did you do to them?"

"Cool it for a minute, kid. I didn't do a *thing*." Fitch pressed his free hand to his temple and kneaded it like a piece of dough, swearing under his breath. "Jesus H. Christ, what a waste. I fired the shot to try to get the doctor's attention, but instead, I get you…and you're not even with him. It wasn't supposed to be you!"

Daniel bowed his head in slight relief. "I'm sorry to disappoint," his knees buckled, "but I think he's a little busy at the moment."

Fitch crouched down, set the gun near his foot, and cradled his head in his fingers.

Daniel considered going for the weapon, but he knew he wouldn't be fast enough. Logan must've known the thought crossed his mind, because he gave Daniel the subtlest shake of the head.

Fitch's expression was strangled with equal parts desperation and injury. Daniel recognized it all.

"Man," Daniel said gently. "You should go home. I'm told these keys can take us pretty much anywhere. Whatever you're planning, I get it. I understand. But it's just not gonna work the way you think it is."

"You *get it*." Fitch's tone was wrapped in iron. "No. I don't think you do. I won't deny you your pain. But you're young, and life hasn't rubbed you raw yet. You got another throw of the dice. Now I want mine."

"Please don't talk to my brother."

At the sound of Zeke's voice, Fitch dove for his gun, then popped up like a spring.

Zeke and Katie made their way down the snow-covered aisle, all hands in the air. Dorian stalked beside them, eyes glowing as he hissed at the detective.

Zeke stepped in front of Daniel, chest puffed. He pointed to his eyes with two fingers. "You don't talk to anyone but *me*."

Daniel's heart rioted in his chest. Zeke used to invoke this tone with reporters when they swarmed the Grimms. In an instant, he could go from Costa Linda's mild-mannered golden boy survivor to broad-shouldered protective brother bear.

"Cassandra! It's the six-month anniversary of your family's tragedy! What does the Queen of Cups want to say to Josiah Retzlaff today?"

"Get away from my aunt's shop now. She has nothing to say to any of you, and neither do I."

Daniel crushed his eyes shut. *Josiah Retzlaff.* Why did that name keep coming up today?

Zeke excelled at scaring the media away, though Katie worked a different kind of magic.

"I think the statement you want is, 'We're strong, we're okay, and we're going to get better.' That's what my parents would want for us, anyway. Have a nice day."

"Zeke." Katie brushed her fingers along Zeke's shoulder. "You're going to let me talk to the detective, okay?"

Zeke's jaw tightened, and when he opened his mouth to protest, Katie slammed a finger to his lips. "No," she said.

"Kate Grimm." Fitch removed his hat and tilted his head. "It's good to see you again."

Katie dipped her chin slightly. "Detective. I wish I could say the same, but it's kind of difficult when you're pointing a Glock 43 at my family. Maybe you can put it away so we can talk?"

Fitch looked impressed that Katie knew the exact model of the weapon, which she'd probably learned from her true crime deep-dives. The detective inclined his head at Zeke. "Tell Top Gun to take a step back. In fact, *everyone* takes a step back. Nobody comes any closer."

Dorian arched his back and hissed at Fitch.

"And if the cat pounces, I shoot," Fitch said. "Contain it."

Katie pinned Zeke with her eyes. "Zeke."

Resigned, Zeke scooped Dorian into his arms.

"You all heard him." Katie flapped a hand at Daniel and Logan. "Step back."

Daniel's mind whirred at full speed, and he knew Zeke was in a similar mindset. They were both grappling with the brotherly instinct to protect Katie and her daughter.

We could tackle him, Daniel thought. *But none of us are faster than a bullet.*

When he snuck a glance at Logan, he saw his friend's chest rising and falling as quickly as Daniel's heart was beating. *I'm sorry for all this,* Daniel mouthed.

They were powerless here. They had to trust Katie.

She extended her palm. "May I have the gun, please?"

Fitch considered the weapon, then pursed his lips. "Sorry, kiddo," he said. "I don't think that'd be smart for any of us. The best I can do is let you walk away. I don't intend to hurt any one of you. So what do you say we just leave each other alone? I move on in peace and forget I ever saw you. Perhaps I'll even offer you a full refund for my past services. After all, I do owe you a thank you. I couldn't have found this place without you."

Daniel's jaw dropped. A full refund? Katie had never shared how much she paid Fitch to investigate Miguel, but she'd been clear that he didn't come cheap.

Katie bit her lip. "I don't know about that, detective. I don't know what you're planning to do with this place."

"Well, I'll tell you exactly what I mean to do," Fitch said. "It's no big secret, sweetheart. I'm here to do what anyone would do, and what your brother already *did*. Are you gonna tell me that's wrong?"

A muscle twitched in Daniel's cheek, and he clamped his lips shut.

"My brother *was* wrong," Katie said, "and he knows it."

"So you'd deny me a few short minutes with my loved ones when the Grimms had three days?" Fitch replaced his hat. "Call me old-fashioned, but that hardly seems fair."

"I agree," Katie said. "It's not fair at all, but it's also not something we get to decide. Our godfather is here to repair the damage, and you're skulking around his collections with a firearm."

"I only intend to use it if he doesn't give me what I want," Fitch said. "Pain ain't my game, sweetheart. I've seen too much of it already."

"Have you considered that this might be pointless in the end?" Katie asked. "Think about it. Say Miguel doesn't give you what you want. Your plan is to put a bullet in him? Fitch…he's a *god*. What do you think that'll do to him, exactly?"

"Only one way to find out." A curious look spread across Fitch's face. "I'll be darned. You don't mean to tell me you're *concerned* for the man? Despite everything he's taken away from you?"

Daniel could see the hurt in Katie's expression. "It is not that simple," she said, her voice blade-edged. "My parents would want me to do the right thing, and I want to raise my daughter to do the same."

"Fitch." Daniel raised his hands in the air, his voice husky. "She's due any day now. My brother and I can't wait to meet our niece. *Please* put the gun away. Don't endanger that baby."

Fitch narrowed his eyes, then pinned his gaze on Katie's belly. "Thought maybe you were cookin' something in there," he said. "A baby girl, huh?"

"Yes." Katie's hands drifted protectively to her middle. "She'll be my first."

"Congratulations," Fitch said, his voice low and sincere. "Truly. I'm sure you love her very much already."

"With *all* my heart," Katie said.

Fitch rubbed his chin. "Well…" in a flash, he cocked the gun and leveled it at Daniel, "then you all had better listen up."

Daniel gasped. For a second, he thought Fitch had softened, that they had broken some ground. Now his expression was rock-hard.

"Fitch, please!" Katie pleaded.

"Come on," Zeke said. "We've been through enough."

"I know it. That's why I'm gonna make this as easy as possible. Maybe we're *all* looking for the same thing in the end. So you, boy," he said to Daniel. "You've been here before. You know this place. If I tell you to look for a certain candle, can you find it?"

"I can't," Daniel said. "I couldn't even find my family again if I tried. This place is organized in a way that only Miguel understands."

"Figured," Fitch said. "Then you'd better get his attention. Call your godfather and get him over here."

"I can't do that either," Daniel said. "Or else I would've found him already."

"I'm curious if a second bullet would be enough to make him listen," Fitch said. "It might not do a damn thing to a god, but if I put it in *you*…right around the knee…Well, I'm sure he's certain to feel some things."

Daniel swallowed.

"You'll sure as hell feel it, too," Fitch said. "Ever been shot before? I'll give you a hint: It's not pleasant."

"Don't point that at him," Logan said.

Fitch swiveled the gun to Logan, keeping his eyes on Daniel. "Maybe we'll try your buddy? How much candlelight does he have left?"

"Stop! We'll help you," Zeke said. "We know where Miguel is."

Fitch lowered the weapon.

Daniel's shoulders deflated, the pressure relenting. But he was also disappointed. He'd wanted to keep Fitch as far from Miguel as possible, regardless of what a bullet could do to him.

"Now, was that so difficult?" Fitch asked.

"We can't get him over here," Zeke said. "But we know where he's going. We were already on our way. We'll take you to him."

Fitch slowly approached Zeke, the gun still trained on the ground. "You're gonna whisper the location in my ear." Fitch tugged on his earlobe. "And then all the rest of you will do the same thing. Your answers had *better* match up. I've been betrayed before, and it will never happen again."

One by one, Fitch coaxed out confirmations of his answer.

By the time he approached Daniel and leaned in, his breath a curious combination of mint and tobacco, he was already confident in his answer. Daniel wanted to keep the words in his throat, but it wouldn't have done any good. He whispered a short phrase.

Fitch turned around and pointed at the horizon. "That tower in the distance, eh?" He adjusted his hat. "I'll be walking behind you. Remember, we all want the same thing here. No stops. No detours. No games. Lead on."

Daniel took a deep breath. Fitch had seemed concerned about wasting a bullet earlier, so maybe he was all bark in the end. Perhaps if they all cooperated, he wouldn't feel compelled to fire a second one.

But the lighter in Daniel's pocket was a constant reminder that good people were capable of dark deeds if they were desperate enough.

And Charleston Fitch had yet to meet the god of death.

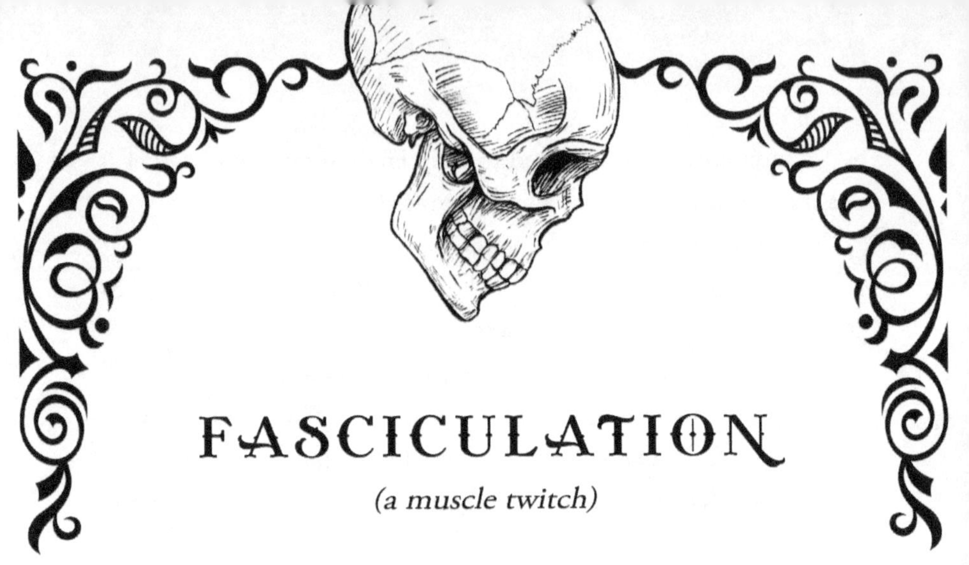

FASCICULATION

(a muscle twitch)

For a while, nobody said a word as they marched to the Column of Time. In certain spots Daniel heard the crackle of a flame or the pop of a jumping ember, but for most of the journey, all he registered was the crunch of snow under his feet. Even his thoughts had softened from a roar to a whisper.

Fitch won't shoot, he'd realized.

The detective was lost in his own mind. In fact, Fitch was often the one to break the silence.

"This place always like this?" He crushed a snowflake in his palm.

Daniel had had ideas about what snow would be like. He thought it would be soft, pillowy, like walking on clouds. But this was nothing like he'd imagined. While there was beauty in the way the ice refracted the candlelight, the chill was like pins in his ears, and the texture constantly threatened his balance. Every time he'd find a steady cadence, his foot would catch something slick. When he slipped, Daniel worried for his sister, then he cursed his bruised knees and the perpetual grit on his palms. No amount of wiping seemed to dry his hands. He and Logan started walking a few steps ahead, making trails and warding Katie away from the slippery patches.

"It's not always like this," he muttered. "If it's always the way it was the last time I was here, it's gorgeous. Watercolor sky. Rolling greens.

Singing birds."

"Singing birds, eh?" Fitch made a face, and Daniel remembered the detective's encounter with the honking seagulls. "Sounds horrid. I'll take the snow."

Katie sighed. "I mean, you do you."

Daniel noticed she had been holding her back a little more, taking the briefest of pauses and catching her breath. Every time he turned around, she'd give him the, *I'm fine* look, wave him along, then pick up her pace.

Even Fitch's expression would contort with concern whenever Katie would stop. He didn't pause, but he didn't nudge her along, either.

"You got a name picked out?" He flicked a bony finger toward Katie's middle. "For the kiddo?"

Daniel wondered if Fitch cared or if he was just filling the silence.

Katie cringed, then wrestled it into a toothy customer service smile. "Nope!" Then she hurried up to her brothers, leaving Fitch a few steps behind.

"If you ever need to slow down—"

"I'm fine." Katie glared at Zeke.

Silence descended again. Logan was the next one to break it. "You know," he said, "the snow sucks, but the walk isn't too bad, right? I'm trying to think of it like we're going hiking. Anyone need a snack or some water?"

Daniel declined. He didn't know how long they'd been wandering, and he didn't want nature to call. Katie accepted some water, offered everyone crackers, and paused a few minutes later.

Zeke and Daniel exchanged a look.

Daniel leaned over and whispered, "What if—"

Don't finish that thought, Zeke said with his eyes, a pointed stab he'd perfected over the years.

Daniel had crafted an equally effective shield for the Zeke stare. "I'm just saying, what if?"

"Daniel."

Katie caught up, all grins. "What if what? What are we talking about?"

"What if," Logan interjected, "Miguel offered to show you your own candle? Danny, have you seen yours? Or has he offered to show you?"

Daniel shook his head.

"Have you thought about it?"

"I almost asked him," Daniel said. "But I think I'm afraid to. Would you want to know?"

Logan bit his lip. "Nah, I don't think so. There's no point. No matter how much time I have left, I don't think I'll live my life any differently."

"I'd think about it," Katie admitted. "I think about that sort of thing a lot, actually. Maybe it's the true crime girly in me, or everything we've already been through. You guys don't ever wonder? Think about your mortality?"

"Well, yeah, all the time," Zeke said. "But what would I do if I knew when? Let's say you have ten years guaranteed. What then? Suddenly you're going bungee jumping? Swimming with sharks just because you can?"

"I've already been bungee jumping," Katie deadpanned. "Justin and I did it together in Costa Rica. Couldn't talk him into the shark excursion."

Daniel's eyes widened. "Seriously?"

"You're more like Mom than I even realized," Zeke said. "You'd do it, wouldn't you? If Miguel offered you a chance to look at your candle, you'd peek. You'd want to know exactly how much time you have with your baby, wouldn't you?"

"Nope," Katie said. "The second I learned about her, I knew how I was going to spend the rest of my life. Whether I die tomorrow or when I'm ninety-five, every breath belongs to my daughter. I'd just want to know when it'll happen so I can go to sleep."

"Doesn't mean it'll be painless," Zeke said. "I think if I peeked, I'd just hear the clock ticking for the rest of my life. And for the last year or so, I'd just be looking over my shoulder, wondering how it'll happen."

"What if Miguel could tell you that, too?"

"Oh, yes, let's play that out." Logan's eyes lit up. "So, Miguel tells me it'll happen at sea on a summer day. Well, if I don't go to the beach all summer, I change my fate, right? I win."

"Maybe we get a freak tsunami," Daniel said. "Or I get kidnapped by pirates that summer and they contact *you* for the ransom. Are you really gonna let them have me?"

"You'd insist I come for you, anyway? When I'm destined to bite it?" Logan slugged his friend's shoulder. "That's *messed up*. You can deal."

"That's enough," Fitch growled, cutting off the conversation with the sweep of an arm. "Why waste your breath with pointless hypotheticals when you're walking through a field of clay? All of this is here, and we found it. We should be strong enough to sculpt our own destinies."

"Because this isn't some art studio," Daniel said. "This is a *museum*. None of this is ours to touch."

Fitch wiggled a brow. "Clever, kid. But even museums are filled with stolen crap that never belonged to them in the first place."

Daniel didn't know how to argue against that. Fitch was right about museums. To some extent, Daniel agreed with him on life as well. *I should be able to give someone more time without breaking the rules.* Why did The Archive have to be so petty? Life could be cruel that way, but Daniel had learned his lesson. *Haven't I? When I find Miguel, I won't try to bargain with him, right? I'll accept things the way they have to go, even if I don't like them. Even if they chew up my heart.*

The conversation broke down to crumbs. Logan offered snacks. They checked in on each other. They huddled up for warmth. They stared in wonder as the Column of Time grew closer and closer. The details bloomed one by one.

First, the tower was a hexagon made of smooth white bricks, with no visible windows. Near the top, some of those bricks jutted out from the facade, but not in any sort of even pattern. It was like somebody had been pushing on them from the inside, and that the effect had rippled upward to the roof. It didn't just remind Daniel of a candle—it reminded him of one that had been burning for a while, the molten wax forming a crust down the sides.

Second, a new fragrance gradually overpowered the traces of memory in the air—the beach, the street fair, and the pancakes. With every step Daniel took, those scents faded. The scents of rain, spices, and cedarwood overtook them until he could no longer ignore them.

"He's here," Daniel said, the hope like a blanket over his shoulders.

He could see the door—two white columns, a glossy black mass between them, and a rounded archway.

Like a gravestone, he thought. A gravestone three times his height. It hadn't been built for mortals. All around the tower, tiny embers glowed in the air, then vanished like mini fireflies. For a second, Daniel thought they were making shapes, like faces or glyphs, but they were all too fleeting for him to hold in his mind.

"Yep." Dorian writhed in Zeke's arms, and Zeke tightened his hold. "We found him. The cat's freakin' out."

"He's a good little fella." Daniel stroked Dorian behind the ears. "We're about to reunite you with your pops."

Dorian mewled, his whiskers twitching.

"Mind if I just…?" Logan plopped down in the snow, lay face up, and spread his arms. He closed his eyes. "Two seconds."

"I'm gonna sit, too." Katie followed suit. "I just need to take this in."

Zeke released Dorian, and the cat immediately bounded for the tower. Halfway to the door, the flickering embers distracted him, and he zipped around, trying to catch them. Zeke crossed his arms and stared up at the top. "It's definitely something to see."

Daniel wanted to sprint the rest of the way and kick the door open.

The only one who didn't share the entrancement, or enthusiasm, was Charleston Fitch.

The detective didn't even look at the tower. He looked more like a hound who had just smelled something, his posture tight with his nose pointed in the air.

"Fitch?" Daniel said.

Fitch spun in a slow circle, focusing on the different aisles that spidered out into the horizon. He reminded Daniel of the compass key, twisting this way and that until he pointed his toes at a specific aisle and relaxed. "I'm gonna wander this way for a minute."

Daniel scrunched his brows together. "Right now? The tower is right in front of us. You're the one who said no stops or detours."

"Call it a detective's hunch." Fitch trudged into the aisle, disappearing from Daniel's view.

Katie rubbed her arms, Mom's blanket still draped over her like a shawl. Her dark nail polish was chipping away. "I just got the weirdest feeling."

Hair stood up on Daniel's neck, and his ears rang. What if Fitch had found his daughter's candle?

Zeke must've had the same idea, because he sprang into a jog and followed Fitch's snow tracks. "Oh, no, you don't…"

Daniel dropped his backpack next to Logan. "Stay here with my sister."

"Wait!"

"We'll be okay," Daniel said.

"Be careful!" Katie said. "And hurry!"

When Daniel sped into a run, he registered the fatigue that had been descending on him for hours upon days upon weeks. His legs protested and his heart skipped a beat. He slammed a cold fist over his chest and gritted his teeth. *Cool it,* he told his body. *Hang in there for just a little bit longer.*

When they rounded the corner, Fitch peered into one of the

windows, one hand over his brow while the other fell to his coat pocket.

Then, the detective drew a lighter.

"Fitch!" Daniel said. "Do not do this. Not now."

Fitch flashed a palm at Daniel and Zeke. "Hold it right there, you two." He made a show out of putting a brand-new cigarette between his teeth. "Relax. I'm just here to *look* for a second. Museum?"

He lit the cigarette, sucked in a long drag, and returned the lighter to his pocket. When he exhaled, Daniel couldn't tell if the man was blowing smoke or cold air. It all obscured the detective's face, rendering his expression impossible to read.

"Well, I'll be damned," Fitch muttered, his tone flat. "Of all the infinite possibilities…"

Zeke's fingers twitched at his sides. "Keep your hands where we can see them."

Fitch flicked a drizzle of ashes into the snow, a low chuckle escaping his throat.

"None of this is a joke, man," Daniel said. "Come back. It's not funny."

"I beg to differ." Fitch removed his hat and scratched his head. "I'm confounded by this place's sense of humor. It's cruel, make no mistake. But I can't help but smirk at Lady Luck. I never guessed that shame would have a smell…whiskey and gunpowder residue."

Daniel caught a breeze that hinted of stale apple turnovers.

"Didn't think it'd lead me here." Fitch retreated from the window with one broad step, then indicated it with both arms. He looked like a ringmaster, inviting the brothers into a circus tent. "Congratulations, boys. This one's for you."

Daniel's heartbeat dragged to a halt, then redoubled, concrete in his knees.

Fitch tapped his watch, a simple timepiece with fraying leather straps. "Tick-tock. Weren't you just holding my feet to the fire a second ago?"

Daniel swallowed, struggling to speak around the lump in his throat. The shape of his grief was sharpening, the words coming out in a croak. "Who did you find?"

"A name that concerns you greatly." Fitch stubbed out his cigarette and replaced his hat. "Do what you will. I'm not gonna touch it."

Daniel's mind raced with possibilities. This wasn't the spot where Miguel had brought him before. *It's not my parents. Not my siblings, unless Miguel rearranged this place.*

Aunt Cass?

Macy?

Grandma Alba?

Or is it me?

"I don't know if I can look," he told Zeke. "Will you tell me who it is?"

His brother nodded once. "I'll go."

Zeke approached the window with a stoic mask. He mouthed a name, and then the stone cracked in his gaze. His shoulders sagged and his breath hitched.

Then he slammed a fist against the window.

To Daniel's horror, it *cracked*, a thin web rippling out where Zeke's knuckles met the glass. For an agonizing second, he thought the window would shatter into confetti, but the cracks only spread a few inches in each direction. The center bore a shallow eye tinged with pink.

Zeke withdrew his fist, spattered with blood.

"Zeke!" Daniel cried. "Who is it?"

His brother shut his eyes and rested his forehead against the window, his fingers trembling.

Daniel approached, observed the bright flame inside, and read the name:

RETZLAFF, JOSIAH D.

He recoiled and put a hand over his writhing stomach.

"Uncanny, isn't it?" Fitch mused. "A stranger blazes into your life like a wildfire and burns up everything you love…leaves nothing. Come to find out the engine that keeps him ticking is only *this* big." Fitch pinched two fingers in front of his nose.

"*Shut up,*" Zeke growled, his voice equal parts venom and pain.

Fitch bowed as if in apology. "Sure thing, Top Gun. Don't let me ruin a moment between brothers. I just find it interesting, that's all." He pivoted on his heel, did a little hop-skip, and whistled under his breath as he browsed the aisle.

Daniel dropped his hands to his sides. Everything started with the paltry flame on that shelf. If that candle had never existed, the Grimms could've lived many more years. Miguel never would've brought Daniel here. Daniel never would've messed things up.

Josiah Retzlaff started it all. He was an atomic bomb.

Zeke's eyes fluttered open, and he considered the candle.

Daniel could barely look at it.

How many times had he woken up in the middle of the night, faced the ceiling, and thought, *Why wasn't it him?*

Why does he get to walk away from all this?

The last time Daniel had seen the man was in a glimpse of a news interview. He could tell the make-up team had exhausted special work into trying to make Josiah look respectable. They had dressed him in a smart brown suit that could've elevated anyone's charisma, but on Josiah, it looked more like a Halloween costume. It fit his gaunt, shrinking form, but he squirmed in it. He fidgeted with the sleeves and the tie like they were handcuffs and a noose. The team had also trimmed his copper-colored hair, as well as his beard, which both had lost luster and fullness over the years. Everything about Josiah seemed…*less.* Smaller.

Daniel remembered the interviewer, Ayana Finfrock, telling him one thing.

"There's a sizable community who believes you did this on purpose. You can bet your bottom dollar they'll be listening to your next words." Ayana crossed her legs and rested her chin on her fist. "Look into that camera, Josiah. Look at the people at home and tell them your side of the story. Tell them what you want them to know."

When Josiah looked at the camera, his eyes betrayed all the work he'd done to appear presentable and strong. The texture of his pain was pointed. He was haunted. There were new wrinkles that Daniel hadn't seen before. He couldn't tell if Josiah was in his thirties or his sixties. But far beyond the dark irises, tiny pinpricks of light flickered. Josiah was *desperately* clinging to something.

"I...I got distracted," Josiah drawled, fighting for control of his voice. "But the thing is, I don't know what I can say. For the Grimms, it doesn't matter why it happened or how it happened. It just... happened. Only thing that matters now is that I tell them I'm sorry. From the bottom of my heart I'm sorry. They may never forgive me, and...that's deserved. I know I'll spend the rest of my life thinking about that day."

Good, Daniel thought.

At that point, Aunt Cass stabbed the TV remote with her pointer finger, killing the power. "So will we," she muttered. Then she cleared her throat and looked at Daniel. "How 'bout we make some cinnamon rolls?"

A pop of thunder pulled Daniel back into The Archive.

Fitch was pacing, meandering.

Zeke was shivering.

"Bro." Daniel looked at Zeke's chapped knuckles.

"You should look away from this." Zeke's voice was both soft and dangerous.

Daniel put a hand on Zeke's shoulder, feeling the tension in his muscles. "You're thinking about it, aren't you?"

Zeke returned his hand to the glass, gentle and flat this time.

"Oh, I'm thinking about it. How simple would it be? The slightest blow…" Zeke exhaled, and his breath clouded the window in a thin sheet of white. "We'd never need to know how it happened…why it happened. It would just…*happen*. Life has its poetry."

Fitch stopped pacing, leaned against a shelf, and crossed his arms, listening.

Daniel forced himself to confront the candle again. His heart twisted, but with less of a burn this time. A rivulet of wax leaked down the side of Josiah's candle, like a teardrop.

"You know we can't do that," Daniel said.

Zeke removed his hand from the window and dug his toe into the snow. "We're just gonna go fix it all, anyway. What's the harm if it's reversible? If *everything's* reversible?"

"Zeke," Daniel said. "No."

His brother's eyes pooled with tears. "This hurts. Every day it hurts. I just want him to feel a fraction of that and know what it's like, you know?"

"I know," Daniel said. "But I bet he feels it, too. We're never gonna know. But we won't feel any better if we blow out his candle. We'd be just like him, and we'd carry that everywhere with us. This doesn't mean we're forgiving him. It's just…we have our own pain. We don't need to carry his, too."

Zeke plucked a splinter of glass from his knuckles and closed his hand over them, cradling the wounds. "God, you sounded like Dad right now. Starting to look like him, too."

"What can I say?" Daniel shrugged. "We all got good genes."

Zeke took one last look at the flickering flame, then turned away. "We're gonna work on our own pain." His posture relaxed, like a blood pressure cuff letting out air. "We're gonna be better."

"Fascinating," Fitch cut in, "if not downright naïve." He took off his hat and fluttered it at the window in front of Josiah's candle. "You could've forgotten that man ever existed."

"Nah," Daniel said. "I don't think we could've." And Daniel wasn't sure he wanted to—he'd already tried. Josiah was even one of the names Dr. Barnes suggested he write to, but instead, Daniel pushed the name far out of his mind. It was like trying not to breathe.

Fitch scratched the stubble on his chin. "You could've chosen the bigger life."

"And we *did*." Zeke wrapped an arm around his brother's shoulder. "This is what that looks like."

And they started retracing their steps back to their sister, the tower looming ahead.

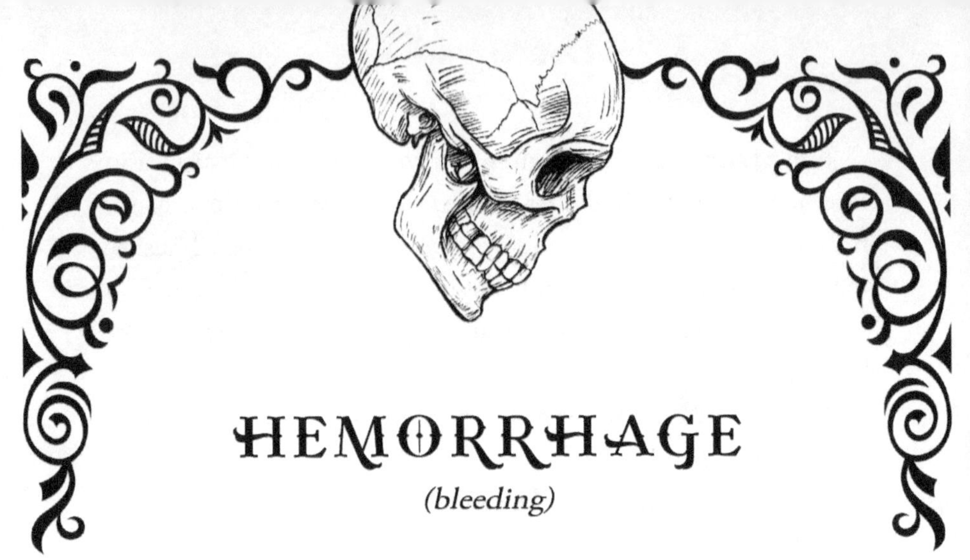

HEMORRHAGE

(bleeding)

On the way out of the aisle, Zeke pulled Daniel aside.

"Real quick," Zeke said. "That key you're holding in your pocket? Does it work both ways?"

Daniel spun the key on his finger. "It should. Miguel told me he could make a door anywhere, in or out."

"Can you give it a try?" Zeke asked. "I'm not backing out; I'm just thinking. If something goes wrong in that tower…do we have a way to get her out of here?"

Daniel squeezed the key, leaving thin grooves in his palm. Then he held it out to his brother. "Here," he said. "You should carry it. My priority is the flame. I won't have time to figure out how to make doors, so if something happens, you'll have it. You can get Katie and Logan out, and then if you need to…you can tell everyone I'm not coming back."

Zeke stared at the key, a muscle churning in his throat. "Danny—"

"No." Daniel shook his head. "We both know it's possible. It's not like that's my plan. This is just a precaution."

"You are the youngest Grimm." Zeke jabbed Daniel's shoulder. "And I'm the oldest. I'm supposed to protect *you*."

Daniel rolled his eyes. *Family.* "Oh, so you want to play the birth order card?" He shoved the key into Zeke's front pocket. "Then I guess I'm supposed to be a manipulative pain in the ass. Let's go."

They found Katie and Logan exactly where they'd left them, resting by the tower while Dorian continued to pounce on twinkling specks.

"Oh, thank God." Katie put a hand over her heart. "What were you doing over there? Zeke, your hand!" She grabbed his wrist, where thin rivulets of blood curled around his knuckles before spilling and dotting the snow. When it leaked onto Katie's palm, Zeke pulled away.

"We can talk about it later." Zeke bit a strip of cloth off his sleeve and began to bind the wound.

Logan returned Daniel's backpack, dangling the handle on one finger. "You good?"

Daniel's jaws cracked in a wide yawn. "I'm good." He put his backpack on, tightened the straps, and a dizzy spell punched him in the brain. He tilted his head as far back as he could, and he could barely see the top of the tower. The smoke had thinned from a husky cloud to a black mist, though the scent of gasoline clung to the bricks. "Hope it's warm in there."

"You're about to light a fire," Logan said. "Let's go bring the heat, my man."

And without another word, Daniel approached the door. His legs were heavy and awkward. He felt like a clumsy giant ambling around, yet he'd never felt so tiny. With every step, he conjured a different name in his mind.

This is for Bobby.

This is for Elena.

For Sam.

For Monica.

And so on, until he was close enough to touch the tower. The door was slick like marble and cold like ice.

"Now what?" Logan said. "No doorknob. No doorbell. No hinges? How do we get in?" He raised a fist and struck the door three times, but the impact barely made a sound.

Everyone watched the door to see if it would open.

A minute stretched by, and then Logan stepped back. "It was worth a try."

"I wonder how long it's been here," Katie murmured. "Or what it's for. Was The Archive ever under attack or something? I mean, towers are built the way they are for a reason. They're fortresses."

"Maybe Miguel just wanted a point of reference," Daniel said. "Some sort of landmark to look to. Or *from*."

"*Maybe.*" Fitch pressed his fingertips to the door's surface. He skimmed it like a book, reading for hidden cracks, dents, and grooves. "Maybe he needs to get a move on. If there's another way in, I'll find it."

Katie put a palm to the door and closed her eyes.

After years of suspicion and anguish, Katie had solved her mystery about Miguel. Was she satisfied? Was she mortified? Was she a little bit of both?

Suddenly, she leapt back with a gasp. "Something's happening."

Fitch narrowed his eyes, continuing to scan the door with his fingertips. "Well, I'll be darned. This thing's hummin' like a tuning fork."

Katie held up her palm for the rest of them to see. "I think it was your blood, Zeke. I'm getting a feeling about this place. No one just walks in without some sort of…"

"Sacrifice," Zeke massaged his knuckles, a scarlet cloud blooming across the white strip of cloth he'd bound it in.

One minute, the solid black door repelled them, unyielding and impenetrable. The next, a translucent wall of crimson light flashed where the door used to be, and Daniel detected faint silhouettes of the room inside.

Katie gasped, "It's open."

"I don't like that color," Logan said, his cheeks reflecting the red light. "Is it safe?"

Dorian purred and trotted through the veil, his tail curling behind him.

Daniel forked his fingers through his hair. "Well, I guess the cat seems to think so."

"But the cat has nine lives," Logan said.

Daniel put a tentative finger to the light, and a faint, warm tingle buzzed from skin to bone. He stepped through, and the light showered him with a feeling like calm sunlight. The snow melted off his boots, and he felt the color trickle into his face again.

But the inside of the tower had no more color than the outside.

He'd stepped inside a ruinous, dingy room made of three concentric hexagons, each dipping lower as they approached the middle. On the outer edge, dusty crates, broken vases, and hefty cauldrons had been strewn about the floor.

Tapestries dripped from each wall, but each had been mangled by the passing of time. Some had lost all their color, while others hung in tatters. The only detail Daniel could make out on any of them was a grain of wheat.

Behind an iron lock, another massive door loomed at the far end of the room. Next to it, cobwebs swarmed in a dreary fireplace, where a careful pile of charred wood sat in its bowels.

Fireplace. Daniel immediately wondered if this was where he needed to light the flame.

He started for the fireplace, only to become startled by a massive shadow passing overhead.

Daniel ducked and covered his head, relieved that nothing had bowled him over or snatched him off the ground. When he looked back up, a large bronze disk swung between opposite walls.

High over Daniel's head, thick, oversized gears kept the pendulum swinging.

He'd found the source of the clock chimes.

The middle tier of the hexagon contained six chairs, each with a different colored cushion and gilded arms. At the foot of each chair, a stone disk had been carved into the ground.

There was that wheat symbol again.

A key.

A fireplace.

A crown.

A trident.

And a lightning bolt.

"Hey, bro?" Logan's voice startled Daniel. He'd been so distracted looking around the tower that he hadn't heard the rest of the group follow him in. "I don't think your godfather needs six chairs. This tower isn't just his, is it?"

"I don't know." Daniel's mind reeled. "I came here for *him*, and it doesn't even look like anyone's here."

He pivoted on his heel, and the red light blinked away. The black door returned, massive and solid to the touch.

"Great." Zeke tapped his bloody knuckles against the door. "We're locked in. You wanna try lighting that fireplace?"

"Hold it." Fitch drew his gun. "You didn't try to pull a fast one on me, did you? We came here for the doctor. You mean to tell me he's not here?"

"Fitch," Daniel growled. "We are just as frustrated as you are. Swinging that thing around isn't gonna do a goddamn thing, so put it away, shut up, and let us *think*!"

Fitch stared back, and Daniel could see how weary the man was. He hated feeling sympathy for a man who was constantly threatening him. *Maybe I'd be a jerk too if someone yanked me out of the grave. I can barely get out of bed sometimes.*

Around that same time, Dorian let out a wistful mew.

He stood in the central hexagon, which was little more than a lacquered wooden floor.

At least, that was what it appeared to be.

Until a voice called out from underneath.

Daniel found the latch at the edge of the hexagon, but he needed Logan's help to wrench the door open.

And six feet under that door, sitting in a pit of black sand, was Miguel Mortiz.

The man looked more mortal than ever, his hair sweaty and disheveled. His feet were bare, and his jeans were torn at the knees. He wore a black undershirt that exposed a pale, wiry physique—one that didn't sync with the healthy figure Daniel had greeted only a day or two ago. Miguel looked up, his eyes red. He appeared to be battling with his eyelids until he locked eyes with Daniel.

"Miguel!" Daniel cried, his heart soaring and breaking all at once.

Dorian leapt into the pit, landing cleanly on all four paws. He nuzzled Miguel's leg, and Miguel flashed a weak smile. "Ah, my friend." His voice was rough and low. "Danny."

"What happened?" Daniel looked for something to toss into the pit. "Are you trapped? Why are you down there?"

Miguel tapped his thumbs together and looked up at the ceiling, worry lines creasing his forehead. "You figured it out. You solved the puzzle. Most excellent. If only the timing aligned a bit more… fortuitously."

"What do you mean?" Daniel asked. "Am I too late? I'm gonna get you out of there. Guys, help me look for a rope or something!"

"*No,* Danny. Not yet. Listen up. You have to leave me down here. We don't have much time." He looked past Daniel and summoned a quick wave. "Hello there, Katie. Zeke. Mr. Thane…Mr. Fitch."

Fitch drew the gun again in a blink, pointing it down into the pit and eliciting a hiss from Dorian.

"Hello, Dr. Mortiz," Fitch said. "You know my name, so I assume you know what I want. How hard do you want to make this?"

"Mr. Fitch," Miguel croaked, "I'm afraid I'm not in the business of making bargains. I strongly recommend you discard the firearm."

"Why would I do that?" Fitch asked. "I have the high ground here. I could put a bullet in any one of your family members right now. But see, you're looking a little pale and weak yourself. Tell me, would you feel it?"

"Intensely," Miguel said. "I'm quite fragile at this moment. You could wound me, perhaps even kill me. But wherever you choose to point that gun, every outcome wounds *you*, and many others outside this tower."

Daniel's mind reeled. *Miguel? Mortal? Trapped?*

The muscle in Fitch's throat made a slow movement, and he worked his jaw. Sweat beaded down his temple. "I'm unconvinced. Try again, doctor."

"*Listen*," Miguel said. "Any minute now, my captors will arrive. They are far more powerful than you, and they will not respond kindly to threats. There are worse fates than death, Charleston. Some of them want my job."

"Your captors?" Fitch scowled. "What kind of deity are you?"

"Who did this to you?" Daniel asked.

"There's still so much I haven't told you, my friend," Miguel said. "I wanted to. I should have. I always knew you were a special young man, yet I clearly underestimated you. I thought you had more than enough on your plate. Even if I strip back the grief…it's not easy to be a young human in your world."

"Miguel," Katie said. "Help us out. Who did this to you?"

Miguel rubbed his wrist, looking around as if searching for the right words floating in the air. But Daniel never expected the two words that followed, simple yet strangled by complications.

"My family," Miguel said. "Who else?"

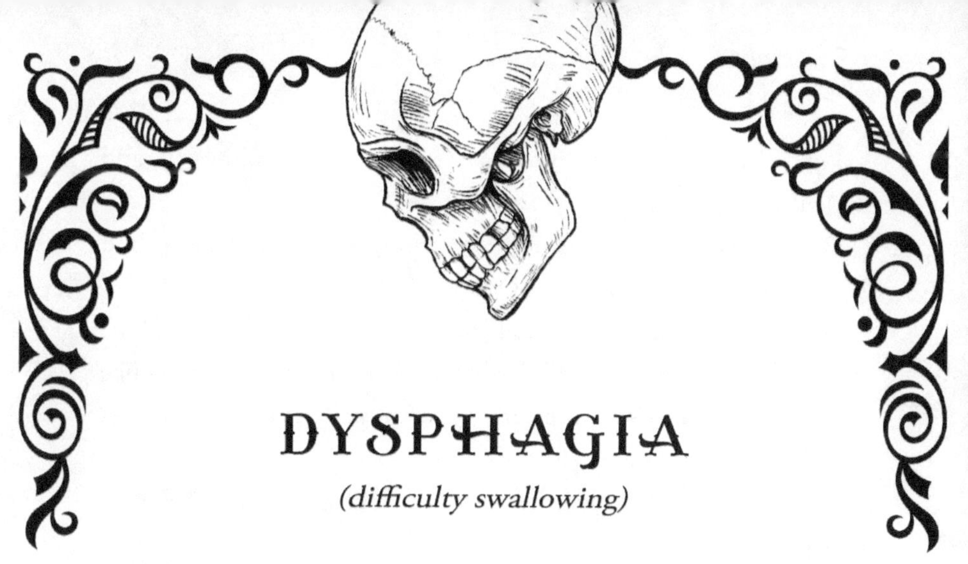

DYSPHAGIA

(difficulty swallowing)

Family?

The earth tilted beneath Daniel, and he grabbed Zeke's shoulder for support.

Katie spoke Daniel's thoughts out loud. "You're not talking about Aunt Cass or any of *us*, are you?"

"You will always be my family, of course," Miguel said. "We've had our disagreements, ups, and downs. As they say, every family has some drama. But the feuds within my *blood*—the family that helped me build this place—those are the bones of legends."

Daniel studied the chairs on the second tier, then the stone disks carved in front of them.

He recognized the trident and the lightning bolt, but he wasn't sure if he dared believe the meanings that popped into his head. He thought of the Grimm Goddesses—the candles his sisters had created.

"*Gods*," Katie breathed.

Miguel's brow furrowed. "That's not exactly the term *I* use, though I'm familiar with the growing mythos. Some of my siblings lean into it a little more heavily than others."

"Siblings," Daniel said. "Of *course*, there are more of you."

"For better or worse, yes," Miguel said. "We each oversee different aspects of our existence. *I'm* the key. My brothers watch over the sea and sky; my sisters women and fertility, home and hearth, and agriculture and sacred law."

Daniel searched his memory for glimpses of mythology he'd learned in literature last year, or world history.

"I can see you trying to recall their names," Miguel said. "Don't bother. My siblings walk the Earth and blend in with the living like I do, and they don't wear the names you know. They try on new lives like they're hats or shoes."

"So *why* have they locked you up in your own tower?" Daniel asked.

"In all fairness, it's what they're supposed to do," Miguel said. "Our father was a little…shall we say, *mad*?"

He watched the pendulum make another journey between the walls, the gears clicking and grinding overhead.

"We do our best to be better than him, but sometimes the apple doesn't fall far from the tree," Miguel said. "What I mean to say is, not even one of us is perfect. My brothers can be cocky and arrogant; my sisters can be short-tempered. We've *all* made mistakes. Imagine if we didn't have a way to keep each other in check? That's what they did here, Danny. I made a mistake, and they put me in check."

"While The Archive is freaking out?!" Daniel asked. "What about the flame?"

Miguel put his fingers to his temples. "Danny, you know how complicated family can be. They dropped me as soon as I walked in, despite knowing exactly why I came here. Perhaps *because* of it. Couldn't even do me the favor of saying hello, let alone hearing me out."

"Wouldn't that end humanity?" Daniel asked. "If the flame went out? Why would your siblings let things get that bad?"

"They won't let humanity die out," Miguel said. "That brazier has been burning since the beginning of time, Daniel. It powers the clock, the order, and *me*. If it goes out, it's proof of my failure to manage The Archive. My time as Death will end, and someone else will be called to take over."

Daniel swallowed. "What can I do? If I can't pull you out of that pit, can I at least light the flame and we can work from there?"

"No," Miguel said. "That was my original plan. You were my failsafe in case my family decided to toss me down here, but I didn't anticipate them staying and holding council. They've been upstairs, where the brazier stands. If you march up there and confront them, they'll only—"

A loud boom sounded over their heads.

Daniel recoiled. Logan stumbled back and tripped over the leg of a chair.

Miguel held a hand in the air, the universal symbol for *wait.*

The pendulum swung five times, louder with every pass.

"You need to *hide*," Miguel whispered, his eyes wide and grave. "All of you. Shut me back in here, get in the crates, and do not make a sound. I cannot stress enough how important this is."

Daniel wiped his sweaty palms on his jeans. When would he know it was safe? Did Miguel's family not understand what was at stake? Did they simply not care about him? "But Miguel—"

"Daniel." Miguel clenched his teeth. "*Now.*"

Zeke and Daniel dropped the door, sealing Miguel in the center of the hexagon, and looked for cover. Only then did they register the distant echo of footsteps coiling around the tower. There were multiple sets, each moving at their own pace. Daniel pinned the closest set of footsteps somewhere behind the wheat tapestry.

"Shit," Logan whispered. "What about the cat? We left him in there with Miguel."

"It's too late." Daniel shoved Logan behind one of the crates. Logan tucked his head down and curled his knees up to his chest, fitting his lanky form to the confines of the wood.

Katie, Zeke, and Fitch all hid themselves near Logan, and Daniel made sure he couldn't see them from the other side.

The trouble was Daniel was running out of spaces to hide.

Katie patted the space next to her, giving him a pleading gaze.

"They'll see me," Daniel mouthed.

This was hopeless. Logan had a point about the cat. With Fitch scowling under his fedora, Zeke struggling to contain his brawny build within the crate, Logan burying his head in his knees, and Katie giving him that worried stare, they all looked like a strange motley crew of adults playing hide and seek.

The footsteps grew louder, closer. The pendulum ticked the seconds away.

Daniel ripped off his backpack and climbed into the nearest cauldron, its innards both slick and gritty with mysterious dregs that smelled like pomegranate. He stuffed himself into the bowl, using his backpack as a sort of pillow. He fit just below the lip of the cauldron, though his bones and joints protested the forced contortion.

He closed his eyes, settled his breaths, and listened as the pendulum passed overhead three more times.

Swish.

Swish.

Swish.

Boom. The far door thundered open, the iron lock clattering against the stone floor.

A chip in the cauldron gave Daniel just enough of a view to see Miguel's trapdoor, as well as the far door that had just opened. He only hoped it wouldn't reveal him to Miguel's captors. The cauldron's acoustics amplified his breaths in his ears, so he pulled his shirt up to his nose and tried to muffle the sound.

Five people entered the room in a single file line.

Daniel couldn't have been more surprised by their appearances. Considering they were siblings, they looked nothing alike.

First, there was a dark-skinned woman with frizzy hair, a black silk dress, and red-rimmed spectacles. She had a stern, tight-lipped expression, and she walked tall as she approached the stone disk with the wheat symbol in front of it. When she reached her chair, she didn't sit down. She folded her hands at her waist and waited.

Then came a sun-tanned man about Miguel's age, with shiny dark hair down to his shoulders. He wore a navy polo shirt and khaki pants, and he sported a gunmetal diving watch on one wrist. He approached the chair with the trident in front of it, stood, and waited.

A red-haired woman wearing a white gown entered, the air smelling like lavender with her arrival. She walked with casual grace, and she had a simple beauty about her. She stood at the crown and waited.

Daniel's jaw dropped when the next woman entered. She was slightly older, though her gray lace dress looked like it belonged in another century. She wore her hair in long ringlets and carried a multi-colored umbrella, closed at her side. She was also the first to carry a smile.

The Gray Lady of Costa Linda. Daniel covered his mouth. *I knew there was something about her.*

She stood at the hearth symbol, rested her umbrella at her feet, and waited.

Finally, there was a tall man in a navy suit, his short silver hair swept in waves. He wore half-moon glasses, and he reminded Daniel of a cross between a classic game show host and a big-time CEO.

Daniel watched the man shut the door, lock it, and descend to the second hexagon. *He must be the lightning bolt.*

Instead of going straight to his chair, the suited man approached the center of the room, took a knee, and opened the trap door. Daniel had needed Logan's help with it earlier, but the suited man just flipped it as simply as the page of a book.

Miguel looked up, groggy and weak, and flashed the man a wan smile.

"Brother."

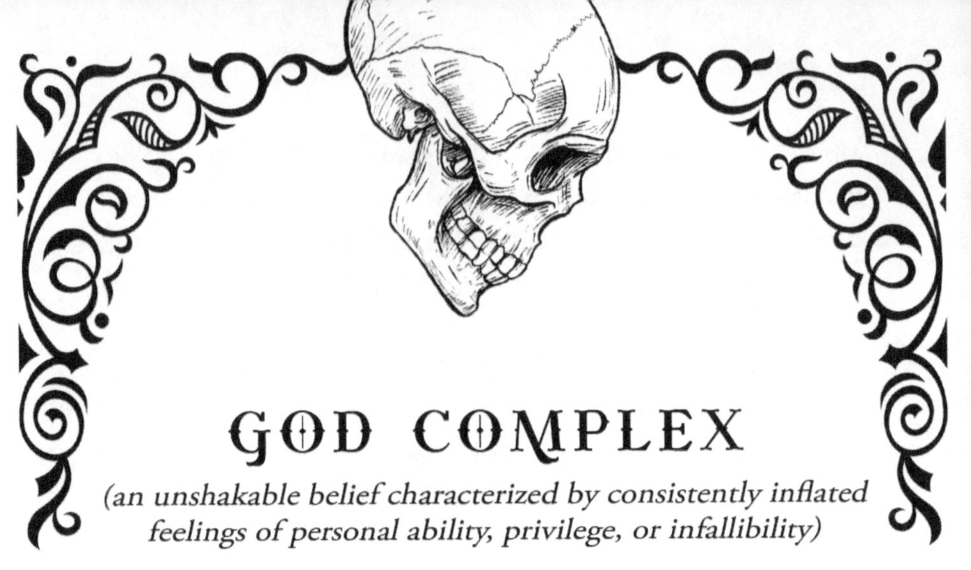

GOD COMPLEX

(an unshakable belief characterized by consistently inflated feelings of personal ability, privilege, or infallibility)

The suited man didn't reply to Miguel. Instead, he went to his seat behind the lightning bolt disk.

When the suited man nodded, all five strangers sat in unison.

Miguel stood and turned in a circle, looking up at each of his siblings one by one. Daniel hated to see him this way—lowered into a pit for others to look down on him. Most of the people were stone-faced and blank, whereas the suited man looked almost murderous. The Gray Lady was the only one who bore a hint of a smile.

The woman in black finally broke the silence. "Brother." Her voice was crisp and powerful. "It's been far too long. I wish we could assemble under kinder circumstances."

Miguel chuckled. "As do I."

Daniel squinted. There was no sign of Dorian anywhere in the pit. *What the heck?*

"Regardless," Miguel said, "it *is* good to see you."

"How do you wish to be addressed this day?" the woman asked.

"I wish to be addressed as Dr. Miguel Mortiz." Miguel bowed his head. "Miguel will do just fine. And my siblings?"

The Gray Lady rested her umbrella across her lap. "You know me as Linda."

The man in the polo shirt flashed a quick wave. "Kai."

"Yumara," the red-haired woman said lightly.

"Niall," the suited man said. For a second, Daniel thought the man had commanded Miguel to *kneel*—that was the ice he carried in his tone.

"And you will address me as Autumn," the first woman said.

Miguel clasped his hands in a sort of *namaste* gesture. "It's great to see you all again. You look great. Divine."

The comment cracked a thin smile from Autumn—a brief quirk of her ruby lips. Kai and Yumara's backs were turned to Daniel, so he couldn't see their expressions. But the way everyone sat, they reminded him of judges in a courtroom.

"You know why we're here, Miguel." Niall stroked the armrest of his chair. "Before we begin, is there anything you wish to confess?"

The pendulum passed overhead, and Miguel responded lightly, "Such as?"

Niall lowered his half-moon glasses, his eyes icy blue. "Such as… is there anyone else inside this tower?"

Something furry tickled Daniel's arm. He flinched, and his heel struck the lip of the cauldron. The metallic *ting* jolted his bones, and he prayed that hadn't just revealed his position.

Dorian curled up on Daniel's chest. *What the hell?* The cat had always had a way of appearing out of nowhere. Long before Daniel learned Miguel's secret, Dorian would sort of slink out of the shadows and show up unannounced. Daniel scratched Dorian behind the ears and let the cat nuzzle into his neck. *Give a guy a heart attack, why don't you?*

But Niall never looked at the cauldron. His gaze remained fixed on Miguel.

"I have no new information for you." Miguel's brow twitched. "Nothing you don't already know."

The corner of Niall's mouth flickered up, but his eyes remained like stone. "Very well." He gestured toward Autumn, and Daniel caught a glimpse of the ring shimmering on his finger. All of them wore rings like Miguel's. "Proceed, Autumn."

"Miguel." Autumn crossed her legs and put her fingertips together. "Our family carries a great gift. It is an honor to walk the earth as we do and watch the people live their lives. We are woven into the early fabrics of their stories. It is a gift to participate in the expanding tapestry of their cultures."

Miguel's siblings nodded in agreement.

"Yes," Miguel said.

"But as keepers of our domains, we also have certain responsibilities, and they are sacred. One of my charges is to ensure that we uphold sacred law," Autumn said. "As the keeper of The Archive, it is *your* charge to uphold the sacred laws of life and death. Even as Miguel Mortiz, you are not exempt from your responsibilities. Do you know what those responsibilities are?"

"Of course, sister. The candles stand to preserve the life and death of every mortal on Earth, along with their storied existence. Each flame may only be—"

"That's good enough." Autumn flashed a palm. "Do you find this charge burdensome, Miguel?"

Miguel took a second, considering his word choice. "On the contrary, I find it beautiful."

"Even after all this time?" Yumara asked.

"Especially so."

Yumara put her hands over her belly. "A beautiful burden can still be cumbersome."

"Challenging, yes. But—"

"Stop," Niall said. "I'd find it hard to believe he would simply *forget* his charge after thousands of years. It's not hard to remember. Our brother doesn't feel burdened. We know the issue at hand is more severe. He has grown *lax*. In spite of our brother's knowledge of the rules, he chose to ignore them, and not for the first time."

"Correct. This is not your first offense. We were quite clear when we recently convened to discuss your actions in France."

Daniel put his fingers to his temple, his mind buzzing. *The fourteenth century? Recent?*

"We discussed what would happen if you allowed another incident in The Archive." Autumn tilted her head, her gaze almost pitying. "Do you recall?"

"Yes, sister. You were abundantly clear."

"And even since then, we've overlooked some of your choices," Yumara said. "For example, you adopted a house pet and gave him nine actual lives."

Dorian licked his paws, and Daniel scoffed.

So that's your story, Daniel thought.

Miguel steepled his hands. "I do thank you for overlooking that. Dorian is a rather loyal companion."

"This is *not* the point," Niall said. "Brothers, sisters, I hardly believe more discussion is needed. Our brother knew the rules; he knew the consequences. He is no longer fit to wear the mantle of Death. He should be stripped of his responsibilities and privileges. Immediately."

Daniel's heart responded with a kick to his ribs.

A world where Miguel wasn't in charge of The Archive? Would that make him mortal? What would change?

I should say something.

Daniel looked to the door where the gods had emerged. If only he could get to that door and up to the top of the tower without being seen. He looked at Dorian. *Teach me your creepy shadow-step thing.*

"No, brother." Kai leaned his elbows on his knees, rubbing his hands together. "That's not how we do things here, not without hearing Miguel's words first."

Niall recoiled as if he'd been slapped. "I beg your pardon?"

Linda stood, marched up to the third tier, and finagled the fireplace. "You are not a peak above the rest of us, Niall, just as Miguel is not a valley below us. We hold council as a family when the time is needed, and every voice is given equal weight." She glared at Niall as a slow, careful fire bloomed in the fireplace. "*Every* voice."

"When was the last time we held a council to discuss *my* actions?" Niall asked. "Or Linda's? Our ability to walk among the mortals must not be taken lightly. Miguel has developed a way of getting too close to them. More than any of us, he should understand the dangers of making that a habit. It's time we faced the truth, brothers and sisters. And that truth is that Miguel is often the source of our troubles."

"Our brother has the right to explain his actions," Autumn said. "Miguel?"

"Autumn. Kai. Linda. Yumara. And Niall." Miguel regarded his siblings one by one as Linda returned to her chair. "Thank you for this opportunity to speak with you. I cherish our time together, however *impassioned* it may be at times."

Niall shooed at something invisible. "Skip the empty platitudes."

"Of course." Miguel folded his hands at his waist. "Folks, I have walked many lives among the people. As Autumn said, it's a gift to be part of their stories. They say our old names and put us on pedestals. We ripple across cultures, and this helps them make meaning of their world…the sea, the sky, their agriculture, their home, birth…and death."

Linda adjusted one of the ringlets that spilled across her shoulder.

"We've become a part of them," Miguel continued. "And in this life, they've become a deeper part of me. They're threaded into my bones, for better or worse. And to be human is to acknowledge and learn from mistakes."

"You're supposed to keep your distance." Kai tapped his fists together. "Humans are tempestuous, brother. Their lives are as fleeting as the waves, and you cannot get caught in their tides."

"Distance," Miguel said. "Why do we bear this gift if we always insist on walking ten feet behind the people? Why live among them without experiencing *life*? Culture?"

"We *are* their culture," Niall said. "What new enlightenment could they possibly have to offer us after all this time?"

"I do recommend you try their bubble tea," Kai said.

"Oh, yes." Yumara made a circle with her thumb and pointer finger. "Superb."

Linda nodded in agreement.

Niall drummed his fingers against his lap. "You can experience bubble tea without growing dangerously attached to the living."

"Yes," Miguel said. "But I find that a thing tastes better when you know the hands that made it…when you take the time to connect with its creator."

That was why Queen of Cups was such a Costa Linda staple. Aunt Cass's concoctions were top-notch, but her connection was the real spice.

"Your folly is that you fail to detach those ties. It is smarter to maintain your distance, Miguel, especially you." Niall clucked his tongue. "To allow them into our hearts is to leave us vulnerable to pain. After all, they will die. *All* of them."

"They will," Miguel said. "That is their plight, brother. Not that they will die, but that they will lose the ones they love. But what do they lose if they never love in the first place? What do *we* lose?"

Linda raised her hand. "I'd like to vouch for our brother. In my time on Earth, I have married, I had children, I loved. I did what I do best: I provided home and comfort…and then I lost them. I *mourned.* I understood what it means to feel their pain. Never have I felt so wounded." She bit her lip, considering her next words. "But to our brother's point, you should know that I would do it all over again if I had the chance."

"That's very touching, Linda." Niall cleaned his glasses on his coat. "The problem is that Miguel struggles to reconcile his connections with his responsibility in The Archive. Your love for the mortals has never distracted you from providing home and hearth. But in France, our brother even fell in *love* with a mortal, and then he made some irresponsible decisions. Did you not?"

Miguel shut his eyes. "I did."

"And you should have learned your lesson then. But this time, you grew attached to an *entire family*. It's one thing to befriend them, but it's another choice entirely to invite them into your domain. After all this time, are you *still* so desperate for their fondness and affection?"

"Niall," Yumara said. "Don't be crass."

Niall took off his glasses and made a broad gesture with his arms. "Have I said anything insincere? Hmm?"

"This is our *family*."

"Indeed," Niall said. "And our love for our brother notwithstanding, it has never been a secret that he is *heavily* unfavored by the mortals. They fashion gruesome monstrosities in his image. They curse his very name, no matter which name he chooses. They blame him for their troubles. Above all, and perhaps more than ever now, they *fear* him."

Linda pointed her umbrella at Niall, her gaze stern. "You cannot cast him out of The Archive, Niall. He may have made mistakes, but he has been a loving caretaker of their departures. There are people who love him dearly."

"On the contrary," Niall said, "I find that Miguel is loathed by many, *especially* the ones he claims to love the most. Let us observe the evidence."

Niall raised his hands to the ceiling, and Daniel watched in awe as a thin veil of storm-gray clouds brewed under the gears of the tower. Flashes of light strobed through the cracks, unbroken by the swinging of the pendulum. Then, the clouds swirled to form an image, like a watercolor painting. An image of Charleston Fitch stared down from the clouds, and his gravelly voice echoed through the tower:

"*Death fucks us all over in the end, doesn't it? If he really walks among us, then he's probably a smug little bastard.*"

Daniel bit his lip. *Fitch said that yesterday.* He wondered how the detective felt hearing his own voice, seeing his own image.

Lightning flashed, and the clouds folded into an image of Josiah Retzlaff, scraggly and haggard at the sparkling seat of a diner. His voice drawled in Daniel's ears.

"*Well, next time you see him, tell him I said he can shove it.*"

Linda shifted in her chair.

A chill scuttled down Daniel's spine, and he buried his fingers in Dorian's fur for support as the clouds shifted into an image of Aunt Cass.

"*Don't paint him with a holy brush, Daniel. You didn't know the whole man. And you don't want to. You can take my word for it,*" her voice echoed. "*If you see him again, walk the other way.*"

"*You broke us! You broke my family!*"

Thunder rolled as the clouds painted an image of Katie in her hoodie, lounging in the library.

"*When it comes to Miguel, I could not care less about that man.*"

Finally, the clouds shifted one more time, weaving an image of Daniel in a dark jacket, his hair wild and his jaws tight.

"*If Death himself walked among us, I'd give him the same thing I'm about to give you.*"

The clouds broke away as Daniel's voice echoed across the walls. Daniel hated hearing his own words hovering in the air. He wanted to return to Mr. Jerricks's office, to early November, and cram that statement back into his throat, but all he could do was endure the deafening silence that followed.

Down in the pit, Miguel paced and massaged the bridge of his nose.

He looked delicate down there.

Lonely.

Defeated.

Daniel was surprised to feel his throat tighten, strangled by guilt.

Niall walked a slow circle around his chair, his shiny oxford shoes clicking against the stone. "We all know what happened next, don't we?" he asked. "Our brother let another human breach The Archive—a human so asphyxiated by his grief that he caused an incident. The effects ripple. The line blurs between the living and the dead."

All of this is my fault… Daniel closed his eyes. *Why is Miguel getting punished for this?*

"Furthermore, I understand a bereaved man fired a gun in your domain tonight." Niall paused and narrowed his eyes at Miguel. "One of the windows has been damaged, struck by yet *another* man. Another incident could have been caused only minutes ago. There have been too many close calls. You are unfit for your responsibilities. Since you love the humans so much, I believe you should join them. Enjoy mortality, Miguel. You're done."

Miguel looked up with weary eyes. "And The Archive?"

"The Archive and the mantle of Death," Niall thundered, "will be taken by me."

Daniel's breath hitched. With everything Niall knew about Fitch and Zeke striking the window, he had to know they were hiding in this room. And yet he'd stripped Miguel down to his mortality and forced everyone to relive the horrible words they'd said about him.

This Niall guy, keeper of The Archive?

I need to speak up. I can't let them do this.

"Niall," Linda said, "with all due respect, I hardly think you're fit for such a role."

"Oh, no?" Niall challenged. "Linda, The Archive needs someone who will follow rules and protocol to the letter. I never would have let things get this out of hand."

"It's not all protocols, Niall. One needs… What do the doctors call it again?"

"Bedside manner," Miguel rasped.

Linda gave her umbrella a triumphant shake. "Precisely. Bedside manner. And on that note, I think it's only fair that we let the *boy* speak now. The one who lit the candles."

Daniel felt like he'd been punched in the throat.

Kai swung a glance over his shoulder, his gaze piercing and dark. "You can come out of the cauldron now."

DIAPHORESIS

(unusually heavy perspiration)

Daniel's muscles throbbed as he clawed his way out of the cauldron, heart slamming against his ribs. He rotated his shoulders to work out the kinks, then massaged the side of his neck. Dorian simply hopped out and joined Miguel in the middle of the hexagon.

As the gods stared at Daniel, their postures straight, tall, and wire-tight, he almost felt naked.

Niall rested two fingers against his temple. "Daniel Grimm, I presume?"

Daniel swatted the dust off his backpack, then put it on. "Yes," he rasped, the words feeling like peanut butter in his throat. "I'm Daniel Grimm, sir."

"Take a seat." Niall pointed to the stone disk with the key on it—Miguel's seat. "Then explain to me how you came to be in this tower."

Miguel's chair was comfortable—a cushioned relief to his aching bones—but it felt wrong, like putting on someone else's shoes. Daniel rubbed the gilded armrest, cool and velvety against his skin. The pleasant sensation helped him find his bearings, and he took a deep breath. "Everything you talked about…" His voice echoed, catching him off guard. "I take full responsibility for it. If anyone should be punished for the incident in The Archive, it's me. I started this."

"You started this," Niall repeated. "Indeed. You lit nearly a dozen candles that had expired a decade ago. That was a grave mistake, Daniel."

"I…I wanted more time," Daniel said. "I never got to say goodbye to my family. I think about the day they died, and I can still smell the car exhaust and the river, and I can hear my aunt screaming, and all I could think about was that it wasn't fair. It wasn't fair the way they were taken from me."

"You missed your family," Linda said. "Of course you did."

"You felt you were cheated," Niall said. "And that you had a better plan. You felt that Death had wronged you."

"That's…that's correct." Daniel's voice trembled, and then Niall flashed a vulpine grin. He looked pleased, like Daniel had proved his point.

A memory of Mr. Jerricks flashed through Daniel's mind.

"You're a victim of terrible circumstances, and anyone in your shoes would be a troubled young man."

He thought of Mrs. Golden's rosary, and Mr. Mikes's loud-mouthed water cooler gossip. *"There oughta be laws against having so many kids. And if you ask me, being number eleven cursed him from the womb."*

Daniel clenched his fists, and when he released the energy, he had gained control of his voice. "But I am *sick* and tired of other people telling me how I feel, or how I should feel, or what *they* know about *my* grief." He rose to his feet. "What you see…what I've done… it has *not* been that simple. Yes, I was angry at Miguel; I hated the idea of him. When he showed me this place, I wanted to tear it apart. I wanted it to burn from the inside out. You'd think this whole system is supposed to make everything fair, but it's not. It's not fair that some of the candles burn for an hour, and some of them burn for a hundred years. It's not fair that Charleston Fitch can't find his daughter. None of this is fair!"

Niall folded up his spectacles and rested them on his lap.

Daniel took a breath and lowered his voice. "But *no one* gets to tell me why I'm here or how I'm feeling now. I'm here because I was wrong to meddle, and my family taught me to take responsibility for my actions."

"Impassioned words, Daniel." Niall crossed his arms, his lips flat. "So do you regret your behavior?"

"Not entirely," Daniel said. "Like I said, it's not simple. I got to hug my family one last time. But…all that time was for me. It wasn't for them. I see the ways it was going to hurt them. Other people started getting hurt. I would never do what I did again."

"And how do you plan to take responsibility?"

Daniel pointed upward. "I want to light the brazier." He paused. "I want Miguel to get his powers back and go free. If anyone should be punished, it's me. Not him."

Miguel pinned Daniel with a gaze. "Danny."

"Those are bold words, Daniel," Kai said.

"I've been punished to the max already," Daniel said. "I don't doubt you could do worse to me if you wanted, but when it comes to Death, I don't think anyone could do any better than my godfather."

Niall stroked his chin, raising a brow. "You would come to his defense after all he's taken from you?"

"He hasn't taken everything from me," Daniel said. "In the time I've known him, he's also given me comfort. He's shown me kindness. I feel like I don't have to be afraid of what happens when my life is over. But I won't take the rest of it for granted."

Dorian nuzzled up against Miguel's ankle, and Miguel stooped down to pet him behind the ears.

"Death might be his charge, but he's more than that. He works his *ass* off at the hospital to keep people going. He plays a mean harmonica. He cooks good food, even though he's had so few people to share it with. He wasn't just some shadow at the end of my family's lives." Daniel looked Miguel in the eyes. "He was there to make the middle more meaningful."

"And because of all of this," Niall said, "you followed him into this tower, unaware of what you would face? And you're telling me you're prepared to suffer even more?"

"If that's what it took to free him, sir…" Daniel said, sounding braver than he felt. "He was ready to do the same for me."

"*No!*" Katie climbed out from behind the crate, her face sticky with tears. She hurried to Daniel as fast as she could, and Zeke popped out and followed. "Danny, no. You can't be saying this right now." She threw her arms around him.

Yumara fixed her gaze on Katie, curiosity in her eyes. Her lips parted, and she tilted her head to the side. She leaned forward, but she didn't say a word.

Niall did a double take as Logan stepped out into the light, then Charleston Fitch did the same, hanging back three steps. Niall looked as if he'd been slapped, his eyes widening.

"Daniel," Autumn said. "Did you drag all these people along with you?"

"We brought ourselves," Logan said. "Ma'am. I chose to be here with my friend. And I don't regret a thing. In fact, if you're gonna punish Danny, you should punish me, too."

"Logan, stop," Daniel said. "All of you, stop. You didn't do anything wrong. You followed me here, and I appreciate you. But now you need to let me deal with this."

"No." Katie buried her head in Daniel's shoulder. "I'm not losing another brother."

"The folly of humans." Niall tilted his head up at Fitch. "And you? Why are *you* here?"

The pendulum whooshed overhead, and Daniel shut his eyes. If Fitch decided to draw his gun, then everything would end. Niall would never let them see the light outside the tower.

Fitch looked at each of the gods one by one. "Me?" He mopped a film of sweat from his forehead and dipped his hand in his coat pocket. "I just…"

Time seemed to stretch, with every swing of the pendulum feeling agonizingly slow. Daniel stared at Fitch, silently pleading for him to keep his cool.

Then the grandfather clock groaned, shaking the floor. The black sand rippled in Miguel's pit, and the mangled tapestries fluttered against the walls. Daniel doubled over in his seat, holding his hands over his ears, while the gods simply sat calm and stoic.

When the vibrations and the echoes subsided, Daniel went up to Fitch, his knees shaking.

"Fitch," Daniel said. "I want you to decide what it all meant and what your daughter would've wanted you to leave behind."

Fitch looked up as if in prayer.

He took the gun from his pocket, his eyes hard with malice.

"I *really* don't like your godfather," he growled, walking along the edge of the room.

Miguel flashed an earnest, crooked smile. "I'm used to that."

Fitch looked at Zeke, Daniel, and finally at Katie.

Then Fitch opened the gun, tipped one remaining bullet into his hand, and tossed the weapon into the fireplace. "But I'm choosing the bigger life." The flames swallowed the metal unceremoniously as Fitch sat down and removed his hat. "I'm done."

A heavy breath left Daniel's lungs as he sat back down.

The gods smirked in their chairs.

"Thank you, Mr. Fitch," Miguel said.

Fitch flapped his hat at Miguel. "Don't you make me regret this." He stole a glance at Katie. "You make sure the girl is comfortable, and that she has a healthy kid. You owe me that much."

Daniel wished he could gaze into the detective's mind. Charleston Fitch had broken into The Archive with dangerous intent, but something had re-routed him along the way. Daniel doubted the gods had changed Fitch's mind. Maybe it was his respect for Katie, dating back to the day she hired him. Maybe he'd seen his daughter in Katie's future kid, or even in Katie herself. Maybe something had softened when they were visiting Josiah Retzlaff's candle.

Maybe it was something I said?

Miguel frowned. "I'm afraid that's not up to me today."

Autumn folded her hands in her lap. "Niall," she said. "Your verdict?"

Niall fidgeted with this tie. "In these mortals alone, we have seen recklessness, folly, even malice. You, Miguel, have become more and more like the mortals every time we meet. You have grown dangerously careless."

Miguel bowed his head.

"And yet, all these people who felt you had wronged them…" Niall continued, "they followed you into The Archive to take accountability and to protect each other."

Miguel nodded. "And what do you make of this, brother?"

Niall tapped his fingertips together, searching the air for words. "Perhaps…perhaps you've done some good as keeper of The Archive. At least, slightly more good than harm."

Daniel almost choked on air. He slammed his feet down on the floor, unsure if he'd heard Niall correctly.

"Perhaps there is good to learn from the mortals, and perhaps they have been right to learn from you." Niall pressed his fingers to his temple and waved Miguel away with his other hand. "Let's get you out of there. You're going take the boy upstairs and rekindle the brazier, before I change my mind."

Daniel thought the brazier would be bigger—a stone bowl not much bigger around than his torso. Ashes and snow mingled inside to create a dark slurry, and a chiseled hourglass adorned each side. The rhythmic, lazy grinding of the clock gears hummed beneath his feet.

A handful of twinkling embers glowed on the brazier's surface, and that was all that remained of the dying flame.

"We're just in the nick of time." Miguel grabbed a long torch from the tower wall. "You've done well, my friend."

Daniel looked out across The Archive. "What happens now? When you light this thing?"

"*You're* going to do the honors." Miguel passed Daniel the torch. "Everything led to this. As soon as you rekindle this, it's all gone, Danny. Time will move forward from *here*, for everyone inside this tower, but everything on the outside will change. The wax will be repaired on the candles. The life you fabricated is over."

"Just like that?" Daniel asked. "Macy will be okay? Aunt Cass? My family won't suffer?"

"All of that will be as it should," Miguel said. "But you may carry the grief for the rest of your life, Danny. And I wish I could ease that."

Daniel took out his lighter and stared at the twinkling phoenix. He'd never asked his dad why he chose that lighter, but it was fitting. For a while, his dad had risen from the ashes, and Daniel would do the same. "It's okay," he said. "I've learned to live with it. In fact, I *need* it. It's a reminder of all they stood for."

"Yes."

Daniel pointed to the ground. "Will the rest of them remember it all? Zeke and them?"

"Those who accompanied you will always remember," Miguel said. "Macy, Billy, and Cassandra may experience some *glimpses* here and there. Be gentle with them."

"What about Fitch? If he's meant to be dead, and he's *here* in the tower...?"

"Once he steps outside," Miguel said, "that's it."

Daniel frowned. "If...if his daughter's been dead all along, then they were dead at the same time for a while." He wrinkled his brows.

"So how come they never found each other?"

This was Daniel's biggest worry—that when he passed on, he wouldn't find his family again.

"*Yet,*" Miguel said simply. "They haven't found each other yet. They will…in time."

That was all Daniel needed to know, because if there was hope for Fitch and his daughter, then this wasn't the end of Daniel's story with his family.

It was merely the end of a chapter.

He flipped the top of his lighter, closed his eyes, and felt the wind on his cheek.

Aunt Cass had always had a thing about wind—that was where she felt the family visited them…where the Grimms could be heard if Daniel only listened hard enough.

He struck the spark wheel.

The flame burst to life.

He touched it to the end of the torch, igniting the tinder.

Daniel didn't hear a thing, but in the warmth of the flame, he felt them.

"I love you," he whispered, hot tears streaming down his face.

Then he dropped the torch into the brazier. Like an orange flower, the flame unfolded and grew, consuming the bowl.

Daniel's knees hit the floor, and his breath left his lungs in a cathartic rush.

In an instant, Miguel was behind him, arms around his shoulders, warmth pouring from his hands.

"It's okay, Danny," he whispered. "It's okay. I know. I've got you."

The snow stopped falling and the clouds parted.

Daniel stood at the top of the tower and looked out across The

Archive. From his view, it didn't look like anything had changed. The heat of the flame behind him told a different tale. *Drops in a bucket,* he thought. Lives were so interconnected. He'd never know how many he'd affected.

"What if you started doing LEDs instead of actual flames?" he asked Miguel. "Is that safer? Can they last longer?"

Miguel shook his head. The color was returning to his face, his body growing stronger. "But who's gonna pay the electric bill?"

"Isn't that like, a Niall thing?" Daniel asked. "Can't he just power them all?"

"I beg you, Danny, leave this place to me."

A new voice sounded behind Daniel and Miguel. "To you, hmm?"

Niall approached. He had unbuttoned his suit jacket and removed his tie, but he still strutted around with that CEO vibe. He gazed at the newly rekindled flame. "My soft spot for you notwithstanding, I still believe you were wrong. That hasn't changed a bit." He crossed his arms. "And the boy was, too."

Daniel's stomach twisted.

Miguel flashed his brother a half-smile. "Niall," he said, "why don't you just keep an eye on *me* from now on? I've got the boy, and I trust he won't be a problem for you."

"I *will* be watching extra carefully from now on," Niall said. "Don't forget your charge. You are the keeper of death and nothing more. Consider this your final warning."

"Sure." Miguel winked. "But in return, I ask that you remember one thing the mortals have taught me."

Niall brushed a flake of lint off his cuff. "And what, pray tell, might that be?"

Miguel clapped Niall on the shoulder. "Life's a circle, brother."

AFTERCARE

(the continued healing of a recovering patient)

Daniel Grimm had always thought the best days of his life were behind him. But after he left The Archive, he knew the days that followed would be some of his favorites. There was nothing wildly exceptional about most of them, but there were memories he'd cherish forever.

Most of them smelled like baby powder.

There was the first morning after Katie's delivery. Daniel had trudged downstairs, yawning all the way, and found Aunt Cass on the couch, cuddling baby Hope against her chest. She cut him a soft glance, smiled, and put a finger to her lips.

The delivery had been smooth, peaceful, and joyous. Daniel, Aunt Cass, Zeke, Miguel, and Justin had all been there. Yumara had assisted.

Then there were the times when Zeke would hold the baby and burst into full, joyful laughter because she had done something simple like sneeze or grip his finger.

There was the time Katie launched into a long story about her college days. Midway through, she fell asleep on the couch, open-mouthed and frizzy-haired.

There was the time Hope spit up on Justin's favorite band T-shirt, and he simply said, "Yum."

And when everyone was conked out, except for the baby, there was the time Daniel walked her around the living room, pointing out the pictures on the walls. "And this is Auntie Monica, and Uncle Victor, and Uncle Bobby, and Auntie Elena…"

He knew she wouldn't register a word, but she followed his finger across every photo, her eyes big and brown. At one point, her arm even twitched, like she was reaching for the Grimms, for her family.

Daniel paused, considered the photos, and bounced Hope lightly in his arms. In his mind's eye, he saw the jungle decorations and the melting popsicles and the sleeping bags on the floor. He heard Victor yelling at the TV and Bowser's tag jingling on his collar. He smelled pancakes in the back of his throat.

He looked into his niece's eyes. "Man, you kind of look like some of them," Daniel said. "And they would've loved you like crazy."

Miguel had been correct. Daniel had most of his life intact again, but it hadn't come free. The grief endured—there was no magic cure. There were undertones of guilt, even the first time he saw Billy Schubert walking through Garney Plaza one afternoon.

Billy had tipped his chin up and flashed Daniel a cocky, crooked grin. "Sup, Grimm Reaper?"

Daniel wanted to bolt and disappear, but he kept on walking, and he returned Billy's nod. "How's life, Schubes? I'm glad to see you."

The words were like an incantation. Billy planted his feet and scratched his head, then he whirled around and pointed a finger at Daniel, the steel bracelets rattling on his wrist. He looked healthy, the color full in his cheeks and his arms swinging with lively energy. "Hold it. What just happened?"

"What?" Daniel shrugged. "I really *am* glad to see you."

Billy scratched his chin. "Did you just call me *Schubes*?"

"I did," Daniel said. "Do you care?"

"Huh." Billy extended his fist. "I don't hate it. You have a kickass day, Grimm."

Daniel tapped Billy's knuckles. "You, too."

Around that same time, Macy sent Daniel a text message.

I have a very important question for you. Be honest.

Something twisted in Daniel's stomach. Macy's follow-up came less than a minute later.

So my parents want me at this dinner they're hosting tomorrow night and I'm kind of dreading it. Will you come? Logan's already in.

Daniel stretched his legs by the coin fountain. There was no wish that would unravel his guilt. It had been difficult to look Macy in the eye ever since The Archive. Same with Aunt Cass.

This may be the second-hardest thing I ever have to do, he thought. But he had to come clean.

First, I have something to tell you.

Her response floored him.

What? That you had a weird adventure with your godfather, ruined one of my multiversal lives, and confronted your Tower, even though none of it would've been possible without me?

I know. I figured it out like, a million years ago, AKA on Tuesday.

I hate you and I love you at the same time. Now, are you coming to dinner or not?

After the new year, the holiday decorations lingered at Queen of Cups. Daniel had offered to take them down between Christmas and New Year's Eve, but Aunt Cass shrugged off the idea. "Nah, why don't we leave 'em for a while?" she said. "It's more fun that way."

He'd been helping her out one morning when she stopped, gripped the edge of the counter, and blew a strand of hair out of her face. "So," she said. "I have something to tell you."

Daniel opened a carton of cream and poured it into his coffee. "What's up?"

Aunt Cass drummed on the counter. "I've invited Miguel to stop by this morning."

Daniel froze, his mouth hanging open until Aunt Cass reached out and tipped the cream carton away from the coffee. He had overfilled his mug, sending a beige waterfall over the edge.

"Are you serious?" Daniel snapped out of his trance and grabbed a towel.

Aunt Cass nodded. "It's time, Danny. I'm done carrying resentment—it's too heavy. Now, that's not to say that I forgive him completely…" She started the grinder and poured in a fresh sack full of beans. "But maybe I can start with a cup of joe. We'll take it one coffee at a time."

The doorbell jingled sometime later, and Miguel stepped in with a tentative energy.

Aunt Cass looked up from a tray of fruity turnovers.

Miguel flashed a vulnerable smile. "Good morning, Cass."

Daniel's mouth twitched. With Miguel, it had always been *Cassandra*.

"May I come in?" Miguel asked.

Aunt Cass put down the tray and wiped her hands on her apron. Her expression was unintelligible, flat, and pensive. But then she stepped out from behind the counter, walked up to Miguel, and they exchanged a careful hug. After a second, she took a breath, leaned into the embrace, and Daniel saw all the tension melt from her shoulders.

"Of course." She gestured to the table closest to the counter. "Um. Can I grab you something? Anything you'd like is on the house."

"No, let me pay." Miguel peeled off his gloves, revealing his wooden ring, and he unwrapped his scarf. "I want to support your shop."

"Miguel," Aunt Cass raised a brow. "Please."

Miguel gave her a polite nod. "In that case, how 'bout a black coffee and whatever pastry Danny recommends?"

While Aunt Cass poured the coffee, Daniel grabbed a warm cherry-vanilla scone and put it on a plate. He brought it to Miguel and took a seat. "Happy New Year, Miguel."

Miguel shrugged out of his jacket and looked around at the holiday decorations. "To you as well," he said. "Fresh start, right?"

Aunt Cass set the coffee down, steam billowing from the dark brew. "Fresh start."

Daniel listened in as they cycled through some awkward formal talk, the bricks of a friendship under repair.

"The weather's been something. I wish it would just pick a side, right?"

"How've you been?"

"And how's work?"

They ignored the elephants, but there would be time.

When Miguel reached the bottom of his coffee, Aunt Cass drummed her fingers on Daniel's shoulder. "I'm gonna step outside for a minute and let you two catch up." Her smile showed a few more teeth than usual. "Holler if you need me, okay?"

"Cass." Miguel raised his mug. "Thank you. For everything."

Aunt Cass bowed her head. "Of course."

When Aunt Cass was out of earshot, Miguel leaned in and folded his arms on the table. "So," he said. "How are you adjusting?"

Daniel picked up Miguel's scarf and folded it absentmindedly, the flannel soft against his fingers. "It's weird being back." He'd gone to the beach with Logan the other day, and they both looked at the ocean a little bit differently. Daniel often looked at the sky and wondered where Miguel's siblings were. It had been a while since he'd seen Linda walking with her umbrella. "I feel like I dreamed the whole thing, but at the same time, everything keeps reminding me how real it all was."

Logan used to say something similar about his grandfather's death.

Those are the stages of grief in a nutshell, Daniel thought. *Love hanging on.*

Miguel flashed Daniel a crooked grin. "I was talking about unclehood."

Daniel looked down, a chuckle bursting from his lungs. "Right." He thought for a second. "Same, I guess? It's crazy how much love I feel for a kid I barely know. I'm already counting down the days until I can hang out with her again."

"I'm willing to bet that kid already loves you in ways she can't express. Love kinda latches on that way."

"Wanna know something funny?" Daniel grinned. "Katie asked me to be the godfather."

Miguel's eyes gleamed as he took a bite of his second scone. He chewed, wiped his mouth, then swallowed. "That's beautiful, Danny," he said. "You'll do an excellent job."

"I learned from one of the best," Daniel said. "Any advice?"

Miguel snorted. "From *me*?"

Daniel tilted his head. "Why is that funny?"

Miguel fidgeted with his ring. "I guess I still feel like an imposter sometimes. Let me think for a minute." He took another bite of his scone, then held up a finger. "Okay. Do you know the story of how I became *Zeke's* godfather? And all the rest of you?"

Daniel shook his head.

"Your parents had asked two friends before they asked me. I was their third choice," Miguel said. "They found out that the first had ties to the mob. He was an old buddy of your father's, and he's no longer around. But he told your parents he'd make sure you and your siblings have everything you ever want—money, fame, fortune—he swore it. Considering the source, your dad wouldn't have it."

Daniel couldn't help but smirk. "The mob? Does Katie know this story yet?"

"I wouldn't be surprised," Miguel said.

"So, who was the second choice?" Daniel asked.

"One of their coworkers," Miguel said. "But he let it go to his head. 'Oh, I'm a saint! I'm an angel!' Apparently, he used to have a huge crush on your mother."

"*Awkward.*"

"When they asked me, I told them the truth," Miguel said. "I felt they needed to know *all* of me. I showed them The Archive, told them about my responsibilities…They doubled down and insisted I was the right man for the job. We grew closer and closer over the years, and apparently, they never blew my cover."

"They never talked about it with me," Daniel said. "Never."

"I hope I've done right by them," Miguel said. "I vowed to make sure their kids would always be treated fairly and equally. That's my advice, Danny. Have fun. Treat the kid fairly. Enjoy it. Sometimes I wonder if I failed them…failed *you.*"

"You've been awesome," Daniel said.

Miguel rested his chin on his fist and looked Daniel in the eye. "Miguel Mortiz can't exist forever, you know," he said. "One day it'll be time for *me* to go away. And I fear it may come sooner than I'd like."

Daniel wrinkled his brows. "This isn't because of your brother?"

"Not at all," Miguel said. "It's the circle of life, Danny. I walk among people and experience their lives, and that also includes facing my own mortality. Keeps my bedside manner strong, I suppose."

Daniel felt like Miguel had just stabbed him with his fork. "That *sucks.*"

"But when that does happen, it's still not forever," Miguel interjected. "You know that now, right? We find ways to go on, both the living and the departed."

Daniel had been thinking about that a lot. Katie and Zeke had talked about feeling Dad's presence at her wedding, but Daniel had yet to experience any sort of presence the way they had. No chills. No whispers. No shoulder taps.

But the smallest things could conjure their memories. They were in smells, in car rides, in songs on the radio, and homemade recipes.

That was how Daniel would go on *now*, but Miguel had activated a deeper question, one Daniel was almost afraid to ask.

"What can you tell me about how it'll happen?" He swallowed. "The end of my life?"

Miguel rubbed his brow. "Danny."

"I'm just curious," Daniel said. "I can't help but wonder sometimes."

His godfather leaned back in his chair. "Are you asking me if you can see what your candle looks like?"

"No," Daniel said quickly. "I don't think I'm equipped for that. Just…tell me something about it. In a way that only you can."

"You break my heart, Danny." Miguel frowned, creases appearing in his forehead. "Once I tell you this, I can't take it back. You'll know it forever."

"That's okay."

Miguel rested his fist against his temple and sighed. "It'll happen on a day that begins just like any other. To you it will seem… unremarkable."

Daniel nodded, taking in Miguel's words.

Miguel had a faraway look in his eyes. "You will be greatly mourned. There will be people who lament that it happened too soon…that there was still too much for you to do, and that they weren't ready to say goodbye to you. You already know some of the people who will say that, but not all. You have yet to meet all the people who will love you, Danny. And when you're gone, they'll grieve, as you do. There will be tears and many temptations to bargain. Some of your loved ones will curse my name, and I'll take it. Some will experience cloudy days for the rest of their lives."

Daniel swallowed a lump in his throat, wondering if he should stop his godfather.

"But then, on the other side of the storm," Miguel said, "or perhaps within the eye of it, those people will find joy. They'll laugh in your honor. They'll remember you. And I promise you, Daniel

Grimm, they'll be made just a little bit better for having known you."

Daniel leaned back in his chair, his eyes prickling.

"There are two more details I will share with you," Miguel continued. "Number one is that you will be ready, even though you'll have plans for the next day… even though you'll have books you didn't read and words you didn't say. And yet, you won't be unsatisfied. Perhaps that's somewhat related to our time together, but more likely, it's because of who you are. You won't take a single day for granted. And the second thing I can tell you is that I will be there when it happens."

"As…you?" Daniel asked. "If *Miguel* will be gone by then, will I even know it's you?"

"You'll see me. You'll recognize me," Miguel said. "And I will do everything I can to make sure you are comfortable."

That afternoon, Daniel wrote three letters by hand.

One would go into his sock drawer and replace his flash drive.

The second went in his backpack, to be delivered at the right time.

The third went out in the mail after some time searching for the right address. The envelope weighed less than a pound, but Daniel felt an enormous weight off his shoulders when he put it in the mailbox.

Six months later, he received a reply.

SIX MONTHS LATER

It had been Katie's idea to choose hydrangeas and peonies for Charleston and Ivy Fitch. She'd read that they symbolized perseverance and healing. Daniel watched her lay them on the grave. Maybe the two would find the flowers. Hopefully, they'd found *each other*.

"It's strange, isn't it?" Zeke said, lightly rubbing his knuckles.

"Seeing their grave, you mean?" Daniel had been wondering if anyone had ever visited Fitch.

Zeke shook his head. "The fact that it took ten and a half years for all of us to come here together."

Daniel took in the summer breeze. Nearby, Aunt Cass had been juggling a growing six-month-old and teaching Hope all about Grandma Alba.

In another part of the cemetery, Macy sat with Logan as he laid a piece of bubblegum, a butterscotch lollipop, and a pair of fuzzy dice on his grandfather's grave.

And Justin carried two coffees, humming some sort of theme park song as he strolled through the grass.

Nothing ever seems to bother that man, Daniel thought. The family was lucky to have someone like Justin Scott around. His boyish, happy-go-lucky naivety was medicine for the soul on stressful days. And Daniel had been losing sleep over this day for over a week.

"You doin' okay?" Justin asked.

Daniel put a hand on his middle. "I'm a little queasy, but ready."

"I think it's badass what you're doing," he said. "Truly. I'm proud of you!"

Daniel cut his gaze to Fitch's grave.

Choose the bigger life.

Katie leveled her palm with her eyebrows and squinted at the parking lot. "Is that him over there?"

A thin man stepped out of a beige truck and began to walk toward Daniel. He had thinning red hair and carried dark red roses in one hand. In the other, he carried a small white box.

"Yep," Daniel said. "That's him."

Justin handed Daniel one of the coffees, still warm. "You got this."

And everyone stood with Daniel as Josiah Retzlaff approached.

"Hello," Josiah said quietly.

Daniel nodded, his heart surprisingly calm in his chest. "Josiah," he said. "Good morning. Thank you for meeting us here."

"No, thank *you*," Josiah said. "Truly. It's the least I could do. I'm sorry it took me so long to answer your letter. Caught me a little off guard, but…I needed it."

Daniel had been surprised to *write* the letter, but he needed it, too. Aunt Cass had inspired him when she first invited Miguel to the café. Daniel still had a long way to go before he could fully forgive Josiah for what he'd done. He wasn't even sure it was possible. But he could follow Aunt Cass's example. He could take the first step.

He held out the coffee cup, filled to the brim with one of Aunt Cass's famous Aztec mochas. "Let's start with a coffee."

Josiah considered the cup.

"It's safe, I promise!" Justin interjected. "I tested it."

A shaky chuckle rippled through the group, breaking the tension.

Josiah accepted the drink, unsure where to look or what to say. "Gosh, I uh…"

"Why don't we walk?" Daniel said. "By the way, these are my best friends, Logan and Macy. I'm sure you know my brother and sister already. My aunt. My brother-in-law. And…this is Hope, my baby niece."

Hope blew a raspberry, drawing another laugh from both Josiah and the rest of the group.

Josiah chuckled and waved a finger at the baby. "I gotta tell ya, I probably won't remember all the new names," he said. "But I'm gonna try, and I…I thank you for the chance to tell you I'm sorry. I'll say it a million times if you'll let me, though it still won't be enough."

"We're glad you're here." Zeke tipped his head toward the package in Josiah's hand. "What you got there?"

"Oh." Josiah set his coffee on a bench, along with the roses. "Used to walk a lot with my friend, and she introduced me to a place that made this special bread. Can't remember the name because it's in Spanish, but I thought I'd bring some for your folks."

He opened the white box and revealed a glittering loaf of bread.

"*Pan de muerto*," Aunt Cass said. "What a beautiful gesture. My mother used to make it and tell stories."

"Gotta confess, this isn't my first time bringing one with me," Josiah said. "I hope it's not overstepping. It's supposed to invite spirits back to the land of the living for a while if you believe in that sort of thing. And even if you don't, I figure what's the harm in sharin' some bread?"

Daniel swallowed. They had arrived at the Grimm family grave, where Daniel had discovered a loaf of *pan de muerto* in the early winter. That day had changed everything.

Maybe there was something to the *pan de muerto,* after all.

Josiah set the bread on the grave, then laid the crimson roses beside it. Daniel followed suit with the letter he had written to his family. He placed the envelope under the column of names.

Hope.

Jonathan.

Nancy.

Alexander.

Victor.

Samuel.

Monica.

Ruthie.

Bobby.

Elena.

A light gust of wind warmed the back of Daniel's neck.

Then, Josiah took the first sip of his drink. It loosened something in him. His shoulders relaxed. He cleared his throat. "Do you think you can tell me something about them?"

"Sure we can," Daniel said. "We'd love that."

Katie opened a binder and showed Josiah the first page. "So, my brother, Sam, once described us all as space wizards. This was the story he was working on. He didn't finish, but I think I know how it ends…"

One by one, Zeke, Katie, Aunt Cass, Justin, Logan, Macy, and Daniel took turns sharing what they knew, what they'd learned, and how the Grimms lived through them. And Josiah listened to every word, often repeating for understanding.

But he wasn't the only one listening.

Hope had been hanging on to every word, wide-eyed and patient. Sometimes she repeated the words, too. When Daniel talked about his mom, Hope would go, "*Muh-muh-muh-muh*" and point to Katie. When the twins came up, she burst into joyful laughter.

And this went on until they had all finished their stories, which was when they saw Hope staring at something on top of the hill.

"Look." Katie tapped Justin's shoulder. "She's all grinning at that tree over there. She's so silly. What are you looking at, baby girl?"

Daniel followed his niece's gaze. That was the sycamore where Miguel had been standing when everything started…where Victor and Xander had been musing about life and death once upon a time.

The breeze swelled, lifting stray leaves and flower petals off the ground, where they gathered and danced in a swirl. Then, as quickly as they came together, they broke away, and the wind grew still.

"That is a *tree*, princess. Just a tree." Justin squinted at the hill as Hope picked up her little hand and bounced it up and down in a wave. "There's nothing else there…"

THE END

ACKNOWLEDGMENTS

When people ask me how the writing's going, there's always a brief moment of panic before I start talking. First, it's hard for me to talk about myself. Second, I know the next question is, "What's it about?" Most of us writers dread the elevator pitch, and it's even more difficult to remember it on the spot! Then I started writing *this* book. I'm a pretty happy-go-lucky dude for the most part, so it was a whole thing when I had to tell people what it was about.

"I'm writing about the god of death this time!"

The Brothers Grimm deserve all the credit for telling the original story. *Godfather Death* (1812) had so many cool ideas. The candles were one of them. I daresay I have too many candles in my home, and they're a writing ritual for me. I loved the idea of lives and flames being tied together. But I was even more compelled by the idea of Death in a mentoring role, and the boy who tries to cheat him. Their version of the story unfolds differently, and I find it haunting, beautiful, and imaginative. What I wanted to do was flesh out that relationship and the details that don't fit in a short story. I wanted to get in both their heads and understand their plights.

And to do that, I had to build out the grief—the five senses of it and the wild ups and downs. I can only speak for my own experience with grief, but I know it doesn't always feel one way. Most days it's a drama. Sometimes it's a mystery. Some days we force comedy out of it. I took a lot of risks experimenting with different tones in one book. It's probably not surprising, then, that this book required some heavy emotional labor.

With that, I really need to thank Avon Van Hassel for being this book's "fairy godmother." I wrote to her one day for advice on the tarot scene, and she offered to look it over. From there, she continued to read and provide constant encouragement and honest feedback even as she processed a recent loss of her own. She pushed me to make this the best it could be, and not to pull any punches! I can't thank you enough, and I hope that this has brought you some comfort and healing along the way.

Katie Salidas also chimed in with valuable feedback, and I credit Macy's advice to her: "Think of this as a weather report. You can't stop the rain, but you can bring your umbrella!"

Maggie Nom has been one of my closest friends for years now, and she cheered me on during the book's Vella run. She also joined me on "themed adventures" that inspired me along the way, including a candlelight concert event and a tarot reading—where the Death card showed up for me. (Thank you, Maria Elena!)

Silvia Curry is my amazing editor, and I continue to be grateful for her watchful eye, enthusiasm, and constant support ever since my first book!

My mom is the best. I showed her the first three chapters in the early stages. I was trying to figure out, "Do I have something here?" And she said, "YES. I want to read more." She might be required to say that, but she continued to check in on its progress, ask how it was going, and she never batted an eye about the subject matter.

Early in my drafting process, a woman lost her life in Tucson. It's the first time I can remember grieving a stranger. Her full story isn't mine to tell, but I felt called to pay some sort of tribute that illuminates how she made me *feel*. To me and many others who live here, she and her umbrella were iconic. Some of us even compared her to a "modern goddess"—a symbol of our home. The Umbrella Lady made Tucson feel like home.

The rest of my thanks go out to my community—the people who maybe don't know that they fuel my creativity just by doing their job. That includes the friendly baristas who remember my coffee order and greet me with kindness in the mornings, the cool folks at Heroes and Villains who learned my name and supported me at Comic Con, my awesome coworkers who support my "5 to 9 life", and you! Thank you for reading and letting me tell you stories. Stories are how we keep going, and how we keep memories alive.

Until the next one, friends. Much love!

ABOUT THE AUTHOR

JACOB DEVLIN is the author of multiple books for teens and pre-teens including *Roses in the Dragon's Den*, which won a Reader's Favorite Silver Medal. Outside of writing, he enjoys drawing, movies, figuring out what he's going to wear to his next Comic Con, and spending time with friends and family. He does most of these things in southern Arizona.

Feel free to connect with him at:
AUTHORJAKEDEVLIN.COM